Remember When

Books by Judith McNaught

Almost Heaven
Double Standards
A Kingdom of Dreams
Once and Always
Paradise
Perfect
Something Wonderful
Tender Triumph
Whitney, My Love
Until You
Remember When

Published by POCKET BOOKS

Judith McNaught

Remember When

POCKET BOOKS
New York   London   Toronto   Sydney   Tokyo   Singapore

POCKET BOOKS, a division of Simon & Schuster Inc.
1230 Avenue of the Americas, New York, NY 10020

ISBN: 0-671-52570-0

First Pocket Books hardcover printing December 1996

10 9 8 7 6 5 4 3 2 1

To St. Jude, Patron Saint of Impossible Things

You put a lot of overtime in on this one—
Thank you.

Acknowledgments

This is the page where, traditionally, authors offer a few words of thanks to those people who have been rather helpful, or extremely tolerant, during the gestation of their novel. In the case of this novel, which has taken forever to write, there is not enough space on this page to *properly* thank even one of the following people for their enormous help, understanding, and support. I can only hope each of you will realize how important you were, and you are, to me . . .

TO

Dr. John M. Lewis, protector of others' hearts, and keeper of mine;
Keith Spalding, always and ever the dearest of friends;
George Bohnenburger, provider of instant answers to complicated questions on boggling subjects;
Betty Mitchell, builder of dreams;
Bruce Monical, artist, adviser, and dearest friend;
Mark Strickler, most patient friend;
Jim Hime, who redefines the concepts of thoroughness and integrity.

And to

John and Whitney Shelley and Clay McNaught—for being my family *and* my friends.

Chapter 1

Houston, 1979

"DIANA, ARE YOU STILL AWAKE? I'D LIKE TO TALK TO YOU."

Diana stopped in the act of turning off the lamp beside her bed and leaned back against the pillows. "Okay," she called.

"How's the jet lag, honey?" her father asked as he walked toward her bed. "Are you exhausted?" At forty-three, Robert Foster was a tall, broad-shouldered Houston oilman with prematurely gray hair who normally exuded self-assurance, but not tonight. Tonight, he looked distinctly uneasy, and Diana knew why. Although she was only fourteen, she wasn't silly enough to think he'd come there to talk about whether she had jet lag. He wanted to talk to her about her new stepmother and stepsister, whom she'd met for the first time this afternoon when she arrived home from a vacation in Europe with school friends. "I'm okay," she said.

"Diana—" he began; then he hesitated, sat down on the bed beside her, and took her hand in his. After a moment, he began again. "I know how strange it must have seemed to you to come home today and find out I'd remarried. Please believe that I would never have married Mary without giving you a chance to get to

1

know each other if I hadn't been positive, absolutely *positive,* that the two of you will learn to love each other. You do like her, don't you?" he asked anxiously, searching her face. "You said you did—"

Diana nodded, but she didn't understand why he'd married someone he hardly knew and she'd never met until today. During the years since her mother died, he'd dated some really beautiful and very nice Houston women, but before things got too serious, he'd always introduced them to Diana and insisted the three of them spend time together. Now he'd actually married someone, but it was a lady she'd never set eyes on before. "Mary seems really nice," she said after a moment. "I just don't understand why you were in such a hurry."

He looked sheepish, but his answer was unquestionably heartfelt. "There will be a few times in your life when all your instincts will tell you to do something, something that defies logic, upsets your plans, and may even seem crazy to others. When that happens, you *do* it. Listen to your instincts and ignore everything else. Ignore logic, ignore the odds, ignore the complications, and just go for it."

"And that's what you did?"

He nodded. "I knew within hours of meeting Mary that she was just what I wanted for myself, and for you, and I knew when I met Corey that the four of us were going to be an exceptionally happy family. However, all my instincts warned me that if I gave Mary more than a little time to decide, she'd start thinking about all the obstacles and agonizing over them, and that in the end she'd turn me down."

Loyalty and common sense made that possibility seem entirely unlikely to Diana. Previous women had gone to absurd lengths to attract and hold her father's interest. "It seems to me that practically every woman you've taken out has wanted you."

"No, honey, most of them wanted what I could give them in the form of financial security and social acceptance. Only a few have truly wanted me."

"But are you sure that Mary truly wanted you?" Diana asked, thinking of his statement that Mary would have turned him down.

Her father grinned, his eyes warming with affection. "I'm *completely* sure she did, and she does."

"Then why would she have turned you down?"

His smile widened. "Because she's the opposite of mercenary and status conscious. Mary is very intelligent, but she and Corey have led a simple life in a tiny little town where no one is wealthy, not by Houston standards. She fell in love with me as quickly and deeply as I fell in love with her, and she agreed to marry me within a week, but when she realized what sort of life we live here, she started trying to back out.

"She was worried that Corey and she wouldn't fit in, that they'd make some sort of inexcusable social blunder and embarrass us. The longer she thought about it, the more convinced she became that she'd fail us."

He reached out and gently smoothed a lock of shining chestnut hair from Diana's cheek. "Just imagine — Mary was willing to toss away all the material things I can give her, all the things everyone else was so anxious to grab, because she didn't want to fail me as a wife or you as a mother. Those are the things that are important to her."

Diana had liked her new stepmother well enough when she met her today, but the tenderness in her father's eyes and the love in his voice when he talked of Mary carried an enormous amount of additional weight with Diana. "I like her a lot," she confessed.

A smile of relief dawned across his face. "I knew you would. She likes you, too. She said you're very sweet and very poised. She said you'd have had every right to get hysterical this afternoon when you walked in the front door and met a stepmother you'd never heard about before. And wait till you meet your new grandparents," he added enthusiastically.

"Corey said they're really neat," Diana replied, thinking back over all the information her thirteen-year-old stepsister had provided during their first day together.

"They are. They're good, honest, hardworking people who laugh a lot and love each other a lot. Corey's grandfather is an excellent gardener, an amateur inventor, and a skillful carpenter. Her grandmother is very artistic and very talented at handcrafts. Now," he said, looking a little tense again, "tell me what you think about Corey."

Diana was quiet for a moment, trying to put her feelings about her new stepsister into words; then she leaned forward, wrapped her arms around her knees, and smiled. "Well, she's different from the other girls I know. She's . . . friendly and honest, and she says what's on her mind. She hasn't been anywhere but Texas, and she doesn't try to act cool and sophisticated, but she's done lots of things I never have. Oh, and she thinks *you're* practically a king," Diana added with a grin.

"What a clever, discerning young lady!"

"Her own father ran out on her mom and her when Corey was just a baby," Diana said, sobered by the thought of such an unspeakable act by a parent.

"His stupidity and irresponsibility are my good luck, and I intend to make certain Mary and Corey feel lucky, too. Want to help me pull that off?" he asked, standing up and smiling at her.

Diana nodded. "You bet," she said.

"Just remember, Corey hasn't had a lot of the advantages you've had, so take it slow and teach her the ropes."

"Okay, I will."

"That's my girl." He leaned over and kissed the top of her head. "You and Mary are going to be wonderful friends."

He started away, but Diana's quiet announcement made him turn back and stop. "Corey would like to call you Dad."

"I didn't know that," Robert Foster said, his voice turning gruff with emotion. "Mary and I hoped she might want to someday, but I thought it might take a long, long time, before she came around to that." He studied Diana for a long moment, and then hesitantly asked, "How do you feel—about Corey calling me Dad—I mean?"

Diana grinned. "It was my idea."

Across the hall, Mary Britton Foster was seated on her thirteen-year-old daughter's bed and running out of small talk. "So you had a nice time with Diana today?" she asked Corey for the third time.

"Yep."

"And you enjoyed going over to the Hayward children's house and riding their horses when Diana took you there this afternoon?"

"Mom, we're all teenagers; you aren't supposed to call us children."

"Sorry," Mary said, idly rubbing Corey's leg beneath the blankets.

"And it wasn't what you'd call a house; it's so big, it's practically a motel!"

"That big?" Mary teased.

Corey nodded. "It's about the size of our house."

The fact that she'd referred to Diana and Robert's house as "our house" was very revealing and immensely reassuring to Mary. "And do the Haywards have a barn at their house?"

"They call it a stable, but it's the same as a barn, only it looks like a beautiful stone house from the outside, and it's as clean as one on the inside. They even have a guy who lives down at the stable and looks after the horses. They call him a groom, and his name is Cole, and the girls think he's a complete hunk. He's just gotten out of college at—I forget where—but I think he said it's here in Houston."

"Imagine that," Mary said, shaking her head in amazement. "Now it takes a college degree just to get a job looking after horses in a barn—er—stable."

Corey suppressed a laugh. "No, I meant he's just finished the semester, and pretty soon he starts another one. The horses are just awesome!" Corey added, switching to the topic of primary interest to her. "I get to ride again at Barb Hayward's birthday party next week. Barb invited me, but I think Diana asked her to do it. I met a bunch of Barb and Diana's friends today. I didn't think they liked me very much, but Diana said I was just imagining it."

"I see. And what do you think of Diana?"

"Diana's . . ." Corey hesitated, thinking. "Diana's cool. She told me she's always wanted a sister, and maybe that's why she's being so nice to me. She's not a snob at all. She even told me I could borrow any of her clothes that I want."

"That's very nice of her."

Corey nodded. "And when I told her I liked the way she wears her hair, she said we could practice different styles on each other."

"And . . . um . . . did she say anything about anyone else?"

"Like who?" Corey asked with sham confusion.

"Like me, and you know it."

"Let me think. Oh, yeah, I remember now! She said you looked mean and sneaky, and she said you'll probably make her stay home and scrub floors while I get to go to balls and dance with princes. I told her she was probably right, but that I'd ask you to let her wear the glass slipper as long as she didn't leave the house."

"Corey!—"

Laughing, Corey leaned forward and hugged her mother as she finally told the truth. "Diana said you seemed very nice and she likes you. She asked if you were strict, and I said you were

5

sometimes, but then you feel guilty and bake up batches of cookies to make up for it."

"Did she really say she likes me?"

Sobering, Corey nodded emphatically. "Diana's mother died when she was only five. I can't imagine what life would be like if I didn't have you, Mom—"

Mary hugged her daughter close and laid her cheek on Corey's blond hair. "Diana hasn't had a lot of the advantages you have. Try to remember that. Having lots of clothes to wear and a big bedroom isn't the same as having Grandpa and Grandma to love you and teach you all the things you learned when we lived with them."

Corey's smile faded a little. "I'm going to miss them something terrible."

"Me, too."

"I told Diana about them, and she was really interested. Could I take her to Long Valley sometime soon so she can meet them?"

"Yes, of course. Or maybe we could ask Robert to let them come for a visit."

Mary stood up and started to leave, but Corey's hesitant voice stopped her. "Mom, Diana said I could call Robert, Dad. Do you think he'd mind?"

"I think he'd *love* it!" She looked a little sad then and added, "Maybe someday Diana might want to call me Mom."

"Tomorrow," Corey said with a knowing smile.

"Tomorrow, what?"

"She's going to call you Mom, starting tomorrow."

"Oh, Corey, isn't she wonderful?" Mary said, her eyes filling with tears.

Corey rolled her eyes, but she didn't deny it. "It was my idea that she call you Mom. All she did was say she wanted to do it."

"You're wonderful, too," Mrs. Foster said with a laugh as she kissed her daughter. She turned out the light and closed the door when she left. Corey lay there, thinking about the conversation and wondering if Diana was asleep. After several moments, she scrambled out of bed and pulled on an old plaid flannel robe over her nightshirt emblazoned with "SAVE THE TURTLES" across the front.

The hallway was dark as pitch as she groped her way across the hall toward the door of Diana's room. Her fingertips finally encountered the doorframe, and she raised her hand to knock just as the door flew open, startling a muffled squeal from her. "I was just coming over to see if you were awake," Diana whispered, backing up and beckoning Corey into her room.

"Did your dad have a talk with you tonight?" Corey asked, perching on the edge of Diana's bed and admiring the cream lace ruffles at the throat and wrists of Diana's high-waisted, pale rose robe and the delicate lace trim on her matching quilted slippers.

Diana nodded and sat down beside her. "Yes. Did you mom have one with you?"

"Yep."

"I think they were afraid we weren't going to like each other."

Corey bit her bottom lip and then blurted, "Did you happen to ask your dad about me calling him Dad?"

"I did, and he loved the idea," Diana said, keeping her voice low so that this cozy pajama party for two wouldn't be ended by parental decree.

"Are you sure?"

"Yes. In fact, he got all choked up." Diana looked down at her lap and drew a long breath, then lifted her eyes to Corey's. "Did you mention to your mom about me calling her Mom?"

"Yes."

"Did she say anything?"

"She said you're wonderful," Corey replied, rolling her eyes in feigned disagreement.

"Did she say anything else?"

"She couldn't," Corey replied. "She was crying."

The two girls eyed one another in smiling silence, then, as if by mutual agreement, flopped onto their backs. "I think," Diana said after a moment's contemplation, "this could turn out to be really, really *cool!*"

Corey nodded with absolute conviction. "Totally cool," she proclaimed.

Yet later that night, as she lay in her own bed, Corey found it hard to believe that things had turned out so well with Diana.

Earlier that day, she would never have believed it was possible. When Diana's father had married Corey's mother after a two-week courtship and brought his new wife and daughter to his Houston home, Corey had dreaded meeting her stepsister. Based on what little she'd already discovered about Diana, Corey figured they were so different they were probably going to hate each other. Besides being born rich and growing up in this huge mansion, Diana was a year older than Corey and a straight-A student; and when Corey took a peek into Diana's feminine bedroom, everything was so neat it gave her the creeps. Based on what she'd heard and seen, she felt sure that Diana was going to be disgustingly perfect and a complete snob. She was even more sure Diana was going to think Corey was a dumb hick and a slob.

Her first glimpse of Diana when she walked into the foyer this morning had confirmed Corey's worst fears. Diana was petite, with a narrow waist, slim hips, and real breasts, which made Corey feel like a deformed, flat-chested giant by contrast. Diana was dressed like a model from *Seventeen* magazine, in a short tan skirt, cream-colored tights, and a tan-and-blue plaid vest topped off by a jaunty tan blazer with an emblem on the front. Corey was wearing jeans and a sweatshirt.

And yet, despite Corey's absolute conviction that Diana would be a conceited snob, Diana had been the one who broke the ice. It was Diana who had admired Corey's hand-painted sweatshirt with the horse on the front, and Diana who'd first admitted that she'd always wanted a sister. Later that afternoon, Diana had taken Corey over to the Haywards' house so Corey could take pictures of the Haywards' horses with the new camera Diana's father had given her.

Diana didn't seem to resent the fancy camera her father had bought for Corey or hate the idea of sharing him with Corey. And if she thought Corey was a dumb hick, she definitely hadn't shown it. Next week, Diana was taking her to Barb Hayward's birthday party, where everyone was going to ride horses. Diana said her friends would become Corey's friends, too, and Corey hoped she was right.

That last part didn't matter nearly as much as having a sister so close to her own age to spend time with and talk to—and Corey wouldn't be doing all the taking either—she had some things to give Diana. For one thing, Diana had led an awfully sheltered life, in Corey's opinion. Earlier that day, she'd admitted she'd never climbed a really big tree, never eaten berries right off the vine, and never skipped rocks across a pond.

Closing her eyes, Corey sighed with relief.

Chapter 2

COLE HARRISON LOOKED OVER HIS SHOULDER AT DIANA FOSTER, WHO was hovering in the open doorway of the stable, her hands clasped behind her back, watching her new stepsister in the riding ring with the other girls who were attending Barbara Hayward's birthday party. He picked up a brush and a currycomb and stopped on his way into one of the stalls. "Would you like me to saddle a horse for you?" he asked.

"No, thank you," she replied, and her soft voice was so very polite and adult that Cole bit back a smile.

He'd been working as a groom at the Hayward estate for the last two years while he went to college, and during that time, he'd seen and heard enough to form some strong impressions about the teenage daughters of Houston's ultrarich. Among those observations was that the thirteen- and fourteen-year-old girls who hung around with Barbara Hayward were all crazy about boys and crazy about horses, and they were desperately eager to perfect their skills with both. In addition to their obsession with boys, they were totally obsessed with their looks, their clothes, and their status with their peers. Their personalities ranged from giddy to sulky, and although they could be charming, they were also demanding, conceited, and catty.

Some of the girls were already raiding their parents' liquor cabinets, most of them wore too much makeup, and *all* of them tried to flirt with him. Last year, their efforts had been amusingly clumsy and easy to deflect, but they were becoming bolder as they grew older. As a result, he was beginning to feel like a sex object for a bunch of single-minded, precocious adolescent girls.

That wouldn't have been nearly as exasperating if they'd restricted themselves to blushing and giggling, but lately they'd progressed to come-hither looks and languishing stares. A month ago, one of Barbara's friends had taken the lead in the "chase" by boldly asking Cole's opinion on French kissing. Haley Vincennes, who was the unchallenged head of the clique, instantly reclaimed her position as lead by informing Cole that she thought he had "a great butt."

Until a week ago, when Diana Foster brought her new stepsister down to the stable to introduce her to Barbara, Cole had rarely seen Diana, but the petite brunette had always struck him as a refreshing exception. Everything about her was appealing and wholesome, and yet he sensed there were depths to her that the other girls lacked. She had hair the color of dark copper and a pair of startlingly large, long-lashed eyes—clear, luminous, mesmerizing green eyes that regarded him, and the rest of her world, with genuine interest. They were expressive eyes, bright with lively intelligence, glowing with wit, and yet filled with a sweetness that never failed to make Cole feel like smiling at her.

When he'd finished brushing the mare, Cole patted her flank and left the stall, closing the heavy oak door behind him. As he turned to put the currycomb and brush on a shelf, he was surprised to see that Diana hadn't left. She was still standing in the doorway, her hands clasped tightly behind her back, her expression anxious as she observed the noisy activities in the riding ring and the practice area outside it.

She was looking so intently at whatever she was watching that Cole leaned to the left to get a better angle of the riding ring. At first, all he noticed was twenty girls who were laughing and shouting as they watched each other trotting in figure eights or jumping low hurdles. Then he noticed that Corey, Diana's new stepsister, was completely alone at the far side of the corral. Corey shouted a compliment to Haley Vincennes as she rode past with three other girls, but Haley stared right through Corey as if a compliment from her was completely meaningless, then said something to the other girls that made them look at Corey and laugh. Corey's shoulders drooped; she turned her horse and trotted out of the ring as if she'd been verbally ejected instead of silently shunned.

Diana's hands tightened convulsively behind her back, and Cole saw her bite down hard on her lower lip, reminding him of a distressed mother bird who knows her chick isn't doing well outside the nest. He was both surprised and impressed by Diana's obvious dismay over her new stepsister's plight, but he also knew her hope of seeing Corey accepted was probably futile.

He'd been present last week when she first brought Corey down to the stables and introduced her to Barbara and several of the other girls who'd come to the stable to see a new foal. He had witnessed the stunned silence that followed Diana's introduction, and he'd seen the expressions of hostile superiority as the young debutantes-to-be discovered Corey's background and judged her an inferior.

That day, Diana had seemed to take for smiling granted that Corey would be made welcome by her wealthy friends. In Cole's opinion, she was in for some sharp and lasting disappointments, and based on Diana's worried frown now, she was arriving at the same conclusion.

Touched by the intensity of the emotions playing across her expressive face, Cole tried to distract her. "Corey's a pretty decent rider. I don't think you have to watch her that closely or worry about her."

She turned partway around and gave him a reassuring smile. "I wasn't worrying just then; I was thinking. Sometimes I frown when I think."

"Oh," Cole said, trying to protect her dignity by pretending he believed her. "A lot of people do that." He thought for something else to say. "What about you, do you like horses?"

"Very much," she said in her strangely adult and oddly endearing way. With her hands still clasped behind her back, she turned fully toward him, obviously willing to continue the conversation. "I brought them a bag of apples," she added, nodding toward a large brown sack just inside the door.

Since she apparently preferred to feed them, not ride them, Cole leapt to the obvious conclusion. "Do you know how to ride?"

She surprised him again by nodding. "Yes."

"Let me see if I have this straight," he joked. "When you come here, you don't ride, even when all your friends are riding, right?"

"Right."

"And you do know how to ride, and you do like horses very much. Right?"

"Right."

"In fact, you like horses so much that you bring apples for them, right?"

"Right again."

He hooked his thumbs in his belt loops and studied her curiously. "I don't understand," he admitted.

"I like them much *better* when I'm on the ground."

There was embarrassed laughter in her voice, and it was so contagious that Cole grinned. "Don't tell me—let me guess. You were thrown and got hurt, is that it?"

"You got it," she admitted. "I rushed a fence and got a broken wrist."

"The only way to get over your fear is to get right back on," Cole lectured.

"I did that," she assured him gravely, but with a twinkle in her green eyes.

"And?"

"And I got a concussion."

Cole's stomach growled, and his thoughts shifted to apples. He lived on a tight budget, and he seemed to have an appetite that was never satisfied. "I'd better put that bag of apples away before it gets stepped on or someone trips over it," he said. Harrison picked up the bag and started toward the rear of the stable, fully intending to share in the horses' bounty. As he passed one of the stalls near the end of the long aisle, an ancient named Buckshot put his head out over the door, his eyes hopeful and inquisitive, his soft nose aimed at the bag in Cole's arm.

"You can't walk and you can't see, but there's nothing wrong with your sense of smell," Cole told the horse as he dug an apple out of the bag and gave it to him. "Just don't go telling your stablemates about these apples. Some of them are mine."

Chapter 3

COLE WAS PUTTING FRESH HAY INTO THE EMPTY STALLS WHEN SEVERAL of the girls who'd been riding marched into the stable. "Diana, we need to talk to you about Corey," Haley Vincennes announced. Cole looked up from his chore, took one look at the group, and knew that the all-girl jury was about to deliver their verdict. And it wasn't going to be a good one.

Diana obviously sensed it, too, and tried to head them off, her voice sweet and persuasive. "I know you'll all like Corey when you get to know her, and then we'll all be good friends."

"That just can't happen," Haley decreed with haughty finality. "None of us have anything in common with somebody from a hick town we've never even heard of. I mean, did you *see* that sweatshirt she was wearing last week when you brought her over here? She said her grandmother *painted* that horse's head on it for her."

"I liked it," Diana said stubbornly. "Corey's grandmother is an artist!"

"Artists paint on canvases not sweatshirts, and you know it. And I will bet you a month's allowance those jeans she's wearing today came from Sears!"

A chorus of murmured laughter from the other girls was proof they agreed; then Barb Hayward finally added her vote to the majority opinion, but she looked a little timid as she decreed poor Corey's fate: "I don't see how she can be our friend, or yours either, Diana."

Cole winced with empathy for Corey and with sympathy for poor little Diana, who he was certain would buckle under the intense peer pressure, but poor little Diana didn't give an inch, even though her voice never lost its softness. "I'm really sorry you all feel that way," she said sincerely, directing her words to Haley, who Cole already knew was the leader in this and the nastiest of the dissenters. "I guess I never realized you'd be afraid of the competition if you gave her a chance."

"What competition?" Barb Hayward asked, looking baffled but concerned.

"Competition with boys. I mean, Corey is very pretty, and she's lots of fun, so naturally the boys are going to be hanging around her wherever she goes."

In the stall across from the girls, Cole paused, pitchfork in hand, a smile of admiration on his mouth, as he realized Diana's strategy. As he'd learned while working there, boys were the most desirable, most valued of commodities to teenage girls, and the possibility that Corey might attract more boys into their collective lair was almost irresistible. He was wondering if that possibility wouldn't be outweighed in their minds by the threat that Corey might steal their existing boyfriends, when Diana interjected smoothly, "Of course, Corey already has a boyfriend back home, and she isn't interested in having another one here."

"I think we should give her a chance and take some time to get to know her before we make up our minds we don't want her in the group," Barb said in the earnest, hesitant tone of a girl who knows the difference between right and wrong, but who lacks the courage to be a leader.

"I'm so glad!" Diana said happily. "I knew you wouldn't let me down. If you had, I'd have missed all of you—I'd have missed sharing some of my best clothes with you, and missed having you go with us to New York next summer."

15

"Missed us? What do you mean?"

"I mean that Corey is going to be my best friend. And best friends have to stick together."

When the others left to return to the party, Cole strolled out of the stall, startling Diana. "Tell me something," he said with a conspiratorial grin. "Does Corey *really* have a boyfriend back home?"

Diana nodded slowly. "Yes."

"Really?" Cole asked dubiously, noticing the guilty laughter in her sparkling eyes. "What's this boyfriend's name?"

She bit her lip. "It's sort of an odd name."

"How odd?"

"Promise you won't tell anyone?"

Enchanted with her face, her voice, her loyalty, and her cleverness, Cole drew an X over his heart with his index finger.

"His name is Sylvester."

"And he's a—?" Cole prompted.

Her gaze mischievously slid away from his, her curly russet lashes casting shadows on her cheekbones as they lowered over the jade of her eyes. "A pig," she confessed.

Her voice had been so low, and Cole had been so certain that Sylvester was a dog or cat, that he thought he had misunderstood. "A pig?" he repeated. "As in *oink?* As in piglet?"

She nodded. "As in 'hog,' actually," she admitted as she lifted glowing green eyes to his. "Corey told me he's huge, and he tags after her at home like a cocker spaniel. At her old home, I mean."

At that moment, Cole decided that Corey was a very lucky girl to have a diminutive but potent champion like Diana Foster to help her bridge the social gulf. Unaware of his silent compliments, Diana glanced at him. "Is there anything to drink in here? I'm really thirsty."

Cole smiled. "Deceit is hard work, isn't it? And there's nothing like going to battle against a half-dozen stuck-up girls to work up a thirst, is there?"

Unabashed, she rolled her eyes at him and smiled. She was spunky as hell, Cole decided, but with a unique soft-spoken style that completely belied her determination and courage. "Sure," he relented, tipping his head to the rear of the stable. "Help yourself."

At the end of the hallway, on the right, Diana found a small room that she assumed was Cole's, with a single bed made up with

16

military perfection and an old desk with an ancient lamp. Books and papers were neatly stacked on the desk and one of them was open. Opposite the bedroom, to the left of the hallway, was a bathroom and tucked behind that was a kitchen area containing only a sink, a small stove, and a miniature refrigerator like the one under Diana's father's bar at home. Diana assumed the refrigerator would be stocked with soft drinks for everyone's use, but when she opened it, there was nothing inside but a package of hot dogs, a carton of milk, and a box of cereal.

She was surprised to see that he kept his cereal in the refrigerator and even more surprised that although this refrigerator was obviously for his use he didn't keep much food in it. Puzzled, she closed the door and filled a paper cup up with water from the sink. When she dropped the cup into the little trash can, she saw two apple cores in it. The apples she brought had been old and soft and completely unappetizing, and she couldn't imagine why he would eat one, let alone two of them. Unless he was hungry. Very, very hungry.

The empty refrigerator and the apple cores were on her mind as she paused to pet a pretty palomino quarter horse; then she returned to the stable entrance to see how Corey was doing. Three girls were talking to her near the corral.

"Do you think you should go out there, in case she needs more help?"

"No, Corey will be fine. She's really great, and they'll find that out. Besides, I don't think she'd like it if she thought I was sort of . . . helping things along."

"You're quite a 'helper outer,'" Cole joked, then realized she was embarrassed, and hastily said, "What if they decide they *don't* like her?"

"Then she'll make lots of other friends on her own. Besides, these girls aren't really close friends of mine, particularly not Haley. Neither is Barbara. It's Doug I really like."

Cole gaped at her, thinking of Barbara's extremely tall and very gangly brother. "Doug is your boyfriend?"

She shot him an odd look and sat down on a bale of hay near the open doors. "No, he's my *friend,* not my boyfriend."

"I thought you were a little short for him," Cole joked, rather enjoying her company. "What's your real boyfriend like?" he asked as he reached for a big red plastic glass he'd left on the windowsill earlier.

"Actually, I don't have a boyfriend. What about you, do you have a girlfriend?"

Cole nodded and took a swallow of water.

"What's she like?" Diana asked.

He propped his foot on the bale of hay near her hip and leaned his forearm on his knee, looking out through a side window that faced the house, and Diana had the feeling that he had drifted very far away. "Her name is Valerie Cooper."

There was a long pause.

"And?" Diana prompted. "Is she blond or dark, short or tall, blue eyes or brown?"

"She's blond and tall."

"I wish I was," she confessed with a wistful look.

"You want to be blond?"

"No," she said, and Cole laughed. "I want to be tall."

"Unless you're planning an amazing growth spurt, you'd better aim for blond," Cole advised lightly. "In your case, blond would be a little easier to achieve."

"What color are her eyes?"

"Blue."

Diana was fascinated. "Have you been going together very long?"

Cole belatedly realized he was not only socializing with one of his employer's guests, which was totally unacceptable, but that the guest was fourteen years old and the conversation was entirely too personal. "Since high school," he said briefly as he straightened and turned to leave.

"Does she live in Houston?" Diana pressed, sensing the conversation was over but rather hoping it wasn't.

"She goes to UCLA. We see each other whenever we can, usually during the holidays."

The birthday party continued for hours, ending with a huge cake served on the lawn, where Barbara opened piles of gifts; then everyone went inside while the servants cleaned up outdoors. Diana had started to follow along when she noticed that half the chocolate birthday cake was still left, and she thought about those lonely hot dogs in Cole's empty refrigerator. On a whim, she walked back to the table and cut a huge chunk off the corner because he'd get more frosting on such a piece; then she took it down to the stable.

Cole's reaction to the chocolate cake was almost comically ecstatic. "You are looking at the owner of the world's biggest sweet tooth, Diana," he said as he took the plate and fork.

He was already eating the cake as he headed down the hall toward his room. Diana watched him for a moment, aware for the first time that people she actually knew, actually came in contact with, didn't always have enough to eat. As she turned away, she decided to bring extra snacks whenever she went to the Haywards, but she sensed instinctively that she'd have to find a way to give them to him that wouldn't make him think it was charity.

She knew nothing about college men, but she knew something about pride, and everything about Cole made her think he had a great deal of it.

Chapter 4

"LIFE IS GOOD," COREY ANNOUNCED TO DIANA TWO MONTHS AFTER Barbara Hayward's birthday party. She'd lowered her voice so they wouldn't be heard by their parents, who had already gone to sleep. The two girls were huddled beneath the quilt on Diana's bed, their backs propped against a pile of feather pillows with lace-edged cases, eating jumbo pretzels and having a gossip session. "I can't wait until you meet Grandma and Grandpa tomorrow. By the time they leave here next week, you'll be crazy about them, you'll see. You'll think of them as if they had always been your very own grandparents."

The truth was that Corey desperately wanted that to be so. She wanted to give Diana something of value to repay her for everything she'd done.

School had started last month, and by that time, Diana had already become Corey's best friend and champion. She helped Corey choose her clothes, helped her fix her hair in different styles, guided her through the social maze at school, and in the end, even

Diana's friends—some of whom *were* snobs—accepted Corey into their inner circle.

Corey spent the first month in a state of gratitude and mounting awe toward her new sister. Unlike Corey, Diana never got flustered, never worried about saying the wrong thing, never made a dumb joke, and never looked like a fool. Her thick, dark reddish-brown hair was always glossy; her complexion was flawless; her figure was perfect. When she climbed out of the swimming pool with her hair soaking wet and no makeup on, she looked like a television commercial. She never even got wrinkles in her clothes!

By then, both girls were already thinking of their respective stepparents as real parents, and now Corey wanted to give Diana some "real grandparents."

"When you meet Gram and Gramps," Corey told her, "you'll see why everybody thinks they're so neat. Gram can figure out a way to make almost anything, and it turns out pretty. She can knit and sew and crochet. She can walk into the woods and come out with ordinary twigs and leaves and stuff, and turn it into amazing things by using just a dab of glue or a little paint. She makes the presents she gives to people, and she makes her own wrapping paper; then she uses things like berries for decoration and everything looks awesome! Mom is just like her. Whenever there's a church auction, everybody in town tries to buy whatever Mom and Gram donated.

"A man who owns a fancy designer gallery in Dallas came to an auction in Long Valley and saw their work. He said they're both really, really talented, and he wanted them to make some things he could sell in his showroom, but Gram said she wouldn't enjoy making things that way. Mom was so tired when she got home from work that she couldn't promise to do what he wanted. Oh, and Gram's a fantastic cook, too. She's really into 'natural,' homegrown stuff—natural food and homegrown veggies and fresh-picked flowers—only you never know whether she's going to decorate with it and put it on the table or put it on your plate. Either way, whatever she makes is just great."

She paused to take a swallow from her can of Coke before she continued, "Gramps loves to garden, and he experiments with ways to grow everything bigger and better. Most of all, he likes to build things."

21

"What sort of things?" Diana asked, fascinated.

"He can build just about anything that can be made out of wood. He can make little rocking chairs for babies, or garden sheds that look like cottages, or tiny furniture for a dollhouse. Gram usually does the painting for him because she's the most artistic one. I can't wait for you to see the dollhouse he built for me! It has fifteen rooms and real shingles and flower boxes on the windows!"

"I'm really looking forward to meeting them. They sound terrific," Diana replied, but Corey was distracted from that discussion by something that had bothered her since the first day she'd peeked into Diana's bedroom, before Diana came home from Europe. "Diana," Corey teased in a dire voice as she surveyed the relentless orderliness of the pretty room, "didn't anyone ever tell you it's *unhealthy* to keep a bedroom this neat?"

Instead of making some sort of deserved rejoinder about Corey's sloppy habits, Diana took a dainty bite of her pretzel and thoughtfully looked around the room. "It probably is," she agreed. "It could be because I have an artistic eye that appreciates symmetry and order. Or it could be because I'm obsessive-compulsive—"

Corey wrinkled her brow. "What's 'obsessive-compulsive' mean?"

"Nuts." Diana paused in her explanation to rub her fingertips free of pretzel dust. "Crazy."

"You're not wacko!" Corey stated loyally and emphatically, taking a bite of her own pretzel. It snapped in two, half of it landing in Diana's lap. Diana's pretzels never broke when she bit into them.

Diana picked it up and handed it back to her. "It could be that I have a neurotic need to keep everything tidy as a way of controlling my surroundings, which was brought about because my mom died when I was little and then my grandparents died a few years later."

"What does your mom dying have to do with why you file your shoes in alphabetical order?"

"The theory is that I think if I keep everything in perfect order and as pretty as possible, then my life will be like that and nothing else bad will happen."

Corey was dumbstruck at the sheer absurdity of such a notion. "Where'd you hear that junk?"

"From the therapist Dad took me to after my grandparents died. The shrink was supposed to help me 'work through' the grief of losing so many people so quickly."

"What a jerk! He's supposed to help you, so he tells you all that stuff to scare you and make you think you're crazy?"

"No, he didn't tell me that. He told Dad, and I eavesdropped."

"What did Dad tell him?"

"He told the shrink that *he* needed a shrink. See, in River Oaks, whenever parents think their kids are getting into trouble, or might someday, they take them to a shrink. Everybody told my dad he should do that and so he did."

Corey digested that and then reverted to her earlier line of thinking. "When I kidded you about being so neat, I was just trying to say that I think it's really amazing that we get along so great even though we're so different. I mean, sometimes I feel like a hopeless charity case who you've taken under your wing, even though I'll never be able to be like you. My grandma always says a leopard can't change its spots, and you can't make a silk purse out of a sow's ear."

"Charity case!" Diana sputtered. "Sow's ear—but—but it isn't like that at all! I've learned lots of new stuff from you, and you have things that I wish I had."

"Name one," Corey said skeptically. "I know it's not my grades or my breasts."

Diana giggled and rolled her eyes; then she said very seriously, "For starters, you have an adventurous side that I don't have."

"One of my 'adventures' will probably land me in jail before I'm eighteen."

"It will not!" Diana said. "What I mean is, when you decide to do something—like take pictures from the top of that scaffolding on that new high-rise—you ignore the danger and just do it!"

"You went up there with me."

"But I didn't want to. I was so scared my legs were shaking."

"But you did it anyway."

"That's what I mean. I never would have done that before. I wish I could be more like you."

Corey considered that for a long moment; then her eyes began to sparkle with mischief. "Well, if you want to be more like me, we should start with this bedroom." She reached behind her head before Diana knew what she was up to.

"What do you mean?"

"Have you ever had a pillow fight?"

"No, wh—" The rest of her question was cut off by a fat pillow stuffed with goose down that landed on her head. Corey swiveled to the foot of the bed and ducked, expecting retribution, but Diana sat very quietly, munching on her pretzel, the pillow lying on her knees. "I can't believe you did that," she said, studying Corey with fascination.

Caught off-guard by her tranquil tone, Corey said, "Why not?"

"Because it makes me have to—*retaliate!*"

Diana lunged so swiftly, and her aim was so good, that Corey didn't have time to duck. Laughing, she dived for another one of the pillows, and so did Diana. Five minutes later, when their concerned parents threw open the bedroom door, they had to peer through a blizzard of drifting feathers to locate the two teenage girls, who were lying on their backs in the middle of the bedroom, shrieking with laughter.

"What in the world is going on in here?" Mr. Foster said, sounding more alarmed than annoyed.

"Pillow fight," Diana provided breathlessly. A feather was stuck to her lips, and she started to remove it with her thumb and forefinger.

"No, just *spit* it out," Corey laughingly instructed her, and then demonstrated, forcing the feathers away from her lips with her breath and the tip of her tongue.

Diana followed suit, then dissolved into giggles at the expression on her father's face. While feathers floated around his head and settled onto his shoulders, he stood stock-still in his robe and pajamas, gaping at them beside Diana's new mom, who was trying to look stern and hide her laughter at the same time. "We'll clean this mess up before we go to bed," Diana promised.

"No we won't," Corey stated implacably. "First you have to sleep in this mess. If you can do that, then there's a slim chance that with more practice you could become a marvelous slob like me!"

Still lying on the floor, Diana turned her head toward Corey and choked back another giggle. "Oh, do you *really* think so?"

"There's a chance," Corey declared solemnly. "If you truly, truly work at it."

Robert Foster looked taken aback at the plan, but his wife put her hand on his sleeve and drew him out of the room, closing the door behind them. In the hallway, he looked at his new wife with a baffled expression. "The girls made that mess, don't you think they should clean it up tonight?"

"Tomorrow is soon enough," Mary Foster said.

"Those pillows are expensive. Diana should have thought of that ahead of time. It's reckless and irresponsible to have destroyed them, honey."

"Bob," she said softly, tucking her arm in his and marching him down the hall and into their bedroom suite. "Diana is the most *responsible* girl I've ever met."

"I've taught her to be that way. It's important for an adult to be conscious of the consequences of their actions and to act accordingly."

"Darling," she whispered. "She *isn't* an adult."

He considered that while a mischievous grin lifted the corners of his mouth. "You're right about that, but do you really think it's important that she also learn how to spit?"

"It's imperative," his wife said with a laugh.

Leaning down, he kissed the smile off her face. "I love you," he whispered.

She kissed him back. "I love Diana," she answered.

"I know, and that makes me love you even more." He got into bed and pulled her on top of him, his hands shifting over her silk negligee. "You know I love Corey, don't you?"

She nodded, her right hand reaching stealthily for the feather pillow on the headboard.

"You've changed our lives," he continued.

"Thank you," she whispered, lifting off his chest into a sitting position beside his hip. "Now let me change your attitude."

"About what?"

"Pillow fights," she said, laughing as she smacked him with her pillow.

Down the hall, in Diana's room, the sisters heard a loud thud. Both girls jumped to their feet in alarm and ran down the hall. "Mom, Dad—" Diana called, knocking on the door. "Is everything okay? We heard a noise!"

"Nothing's wrong," Mary Foster called, "but I could use a little help in here."

Diana and Corey exchanged puzzled looks; then Diana turned the knob and opened the door. They stopped dead. Openmouthed, they gaped at their parents, then at each other.

And they burst into shrieks of laughter.

On the floor, amid another blizzard of feathers, their father had pinned their mother beneath him and was holding her forearms against the carpet. "Say uncle," he ordered.

His wife laughed harder.

"Say uncle, or I won't let you up."

In response to that arrogant masculine command, Mary Foster looked at her daughters, struggled for breath, and managed to say between laughs, "I think women have to . . . to stick together . . . at times like . . . this."

The girls stuck together. The score that night was 12 to 2; twelve feather pillows that met their demise against two foam-rubber pillows that survived.

Chapter 5

BRIMMING WITH GOOD NEWS, DIANA SNATCHED HER SCHOOLBOOKS from the leather seat of the new BMW her father had given her last month for her sixteenth birthday and raced up the steps of the stately Georgian mansion that had been her first and only home. In the two years since her stepmother, and then her stepgrandparents, had come to live with them in River Oaks, the house and grounds had changed in atmosphere and appearance. Laughter and conversation had filled the empty silences; wonderful smells emanated from the kitchen; flowers bloomed in rampant splendor in the gardens and splashed their colors in beautiful arrangements all over the house.

Everyone was happy with the new look, the new atmosphere, and the new family arrangements—everyone except Glenna, the housekeeper who'd helped raise Diana after her mother died. It was Glenna who was in the foyer when Diana ran into the house. "Glenna, is Corey home?"

"I think she's out in back with everyone else, talking about tomorrow night's party." Glenna finished dusting a walnut console

27

table and straightened, giving it a close look. "When your mama was alive, she called in caterers and florists when she wanted to give a party. She used to let *them* do all the work," she added pointedly. "That's the way most rich folks entertain each other, but not us."

"Nope, not us," Diana said with a quick smile. "Now we're trendsetters." She headed down the hall, toward the back of the house, with Glenna walking beside her, irritably swiping her dustcloth at nonexistent specks of dust on tables and chairs as they passed.

"Used to be, when we gave a party," Glenna continued doggedly, "that everything only had to look pretty and taste good. But now, that's not good enough. Now everything has to be *fresh* and everything has to be *natural* and everything has to be *homegrown* and *homemade*. Homegrown and homemade is for country folks. I realize your grandparents are country folks, and they don't understand that . . ."

Glenna had become perpetually miffed ever since Diana's new mother and grandmother had taken over the household.

Corey's grandparents and Diana had fallen in love with one another during their first visit together. After several months of the girls splitting their time between Long Valley, where Rose and Henry Britton lived, and River Oaks, Robert instructed an architect and a building contractor to renovate and enlarge the estate's guest cottage. The next step was a greenhouse for Rose and a vegetable garden for Henry.

Robert was rewarded for his generosity with fresh fruits and vegetables grown on his own property and mouthwatering meals served in an endless variety of delightful ways and changing locations.

Robert had never liked to eat in the vast kitchen at the back of his house. It had been designed to accommodate the small army of caterers who were needed on those occasions when a large party was being given. With its white tile walls, oversize stainless-steel appliances, and uninspiring view from its single window, it struck Robert as institutional, sterile, and uninviting.

Until Mary and her family had come into his life, he had contented himself with the fiery fare that his cook, Conchita, prepared, which he had eaten as quickly as possible in the rigid formality of his dining room. He would never have considered eating under a tree in his pleasant but uninspiring backyard or dining beside the Olympic-size rectangular pool that his builder had unimaginatively stuck near the middle of the yard and surrounded with an ocean of concrete.

Now, however, Robert was a changed man, living in a greatly altered environment, enjoying savory meals, and he loved it. The kitchen he had once avoided had become his favorite room. Gone was the sterility of white tile walls and blank, gloomy spaces. On one end, Henry had created a solarium by installing skylights in the ceiling and tall windows along the outside wall. In this cozy, bright area were comfortable sofas and chairs for lounging in while dinner preparations were underway. Mary and Rose had hand-stenciled vines and flowers on each piece and covered the thick cushions with fabric of the same pattern. Then they'd filled the area with a profusion of green plants growing in white pots.

At the opposite end of the refurbished kitchen, the ordinary white tiles had been ornamented with a festive border of hand-painted ones. Mellow old bricks gathered from a torn-down building now covered one wall and formed a wide arch over the stoves, above which hung copper pots and pans in every size and shape.

His wife and her family had transformed his surroundings, bringing breathtaking natural beauty to the grounds and inviting charm to interior spaces. Whether their current project was unique place mats, elaborate picture frames, graceful, hand-painted furniture, gilded vegetable centerpieces, or elegant foil gift-wrap, it was created with a wealth of love.

A year after her marriage to Robert, Mary had made her formal debut as his hostess by planning and executing a lavish garden luau for the sophisticated, somewhat world-weary Houston socialites who were Robert's peers and friends.

Instead of calling in professional caterers and florists, Mary and Rose supervised the preparation and presentation of food, which was cooked according to their own recipes, seasoned with herbs from Henry's garden, and served by flickering torchlight on tables covered with hand-appliquéd linens lavishly strewn with Henry's showy blossoms.

In keeping with the luau theme, Mary and her mother gathered hundreds of orchids from their own greenhouse; then Diana and Corey and four of their friends were put to work making elegant leis. Mary and Rose decided that each lady should receive a small lacquered ring box decorated with tiny painted orchids in the same hues as the real ones used for the leis. Clinging to the belief that even jaded Houston millionaires would surely appreciate the merits and uniqueness of her handcrafted table decorations, homegrown edibles, and the changes she'd made to soften and brighten the house's austere formality, Mary and her mother spent many happy hours in the kitchen planning and creating.

Two hours before the party, Mary inspected the grounds and the house, and burst into tears in her husband's arms. "Oh, darling, you shouldn't have let me do this!" she moaned. "Everyone will think I've ruined your beautiful home with homemade j-junk. Your friends are world travelers accustomed to five-star restaurants, formal balls, and priceless antiques, and I'm putting on a—a fancy backyard barbeque for them." Tears dripped from her eyes as she clung to him, her wet face pressed to his chest. "They're going to think you married the Beverly Hillbillies!"

Robert stroked her back and smiled over her shoulder. He, too, had taken a tour of his house and grounds that day, looking at everything through the eyes of an outsider. What he saw filled him with pride and anticipation. He truly felt that Mary and her parents had brought a whole new meaning to the term "homemade." They had redefined and elevated it to a creative act that personalized the impersonal and transformed commonplace things into items of remarkable beauty and significance. He was convinced his guests were discerning enough to recognize and value the uniqueness and beauty of Mary's efforts. He thought they were going to be amazed by her as well as everything she had done. "You're going to dazzle them, Mary girl," he whispered. "You'll see."

Robert was right.

The guests raved about the delicious food, the decorations, the flowers, the gardens, the house, and, most particularly, the unaffected graciousness of the hostess. The same acquaintances who had expressed amused shock months ago when they discovered Robert had plowed up part of his lawn for a vegetable garden tasted the vegetables it had produced and asked to have a look at it. As a result, Henry spent several hours proudly giving moonlight tours of the garden. As he guided them along the neat rows of organically grown vegetables, his enthusiasm was so contagious that before the night was over, several of the men had announced their desire to have vegetable gardens of their own.

Marge Crumbaker, the society gossip columnist for the *Houston Post* who covered the party, summarized the reactions of the guests in her next column.

As she presided over this lovely party and looked after her guests, Mrs. Robert Foster III (the former Mary Britton of Long Valley) displayed a graciousness, a hospitality, and an attention to her guests that will surely make her one of Houston's leading hostesses. Also present at the festivities were Mrs. Foster's parents, Mr. and Mrs. Henry Britton, who were kind enough to escort many fascinated guests and would-be gardeners and handymen (if we only had the time!) through the new garden, greenhouse, and workshop that Bob Foster has erected on the grounds of his River Oaks mansion. . . .

Now, a year later, Diana thought of all that as Glenna continued her litany of complaints about the upcoming party. To keep from getting angry, she reminded herself that Glenna didn't really dislike her stepmother or grandparents; Glenna simply disliked being replaced as head of "domestic affairs." As far as Diana was concerned, life was wonderful, so filled with people and activities, with love and laughter . . .

"I'm the last one to point a finger at a person's upbringing," Glenna confided, "but if Mrs. Foster had been from a nice high-society family, instead of from some rinky-dink little town, then she'd know how rich people are *supposed* to do things. Last year, when your daddy told me he was bringing her parents here to live in the guesthouse, I figured things couldn't get any worse. Next thing I knew, your new grandpa was digging himself a vegetable patch and a compost heap, right in our backyard; then he turned the garage into a—a toolshed and a greenhouse! And before I could catch a breath, your new grandma was diggin' up the grass for an herb garden and making clay pots with her own hands. It's a miracle that gossip-column lady—Marge somebody—didn't call us hicks in her column after she came here for the first party."

"Glenna, that's completely unfair, and you know it," Diana said, pausing to put down her schoolbooks. "Everybody who meets Mom or Gram or Gramps thinks they're wonderful and special, and they are! Why, we're getting famous in Houston for what Mom calls 'Getting Back to Basics.' That's why *Southern Living* magazine is coming to photograph our party tomorrow night."

"It'll be a miracle if they don't make us look ridiculous!"

"They don't think we're ridiculous," Diana said as she shoved open the back door. *"Southern Living* saw those pictures of our last party that were in the *Houston Chronicle,* and the magazine wants to do a story about the way we do things."

Recalling what her father had said about the need to be patient and understanding with Glenna, Diana smiled at her. She knew that she and her father were about all the family Glenna had. "Daddy and I know it's harder for you with four extra people to look after, especially when they're busy with their hobbies and things. We worry about you being overworked, and that's why he wants you to hire someone to help you."

Much of the ire drained from Glenna's face at this proof she was appreciated. "I don't need help. I've managed well enough on my own to take care of this family, haven't I?"

Diana patted her arm fondly as she walked outside, her mind on finding Corey. "You were like a mother to me for years. Daddy and I could never have gotten along without you before, and we couldn't now." The last part of that wasn't entirely true, but Diana felt the small fib was excusable because it brought an instant look of relief and pleasure to Glenna's dour face.

Diana stood beneath the upper balcony, looking for a sign of Corey amidst the chaos and temporary helpers hired for the party preparations.

Originally, the three-acre backyard had been spacious but unremarkable, with a large swimming pool in the middle, a guesthouse at the rear, tennis courts on the left, and a six-car garage on the right that was attached to the main house by a porte cochere. Diana had played out there for as long as she could remember, and it had always felt a little lonely and barren to her, just as the big rambling house had. Now all that had changed.

Despite her pleasure in the changes to her home and her family, Diana felt a little worried at the current state of affairs in the backyard. With little more than a day before the crew from *Southern*

Living was due to arrive, nothing was ready. Tables and chairs were scattered everywhere, along with umbrellas on the ground, waiting to be put up; her grandfather was on a ladder, trying to finish a gazebo by tomorrow night; her grandmother was arguing with two gardeners about the best way to clip the magnolia branches that were going to be used in the centerpieces; and her mother was reading from a list to two maids who'd been hired for the week.

Diana was still looking for Corey when her father emerged from the garage with his briefcase in hand and his suit coat over his arm. "Hi, Daddy," she said, leaning up and giving him a kiss. "You're home early."

He put his arm around her shoulders, his gaze taking in the elaborate confusion. "I thought I'd come see how the troops are doing. How are things at school?"

"Okay. I got elected class president today."

His arm tightened in an affectionate squeeze. "That's great. Now, don't forget all the ways you were going to make things better." His eyes smiled down at her, then shifted to his wife and his mother-in-law, who'd seen him and were heading his way with warm smiles and purposeful strides. "Well, Madame President, something tells me I'm about to be put to work," he teased. "I'm surprised you and Corey haven't been enlisted."

"Our job is to 'stay out from underfoot,'" she recited. "I came home to get Corey because Barb Hayward invited us over to ride today."

"I think Corey is in her bathroom," their mother offered, "developing some film."

"Oh, I think she'll want to go over to the Haywards'," Diana said, already turning and heading into the house. Actually, she was positive Corey would want to go, not to ride horses, but to see Spencer Addison, who was supposed to be at the Haywards' stable that afternoon.

Corey's bedroom was directly across the hall from Diana's. Both rooms were identical in size and layout, with private bathrooms, separate dressing rooms, and large closets. Beyond that, the bedrooms were as radically different as the personalities and interests of the two girls who inhabited them.

At sixteen, Diana was petite, poised, and charmingly feminine.

33

She was still a straight-A student and an avid reader, with a propensity for neatness, a talent for organization, and a tendency to be a little reserved with strangers.

Her bedroom was furnished in French antiques, including a graceful painted armoire and a canopy bed upholstered in yellow chintz. Against the opposite wall was a French writing desk, where she did her homework. There was not a paper or pen out of place.

Diana went into her room, put her books down on the desk, and went into her closet. She took off her red cotton sweater, folded it neatly, and placed it on an empty shelf amid dozens of other identically folded sweaters that were all displayed and divided according to color hue, rather than style or sleeve length.

She peeled off her pleated navy slacks and hung them on a pants hanger in the section with blue slacks and shorts; then she padded barefoot along the row to the white section and removed a pair of pleated white shorts. From the sweater shelves she took down a navy polo trimmed in white piping and pulled it over her head. After slipping her feet into a pair of white sandals from the neat row of shoes along the floor of her closet, she stopped at her dressing table and ran a brush through her hair. Automatically, she picked up a tube of light pink lipstick, used it, and stepped back to study her reflection.

The face that looked back at her seemed extremely ordinary and unnoteworthy to her, and it wasn't changing in any noticeable way with maturity. The same green eyes and dark lashes were in the same place they'd always been, and even a touch of eye shadow made them look garish, instead of more pronounced, to her. Her cheekbones were high, but blusher made her feel as though she were made up for a masquerade, and liquid makeup didn't seem to make any difference in her skin at all, so she skipped that, too. She had a tiny dent in the center of her chin, which refused to shrink or go away. Her hair was her best feature, thick and gleaming from careful washing and brushing, but she preferred to wear it in simple styles that didn't require a lot of bother or maintenance, and she thought those looked the best on her anyway. After considering the wilting heat and humidity outside, she pulled it back into a ponytail with quick deft movements; then she went to find Corey to impart her news.

Corey's bedroom door was open, but she was nowhere in sight.

The door to her bathroom was closed, however, and Diana gingerly picked her way toward it through the jungle of clothing, shoes, scarves, photograph albums, camera equipment, and miscellaneous debris that covered every surface of the room. "Corey?" she called. "Are you in there?"

"Be out in a sec," Corey answered from inside. "I just need to hang this film up to dry. It looks like I got a great shot of Spence when he was playing night tennis at the club last week! I think I'm finally getting the hang of night photography."

"Hurry up. I have great news," Diana said with a smile as she turned away from the closed door.

Corey's interest in photography had begun two years ago, when Mr. Foster had given Corey her first camera, and it had grown into a full-fledged hobby. Her interest in Spencer Addison had begun one year ago, when she spotted him at a party, and it had grown into a full-fledged obsession. Pictures of him at home, at parties, at sports events, and even at the McDonald's drive-through in his car were taped to her mirror, tacked to her bulletin board, and framed on her wall.

Despite the fact that Spence was a football star at Southern Methodist University, where he dated beautiful coeds who drooled over his good looks and sports prowess, Corey never stopped believing that luck, persistence, and prayer would someday make him hers and hers alone.

"I was right," Corey said, emerging with a strip of wet negatives in her hand. "Just look at this shot of Spence making that serve!"

Diana grinned at her. "Why don't we go over to the Haywards' so you can see him in person?"

Corey's face lit up with joy. "He's home from school? You're sure?" Before Diana could reply, Corey ran back into the bathroom to hang up the film, then raced back out to the mirror over her dresser. "What should I wear? Do I have time to wash my hair?" Sounding as if she would die of disappointment if Diana was wrong, she said, "Are you *sure* he's going to be there?"

"I'm sure. Doug Hayward happened to mention that Spence was going over to their place after dinner to try out Doug's new polo pony. As soon as he told me, I found Barb and—very casually— wrangled an invitation for us to come over there tonight. I put gas in the car, and as soon as dinner's over, we can go."

Corey knew Diana didn't like to ride horses, and she knew it was boring for Diana to watch everyone else ride when the two of them went to the Haywards', but Diana was always willing to tag along because Corey loved to ride. Now she'd gotten them an invitation to go to the Haywards' because Spence was going to be there. "You're an awesome sister!" Corey said, giving her an impulsive hug.

Diana returned it and stepped back. "Hurry up and get ready, so we can eat and get there before Spence does. If you're already there, then it can't look to anyone as if you're chasing him."

"You're right!" Corey said, impressed yet again by Diana's foresight. No matter what Corey wanted to do, Diana tried to help her accomplish it, but Diana also thought ahead, looking for ways to keep Corey from getting embarrassed or into a mess. Diana excelled at looking ahead and thinking of the risks, but Corey was so impulsive and so persuasive that she still landed in deep water now and then, and Diana usually landed in it right beside her.

It was inevitable that some of their ill-fated escapades would come to the attention of their parents, and when that happened, Corey's mother usually took it in stride and pointed out that there was no real harm done.

Diana's father, however, was less philosophical about such things as having his daughters lost overnight in Yellowstone National Park because Corey wanted to photograph a sunrise with elk in the shot. He was not pleased to discover from the newspaper that his daughters had been rescued from a construction elevator on the thirtieth floor of an unfinished high-rise that was surrounded by an eight-foot fence and posted "Absolutely No Admittance."

"While you're getting dressed," Diana said as she turned and started toward the back stairs that led down to the kitchen, "I'll go downstairs and see what kind of food I can find to bring for Cole."

"For who?" Corey said, her mind fixated on the unexpected thrill of seeing Spence.

"Cole Harrison. You know—at the Haywards' stable. Doug said Cole's back from his vacation," she explained with a smile and a breathless catch in her voice. "Unless something's changed, he'll be short of food, as usual."

Corey watched her walk away, immobilized by the unmistakable undercurrent of excitement she'd just witnessed in Diana. Not once had Diana ever said anything to indicate she had secret feelings for the Haywards' stable hand, but then Diana didn't blurt out every thought that came into her mind the way Corey did.

Once the idea of Diana and Cole had taken root, Corey couldn't seem to shake it loose. In the shower, as she worked shampoo into a thick lather, she tried to envision Diana and Cole as a twosome, but it was just too ludicrous.

Diana was sweet and pretty and popular, and she had her choice among the wealthy guys from backgrounds like her own — guys like Spencer Addison, who never made social blunders and who were sophisticated and well-traveled by the time they were seventeen or eighteen. They grew up in country clubs, where they played golf and tennis, and wore custom-made tuxedos to formal dinners by the time they were sixteen.

Wrapped in a towel, Corey pulled a brush through her long, blond hair, still trying to understand how Diana could possibly prefer someone like Cole, who had none of Spence's polish or charisma. Spence looked like heaven in a navy blue sport jacket and khaki slacks, or tennis whites, or a white dinner jacket. Whatever he did or whatever he wore, Spencer Addison looked as if he was "born to the blue," as Gram often said of wealthy Houston youths. With his sun-streaked, tawny hair, smiling amber eyes, and refined good looks, Spence was handsome, polished, and warm.

Cole was Spence's opposite in every way. His hair was black, his face was tanned, his features were rugged, and his eyes were the cool, unsettling gray of a stormy sky. Corey'd never seen him in anything except faded jeans and a T-shirt or sweatshirt, and she couldn't even imagine him playing tennis with Diana at the club in tennis whites or dancing with her in a tuxedo.

She'd heard the saying that "opposites attract," but in this case the differences were too extreme. It was almost impossible to believe that practical, sweet, fastidious Diana would actually be attracted to all that raw sex appeal and macho ruggedness. He wasn't even very friendly to anyone! He did have a great physique, but Diana was so petite and dainty that he'd tower over her if they went anywhere together.

To the best of Corey's knowledge, Diana had never had a real crush on anyone, not even on Matt Dillon or Richard Gere. It seemed impossible to believe she'd go and get a crush on a guy like Cole, who didn't seem to care what he wore or where he slept. Not that there was anything wrong with how he lived or dressed; it was just that it seemed so wrong for someone like Diana.

Corey paused, a pair of tan riding breeches in her hand, when she remembered that Barb Hayward and the other girls didn't share Corey's indifference to Cole, either. In fact, he was the object of a great many secret fantasies and a whole lot of speculation. Barb Hayward thought Cole made all the other guys they knew look like wimps in comparison. Haley Vincennes thought he was "sexy."

Corey was so bewildered that for a moment she had forgotten she was going to see Spence tonight. When she remembered, she felt the same sharp stab of longing and delight that she'd experienced the first time she had set eyes on him and every time since.

Chapter 6

Corey was too excited to eat more than a few bites of her dinner, and when her grandmother remarked on it, the conversation at the large oak kitchen table came to a halt and everyone except Diana turned to her with concern. "You've hardly touched your dinner, Corey. Is anything wrong, dear?"

"No, nothing's wrong. I'm just not very hungry," she said.

"Are you in a hurry?" her mother asked.

"Why do you think that?" she asked innocently.

"Because you keep looking at your watch," Grandpa observed.

"Oh, that's because Diana and I are going over to the Haywards' to ride tonight," Corey said, feeling harassed by all this scrutiny. "Doug has a new polo pony, and we're going to watch him work in the ring. Mr. Hayward had big lights put up so the ring can be used at night, when it's cooler."

"A new polo pony!" her father exclaimed with a knowing smile at her perfect hair and carefully applied makeup. "I guess you're hoping to make a good impression on him when you see him for the first time."

39

To satisfy everyone, Corey had taken a large bite of chicken. Now she swallowed it and looked at her father with a puzzled smile. "Why do you say that?"

"Well, because your hair looks like you spent the day at the beauty shop, and you're wearing lipstick and that pink powdery stuff on your cheeks, and is that—" Suppressing a laugh, he peered at her eyelids. "Is that mascara I see on your lashes?"

"I don't think there's anything wrong with getting dressed up for a family dinner now and then, do you?"

"Certainly not," he agreed at once. Pretending to address his remarks to his wife, he said, "I had lunch at the club today, and I ran into Spence's grandmother. She was playing bridge in the ladies' card room."

"How is Mrs. Bradley?" Diana asked hastily. Spence had lived with his grandmother since he was a little boy, and Diana had a feeling she knew what her father was getting at. Trying to spare Corey the inevitable teasing, she added, "I haven't seen her in months."

"Mrs. Bradley is very well. In fact, she was in remarkably high spirits today. The reason she was in such—"

"She has so much energy for someone her age, doesn't she, Mom?" Diana asked.

Diana had rushed in, but her father wasn't going to be deterred. "—high spirits was because Spence surprised her by coming home for the weekend to celebrate her birthday with her."

"He's such a nice young man," Gram said. "So charming and thoughtful."

"And so fond of polo, too," Grandpa provided with a meaningful smile aimed straight at Corey. "And such a good friend of the Haywards, isn't he?" Four faces gazed at Corey with identical expressions of knowing amusement. Only Diana abstained.

"The problem with this family is that everybody pays too much attention to what everybody else is doing and thinking."

"You're right, dear," Gram said, giving Corey's shoulder an affectionate pat as she got up to help Glenna clear away the dinner dishes. "It's not good to eat on a nervous stomach. Why don't you run upstairs and fix your lipstick so it looks as nice as it did when you came down to dinner."

Relieved, Corey slid out of her chair and carried her plate over to the sink; then she headed upstairs. Over her shoulder, she said to Diana, "Let's leave in fifteen minutes."

Diana nodded, but her thoughts were on Cole. "Gram," she said, "can I take that leftover chicken to the Haywards'?"

Her grandmother said yes immediately, but at the table, her mother, father, and grandfather exchanged startled looks. "Diana," her father said, sounding baffled, "What would the Haywards do with our leftover chicken?"

"Oh, it's not for them," Diana said as she opened the refrigerator and took out several apples and oranges. "It's for Cole."

"Coal?" He repeated, nonplussed. "As in the black rock we used for fuel in the old days?"

Diana laughed. "No, *Cole* as in your friend *Cole Martins*," Diana explained, referring to a wealthy rancher friend of her father's. She opened the pantry doors, surveying the contents as she continued, "This Cole works at the Haywards' stable and lives there, too, but he's thin, and I don't think he wants to 'waste' what little money he has on food."

"Poor old feller," Grandpa said, filled with misplaced sympathy for the plight of the elderly.

"He's not old," Diana said absently as she eyed the rows of home-canned fruits and vegetables on the shelves. "He doesn't like to talk much about himself, but I know he is in college, and he's had to work to put himself through school." Diana glanced over her shoulder at her grandmother, who was already piling broiled chicken breasts and steamed vegetables into a large plastic container. "Gram, could I take some of your canned peaches and a few of these jams, too?"

"Yes, of course you can." Mrs. Britton wiped her hands on a towel and walked into the pantry to assist Diana. She got down a paper bag and put three jars of each item into it.

"The last time I brought Cole some of your strawberry preserves," Diana added, "he said it was better than candy, and he's crazy about candy."

Aglow at this praise from a hungry stranger, Mrs. Britton promptly added four more jars of strawberry preserves to the bag, then headed for an antique blue transfer ware china platter on the kitchen countertop. "If he likes sweets, he should have some of these blueberry muffins. There's no sugar and hardly any fat in

41

them, so they're very healthy." She piled a half dozen of them on a plate. "Oh, and he really ought to have some of those hazelnut brownies I made yesterday."

When she reached for a second paper bag and headed back into the pantry, Diana stopped her. "I don't want him to think this is charity, Gram." With an apologetic grin, she added, "I have him completely convinced that you're sort of a 'compulsive canning addict' and that we always have piles of leftovers after every meal."

Grandpa had gotten up to refill his coffee cup, and he chuckled at Diana's fabrication. Putting his arm around her shoulders, he said, "He must think we're either addled or wasteful."

"I'm sure he thinks both," Diana admitted, blissfully unaware that her parents were eyeing her with barely concealed fascination. "I figured it was better to let him think that than to let him feel like a charity case," she explained with a smile as she picked up the heavy brown paper bag and wrapped both her arms around it.

"I haven't heard a word about this young man before tonight," her father said flatly. "What's he like?"

"Like? He's . . . well . . . he's different—from any of the other boys we know."

"Different how?" her father asked. "Different as in a rebel—a renegade—a malcontent?"

Diana considered that from the kitchen doorway, shifting the heavy bag into her right arm for better balance. "He's probably a renegade, but not in a bad way. He's . . ." She looked at them, and finally added, ". . . special. He's just special. I can't explain why or how, but I know he is. He's not like the other boys I've known. He seems much older, more worldly. He's—he's just not like any other boy," she finished lamely. She wiggled her hand in a cheerful wave, too eager to be on her way to notice the speculative looks on the faces she left behind. "Bye, everybody."

After several moments of silence, her father looked from his wife to his in-laws. "I happen to *like* the other boys she's known."

"This one is different," Gram echoed.

"Which is why I feel sure I won't like him."

"Robert," his wife soothed, "this is the first young man Diana has showed a particular interest in, and you're a little jealous. You acted the same way last year when Corey started talking about Spence all the time."

"I'm used to that now," he said, a little disgruntled. "I never thought in my wildest dreams her crush on Spence would last a month. It's lasted a year, and it's gotten worse, instead of better."

"She thinks she's in love with him," Mary Foster said wryly.

"She *thought* she was in love with him the night she met him. Now she's sure she wants to marry him. Have you looked in her bedroom lately? She's wallpapered her walls with his pictures. She's turned it into a shrine. The whole thing's ridiculous."

Grandpa Britton shared a little of his son-in-law's pique over being replaced in the girls' lives by other males. "Corey will get over it. It won't last. Girls don't fall in love when they're fourteen; they only think they're in love."

His wife picked up a pencil to put the finishing touches on a simple but elegant stencil design she was creating for a border along the top of the guest bathroom walls. "Henry, I fell in love with you when *I* was fourteen."

Robert Foster had lost the thread of the conversation. Staring toward the doorway where he'd last seen Diana, he said, "Was it just me, or did it look to anyone else like Diana was blushing when she talked about that stableboy?"

"College student," Mary corrected quietly; then she laid her hand over his and gave it a reassuring squeeze. He relaxed and smiled sheepishly. "It's just that I have such big plans for the girls. I don't want them to get absorbed with boys and all that too early to realize what they'll miss if they get married too young."

"Don't make any plans for Corey," Gram said dryly. "She's already made her own. She wants to marry Spence, and she wants to become a famous photographer."

"Not, I hope, in that order," Robert said.

Gram ignored that. "As for Diana, I can see her becoming an interior designer, or maybe an architect, or maybe a writer. She has a lot of talent for all of those things, but she doesn't seem too eager to be any of them. I hate to see gifts like hers go to waste."

"Her real gift won't go to waste," he argued. When everyone looked expectantly at him, he said proudly, "She may have gotten her mother's artistic eye, but she has *my* brain. In time, she'll find her own ways of putting it to use. She's always been interested in business."

"Business is good," his wife said with a nod and a smile.

"Business is very good," Grandpa said.

The women looked at each other and both of them got up. "There's only a half hour of daylight left, Mom. I could use some advice about the table arrangements."

Mrs. Britton hesitated and looked at the men. "Are you both sure you don't want some fresh strawberries with yogurt topping for dessert?"

"I couldn't eat another bite," Mr. Foster said.

"Me, either," Henry Britton agreed, patting his stomach to indicate it was stuffed to capacity. "You're right about these all-natural, low-fat meals, Rosie. They're very satisfying once you get used to them. That broiled chicken hit the spot; it really did. You girls go ahead outdoors and do what you need to do."

The two men sat there in innocent silence, listening for the sound of the back door opening. The moment it closed behind their wives, they got up. Robert Foster headed straight for the freezer and took out French vanilla ice cream, while Henry Britton hurried to a lower cupboard and removed a Dutch apple pie that Glenna had bought at the bakery earlier and hidden there for them.

Henry cut into the deep-dish pie and glanced at his coconspirator. "Large piece or medium?" he asked his son-in-law.

"Large."

Henry cut two hefty pieces of the pie and laid them carefully on plates, while Robert dug the ice cream scoop deep into the container and came out with a heaping portion.

"One scoop or two, Hank?"

"Two," Henry said.

They glanced up at Glenna as she moved efficiently around the kitchen, tidying up. "You're a saint, Glenna."

"I'm a traitor."

"You have job security for as long as I live," Robert countered with a grin.

"Your wives would fire me if they knew what you two make me do."

"We'd hire you right back," Henry said, closing his eyes and savoring the sublime taste of forbidden sugar and fats. He looked at his son-in-law, whose expression of utter contentment matched his. "I thought Mary and Rose were never going to leave us alone in here tonight. I was afraid we'd have to wait until after they'd gone to sleep to raid the kitchen."

Outside on the lawn, Mary stood with her back to the kitchen window, discussing rearranging the tables for tomorrow night's party. "I think we should," Rose said. "I'll get Henry and Robert to help us."

"Not yet," Mary said dryly. "They haven't finished their dessert."

Rose plunked her hands indignantly on her hips. "What is it this time?"

"Dutch apple pie."

"We ought to fire that Glenna. Before Conchita retired, she kept Glenna out of the kitchen."

Mary sighed with resignation and shook her head. "Glenna's only following orders. Besides, they'd just hire her back. Except for the desserts they sneak, we've got them both on a sound low-fat diet, and I know Robert sticks with it at breakfast and lunch." She started to move the heavy table into position a little at a time, and Rose pitched in to help her. "His doctor told him yesterday that his cholesterol level was finally coming down," Mary added.

"What about his blood pressure?"

"Don't ask."

Chapter 7

THE RIDING RING WAS ON A SLIGHT INCLINE, THIRTY YARDS TO THE right of the stable. It was surrounded by a low, white fence and brightly lit now by huge, new mercury-vapor lights on high poles that shone almost as bright as daylight on the ring and simultaneously cast everything else into shadow.

From her vantage point just outside the stable, Diana watched Spence dismount and begin leading the handsome sorrel around the ring to cool him down. He said something to Corey that made her laugh as she walked along beside him, and Diana smiled with pleasure that Corey's evening was turning out so well.

Instead of having to share him with Doug and Barb Hayward and Doug's father plus one of Spence's innumerable and inevitable girlfriends, as Corey and Diana had expected, Corey had him entirely to herself. The Haywards had at the last minute remembered a relative's birthday party and were attending that, and Spence was by himself.

Diana's evening hadn't turned out badly, either. She'd had Cole entirely to herself. Managing to see him as often as she could

46

without having it seem contrived had been the second hardest thing she'd ever done — second only to keeping her feelings for him a complete secret from him and everyone else.

Nearly all of Barb's friends had wild crushes on him. He was tall, tanned, wide-shouldered, and narrow-hipped. In snug, soft jeans and a short-sleeved shirt, every inch of his muscled body exuded power and raw sex appeal. His complete lack of social standing, his lack of money, and his lowly job at the stable made him off-limits to them. Which made him infinitely more attractive.

He refused to talk about himself to them, which made him mysterious and all the more fascinating.

He was unattainable, which made him even more desirable.

He was immune to their looks, their money, and their ploys. And that made him a challenge.

Since Cole couldn't be coerced or tricked into talking about himself, they spent endless hours speculating about his family and his friends back home and inventing dire experiences that might have made him want to forget or bury his past.

They did everything to get his attention, from trying to flirt with him, to wearing their tightest pants and most revealing tops, to asking him to examine nonexistent ankle sprains and hurt wrists, to pretending to fall against him when they dismounted.

One by one, Diana had watched Cole's reactions to each girl's attempt to flirt with him, and she soon realized that the more blatant the attempt was, the stronger his retaliation. Milder transgressors were treated like children, subjected to his open amusement and spoken to in a condescendingly superior way that made the transgressor squirm. More daring transgressors received a much more unbearable punishment: they were subjected to weeks of cool and distant behavior. Unfortunately, both of his tactics made it necessary to find ways to get back into his good graces, which made him seem even more powerful and desirable.

At one point or another, during the last two years, practically every girl who rode at the Haywards' place had claimed that he'd done or said something to indicate he had some secret interest in *her*. In April of this year, nine of the girls had each bet ten dollars on who would be the first to kiss him. Diana had abstained, claiming he simply didn't appeal to her, but she volunteered to be the treasurer — and silently prayed she'd never have to hand the booty over to a winner. Earlier that spring, at a sleepover at the Haywards', Barb had claimed she'd won the bet the night before. For a half hour, she provided her girlfriends with dozens of titillating, imaginative, and highly improbable details about the nature of the kissing and the extent of the petting that followed.

Just when Diana thought she would surely throw up if she had to listen to another description of their body positions, Barb had flopped back on the bed and burst out laughing. "April Fools!" she called, and was immediately bombarded with handfuls of popcorn for her joke.

As miserable as Diana had been before Barb admitted to the joke, Diana hadn't betrayed by expression or word how she felt. Not then and not now.

She glanced over her shoulder and saw Cole pouring feed into the bucket in the last stall, and she knew he'd come back outside to join her in a minute. She knew a lot more about him than the other girls did, because she alone had spent substantial amounts of time with him.

She knew exactly how sunlight turned his hair to polished ebony; she'd seen the way his sudden white smile could soften the hard planes of his face and turn his eyes to liquid silver; she'd felt his hands at her waist when he came up behind her and jokingly picked her up to lift her out of his way. She'd heard the awful fury in his voice when he dragged outside one of Doug's friends who was smoking in the stable and verbally flayed him for creating a fire hazard for the horses.

She'd also seen him deliver a litter of kittens while he murmured gentle encouragement to the mother, and she'd seen him revive what had appeared to be a stillborn kitten by massaging it with his fingers.

She'd actually experienced some of the fantasies the other girls could only dream of, but there were two enormous differences between Diana and the others: she was smart enough not to try to make her fantasies into reality, and she was wise enough to understand and accept that this casual friendship she shared with him was all there was ever going to be.

She realized that she would never know how it felt to have his mouth cover hers in a kiss, or his arms close around her, or his hands press her tightly against him. She accepted all that with only a little regret. Because she was also smart enough to know that if he ever made up his mind to kiss her, she probably wouldn't be able to handle it or control him.

Cole wouldn't bother with a lot of smooth talk and rehearsed strategies; he'd expect her to be a match for him in every way. But she wasn't, and she knew it. Even if she weren't hopelessly naive compared to him, they were as different as two people could possibly be.

Cole was blunt, reckless, and earthy. Diana was reserved, cautious, and hopelessly proper.

He was motorcycles and blue jeans and battered duffel bags, with a need to blaze his own trails through life.

She was BMWs and prom gowns and matched luggage, with a need to stay on smooth, paved roads.

Despite her philosophical understanding of the situation, Diana sighed as she watched Corey walking beside Spence. Corey was inviting disappointment and unhappiness by chasing Spencer Addison, but she was willing to take all the risks. Diana couldn't and wouldn't.

Cole finished feeding the horses and walked up silently behind her. "I sincerely hope all that sighing you're doing isn't because of Addison," he said dryly.

Diana jumped guiltily, her senses going into instant overload at his nearness. His voice sounded as dark and sultry as the night; he smelled like soap and fresh hay; he seemed to loom over her—as indomitable and rugged as the mountains in the Texas hill country to the west. "What do you mean by that?"

Moving to a position beside her, he braced his foot on the lowest railing of the fence and tipped his head toward the couple coming slowly toward them. "I mean I'd hate to see anything come between you and Corey. The two of you are closer than any natural sisters I've ever known, and it's embarrassingly obvious that Corey wants him for herself."

"Is it that obvious?" Diana asked, peering at him in the darkness, trying not to notice that his shirt sleeve was touching her upper arm.

"Not at first. You have to watch her for thirty seconds or so when he's around to see what's going on in her mind."

Ill at ease with that topic, and unable to think of a different one when he was standing so close, Diana followed his gaze. "Spence is a terrific horseman," she said.

Cole shrugged. "He's not bad."

Diana had known Spence since she was a little girl, and she couldn't let that slur on his ability pass without argument. "He's better than 'not bad'! Everyone says he could become a professional polo player!"

"What a paragon," Cole said in a scoffing tone she'd never heard him use before. "A college football hero, a 'professional' polo player, *and* an Olympic-class ladies' man."

"What makes you say that last thing?" Diana asked, worried for Corey's sake.

He shot her a sardonic look. "I've never seen him here when he didn't have a beautiful girl along to lavish him with the sort of hero worship he's getting from Corey and you tonight."

"Me?" Diana burst out, gaping at him and on the verge of laughter. "Me?"

Cole surveyed her upturned face. "Evidently not," he admitted with a slow grin. He looked back at Corey and Spence who were making their slow way toward the stable now. "I hope Corey doesn't get her heart broken. She's got one hell of a crush on Addison. She used up a roll of film on him tonight."

"That doesn't mean anything," Diana fibbed. "You know how serious Corey is about her photography. She's working on action shots now, and since Spence was riding . . ."

"He hadn't gotten on the horse yet, Diana."

"Oh." Diana bit her lip, and then hesitantly asked, "Do you think Spence notices how she feels?"

Cole knew the answer to that was an emphatic yes, but he didn't want to distress Diana, and now that he knew she wasn't another one of Addison's army of admirers, he felt charitable enough to give the man some credit. "If he does know, he either doesn't find it annoying, or else he's too much of a gentleman to hurt her feelings."

Cole propped both of his elbows on the fence, and he and Diana lapsed into companionable silence for several moments. Finally, Cole said, "If it isn't Addison, then who's the latest guy who makes your heart beat faster?"

"George Sigourney," Diana quipped.

"And is this Sigourney a jock like Addison? Or is he just a rich preppie?"

"Mr. Sigourney happens to be the dean of admissions at Southern Methodist—he signed my college admission letter and made my little heart flutter."

"Diana, that's wonderful!" he interrupted with a heart-stopping smile. "Why didn't you tell me earlier?"

Because when I'm with you, nothing else seems to matter, Diana thought. "I was waiting for the right moment," she said.

He gave her a puzzled look, but he didn't argue. "Have you decided on a major?"

When she shook her head, he adopted the patronizing tone of a wise old adult counseling a mere child. "Don't worry about it. You have plenty of time to decide all that."

"Thank you," Diana returned with a sideways smile. "And what about you? Have you already decided what *you're* going to be when *you* grow up?"

He chuckled at her impertinent question. "Yep," he said.

"What?"

"Rich," he replied with absolute conviction.

Diana knew that he was a finance major at college, but the details of his objective were unknown. "Do you have some sort of plan in mind?"

"I have some ideas."

In the riding ring, Spence turned the horse toward the stable, and Corey knew her time with him was coming to an end even before Spence said, "I have to get going." She tried to think of something clever or witty to say, but whenever he was near, Corey could hardly think at all. "I promised Lisa I'd pick her up at nine," he added.

"Oh," she said glumly, her spirits plummeting with this new piece of depressing information. "Lisa."

"Don't you like her?" Spence asked, looking surprised.

Corey marveled at the denseness of the human male. She positively *loathed* Lisa Murphy, and Lisa returned the feeling.

A month before, Corey's family had attended a charity horse show near San Antonio, and Corey had been surprised and elated to see Spence there. Since she'd brought her camera, she managed to get several excellent candid shots of Spence along with some fine shots of the horses. When Lisa led her horse back into the barn after taking a blue ribbon in the gaited-pleasure-horse class, Spence accompanied her, and Corey naturally followed at a discreet distance, hoping for a few more glimpses of him.

The huge barn was crowded with horses, grooms, trainers, owners, and riders, and Corey felt certain she wouldn't be noticed. Pretending to inspect the horses, she moved slowly down the gangway, pausing now and then as if to talk to some of the riders. She was almost directly across from Lisa's assigned stall when Spence passed her en route to get a Coke for his current flame. Corey turned her back quickly, and he didn't see her, but Lisa did. She marched out of her horse's stall and stormed up behind Corey. "Why do you have to be such a pest!" Lisa exploded in a low, incensed voice. "Can't you see that you're making a fool of yourself by tagging after Spence everywhere he goes? Now, go away and stay away!"

Humiliated and angry, Corey had returned to the arena and joined her family in the bleachers, but she'd kept her camera ready in case she saw Spence again. That turned out to be a very good thing because, although she didn't see Spence, she did see Lisa get thrown from her horse in the next round. As Lisa landed on her rump in the dirt with her hat off and her hair in her face, Corey had gotten that shot and several others. One of them became a favorite of hers, and it was prominently displayed in her room even though Spence wasn't in it.

Since Spence was still waiting for an answer, she shrugged and said mildly, "Lisa isn't my favorite of your girlfriends."

"Why not?"

"You'd probably think it isn't important."

"Let's hear it," he ordered.

"Okay, she's meaner than a two-headed snake!"

He laughed at that, and in a rare gesture of open affection, he put his arm around her shoulders and gave her a quick squeeze. Corey knew it had been a brotherly hug, but she was so ecstatic that she almost overlooked a highly revealing sight: Diana was standing at the fence beside Cole, and his arm was so close to hers that they were nearly touching. What's more, Diana and the Haywards' sexy, uncommunicative stable hand seemed to be completely absorbed in their conversation.

It had seemed incredible to her earlier, but seeing them together that way was enough to convince her that no matter how ill-suited they seemed, or how well Diana had hidden it, she was in love with him. Corey immediately racked her brain for some way to prolong their time together, and in the process she hit upon a possible means to spend a little more time with Spence as well. "Spence," she burst out, "could you give me a ride home?"

He shifted his glance from the couple at the fence to hers. "Isn't Diana going to take you home when she leaves?"

"That was the plan," Corey admitted; then she flashed him a conspiratorial smile and nodded toward her unsuspecting sister. "It's just that I hate to break up their evening."

His gaze narrowed on her face; then it sliced to Diana and Cole, and his expression went from disbelief to amused skepticism. "You aren't actually implying that Diana is interested in Cole Harrison, are you?"

"You don't think it's possible?"

"No, I don't."

"Why, because he works in a stable?" Corey held her breath, hoping her idol wouldn't betray the flaw of snobbery.

"No, that's not it."

"Then why isn't it possible?"

He looked at Diana and shook his head, chuckling. "I can't believe you haven't realized that Diana is the last girl on earth to go for the dark, brooding, earthy type. Among other things, he'd completely intimidate her."

"What makes you so sure?" Corey asked, even though she'd felt exactly the same way earlier that day, when she first suspected how Diana really felt.

"My superior knowledge of women," he said with an outrageous sense of male arrogance, "combined with excellent insight."

"Insight!" she scoffed indignantly, thinking of how Lisa Murphy was getting her claws into him. "How can you talk about insight when you think Lisa Murphy is a cream puff?"

"We're talking about Diana, not Lisa," he reminded her in a pleasant, but firm tone.

Since he obviously wasn't going to believe Diana was romantically interested in Cole, Corey thought madly for some other reason to explain why Diana should stay and Spence should take her home. Diana wanted to spend time with Cole, and Corey uttered the only feasible explanation that came to mind. "Okay, but you're ruining the surprise if you make me tell you more than this: Diana got thrown a couple years ago, and she's been afraid to ride ever since."

"I know that."

Trying very hard to stick to the truth, she said, "And Cole's been urging her to ride, but you know how Diana is—she doesn't like anyone to see that she's really nervous or afraid—"

Understanding dawned and Spence grinned. "Diana's getting some private riding lessons!" he concluded—appropriately, if incorrectly. "That's great!" He nodded toward his white Jeep Cherokee as they neared the couple at the fence. "Get your things together, and I'll drop you off on the way home."

Corey nodded and hurried forward in hopes of preventing Diana from objecting and spoiling Corey's ploy. "Spence said he'd drop me off at home," she said, giving Diana a pleading look that was so obvious that Cole had to bite back a smile. "That way, you can stay here as long as you like."

Diana stared at her in embarrassed dismay. Without Corey as an excuse, she couldn't and wouldn't linger with Cole; yet she wanted Corey to be able to ride home with Spence. "Okay," she said, deciding she'd leave immediately after they did.

While Cole took the reins of the sorrel and led the stable's newest resident back into his stall, Diana watched her sister and Spence get into his car. She waited until the Jeep's taillights vanished around a curve; then she went into the stable to get her purse and car keys. At the end of the long hallway around a corner, Cole was emptying the grocery bag of goodies she'd brought onto the sink counter beside his small refrigerator, and Diana walked back there to say good-bye. "Thanks for the company," she said.

"You can't leave yet," he said, and Diana's heart soared. "If you leave too soon, you'll end up passing them on the way home," he added with a knowing smile. "Which will completely confuse Addison and embarrass the hell out of Corey. Why don't you stay and share some of this food with me?"

It occurred to Diana that she could avoid encountering Corey and

Spence simply by taking a circuitous route home, but since that evidently hadn't occurred to Cole, she accepted his invitation with a happy smile. "I've already eaten, but I'll have a cookie for dessert with you."

"We can eat on our laps," he said, ruling out the desk in his bedroom as an unsuitable locale.

"I'll figure something else out," she called, already turning the corner into the corridor.

While the chicken and vegetables were heating, Cole finished unpacking the groceries; then he filled his plate with the delicious leftovers and stepped into the main hall from the small kitchen.

"All set," Diana said, straightening and reaching for the light switch. "But a little less light will make this look a whole lot better, believe me." As she spoke, she turned off the bright corridor lights, and Cole was startled by the effect she'd achieved.

In less than ten minutes, Diana had turned three bales of hay and a piece of plywood into a lamplit table covered with a red, yellow, and orange beach towel from the trunk of her car and a makeshift L-shaped bench. In the center of the table, between two kerosene lamps, was an old stainless steel bowl filled with lush hibiscus leaves and its vivid orange blossoms. "This is very nice," he said.

Diana dismissed that with a smiling shrug. "My mother and grandmother are convinced that atmosphere and presentation are seventy percent of what makes a meal taste good."

"They're probably right," Cole said as he put his meal and a plate of cookies on the makeshift table and slid onto his bale of hay. The entire concept of "presentation" as it applied to dining was completely unknown to him. He had a great deal to learn about the hundreds of little niceties and refinements that went with being wealthy and successful, but he was more concerned right now with acquiring wealth than the social polish he'd need later to go with it. "I'm awed," he added, stretching his long legs out beside the table. She sat down on the bale at his left.

"Why?" she asked, breaking off a small piece of cookie.

"Because you're remarkable." Cole hadn't meant to say that aloud, but it was true. Among other things, she was very bright and very poised. She was soft-spoken and amazingly witty, but her wit was so subtle and her voice so softly musical that her sense of humor either caught him off-guard or almost slid by his notice. But what he liked most about Diana Foster was the democratic impartiality she showed to him, a lowly stable hand.

She spoke to him with a friendly interest that was genuine and yet devoid of any hint of flirtatiousness. In the years he'd worked for the Haywards, nearly all of Barbara's teenage girlfriends had made some sort of romantic overture toward Cole, all of which he wisely and carefully dodged.

Their tactics were often blatant, usually transparent, and frequently amusing. What he found most irritating was that these wealthy, young femme fatales seemed to think they could attempt to seduce an "inferior being" without the slightest risk of repercussions. What they needed, in his opinion, was a sound spanking, though it was too late now for such parental discipline, even if their parents had been so inclined.

In this, as in everything else, Diana Foster was a delightful exception. She had been a constant surprise almost from their very first meeting, and now she surprised him more than ever before, because his honest compliment had made her shy and self-conscious. In what he knew was an attempt to avoid his scrutiny, she called out to one of the kittens she'd helped him deliver, and it bounded over to her.

"Just look how you've grown, Samantha!" she exclaimed as she scooped the tan cat into her arms and gave it a piece of cookie. A short black-and-white dog with long hair and no discernible link to any known pedigree on earth had been at her heels all evening, and she broke off a piece of cookie for him, too. "Sit up, Luke," she ordered, and when the dog eagerly obeyed, she gave him his reward.

"How many dogs and cats of your own do you have?" Cole asked, watching her fingers lovingly stroke the dog's matted fur as if it were sable instead of canine.

"We don't have any of either."

Cole was dumbfounded. When the litter of kittens was born, she'd fussed over them, played with them, and then managed to find homes for all but Samantha, whom she'd persuaded Cole to keep. Last winter, she'd appeared with a scroungy stray dog in her arms and managed to persuade him to keep that at the barn, too. "I'll help you name him," she'd volunteered while Cole was still arguing against keeping the animal. "How about calling him Luke?"

"He looks more like a Rover," Cole had argued. "Or a Fleabag."

"He'll look like a Luke when he's cleaned up."

Cole hadn't been proof against those big green eyes of hers. Taking the dog by the scruff of its neck, he'd held it away from himself and gone in search of flea soap and a metal tub. Naturally, he'd assumed she'd already inflicted the maximum quota of homeless beasts on her own family.

He seized on that subject as a way of getting her over her sudden attack of shyness. "Kitten, didn't anyone ever tell you that charity begins at home?" he asked dryly, using the nickname he'd teasingly begun calling her after she'd persuaded him to take in Luke and Samantha.

She put Samantha on the floor and picked up Luke, cradling him in her lap; then she shot Cole a quizzical glance. "What do you mean?"

"Why did *I* end up playing surrogate parent to that mangy waif of a dog, instead of you? I naturally assumed you had already done *your* fair share of providing a 'home to the homeless' before you turned to me."

She curled one tanned leg beneath her and turned sideways, so that Luke and Sam could both enjoy her petting. "My father's terribly allergic to dogs and cats. Otherwise," she told the adoring dog, "I'd have taken you straight home with me! You could have slept in my bed . . ."

Lucky dog. The words drifted so softly through Cole's mind that he didn't notice at first what direction his thoughts had taken. He watched the lamplight dancing on the wall behind her, casting cheerful shadows to dispel the gloom. Diana had that same ability to brighten and beautify her surroundings simply by being there. She was going to be a very special woman someday . . . and also a very beautiful one, he decided.

She had hair the color of dark copper and the texture of heavy silk, and soft, dewy skin. Every time he had seen her during this past year, she seemed to have grown prettier, her skin fairer, her eyes greener. She was no more than five feet two inches tall, barely reaching his shoulder, but in yellow knit shorts and a matching Vneck top, she had the figure of a petite goddess, with long shapely legs, full breasts, and a tiny waist. She also had a way of looking at him that made him feel mesmerized by her eyes. His gaze slid from her russet eyelashes to the gentle swell of her breasts, pausing to contemplate the curve of her smooth cheek and the softness of her lips . . .

Realizing that he was inventorying the feminine assets of an innocent child, Cole diverted them both with a question, but he was furious with himself for what he'd been thinking . . . and wanting. "It's ridiculous that you keep refusing to ride a horse!" he said brusquely. His voice made the dog, the cat, and the girl all look at him in consternation, but Cole was so angry at himself for thinking like a pervert that his tone remained harsh. "Don't you have any guts?"

Diana couldn't believe he was speaking to her like this. Simultaneously she felt the desire to cry and had the impulse to leap to her feet, put her hands on her waist, and demand an explanation. Instead of doing either, she gave him a long look and said quietly, "I'm not a coward, if that's what you mean."

"I didn't mean that at all," Cole said, feeling like a complete bastard. Inch for inch, Diana Foster was undoubtedly one of the most courageous, kind, independent females he'd ever known. "As a matter of fact, I cried my eyes out the first time I got thrown," he lied to make her feel better.

"I didn't cry," Diana said, helplessly beguiled by the image of a little boy with dark, curly hair, crying with his fists pressed to his eyes.

"You didn't?" Cole teased.

"Nope, not me. Not when I broke my wrist and not while Dr. Paltrona was setting it."

"Not even one tear?"

"Not even one."

"Good for you," he said.

"Not really." She sighed. "I fainted instead."

Cole threw back his head and burst out laughing; then he sobered and looked at her with an expression so tender that Diana's heart began to hammer. "Don't change," he said huskily. "Stay just the way you are."

Diana could hardly believe this night was actually happening, that he was really talking to her and looking at her this way. She didn't know what had finally brought it on, but she didn't want it to stop. Not yet. "Is it all right if I get a little taller?" she teased shakily.

She'd tipped her head back, gazing up at him in a way that unconsciously invited him to lower his mouth to her smiling lips, and Cole noticed it. "Yes, but don't change anything else," he said, trying to ignore her provocative pose. "Someday, some lucky guy will come along and realize what a rare treasure you are."

Having him cheerfully predict that another man would win her heart was enough to douse Diana's happy glow. She straightened and put the dog down, but she bore Cole no ill will for his impersonal attitude, and she was genuinely interested in his opinion. "What if I don't feel that way about him?"

"You will."

"It hasn't happened yet. I'm the only girl I know of who isn't madly in love with someone and convinced he's the one I want to marry." Lifting her hand, she began counting off her friends on her fingers. "Corey is in love with Spencer—Haley is in love with Peter Mitchell—Denise is in love with Doug Hayward—Missy is in love with Michael Murchison—" With a disgusted wave of her hand, she finished, "I could go on and on forever."

She sounded so despondent that Cole felt obliged to cheer her up before he could let the topic drop. "Come on, there must be at least one other girl your age with enough sense to look beyond the moment toward the future." Although Cole privately regarded Barbara Hayward as an airhead, Diana hadn't mentioned her name, so he seized on her as a possible illustration of his point. "How about Barb? Who is she hoping to marry?"

Diana rolled her eyes in disgust. "Harrison Ford."

"That figures," Cole said dryly.

"And then there's you," Diana continued, provoked into bringing up Valerie, even though she knew it would distract him completely from herself.

"What about me?"

He looked so bewildered that Diana's heart soared with hope. During their many talks over the last two years, she'd heard all about the beautiful blond from Jeffersonville who went to school at UCLA. She knew they exchanged letters and phone calls several times a month and that he managed to see her occasionally, usually during summer vacations when she was home. "I was referring to Valerie."

"Oh." He nodded with emphasis, but that was uninformative enough to spur Diana's curiosity and hope even higher. "Have you heard from her lately?"

"I saw her a few weeks ago during spring break."

Diana had a vivid and unwanted picture of Cole and Valerie making wild, passionate love together in some scenic glade beneath a starlit sky. Somehow a primitive outdoor setting seemed better suited to his rugged good looks. In a moment of weakness Diana had requested a copy of the UCLA yearbook through Houston's main library. From it, she'd discovered that Valerie was not only active in her sorority, she seemed to be dating the captain of the college's soccer team. Besides that, she was tall and beautiful, as well as older and undoubtedly more worldly than Diana. She had the face and eyes of a Nordic princess and a smile straight out of a toothpaste ad. Diana had to make an effort not to hate her. In fact, the only thing Valerie didn't have was good grades. That at least was something Diana had in common with Cole. He had a 3.9 grade-point average and so did Diana. "How were Valerie's grades at the end of the semester?" she asked, descending to petty competitiveness and hating herself for it.

"She's on scholastic probation."

"That's too bad," Diana murmured. "Does that mean she'll have to go to summer school and you won't be able to see her when you go home?"

"I don't go home unless it's to see her," Cole said.

Diana had assumed as much. Although she knew relatively little about his life before he came to Houston, she'd managed to discover that he was from a town in Texas called Kingdom City and he had no family except a great-uncle and a cousin who was five years older than he. She'd soon learned that any attempt to pry deeper into the details of his past gained her little beyond an offhand answer or a premature end to the camaraderie she treasured.

As he lifted his Coke to his mouth, Diana watched the golden lamplight flicker on the tanned column of his neck and gild the hard contours of his square chin and firm jaw, but the flame was too feeble to pierce the midnight darkness of his thick hair.

She hoped Valerie appreciated Cole's loyalty and devotion; she hoped his girlfriend wasn't going to try to make him into a tame, well-groomed, Labrador retriever instead of the panther he resembled. There was something about the girl with the toothpaste smile that made her look all wrong for Cole. It was wrong to covet, but Diana just couldn't help it!

Beside her, Cole lowered his soft drink can an inch and warily studied the ferocious, possessive scowl on Diana's face. "By any chance, am I drinking your Coke?" he asked.

Diana snapped out of her fanciful dreams and quickly shook her head. It was time to leave . . . long past time to leave, because tonight her common sense, her logic and self-control weren't operating very well. "I'll help you clear all this away," she said, already standing up and gathering plates and silverware.

"I have to study for finals," he said as he blew out the two lamps and picked up the bowl of orange hibiscus, "but I have enough time for a hand of pinochle before you go."

He flipped on the bright corridor lights as he made that offer, and the harsh light banished the last traces of her romantic fantasies. She'd taught him pinochle and hearts last year, during one of those rare and wonderful afternoons when Corey came to help exercise the horses, as she loved to do, and no one else was around. All that was over now, Diana realized. It had to end because she suddenly realized that she was no longer able to keep her fantasies about him in their proper place. They were getting completely out of control. Tonight, if he'd kissed her, she'd have ignored all the dangers and let him. Let him? If he'd given her just a little bit more encouragement, *she* would have kissed *him!* Somehow, during the last few weeks, she'd begun to truly risk her whole heart on him, and that made the stakes much too big for a sensible girl who already knew that the odds against her were so high she couldn't possibly win.

"You're too good now," she said with a bright smile over her shoulder.

"Not for a cardshark like you, I'm not."

"I really do have to go."

"I understand." He sounded a little disappointed, and Diana fought against the temptation to stay awhile longer. She was still wavering when he turned and disappeared into his room. By the time he emerged to walk her out to her car, she'd put the dishes in the sink and her friendly, impersonal facade firmly in place. She was congratulating herself for resisting the temptation to stay as he reached out with his right hand to open her car door. "By the way—" he said as she turned to him to say good night, "I heard some of the girls talking about the sweet sixteen party your parents threw for you a couple weeks ago."

Diana was too preoccupied with the inexplicable smile hovering at the corner of his mouth to say anything intelligent. "It was my sixteenth birthday."

"I know," he said with a sudden grin at her flustered answer. "And where I come from it's customary to give a girl something special on her sixteenth birthday—"

A kiss! He was going to kiss her, Diana realized, and all her defenses and fears collapsed beneath the weight of her joy and nervous anticipation. She dropped her gaze from his gleaming silver eyes to his sensual mouth. "What do you give a girl back home," she breathed shakily and closed her eyes, "when she turns sixteen?"

"A present!" he exclaimed triumphantly as he took his left hand from behind his back. Diana's eyes snapped open, and she clutched the car door for balance as she stared in mortified surprise at his outstretched hand. In it was a large, oddly shaped item that he'd obviously wrapped himself in a sheet of newspaper and tied with what looked like a shoelace. Seemingly oblivious to her inner turmoil, he held it closer. "Go ahead, open it."

Diana recovered her manners, gave him an overbright smile, and pulled on the end of the broken white shoelace.

"It isn't much," he warned, sounding suddenly uncertain.

The paper fell away to reveal a stuffed toy—a life-size white cat with a pink tongue, green eyes, and a tag around its neck that said, "My name is Pinkerton."

"You've probably had dozens of really exotic stuffed animals," he added uneasily when she didn't immediately react. "In fact, you're probably too old for stuffed animals, period."

He was right on both counts, but none of that mattered to Diana. To save money, he did without all sorts of things, including good food, but he'd actually gone out and gotten her a present. Speechless, she lifted the ordinary, inexpensive toy from his hands as carefully as if it were priceless porcelain; then she held it in front of her to admire it.

Cole looked at the toy and realized how cheap it would look to someone like her. "It's just something I picked up—a token—" he began defensively. He broke off in surprise as Diana shook her head to silence him, then clutched the stuffed animal to her chest and wrapped her arms tightly around it.

"Thank you, Cole," she whispered, laying her cheek against its furry head. Smiling, she lifted her glowing gaze to his. "Thank you," she said again.

You're welcome, Cole thought, but the incredible warmth of her reaction seemed to have momentarily melted his ability to speak and his ability to think. In silence he closed the car door after she'd settled into her seat, and in silence he watched her taillights vanish around a curve in the long drive that wound through the trees and along the side of the house.

Chapter 8

*D*IANA HAD BEEN GONE FOR THREE HOURS WHEN COLE FINALLY closed his economics textbook and shoved his notes aside. His shoulders ached from being hunched over his desk, and his brain felt saturated. There was no point in more studying; he was prepared enough to ace the final exam, but good grades had never been his goal. It was knowledge that he pursued, the knowledge he needed to achieve and enjoy his goals.

Absently, he rubbed his aching shoulders; then he leaned his head back and closed his eyes, resting them, while he thought about his uncle's letter. The letter had arrived in the morning's mail, and the news was so good, so unbelievably good, that Cole smiled as he rotated his shoulders trying to work the kinks out of them.

Four years ago, a drilling company had approached Calvin and offered him a contract and ten thousand dollars for the right to drill a test well on Cal's land. The first well hadn't produced, but the following year they tried a second time for an additional five thousand dollars. When the second well failed to produce enough natural gas to make operation profitable, they'd given up and so had Cal and Cole.

A few months ago, however, a much larger drilling company had paid a visit to Cal and asked to drill in a different area of his land. Cal said they were wasting their time, and Cole privately agreed with him, but the two of them had been wrong. In the mail today was a letter from Cal that contained the staggering news that the new well was hugely successful and that the "money's going to be pouring in."

Straightening, Cole opened his eyes and reached for the thick envelope that contained his uncle's letter and a copy of the contract that the drilling company wanted Cal to sign.

Based on Cal's own calculations, he would make $250,000 in the next year—more money than the old rancher had netted in a lifetime, Cole knew. It was ironic, Cole thought with amusement as he unfolded the bulky contract, that of all the Harrisons who might have struck it rich over the years, Calvin Patrick Downing was the least likely to spend or enjoy the windfall. He was, by nature and inclination, a miser, and a quarter of a million dollars wasn't going to change that.

Instead of spending two dollars to call Cole long distance and tell him the fantastic news, he'd sent him a letter and a copy of the contract by ordinary first-class mail. And the reason he'd sent Cole the contract, according to his letter, was because "the drilling company says these are standard contracts and they can't be changed. I figure there's no sense in paying a bloodsucking lawyer to read all this mumbo jumbo just so he can tell me the same thing, but you've got a law school right there at your university. Get one of those student bloodsuckers to look this over, will you—or else look it over yourself and tell me if you think Southfield Exploration has any tricks up their sleeve."

That was Cal—thrifty to a fault. Cheap. Miserly.

Cal clipped coupons out of the newspapers, cut his own hair, patched his jeans, and dickered furiously over an extra penny per foot for chicken wire. He hated more than anything to part with a dollar.

But he'd handed over his first ten-thousand-dollar check for the test well to Cole so he could go to college.

And one year later, Cal had handed over his second check for five thousand dollars.

As a lonely, rebellious youth, Cole had often hitchhiked the forty miles to Calvin's place, and there, with Cal, Cole found the understanding and warmth that his own father was incapable of feeling. Calvin alone had understood his frustration and believed in his dreams, and for that Cole loved him. But Calvin hadn't just given lip service and encouraging words to Cole; he'd given him his money so that Cole could have a real future, away from Kingdom City—a bright, promising future with unlimited possibilities. For that, Cole felt a sense of loyalty and indebtedness that surpassed all his other emotions.

The contract that Cal had sent him was fifteen pages long, covered with fine print and legalese. In the margins, Calvin had penciled in some comments of his own, and Cole smiled at the wily old man's astuteness. Calvin had dropped out of school after the tenth grade to go to work, but he was a voracious reader who'd educated himself, probably well enough to merit an honorary college degree. Cole, however, had no intention of allowing his uncle to sign these documents until they'd been reviewed by a competent, practicing lawyer—one who specialized in oil and gas leases. Cal was wily, but in this case Cole knew the older man was totally out of his league. After four years in Houston, Cole had heard, read, and seen enough to know how business really worked. He knew there was no such thing as a standard contract that couldn't be changed—and he knew whose interests were usually protected by the originator of any contract.

Tomorrow, when Charles Hayward returned from his business trip to Philadelphia, Cole intended to ask Hayward for the name of the most prominent oil-and-gas-lease attorney in Houston. It was common knowledge that Cole's employer had made his initial fortune in the oil business. Hayward would know whom Cole should consult about this contract, and he'd be willing to offer advice as well.

Unlike many of the socialites Cole had met in the course of his job, Charles Hayward was neither pompous, soft, nor filled with self-importance. At fifty, he was energetic, hardworking, blunt, and fair. He had exacting standards for everything, from his staff to his family to his horses. Those who fell short of his expectations—be it employees, hunting dogs, or horses—were soon gone from the premises, but he treated those who met his standards with respect. When he was home, he visited the stable every evening and strolled down the wide corridor dispensing carrots and friendly pats to each of the splendid horses who inhabited the ultramodern stalls.

As time passed, he'd developed an increasing appreciation of Cole's knowledge and his vigilant care of the horses, and that had eventually led to a kind of friendship between the two men. Often when Hayward paid his nightly visit to his beloved animals, he stayed for coffee and conversation with Cole, and slowly, he'd become a kind of mentor to the younger man, offering advice and insight on the two subjects Cole was most interested in: business and money.

When it came to those topics, Charles was incisive, brilliant, and perceptive. In fact, the man had only one blind spot that Cole had ever discovered, and that was his family. Hayward's first wife and their only child had been killed in an airplane accident twenty-five years before, and his grief had been so deep and so prolonged that it was still a topic of whispered conversation among his friends when they gathered at the stable.

Seventeen years ago, he'd remarried, and his new wife had promptly given him a son and a daughter within two years. Hayward positively doted on his new wife, Jessica; he gave her and their children the very best money could buy, and he seemed to automatically assume that they either did, or would eventually, live up to all his hopes and expectations.

Cole could have told him he was wrong. In this one area, Cole could have offered his mentor some painfully enlightening examples of the results of overindulging children and trusting a faithless wife.

As Cole knew from personal observation and experience, Jessica Hayward was a beautiful, spoiled, promiscuous, amoral, forty-year-old bitch.

Her fifteen-year-old daughter, Barbara, was so awed and intimidated by her that the homely teenager was completely spineless—a born follower who had been rendered even more helpless by all the material goods that Charles showered on her, luxuries that she wasn't challenged to earn with decent grades or anything else.

Doug Hayward was a completely charming, irresponsible, handsome sixteen-year-old, but Cole thought there was still hope for him. Despite his frivolous immaturity, Cole occasionally glimpsed Charles Hayward's bluntness and some of the older man's sharp intellect in Doug. His grades were average, but as he'd confided to Cole, his SAT scores were very high.

Cole glanced at his watch, saw that it was after eleven o'clock, and stretched his arms, stifling a yawn. He walked out into the corridor and took a last stroll down the long walkway to make certain everything looked all right for the night.

Chapter 9

$\mathcal{J}$ESSICA HAYWARD STEPPED OFF THE TREADMILL IN THE WORKOUT room that was part of the master bedroom suite and grabbed a towel, looping it around her neck. Clad in thin white shorts and a clingy red-and-white tank top, she walked into the bedroom, feeling energized and restless and alone. Her husband wasn't due home until the following day, but even if Charles had been there, he wouldn't have been able to give her what she wanted.

She wanted sex . . . hot, rough, mind-drugging, demanding, passionate sex. She did not want the sort of lukewarm, polite, predictably boring sex that Charles called "making love." She didn't want to make love at all; she wanted to make madness. She didn't want Charles . . .

She wanted Cole.

Furious with herself for helplessly lusting after an arrogant, disobliging, macho employee who was nowhere near her social equal, she went over to the bar built into the closet and took an expensive bottle of chardonnay out of the cooler. She opened it and poured some into a gold-rimmed glass; then she walked over to the windows that overlooked the back lawn and the stables off to the left. Closing her eyes, she conjured up a vivid image of Cole, his shoulders broad and heavy with muscle, his skin sleek with sweat as he drove into her with the tireless brute force she preferred most of the time.

Her thighs tightened involuntarily against the delicious recollections, and she tossed down the rest of the wine in her glass and turned away from the window. Tugging off the towel, she stopped long enough to run a brush through her hair; then she picked up the bottle of wine and another glass and brought them with her.

Her daughter's bedroom door was closed, but a strip of light was visible beneath it, and Jessica moved cautiously along the hall then down the back stairs.

Outside, the night was hot and sultry, heavy with the scent of gardenias blooming in beds along the path that led to the stable. Moonlight lit the flagstone path that wound through the oaks, but Jessica didn't need it to find her way; she'd made this nocturnal journey many times in her dreams and often enough in reality. Balancing the bottle of wine and two glasses, she slipped in a side door of the stable, glad when the air-conditioning touched her damp skin.

Without bothering to turn on the main corridor lights, she walked quietly around the corner and stopped in his doorway. His back was turned, and she watched in anticipation as he stripped off his shirt and tossed it aside. The soft glow of light from the lamp on his desk highlighted the rippling muscles of his shoulders and tapered back, and when he reached for the snap on his jeans, her breath came a little faster.

Perhaps that almost imperceptible sound alerted him, because he swung around and pinned her with a look that was at first alarmed and then annoyed. "You scared the hell out of me, Jessica!"

Jessica held up the glasses and wine bottle and strolled into his room as if she owned it, which she did. "I saw the lights on down here and since neither of us seemed to be able to sleep, I thought we could share this."

"As a matter of fact, I'm tired and I don't expect to have any trouble sleeping."

"There's no need to snap my head off," Jessica said as she perched on the edge of his desk and crossed one long, slender leg over the other, letting her sandal dangle from her lacquered toes. "I haven't seen you in ages, and I decided to come for a visit, that's all," she added as she leaned sideways and poured wine into both glasses.

"Really, that's all?" Cole said sarcastically as his gaze took in her scanty tank top, revealing shorts, and seductive smile. Deliberately, he reached for his shirt, but she shook her head, her smile turning hard and determined.

"Don't get dressed, darling. I like looking at you just the way you are."

"Jessica," he said sharply, "we aren't going to go through all this again. It's over, done with, finished. I told you, I'm tired."

"That's a very disrespectful way to speak to your employer," she said, sliding off the desk and reaching for his cheek.

"Dammit, knock it off!" Cole snapped, jerking his head aside. For the moment, that was the only evasionary tactic available to him. As a last resort, he was prepared to physically force her out of his way, but he really didn't want to touch her. For one thing, he wasn't certain whether touching her would ignite her formidable temper or worse—ignite her passion. The bed was behind him, and short of physically lifting her out of his way, he was trapped for the moment. Jessica realized he was trapped, and she moved forward, a smile of victory on her face.

"Jessica—" Cole warned darkly. "You're married, for God's sake!"

"I know that," she replied, pulling off her top and tossing it behind him on the bed.

"I like your husband," Cole said, trying unsuccessfully to sidestep her.

She gazed at him in wide-eyed wonder as she reached behind her back to unclip her bra. "I like him, too," she said.

If his predicament hadn't been so sordid and so dire, Cole would have laughed at the sheer ridiculousness of it: a beautiful woman was stripping in front of him, using her body to block his escape, while she innocently professed to like her husband, whom she was trying to cuckold. "I'm not in the mood for a striptease," he warned her.

"You will be pretty soon," she promised, the bra straps sliding down her arms.

"You don't even know the concept of marital fidelity, do you?" he said, putting his hands on the straps to stop them from sliding off her wrists.

"I'm always faithful when Charles is in town," she said, her eyes turning hot, her hands sliding up the matted dark hair on his chest. "Only he's not here tonight, and you are, and I'm bored."

"Then take up a hobby," Cole said as he clamped his hands on hers.

She laughed low in her throat, wrapped her arms tightly around his neck, and began rubbing herself against his thighs.

Cole was not enticed, not excited, and he was losing his temper and patience. "I'm warning you," he said, grabbing her wrists and yanking them free. "Don't make this hard for both of us."

She shifted her hips sensuously against his and laughed suggestively in her throat as she deliberately misinterpreted his words. "No, I wouldn't say it's very *hard.* I'd say it's very *big,* but not—"

Fluorescent light suddenly burst down the corridor outside his room as someone turned on the main stable lights, and Cole clamped his hand over her mouth.

"Cole?" Charles Hayward called out in a deep, friendly voice from thirty feet away. "I saw your light on and decided to have a look at our new resident. What do you think of him?"

Beneath Cole's hand, Jessica's lips began to tremble and her eyes were huge with panic.

"I'll be right there!" Cole called out as he pulled his hand from her mouth.

"Oh, my God! I have to get out of here!" Jessica said, her entire body rigid.

She was shaking so hard that Cole would have pitied her if she hadn't just put both of them in jeopardy. As he knew from Charles Hayward's past nocturnal visits to the stable, the man would walk down to the tiny kitchenette and make himself a cup of instant coffee; then he'd expect Cole to join him as he walked along the stalls, discussing each occupant. That had become a pleasant ritual for both men over the years, and normally Cole thoroughly enjoyed the visits, particularly when Hayward stayed on and the conversation drifted to other topics. Hayward was well-read and well-informed on a staggering variety of topics . . . that did not include his wife.

"Listen to me!" Cole said, his voice low and fierce as he snatched her discarded shirt and thrust it into her hands. "He's in the kitchenette, fixing himself a cup of instant coffee."

"Then he's blocking the only door out of here!" she panted. "I'm trapped!"

Cole didn't bother to comment on that. "Don't panic yet," he warned because she looked crazy with fear. "I'll close my door, and he won't come in here or see you."

"I have to get back to the house!"

"Cole?" Charles called out. "Do you want some coffee?"

"No. No thanks," Cole answered, already backing toward the door, using his body to block any view Charles might have of his room and the half-naked, wild-eyed woman standing in the middle of it, clutching her shirt to her bosom.

He left her there, closing the door behind him, and walked, barefooted and barechested into the kitchenette, where Charles had just finished stirring instant coffee into a cup of hot tap water. "Well," the older man said, looking at Cole with an expectant smile, "what do you think of the polo pony?"

"Not bad," Cole said; then he forced himself to come up with a lame joke. "I don't know how well he plays polo, but as a horse, he's a fine-looking animal." The polo pony was only a few stalls away from the doorway into Cole's room, and Cole was instinctively afraid that Jessica was going to try to bolt from the scene of her attempted crime and probably get herself caught in the process. "You might want to have a look at the chestnut mare's foreleg," he suggested, walking deliberately toward the far end of the stable.

Charles looked up in concern and instantly followed Cole down the wide hallway. "What's wrong with her leg?"

"She hurt it when she took a jump yesterday."

"Who was riding her?" Charles asked, all his sympathies with the splendid hunter-jumper whom he often preferred to ride.

"Barbara," Cole said.

"That figures," Hayward said with a disgusted grimace. "I try not to be impatient with Barb, but so far, she's not good at anything she does. Except talking on the telephone about boys. She does that very well."

Without replying, Cole opened the heavy oak stall door, and Charles followed him inside. Handing Cole his cup of coffee he bent down to personally inspect the big mare's bandaged leg. "Not too swollen," he said. "That liniment you mix smells like hell, but it does a great job. I still think you should become a vet," he added, straightening much more quickly than Cole would have liked and giving the mare a farewell pat. "I've never seen a man who had a better way with animals."

"They wouldn't be nearly as fond of me if I were shoving worming tubes down their noses," Cole said with a distracted glance down the hallway. His breath caught as Jessica's face appeared in the doorway of his room; then she made a wild dash across the hallway, holding her red-and-white top over her bare breasts. Cole swung around to block Charles Hayward from leaving the stall, and in the process he hit the coffee mug against the man's arm and sent coffee spewing over hay and trickling down Charles's shirt.

"What the—" Hayward began; then he choked off his startled exclamation and began brushing at the drops.

"I'm sorry," Cole said.

"That's okay, I'll get another one. Why don't you put our new resident on a longer line and see how he goes. I only spent a half hour looking him over in Memphis in a stall because that was all the time I had." He peered at Cole, who'd started to turn, and said, "Is anything wrong? You seem a little edgy tonight."

Cole shook his head in the negative and followed him down the hallway, actually beginning to believe that Jessica had made a safe escape and nothing worse would come of her antics tonight. His relief came a moment too soon. "That's odd," Charles Hayward said as he passed Cole's room. "I distinctly saw you close that door behind you tonight when you came out of your room."

"It probably swung open on its own—" Cole began, but his voice trailed off as Hayward came to a sudden halt, a puzzled smile still on his lips, his eyes riveted on something in Cole's room.

"I gather you were entertaining, and I interrupted," Hayward said. "And now the young lady's run off or in hiding—"

Cole's gaze followed his to the lacy white bra on the floor near Cole's rumpled bed, but before he could react, the older man had noticed something much more damning than the bra, and his expression went from startled, to accusing, to furious. "Aren't those my wineglasses?" he demanded; then he stepped forward and jerked the bottle of wine up to see its label. "And this is Jessica's favorite—"

74

"I borrowed it—" Cole began. "No, I stole it—" he said, trying to prevent the inevitable even as Hayward stalked toward the rear doorway of the stable, peering toward the flash of white racing toward the back door of the house.

"You son of a bitch!" Hayward exploded as he whirled and swung with his right arm, his fist connecting with Cole's jaw with stunning force. "You fucking bastard!"

Momentarily free of imminent discovery, Jessica fled to the house and up the stairs to her room, but when she peeked out the window, she saw her husband moving at an infuriated half-run from the stable toward the house. "Oh, my God," she breathed, quaking in terror as her comfortable life began to shatter around her. "What'll I do—?" she whispered, looking wildly around the dark room for some way to avoid disaster.

Down the hall, Barbara turned her stereo up another notch, and inspiration struck.

"Barbara!" Jessica cried, racing into her startled daughter's room and slamming and locking the door behind her.

Barbara looked up from the magazine she was reading, her expression first startled and then alarmed. "Mom—what's wrong?"

"You have to help me, darling. Just do what I tell you, and don't ask questions. I'll make it worth your while—"

Chapter 10

Dallas, 1996

GOOD AFTERNOON, MR. HARRISON. AND, CONGRATULATIONS," THE guard called as Cole's limousine passed through the main entrance of Unified Industries' ultramodern fifty-acre campus not far from Ross Perot's E-Systems. A smooth four-lane drive meandered through a gently rolling landscape dotted with trees, past a massive fountain and man-made lake. In fine weather, employees who worked in the seven sprawling, mirrored-glass buildings that were linked together by enclosed crosswalks frequently gathered there to eat their lunch.

The limo glided past Unified's administration building and continued past the research laboratories, where three men in white lab coats were engaged in a lively debate as they approached the front door. The limo finally rolled to a stop in front of a discreet sign at the curb that said, "Executive Offices."

"Congratulations, Mr. Harrison," the receptionist said as Cole stepped out of the elevator on the sixth floor.

Cole replied with a brief, preoccupied nod and continued through the executive reception area, which was separated from the offices by a tall teak-paneled wall bearing the corporation's insignia. There, visitors with appointments waited in luxurious comfort on pale green leather sofas, surrounded by a sea of thick oriental carpeting dotted with graceful mahogany tables and accent pieces inlaid with mother-of-pearl or trimmed with brass.

Oblivious to the restrained splendor of the reception area, Cole turned to the right behind the teak-paneled wall and continued down the carpeted hallway toward his office, only vaguely aware that the place was unnaturally silent.

As Cole passed by the main conference room, Dick Rowse, the head of advertising and public relations, stopped him. "Cole, could you come in here a moment?"

As soon as Cole stepped into the crowded room, champagne corks began popping, and forty employees burst into applause in honor of the corporation's latest coup—the acquisition of a profitable electronics firm with fat government contracts to sweeten their balance sheet and a new computer chip that was in the testing phase. Cushman Electronics, owned by two brothers, Kendall and Prentice Cushman, had been the object of hostile takeover attempts launched by several major corporations, and the widely publicized battle had been bloody and fierce. Today, Unified Industries had emerged victorious, and the media was going crazy.

"Congratulations, Cole," Corbin Driscoll, the company's controller, said as he pressed a glass of champagne into Cole's hand.

"Speech!" Dick Rowse called out. "We want a speech," he persisted determinedly in the jocular tone of a man who feels compelled to make everyone feel relaxed and everything look rosy, and who has also had too much to drink. In this case his efforts struck a particularly false note, because jovial camaraderie between the executive staff and the corporation's hard-driving CEO simply did not exist.

Cole glanced impatiently at him, then relented and gave his "speech." "Ladies and gentlemen," he said with a brief, perfunctory smile, "we've just spent one hundred and fifty million dollars to acquire a company that won't be worth half that if we can't market that computer chip. I suggest we all get busy thinking up ways to cut our losses if that happens."

"I was hoping for a quote I could use for the media," Rowse said.

"My phone's been ringing off the hook since the announcement was made two hours ago."

"I'll leave that to you. Thinking up quotable quotes for the media is your job, Dick, not mine," he replied; then he turned and headed toward his office, leaving Dick Rowse feeling reprimanded and everyone else feeling a little deflated.

Within minutes the group had disbanded, leaving only Rowse, his new assistant director, Gloria Quigley, and Corbin Driscoll in the conference room.

Gloria Quigley was the first to speak. Tall, blond, and glamorous, the thirty-year-old was the youngest, and newest, member of the senior staff. "What a letdown," she said with an exasperated sigh. "Wall Street is in an uproar because Unified Industries wrested Cushman away from Matt Farrell's Intercorp and two other major players. *We're* all euphoric, the clerical staff is proud, and the janitorial people are probably dancing a jig," she finished, "but the man who masterminded the whole buyout doesn't seem to care."

"Oh, he cares," Dick Rowse told her. "When you've been here for six months, you'll realize that you've just seen Cole Harrison exhibiting extreme pleasure. In fact, he was happier just now than I've ever seen him."

Gloria looked at the two executives in disbelief. "What's he like when he's *un*happy?"

Corbin Driscoll shook his head. "You don't want to see that."

"He can't be that bad," Gloria argued.

"Oh, yeah?" Corbin joked. He pointed to his thick, immaculately groomed gray hair. "I didn't have a strand of gray hair two years ago, when I went to work for Cole." The other two laughed, and he added, "That nice, fat salary and benefit package you got when you came to work here comes with a few strings attached."

"Like what?" Gloria asked.

"Like phone calls at midnight because Cole has some new idea and wants you to act on it," Dick Rowse said.

"And you'd better learn how to pack a suitcase and catch a plane with an hour's notice on a weekend," Corbin added, "because our CEO doesn't live by clocks or calendars."

"*Weekends?*" Gloria exclaimed in mock horror. "I'll have to start turning off my answering machine at home on Friday nights!"

"I'm glad you mentioned that," Rowse said with a wry chuckle as he reached into his pocket and withdrew a small, black object. "This is a present for you—something to replace your answering machine and a token proof that you have a position of some importance here."

Gloria automatically opened her hand, and Rowse slapped a pager into her palm. "Welcome to Unified Industries," he said dryly. "If you're wise, you'll sleep with that pager."

Everyone laughed, but Gloria had known when she applied for this job that a great many demands were going to be made of her. The challenge had been much of its appeal.

Before giving up her own Dallas PR firm to come to work for Unified Industries, she'd read every article she could find about the aggressive, enigmatic entrepreneur who had made history by putting together a very large, very profitable conglomerate before he was thirty years old.

From personal experience, she'd already learned that he was an exacting and demanding employer, with an aloof, impatient attitude that discouraged familiarity, even among his senior executives, who all treated him with caution and deference.

He seemed to be as unconcerned about making enemies as he was about his public image, and yet, he was ferociously protective of the corporation's reputation.

Customer service was his personal "hot spot." As a result of his rigid high standards, Unified Industries had received justifiable acclaim for the unparalleled customer service offered by every one of the companies beneath its corporate umbrella. Whether the newly acquired subsidiary was a floundering drug manufacturer, a small fast-food chain, or a large textile company, the first order of business for Harrison's takeover team was to bring the customer-service area up to Unified Industries' superior standards.

"He's a complete mystery to everyone in the business world, including the people around here," Gloria said, thinking aloud. "No one really knows anything about him. I've been interested in him ever since he made headlines during the Erie Plastics takeover two years ago. A friend told me that MBA candidates are studying his takeover techniques."

"Well, Erie Plastics wasn't that complicated. I can give you a concise view of what really happened there, and you don't need to be a candidate for a master's degree to understand it," Corbin offered wryly.

She looked at him intently. "Please do."

"Basically, the reason Cole succeeded was he ran the competition out of time and money. When other corporations decide to acquire a company, they weigh the acquisition's value to them against its cost in money and time. If the cost gets too high, they cut their losses and back off. That's the established practice among successful corporations all over the world. That's the way Cole's adversaries play the game. While the battle is raging, they constantly reassess what they have to lose against what they have to gain; then they try to predict their adversary's next move based on their estimation of what *he* has to lose and gain.

"Cole is different. When he wants something, he won't stop until he gets it, no matter how high the cost goes. His adversaries have finally realized that, which gives Cole an even bigger edge. These days, when he decides to acquire something, other potential buyers generally pull out and let him have it, rather than go to the trouble and expense of fighting him. Basically, that's his weapon and why he wins."

"What about Erie Plastics? That's what made him a legend."

Corbin nodded. "In the case of Erie Plastics, there were originally five suitors who courted them, and we were the first. Erie's board of directors had agreed in principle to our generous offer, but when the other companies suddenly jumped in, Erie's board decided to take advantage of the competition among us by upping the ante. The price and the concessions Erie wanted kept escalating until the three smaller companies finally dropped out of the bidding. That left only Intercorp and us in the game, but just as the other companies dropped out of the bidding, another plastics company that Intercorp liked even better approached them with an offer to sell. Intercorp pulled out and that left us as Erie's only remaining suitor. The day after Intercorp pulled out, Cole retaliated against Erie's board by offering them *less* than he'd originally offered in the very beginning. Erie screamed 'foul' all over Wall Street. They got some sympathy, but no other suitors came forward with an offer because buyouts and takeovers cost a fortune, win or lose, and Cole was still standing in the ring—like a heavyweight champion with gloves on and fists raised—ready to take on the next contender if they made a move on Erie. The rest is history—Unified got a plastics company for less than it was worth, and Cole got some bad publicity and a whole new set of enemies."

"I can't do anything about his enemies," Gloria said, "but I intend to do something about our public relations."

"Cole doesn't care about making enemies. He cares about Unified and about winning. That's the point I was trying to make earlier: Cole Harrison would have paid whatever it took to get Erie, no matter how much it was. It's as if winning is as important to him as the thing he's after, maybe even more important."

"With that kind of tunnel vision, I'd have expected him to be a failure in business instead of such a dramatic success."

"You'd have been right, except that Cole Harrison has a very special gift—in addition to tenacity," Dick Rowse said grudgingly as he poured scotch from the conference room's bar into his glass.

"What gift is that?"

"Foresight," he said. "He has an extraordinary ability to foresee a trend, a change, a need, and to be ready to capitalize on it long before most of his competition."

"You don't sound as if you admire that," Gloria said, puzzled.

"I admire the talent, but not the man," Rowse said bluntly. "Whatever he does, he does it with some sort of intricate hidden agenda in mind. He drives the Wall Street analysts crazy trying to second-guess him, and they rarely succeed. He drives *all* of us crazy trying to second-guess him."

"He sounds like an intriguing man," Gloria said with an apologetic shrug for her dissenting opinion.

"What makes you think Cole Harrison is a man?" Rowse replied half seriously. "I have reason to believe he's actually a six-foot-two robot with artificial intelligence in an eight-thousand-dollar suit." When the other two laughed, he lightened up a little. "You're laughing, but there's data to support my opinion. He doesn't play golf, he doesn't play tennis, and he's not interested in professional sports or any sort of social life. If he has a friend in the world, no one knows who it is. His former secretary told me the only nonbusiness calls he gets are from women. Women," Rowse finished with an accusing glance at Gloria, "*all* seem to find him fascinating."

"That shoots down your robot theory right there, Dick," Corbin joked.

"Not necessarily," Rowse replied. "How do we know that the latest robotics technology can't produce a male robot with a—"

"I hate to interrupt this enlightening discussion," Gloria lied as she stood up and put her glass on the table, "but I have a job to do, and I'd better get at it. Mr. Harrison may not care about his public image, but it affects the corporation, and we're being paid to enhance it. While he's here today, let's talk him into a press conference about the Cushman deal—future corporate plans, and all that."

"He won't do it," Rowse warned as he stood up. "I've tried."

"Let's double-team him then and see if the two of us can prevail upon his good sense."

"He's already turned me down. Maybe you'll have beginner's luck if you try it alone—assuming you can even get in to see him."

Getting in to see Cole Harrison was much easier than getting his attention, Gloria had realized within moments of being admitted to the chrome-and-glass inner sanctum with its silver-gray carpeting and burgundy suede furnishings.

For the past ten minutes, she had been seated in front of Cole Harrison's desk, trying to convince him to agree to a press conference while he signed documents, talked to his secretary, made several phone calls, and mostly ignored her.

Suddenly his eyes leveled on her. "You were saying?" he said in the clipped tone of one issuing a command to continue, which of course he was.

"I—" Gloria faltered beneath that cold, assessing gaze, then forged ahead. "I was trying to explain that a press conference now is not merely helpful, it's vital. The press has already made the Cushman takeover look like a bloodbath. The losers were screaming 'foul' before the game was over—"

"I play to win. I won. They lost. That's all that matters."

Gloria looked him squarely in the eye and then decided to test her job security. "According to your opponents, and a lot of people on Wall Street, sir, you play unnecessarily rough, you don't take prisoners. The press has been making you look like some sort of rapacious wolf who enjoys the kill more than the food."

"That's *very* colorful, Miss Quigley," he replied with scathing mockery.

"It's *fact*," she argued, smarting from his snide tone.

"No," he countered, *"this* is fact: Cushman Electronics was founded by a genius six decades ago, but his heirs grew more lazy and more stupid with each successive generation. Those heirs—who happen to make up the board of directors—were born to great wealth, educated in the best schools, and despite the fact that they were letting Cushman, and its shareholders' investments, go down the toilet, they *still* remained so convinced of their own superiority that they couldn't see what was coming. They couldn't believe that some school chum from their 'old-boy fraternity' wasn't going to step in and rescue them with an infusion of cash that they could squander either on themselves or on fighting off more takeover attempts.

"Instead of that, they lost to me—to an upstart from the wrong side of the social tracks—and it's humiliating to them; it offends all of their cultured sensibilities. That's why they're screaming 'foul.' We weren't engaged in a tea party with polite rituals; we were engaged in a battle. In a battle, there are only winners, and losers, and bad losers."

Cole waited for her to admit defeat and retreat, but she sat there in stubborn silence, refusing to agree. "Well?" he demanded after a moment.

"There are ways to fight the battle so that the winner doesn't look like a barbarian, and public relations is the key to that."

She had a point and Cole knew it, but he didn't particularly appreciate having to face it or admit it. Time and again, as Cole had built his company into a major conglomerate composed of profitable subsidiaries, he'd waged legal and economic battles with complacent aristocrats like the ones on Cushman's board, and each time he'd emerged victorious, he had the feeling that they hated him as virulently for successfully invading their ranks as for taking whatever prize he had wrested from them. It was as if the damage Cole did to their sense of invulnerable superiority was as loathsome to them as the financial damage he did to their bank accounts and stock portfolios.

Personally, Cole found their attitude funny rather than insulting, and he was amused that, when it came down to a corporate battle over the takeover of another company, he was always portrayed as a ruthless marauder swinging a mace, while his targets were innocent victims and his competitors were chivalrous white knights. The real truth was that those courteous knights hired mercenaries in the form of lawyers and accountants and stock analysts to do their "dirty" fighting and maneuvering behind the scenes; then when their opponent was too weak to put up more than token resistance, they strolled gracefully onto the corporate battlefield wielding a gentlemanly saber. After a brief, symbolic duel, they lifted the blade to their forehead for a courteous salute to their victim, plunged the blade into him, and then strolled off the field, leaving more hired mercenaries to clean up the legal mess and bury the victim.

In contrast to these corporate duelists, Cole was a brawler, a street fighter who was interested only in victory, not in his reputation or in making friends or in showing off his grace and prowess on the battlefield. As a result, he'd acquired many enemies and few friends over the years, along with a reputation for ruthlessness that he partially deserved and one for unscrupulousness that he didn't deserve at all.

None of that bothered him. Lifelong enemies, unjust public accusations, and hard feelings were the dues that one paid for success. Cole paid his without complaint, as did those other determined visionaries who, like him, had managed in the last two decades to harvest vast personal fortunes from soil that was no longer fertile, in an economic climate that was considered unhealthy.

"They said the same thing about Matt Farrell and Intercorp in the late eighties," Cole reminded her pointedly. "Now he's the Prince Charming of Wall Street."

"Yes, he is. And part of that is due to some very good publicity that resulted from his tumultuous marriage to a well-loved heiress and from a more open, public profile."

Cole glanced toward the doorway and nodded a greeting to the corporation's head counsel, John Nederly, who was being ushered into the office by Cole's secretary. Gloria assumed her time with Cole Harrison was at an end, and she stood up, defeated.

"When do you want to have the press conference?"

For a split second, Gloria couldn't believe her ears. "I—As soon as possible. How about tomorrow? That's enough time to set it up."

He was signing more papers handed to him by his secretary, but he glanced up at her and shook his head. "I'm leaving for Los Angeles tonight, and I'll be there until Wednesday."

"What about Thursday?"

He shook his head again. "I'll be in Jeffersonville, Thursday and Friday, handling a family matter."

"Saturday then?" Gloria said hopefully.

"That's fine."

Gloria's mental cheer was strangled by the secretary, who turned over the page in his desk calendar, pointed to something written on it, and said, "I'm afraid Saturday's out of the question. You're to be in Houston that night."

"Houston?" he demanded, sounding disgusted and irate at the prospect. "For what?"

"For the White Orchid Ball. You donated a Klineman sculpture to the charity auction that precedes the ball, and you're to be honored for your generosity."

"Send someone else."

They all looked up in surprise as Gloria negated that suggestion. "I put the Orchid thing together. The Klineman will be the most valuable item to be auctioned off—"

"It will also be the ugliest," Cole interjected in such a mild, factual tone that Gloria choked back an inappropriate giggle. "Why did you buy it?" she asked before she could stop herself.

"I was told it would be a good investment, and it's gone up substantially in value over the last five years. Unfortunately, I don't like it any better now than I did when I bought it. Let someone else go to Houston in the corporation's name and take the bow."

"It has to be you," Gloria stubbornly persisted. "When public relations suggested you make a donation, you made a very generous one. The proceeds go to the American Cancer Society, and the ball is a major national media event. The timing is perfect for a little publicity there, followed by a press conference here next week."

Cole stopped writing and stared hard at her, but he couldn't find an argument to outweigh her logic, and in a small way, he approved of her resolute determination to do the job the company was paying her to do, despite his personal opposition and lack of cooperation. "Fine," he said curtly.

Dismissed, she got up and started to leave. A few steps away, she turned around and found the two men watching her. "The networks are going to play up the Cushman deal," she said to Cole. "If you have a chance to catch any of that on the news, I'd like to go over it with you and make some plans for countermeasures at your press conference."

When he replied, he sounded as if she was in danger of exhausting his patience. "I'll put the news on while I pack for Los Angeles." Gloria began to retreat.

As she left, Cole leaned back in his chair and looked at the corporation's chief counsel, who, with an appreciative gleam in his eyes, was watching Gloria exit. "Tenacious, isn't she," John remarked when she was out of earshot.

"Very."

"Great legs, too." The door closed behind her, and John switched his attention to the matters at hand. "These are the proxies your uncle needs to sign for the board meeting," he said, sliding some papers across the clear glass desktop which rested on a random pattern of free-form chrome tubes that always reminded John of twisted chrome Tinkertoys. "Cole, I hate to sound like a purveyor of gloom and doom, but your uncle really needs to sign over his shares in the corporation to you, instead of giving you his proxy each time. I know his will stipulates that you're the sole heir to his shares, but I lie awake at night in a cold sweat, thinking of the disaster we would have on our hands if he should get senile or something and decide to withhold his proxy."

Cole flicked a wry glance in the attorney's direction as he slid the proxy forms into his briefcase. "You've been losing sleep over nothing," he said. He swiveled his chair around and began removing files from the credenza behind his desk. "Cal's mind is as sharp as a razor blade."

"Even so," John persevered, addressing Cole's back, "he's in his seventies, and elderly people can be tricked into doing some very peculiar and damaging things. Last year, for example, a group of small shareholders of an Indiana chemical company decided to oppose a merger its board was trying to push through. The shareholders located an elderly woman in California who owned a major block of shares she'd inherited from her husband, then convinced the old lady that the board's action would cause massive layoffs and vastly decrease the value of her shares. They then escorted her back to Indiana, where she *personally* voted her shares against the merger and got the damned thing blocked. A few weeks later, she wrote a letter to the board claiming she was forced to do what she did!"

Cole locked the credenza, turned back around in his chair, and regarded the worried attorney with unconcealed amusement while he put the files into his briefcase. Calvin Downing was his mother's uncle, and Cole was not only closer to him than he'd ever been to his real father, he also understood him well enough to know that the attorney's fears were ludicrous in Cal's case. "To the best of my knowledge, no one, including me, has ever been able to convince, coerce, or force Calvin to do anything he didn't want to do—or prevent him from doing something he did."

When the attorney continued to look dubious, Cole cited the first example that came to mind. "For five years, I campaigned for him to leave the ranch and move to Dallas, but he wouldn't. I spent the next five years trying to convince him to build a nicer house at the ranch, but he argued that he didn't want a new house and it was a waste of money. By then he was worth at least fifty million dollars, and he was still living in the same two-bedroom, drafty old place he was born in. Finally, two years ago, he decided to take his first—and last—real vacation. While he was gone for six weeks, I hired a contractor who brought in an army of carpenters, and they built him a beautiful place on the west side of the ranch." Cole closed the briefcase and stood up. "Do you know where he lives today?"

John heard the ironic note in Cole's voice and made an accurate guess: "In the same old house?"

"Exactly."

"What does he do out there, all by himself in an old house?"

"He's not entirely alone. He's had the same housekeeper for decades, and he has a few ranch hands to help out on the place. He spends his time either interfering with them or else reading, which has always been his favorite pastime. He's a voracious reader."

That last piece of information didn't fit at all into John's preconceived Yankee notion of an elderly, weathered Texas rancher. "What does he read?"

"He reads everything he can get his hands on that pertains to whatever happens to fascinate him at a particular stage in his life. His 'stages' usually last three or four years, during which he devours dozens of tomes on his current subject. He went through a period where all he read were biographies about war heroes from the beginning of recorded history; then he switched to mythology for a while. After that came psychology, philosophy, history, and finally westerns and murder mysteries." Cole paused to make an entry in his desk calendar before he added, "A year ago, he developed an acute interest in popular magazines, and he's been reading everything from *GQ* to *Playboy* to *Ladies' Home Journal* and *Cosmopolitan*. He says popular magazines are the truest reflection of the state of a modern society's collective mind."

"Really?" John said, carefully hiding his instinctive unease with the eccentricities and obsessions of a stubborn, elderly millionaire who happened to hold an enormous block of shares in Unified Industries—and who could, if he chose, wreak havoc on Unified's complex corporate structure of subsidiaries, divisions, joint ventures, and limited partnerships. "Has he drawn any conclusions from his reading?"

"Yes." Cole shot him an ironic smile, glanced at his watch, and stood up to leave. "According to Cal, our generation has flagrantly violated the rules of morality, decency, ethics, and personal responsibility, and we are further guilty of breeding a new generation of children who don't even understand those *concepts*. In short, Cal has surmised from his reading that America is going down the toilet in the same way as ancient Greece and Rome and for the same reasons that caused their decline and collapse when they were world powers. That impossible metaphor, by the way, is Cal's not mine."

John got up and walked toward the office door with him, but Cole paused with his hand on the knob and said, "You're right about the need for Cal to transfer his shares over to me. That's a loose end that I should have tied up years ago, but for a variety of reasons I've postponed it. I'll work it out with Cal when I see him later this week."

"Work it out?" John repeated worriedly. "Is there some sort of problem?"

"No," Cole said, somewhat disingenuously. The truth was that he had no desire to try to explain to a stranger the role that Cal had played in his life, or the gratitude Cole felt for him . . . or the love. Even if he had wanted to try, Cole knew he could never explain or justify to a corporate attorney that sheer sentimentality alone had prevented Cole from asking his uncle to sign back to Cole the stock Cole had issued to him fourteen years ago.

Back then, Unified Industries had been only a vague, far-fetched dream of Cole's, but Cal had listened to his plans. With boundless faith in Cole's ability to turn his grand scheme into a reality, Cal had lent him a half million dollars to get it started—an investment that, at the time, constituted all his profits from the oil and gas leases on his land as well as an additional two hundred thousand dollars he borrowed from a bank. Cole had then approached a Dallas banker for a loan of an additional $750,000, using the future income of Cal's wells as collateral. Armed with more than a million dollars, a quick intellect, and a wealth of inside knowledge he'd obtained merely by listening to Charles Hayward and the other millionaires who gathered at the Haywards' stable, Cole made his first gamble in the high-stakes world of business and finance. He placed his opening bet on one of the riskiest, and potentially most profitable, of all ventures—oil and gas leases.

Having seen one large drilling company try twice and fail on Cal's ranch, he decided to buy an interest in the second and smaller company, the one that had ultimately succeeded. Southfield Exploration was owned and badly managed by Alan South, a cocky thirty-three-year-old, third generation "prospector," as he called himself, who loved nothing more than finding oil and gas where major drilling companies had failed.

The challenge was what drove Alan; the adrenaline of success was what he sought, rather than making and maintaining profits. As a result, he was low on funds and anxious to acquire a partner when Cole approached him with a million dollars to invest. Alan was not nearly so anxious to turn over full financial control of the operation to Cole, but Cole was adamant and Alan had no choice.

Cal had wanted Cole to consider his investment a loan, but Cole's pride made him go one step further. He had insisted that Cal be a full partner, as well as insisting on paying back the loan, and he'd had the documents drawn up by a lawyer. In the three years that followed, Alan made strike after strike—and had fight after fight with Cole, who flatly refused to let him overextend again, no matter how promising various locales looked. At the end of that time, Cole allowed Alan to buy him out for five million dollars, and the two men parted friends.

With Cal's approval, Cole used his profits from the drilling company to buy three carefully selected, small manufacturing companies. He hired a new management team, shored up the companies with new equipment, emphasized customer service, and boosted the morale of the sales staff. As soon as each company's balance sheet looked good, he sold the company. In what he considered his spare time, he studied the stock market and analyzed the philosophies of successful brokers and money managers. Based on the fact that most of the experts disagreed radically with each other on one or all of the important points, Cole concluded that luck and timing mattered as much or more than skill and knowledge. Since luck and timing had been on his side thus far, he tried his hand in some serious investing.

At the end of three years, Cole had turned five million dollars into sixty-five million. During all that time, the only condition Cal put on Cole was that Cal's other nephew, Travis Jerrold, be given a place in Cole's next business venture. Travis was five years older than Cole and from a town on the other side of Texas, where he worked for a failing tool manufacturer. He had a college degree, a pretty wife named Elaine, whom Cole liked very much, and two spoiled children named Donna Jean and Ted, whom Cole did not like at all. Although Cole had only seen Travis once as a teenager, he liked the loyalty that Travis as "family" would bring to the business, and he was perfectly amenable to Cal's request.

Cole began looking around for a profitable company on which he could found his corporate dynasty—a company that provided a product or service for which there was likely to be an ever-increasing need. Predicting that need was the key to success, and it was there that Cole discovered he had a genuine gift. Although everyone else seemed to believe that IBM and Apple would soon own the entire computer hardware market, Cole was convinced that lower-priced, but high-quality, generic brands could seize a large share of the personal computer market.

Against everyone else's judgment and advice, he bought a small company called Hancock and invented his own new "name brand."

He tripled the size of the company's sales force, beefed up quality control, and poured money into an ongoing advertising campaign. Within two years, Hancock computers were sold in retail markets all over the country and winning praise for their reliability and flexibility. When all that was in place, Cole named Travis as Hancock's new president and put him in charge, which caused Travis's ecstatic wife to burst into tears of gratitude and Travis to break out in a nervous rash.

Travis proved to be an asset to what was now a family venture. What Travis lacked in imagination, he made up for in loyalty and determination and scrupulous adherence to Cole's instructions. When Cole created Unified's new research and development division four years later, he named Travis to head it.

Chapter 11

"I'M A BIG FAN OF YOURS, MISS FOSTER," THE MAKEUP ARTIST AT CNN remarked as she made slow, careful strokes over Diana's shiny shoulder-length hair. "My mother and my sister and I all read your magazine from cover to cover, every month."

The room where makeup was applied to guests while they waited to go on the air was like most of its kind in every television studio in the country, except CNN's was a little larger. Two long Formica countertops stretched the length of both sides of the narrow room, with chairs spaced at six-foot intervals along them and brightly lit mirrors lining the walls. At each makeup station, jars and bottles of cosmetics fought for counterspace with lipsticks, eyeliners, eye shadows, and an assortment of brushes and combs.

Sometimes all the stations were occupied by guests being made up for television, but this afternoon, Diana was the only one scheduled for an interview, and the young woman who was applying her makeup was bursting with enthusiasm: "For my sister's birthday, we used your grandmother's recipe for vanilla pudding cake. We topped it with fresh sugar-glazed blueberries, just like the picture in magazine. Then we gathered armfuls of peonies for a centerpiece, and we decorated our own gift wrap by using rubber stamps cut in the shape of peonies. I used a gold stamp pad for mine, but my mom used a silver one, and they were both really great!"

"That's very nice to hear." Diana flashed her an absentminded smile, without taking her attention from the urgent memos that had arrived by fax at her hotel late that morning.

"My mom finally got my dad to try your grandpa's special trick for raising giant, juicy strawberries, and they turned out *huge,* and were they ever delicious! When my dad first looked at the picture of them in the magazine, he said you were using trick photography and they were probably crab apples, but his turned out fantastic, too! Next, he built that compost box your grandpa showed in the magazine. Now he reads *Foster's Beautiful Living* from cover to cover, just like we do!"

Feeling that some response was again required, Diana gave her another smile before she turned to the second page of the fax from the Foster Enterprises office in Houston. The smile was all the encouragement the enthusiastic young woman needed. "Practically everybody I know reads your magazine. We just love the ideas you put in it, and the pictures your sister takes are really gorgeous! Gosh, the way your mom writes about all of you, I feel like I know your whole family. When Corey had her babies—the twins—we sat right down and crocheted those adorable little booties for them. You know—the ones that look sort of like high-top running shoes? I hope she got them."

Diana looked up and smiled for the third time. "I'm sure she did."

The young woman dusted a light coat of blusher on Diana's high cheekbones and stepped back. "I'm finished," she said almost regretfully. "You're even prettier in real life than you are in that picture at the front of the magazine."

"Thank you very much," Diana replied, laying the faxes aside and looking up at her.

"You have about ten minutes before they'll come and get you and take you into the studio."

When she left, Diana looked over at Cindy Bertrillo, the public relations director at *Foster's Beautiful Living* magazine, who had accompanied her to Atlanta and had been sitting nearby while

Diana's makeup was applied. "Are there any other faxes?" Diana asked as she scribbled instructions on two of the faxed memos and handed them to Cindy to send to the office when they got back to the hotel.

"Nope, that's it," Cindy said, stuffing the memos into her brief-case. With her short-cropped black hair, oversize glasses, and swift, energetic movements, the tireless thirty-two-year-old publicist looked, Diana thought, as if she was constantly searching for new things to benefit *Foster's*. And she was.

Diana glanced at her watch and grimaced. "I hate these inter-views. They take away too much time from work. I have six meetings tomorrow, the accountants want to go over the prelimi-nary P-and-Ls, and I should be finalizing the arrangements for the new coffee-table book. I'm behind schedule on everything!"

Cindy was very familiar with Diana's killing work schedule. At thirty-one, Diana was more than a successful businesswoman; she had become a reluctant celebrity, an unwilling idol—a state of affairs that owed itself to her remarkably photogenic features and her ability to look outwardly serene even when the situation was chaotic and her nerves were unraveled. Despite Diana's wish to maintain her privacy and keep a low profile, her classic features, vivid coloring, and natural elegance had made her an increasingly popular subject for journalists and photographers—and television talk-show hosts.

Cindy smiled sympathetically as she repeated what she always said in these circumstances. "I know, but the television cameras love you, and interviews help sell magazines." She tipped her head to one side, assessing the effect of Diana's buttercup yellow crepe suit against the auburn highlights in her hair and striking green eyes. "You look terrific," she said.

Diana rolled her eyes, dismissing the remark. "Please try to book Gram and Mom for more of these interview shows, or even my grandfather, but not me. Gram and Mom *are* the Foster Ideal; they're the soul and spirit of the whole concept; they *are* the magazine. Put Corey on television, for heaven's sake; she's the one with the photographic genius that makes the magazine look so spectacular. I'm just the figurehead; I'm the business end, and I always feel like a complete phony when I do these shows. Besides, I'm just too *busy* for this."

When she ran out of argument, Cindy said very pleasantly, and very firmly, "The media wants *you*, Diana. And anyway," she added with a rueful smile, "we can't let Gram do any more live interview shows. She's gotten much too outspoken in her advancing years. I didn't tell you this, but last month, when she taped the show for the Dallas CBS channel, the host asked her to explain the difference between *Foster's Beautiful Living* magazine and its closest competitor, *New Style*."

Cindy waited, with raised brows and an expression of ill-suppressed mirth, for Diana to ask the obvious question. "What," Diana asked warily, noting the telltale look, "did Gram say?"

"She said when she followed *New Style*'s instructions for making a hand-decorated lamp, she nearly burned the house down."

Diana muffled a horrified laugh.

"Then she said she'd eaten better-tasting plaster than *New Style*'s special wedding cake."

"Good God!" Diana said, laughing in earnest now.

"If that show had been live, instead of taped, Gram's candor would have gotten us a nice fat lawsuit," Cindy continued wryly. "As it was, I threw myself on the host's mercy and begged him not to use what would have been the juciest part of the interview." Cindy leaned forward and jokingly confided, "He agreed, but I have to sleep with him the next time I go to Dallas."

"That sounds reasonable," Diana said, straight-faced, and then they both laughed. "Gram doesn't say things like that to be spiteful," she explained, sobering. "In her advancing years, she's suddenly decided that she doesn't want to waste what breath she has left on polite lies—or something like that."

"So she informed me in Dallas. Anyway, I do book your mom and Corey or your grandparents whenever I can; you know that. I can arrange network specials for them, where they demonstrate all their wonderful projects, and the shows are always a big hit, but when it comes to talk shows and personal interviews, it's *you* the public wants to see."

"I wish you'd do something to change their minds."

"Change your face, and maybe I could," Cindy countered with a grin. "Get ugly, get fat. Get a little conceited, or a little pushy, or a little crude. The public will spot that instantly, and you'll lose your commercial appeal."

"Thanks, you're a big help," Diana said.

"Can I help it if you've become an icon? Is it my fault the public sees you as America's Favorite Domestic Goddess?"

Diana made a comic face at that phrase, which had been coined by a CBS commentator when he interviewed Diana last year. "Don't tell anyone that I haven't had time to cook a real meal at home in two years, will you?—or that I had to pay an interior designer to fix up my apartment because I'm too busy working."

"They couldn't pry it out of me with pliers," Cindy joked, then she sobered. Shoving cosmetics aside, Cindy perched her hip on the edge of the countertop and said very seriously, "Diana, I've heard you joke about things like that several times in the last few months, and it's been making me increasingly nervous. When you first started the magazine, you had a wide-open field, but all that's changed radically in the last two years. I know I don't have to tell you how much the competition has grown, or how much money they have behind them, or how far they would go just to topple you and *Foster's Beautiful Living* out of first place. You have major publishers putting out their own magazines and books and trying to build their own 'icons.'

"If they find just one real weak spot in you, they'll use it to bludgeon you—and the entire Foster Ideal—all over the media. No matter how inventive or talented your mother and grandmother and all the assistants at the magazine may be, it's *you* the women of America see as the real Foster Ideal.

"I know you're exhausted, and I know you resent the hell out of having your private life mixed with your business life, but until you and Dan Penworth are married and in a house of your own, decorated with lots of pretty projects we've featured in the magazine, you cannot afford even to *joke* about your lack of domesticity. If our competitors get wind of it, they'll make you look like a complete fake in the press."

Diana tipped her head back, fighting to keep the angry resentment out of her voice. "I'm an executive with a large and growing corporation. I do *not* have the time to stencil borders on my wallpaper."

Cindy was stunned by the sound of tears in Diana's voice, and for the first time, she realized that Diana, who always seemed to be the embodiment of vitality, optimism, and serenity, was actually strained to the breaking point. It was little wonder, considering the responsibility she shouldered. Her work schedule practically eliminated any personal life. In addition, she had kept her fiancé waiting patiently in the wings for nearly two years for a wedding that had to be the embodiment of the Foster Ideal. "I'm sorry," Cindy said gently. "I wouldn't have upset you for the world. Let me get you something. How about some coffee?"

"Thanks," Diana replied, flashing a rueful smile at Cindy. "I'd love some."

Cindy left, closing the door behind her, and Diana turned in her chair. Her face gazed back at her from the mirror, and she shook her head in amused irony at the vagaries of fate. "Tell me something," she softly said to her reflection. "How did a nice girl like you end up in a place like this?"

The woman in the mirror looked back at her with a wry smile. The answer was so obvious: necessity and desperation after her father's sudden death after a stroke eight years ago had driven her to take risks and defy the odds in order to keep the family together. Timing and luck had propelled the family far beyond their modest hopes. Timing and luck—and probably a little celestial help from Robert Foster.

After the funeral, when her father's lawyer revealed the true state of their finances—he'd finished droning on to the grief-stricken family about cross-collateralized assets and the stock market's fatal plunge a few months before—Diana alone had been capable of absorbing the meaning of it all: after her father's debts were paid, the family would have nothing except the house they were living in and the furniture in it.

In a desperate effort to keep everyone together, Diana had decided to try to turn the family's locally acclaimed flair for style into a money-making proposition. Somehow, she had managed to get good advice, draw up a business plan, and borrow the start-up money they needed. And in the end, she had managed to turn her family's unique way of life into a multimillion-dollar business.

Chapter 12

STANDING IN FRONT OF A DARK GRAY MARBLE SINK WITH HIS FACE covered in shaving lather and his chest bare, Cole stroked the razor up his neck while he listened to the news on the television. In the study adjoining the bedroom, a large television screen was built into the wall behind a sliding panel.

His suitcase was open on the bed, packed for his trip to Los Angeles, and Michelle was mixing drinks for them in the dining room. CNN was introducing a guest they were about to interview: "In the years since Diana Foster conceived and executed a plan to turn her family's 'hobby' into a business, she's become not only the publisher of *Foster's Beautiful Living* magazine, but the president of a thriving Houston-based corporation that, under her leadership, has diversified into many areas, including television as well as the manufacture and sale of Foster's Products for the Home — a line of all-natural cleaning products.

Cole was rinsing his face when he heard the guest's name, and he assumed it was pure coincidence, but when the show's host also threw Houston into the equation, Cole straightened and grabbed a towel. He dabbed leftover shaving cream from his face as he strolled into the library and halted in front of the television.

A slow smile of pleasure and disbelief worked its way across his face as he gazed at Diana Foster's lovely image while the show's host continued with her bio: "In the last two years, Diana has appeared on the covers of *People* and *Working Woman* magazine. Articles have been written about her in newspapers from *The New York Times* to the *Enquirer* and *Star*. *Working Woman* called her 'an example of what a woman executive could—and should—be.' *Cosmopolitan* featured her in a cover story entitled 'Women with Beauty, Brains, and Bravery.'"

The host turned to his guest. "Diana, one news commentator dubbed you the 'High Priestess of Domestic Grace and Beauty.' How does all this make you feel?"

She laughed—the soft musical laugh Cole remembered from years gone by—and after all this time, the sight of those entrancing eyes and radiant smile still warmed him. "Flattered, of course," she said. "Unduly flattered, actually. *Foster's Beautiful Living* is a massive family effort, and I'm only one small part of it."

"You were only twenty-two when you decided to try to market what was, until then, only a well-known family lifestyle in Houston. Were you filled with youthful optimism, or did you have some fears about the risk you were taking when you founded the magazine?"

"I had only one fear," she said solemnly, but Cole grinned because he had known her well and he caught the almost imperceptible note of humor in her voice, "but it kept me awake nights for the first two years."

The host took her very seriously. "What was that one fear?"

She laughed. "Failure!" The host was still chuckling when she added, "And I really have to confess that some of my ancestors' wealth and prominence came from robbing banks and rustling cattle. In fact, until 1900, the most reputable one of them all was a professional gambler, and he was shot for cheating at cards in a Fort Worth saloon."

Standing in the center of the library with his feet bare, his fists on his hips, and a grin on his lips, Cole chuckled at her unaffected candor and wit.

Behind him, Michelle entered with a tray of drinks and hors d'oeuvres. "What's so funny?" she asked as she put the tray on the table and straightened, smoothing the wrinkles from her silk pants and shirt.

Cole shook his head without taking his eyes from Diana's face on the television screen.

"That's Diana Foster," she told him. Michelle was from a prominent Dallas family with important connections in Houston, and so she knew about all the proverbial skeletons in the closets of her own social set. "She capitalized on her family's reputation, borrowed a lot of money, and used it to start up a little business that the whole family worked in. No one figured they'd make it, but they've made it really big. Originally, Diana raised a lot of eyebrows when she started the whole thing up. Now she's made a lot of enemies, too."

Cole was instantly irate on Diana's behalf. "Why?"

"This is Texas, honey, remember? This is the home of the 'good-old-boy' network, where the myth of male superiority still prospers and where 'macho' is a holy word. In Texas, rich men pamper and patronize their wives and daughters. Wives and daughters are *not* supposed to strike out on their own, and if they do, they are definitely not supposed to succeed in a big way, let alone become more famous than the menfolk."

While Cole was still absorbing the unquestionable truth of what she said, Michelle ran her fingers through the short black hairs on his chest. "Diana Foster is also beautiful, unmarried, and very classy. When you add all that together, she's more likely to be envied than liked by my sex."

Cole looked down at her long aristocratic fingers with their vermilion nails as they played enticingly with the nerve endings in his chest. "Would that include you?" he asked, but he knew it wouldn't. At thirty-two, Michelle was too intelligent, too wise, and too clever to waste her time envying another woman. Besides, she had already picked out her candidate for her third husband, and Diana Foster was no threat to her.

"No," she said, tipping her head back and gazing into his eyes. "But, I'd trade places with her in ten seconds, if I could. I've already been a victim of all that 'pampering and patronizing' from my father and two husbands."

She was beautiful, candid, and a wildcat in bed. In addition to his sexual and intellectual attraction to her, Cole genuinely liked her.

He linked his hands behind her back, pulling her close. "Why don't we go to bed so I can pamper and patronize you myself?"

She shook her head no and smiled seductively into his eyes.

"In that case," he countered in a husky, sensual voice, "we'll go to bed and I'll let *you* pamper and patronize *me.*" Michelle never turned down a chance to go to bed with him, under any circumstances, and so he was surprised when she declined again. "Why don't you marry me instead?"

Cole's expression didn't change. He whispered one word, then bent his head and silenced her protests with his mouth. "No," he said.

"I could give you children," she said shakily when he lifted his head. "I'd like to have children."

Cole tightened his arms and seized her lips with a steamy passion that was in complete contrast to the icy finality of words. "I do not *want* children, Michelle."

Chapter 13

$\mathcal{T}$HE TELEPHONE AT THE RECEPTIONIST'S DESK RANG, AND TINA Frederick picked it up. *"Foster's Beautiful Living,"* she said with a bright, energetic voice that reflected the general attitude of all Foster's employees.

"Tina, this is Cindy Bertrillo. Has Diana Foster come back from lunch?"

The magazine's publicist sounded so tense and desperate that Tina automatically looked over her shoulder to double-check that the lobby's revolving doors weren't moving. "No, not yet."

"As soon as you see her, tell her I have to talk to her. It's urgent."

"Okay, I will."

"You're the first person she'll pass when she enters the building. Don't leave your desk for any reason until you've given her my message."

"I won't." When she hung up the phone, Tina tried to imagine what sort of urgent matter might have come up, but she was positive that whatever it was, Diana would handle it with ease and not show any of the anxiety that had permeated Cindy's voice.

Diana Foster's tranquility and humor were admired by all 260 of the Foster Enterprises' employees who worked in the downtown Houston offices. From the mail room to the executive suite, Diana was famous among the staff for the courtesy and respect she showed to everyone who worked for her and with her. No matter how much stress she was under or how long the hours she worked, she rarely passed an employee without a smile or some gesture of acknowledgment.

Given all that, it was little wonder that Tina rose from her chair in shock when Diana blasted through the revolving doors several minutes later with a folded newspaper under her elbow and stalked right past Tina's desk. "Miss Foster—" she called, but her normally gracious employer didn't so much as glance her way.

Diana stalked down aisles lined with secretarial cubicles and executive offices without a word or glance in any direction, her face pale and rigid. She walked past the art department without saying a word about the next issue, pressed the button for the elevator, and, when the doors opened, disappeared into it.

Diana's secretary, Sally, saw her get off the elevator, and she automatically gathered up her phone messages because Diana always asked about messages the moment she came back to her office. Instead, Diana walked around Sally's cubicle as if it were invisible and vanished into her office. Sally stood up with the message slips in her hand and, as she moved around her desk, noticed several other secretaries peering curiosly toward Diana's office.

Preoccupied with the desire to give Diana her messages so that she wouldn't have to ask for them, Sally doggedly followed Diana into her office. "Mrs. Paul Underwood called about the White Orchid Ball," Sally began, reading the first of the three slips of paper. "She said to tell you that the amethyst-and-diamond necklace you'll be modeling at the charity auction is spectacular and that if it weren't understood that Dan Penworth will buy the necklace for you, she'd insist her husband buy it for her." Sally paused and glanced up. "I think she was sort of, well, joking a little."

She waited, expecting some sort of humorous reaction to this, but Diana only nodded stiffly as she flung the newspaper on her desk and pulled off the jacket of her cherry wool-crepe suit, dropping it haphazardly on the back of the suede swivel chair behind her desk. "Any other calls?" she asked, her head down, her voice strained.

"Yes. The bridal salon called to say they have several new gowns in from Paris, which they think you'll love."

Diana seemed to freeze; then she turned away from her desk and walked over to the glass wall that looked out across a sunny Houston skyline. In silence, Sally watched Diana cross her arms over her chest, rubbing the sleeves of her white silk blouse as if her arms were cold. "Anything else?" she asked in a voice so low that Sally moved a little closer, trying to hear her.

"Bert Peters called. There was a problem with two of the photo layouts in the next issue, and his group is scrambling to get it fixed. Bert asked if you'd let him reschedule the produciton meeting you wanted from three o'clock today to four?"

Diana's voice dropped lower, but it was filled with resolution. "Cancel it."

"Cancel it?" Sally repeated in disbelief.

Diana swallowed. "Reschedule it for eight **A.M.** tomorrow." After a moment, she added, "If my sister's in the building, ask her to come here."

Sally nodded and reached for the phone on Diana's desk, calling the extension where she knew Corey Foster could be reached. "Corey's downstairs with the production staff, helping with the layouts," she explained to Diana's back. "Bert said she had a solution that will work."

Sally repeated Diana's request to Corey on the telephone; then she hung up and stared worriedly at Diana's still form and stiff shoulders. People who didn't know Diana were normally so dazzled and disarmed by her classic features, vivid coloring, soft voice, and quiet elegance that they were misled into thinking of her as a languid young socialite who spent her days dabbling in charity work or dropping by her office for an occasional board meeting and spent her evenings being pampered in order to keep worry lines from marring her fragile beauty. However, those people who worked closely with her, as did Sally, knew that Diana was a tireless worker with seemingly endless supplies of energy and enthusiasm.

When the magazine's monthly deadlines drew near, it was not unusual for the staff to work each night until midnight. When everyone was too exhausted or too stressed-out to do more than droop in their chairs, Diana—whose administrative duties often kept her working late in her office on the top floor—would frequently appear in the production department with an encouraging smile on her face and a tray of coffee and sandwiches in her arms.

The following morning, the production staff would stagger in a little late, their eyes bleary and their brains foggy, while Diana would look fresh and rested and be filled with sympathetic appreciation for the long hours they'd worked. The wide difference between the effect of stress and lack of sleep on Diana versus its effect on others almost always evoked some sort of good-natured grumbling comment from someone who'd worked late the night before. Diana would bear it with a smile or laugh it off with some remark about it all catching up with her someday, then turn the discussion to the next issue and the next set of problems they would invariably face.

Considering the fact that she never showed the slightest pessimism about even the largest problems, and considering her ability to juggle a dozen different projects and a hundred different details without ever seeming to be rattled, Sally had found it both amazing and endearing when she discovered that Diana actually had two weaknesses: she required a basic framework of routine within which to operate, and she required a state of absolute orderliness in her office. The lack of either of these could throw her into a state of confusion and dismay like nothing else could.

Diana could stand serenely in the chaos and disorder of the production department, the floors and drawing boards littered with proposed layouts and copy proofs, and make vital decisions with flawless judgment—but she could not sit at her own desk and concentrate on a problem or make a decision unless the top of her Louis XIV desk was perfectly neat, with each item in its proper place.

Last week, before leaving the building for a luncheon meeting with the corporation's attorney's, Diana had attended the regular Monday-morning budget meeting. While there, she ended up simultaneously arbitrating an argument between two extremely talented and temperamental artists, issuing instructions to the

105

corporation's controller, and reviewing the contents of a contract Sally had brought her to sign. She managed all that without missing a written or spoken word, but when she was ready to sign the contract and reached into her briefcase for the gold pen she kept there and couldn't find it, she lost all concentration on everything.

She used the controller's pen to sign the document, but she continued to search through her briefcase and then her purse for her own pen, and when the two verbal combatants demanded to know if she had a compromise to suggest to settle the dispute, Diana glanced blankly at them and mumbled, "What dispute was that?"

As Sally had soon discovered, the "secret" Diana was a creature of habit with a need for orderliness in her personal surroundings. Each Friday morning at seven-thirty, come hell or hurricane, she had a massage at the Houstonian Hotel and Health Club, followed by a simultaneous manicure and pedicure at her favorite salon. She returned to the office at ten A.M., where a local car-care service picked up her car keys, washed her car, filled it up with gasoline, and returned it by noon, so that it would be available if she went out to lunch. She wrote checks for her personal bills on the first and fifteenth of the month, regardless of where she was or what day of the week the dates fell upon, and she went to church every Sunday morning at ten. And always, always, when Diana returned from lunch, she asked Sally to tell her, first, who had called while she was out and then what items were on her schedule for the afternoon.

Today, however, she'd done neither, and Sally's uneasiness grew as she looked at the newspaper Diana had tossed on her desk, on top of a treasured Steuben crystal frog, and at the red wool jacket that was hanging by only one shoulder over the back of her chair. "Diana?" Sally said hesitantly, "I don't mean to pry, but is something wrong?"

For a moment, Sally thought Diana either hadn't heard her or didn't want to answer; then Diana lifted her head and glanced over her shoulder, her green eyes bright with some emotion. "I think you could say that," she said in a shaky whisper. When Sally stared at her in helpless confusion, Diana tipped her head toward the newspaper. "I've just made the front page of the *National Enquirer.*"

Sally turned to the desk and reached for the newspaper, her apprehension already outweighed by outraged loyalty and indignation at whatever she was about to see that had so upset Diana. And even though she was braced for an affront, the headline and pictures that were sprawled across the front page had the effect of a punch in the stomach.

TROUBLE IN PARADISE
DIANA FOSTER IS JILTED BY FIANCÉ

Below the headline was a huge picture of Diana's handsome fiancé, Dan Penworth, who was lying on a beach beside a curvaceous blond. The caption read, *"Diana Foster's fiancé, Dan Penworth, honeymooning with his new bride, 18-year-old Italian model and heiress Christina Delmonte."* Sally scanned the story, her stomach churning. *"Yesterday, in Rome, Christina Delmonte got the 'scoop' on* Foster's Beautiful Living *magazine's publisher, Diana Foster. . . . Lately, the Foster Empire has been under siege from rival magazines who've scoffed at Ms. Foster's steadfast avoidance of matrimony and motherhood while her magazine preaches the bliss and beauty to be found in both. . . ."*

"That weasel!" Sally breathed. "That sneak, that—" She broke off as Corey walked into the office, looking rushed but blissfully unaware of any disaster.

"I think we've got the problem with the layout settled," Corey said, peering at Diana's averted face and then at Sally's stricken one. "What's wrong?"

In answer, Sally held out the newspaper, and Corey took it. A moment later, she hissed, "That bastard! That—"

"Coward!" Sally provided.

"He's a scumbag," Corey added.

"A jerk—"

"Thank you both," Diana said with a teary, forced laugh. "At a time like this, loyalty counts for a lot."

Corey and Sally exchanged sympathetic glances; then Sally turned and left, closing the office door behind her, and Corey headed for her sister. "I'm so sorry," she whispered, wrapping her in a fierce hug.

"Me, too," Diana said, sounding as meek and bewildered as a child who has been punished for something they didn't do.

"C'mon," Corey urged, turning Diana away from the window and

107

toward her desk. "Get your jacket and purse and let's get out of here. We'll go home and break the news to Mom and Gram and Gramps together."

"I can't leave early." Diana managed to lift her chin a notch, but her eyes were still wounded and glazed with shock. "I can't run away. By tonight, everyone in the office will have seen or heard about that article. They'll remember that I left early, and they'll think it's because I couldn't face people."

"Diana," Corey said very firmly, "there cannot be any other president of a large company who is as thoroughly liked and as much admired by their employees as you are by yours. They'll feel terrible for you."

"I don't want pity," Diana said, getting her voice under control and her features into a semblance of their normal expression.

Corey knew it was useless to argue. Diana had a great deal of pride and courage, and both those things would force her to brave out the day no matter how shattered she was. "Okay, but don't work late. I'll phone Mom and tell her we'll both be home for dinner at six-thirty. With any luck we'll be able to break the news to the family before they've heard it elsewhere."

She half expected Diana to proudly decline that offer of support, but she didn't. "Thanks," she said.

Chapter 14

*B*Y THE TIME SHE LEFT THE OFFICE THAT NIGHT, WORD HAD ALREADY
spread, making her the object of pitying glances from her employees, the security guards in the lobby, and even the parking lot
attendant. While Corey waited outside in her car, Diana went into
her apartment to change clothes. Her answering machine was full
of messages from reporters, from friends, and from distant acquaintances who rarely called—all of them, Diana was certain,
eager for more of the juicy details. She was furious with Dan and
thoroughly humiliated.

As soon as Diana and Corey walked through the doorway of the
River Oaks house, it was obvious from the indignant, dismayed
expressions on the faces of their mother and grandparents that the
rest of the family had also heard the news. "We heard it on the
television, just before you got home. I can't believe Dan did this—
not this way, not without a phone call or a telegram to let you
know," Mrs. Foster said as they waited in the dining room for
dinner to be served.

Diana stared bleakly at her hands, twisting the four-carat diamond engagement ring on her finger. "Dan called from Italy the day before yesterday, but we were on deadline and I couldn't take the call. Last night, we worked until midnight, and with the time difference, it would have been perfect for me to call him when I got home, but I fell asleep sitting up in bed, with my hand on the phone. This morning, I woke up late, and as soon as I got to work, I got involved with a half-dozen crises. He probably wanted to tell me about this, but I was too busy to call him back," she said bitterly. "It's my own fault for finding out about his marriage in the newspaper . . ."

"Don't you dare blame yourself for this, young lady," Diana's grandfather exclaimed loyally as he shifted in his chair, his left leg stiff from recent surgery. "He was engaged to you when he married someone else. He ought to be horsewhipped!"

"I never liked Dan Penworth!" Corey's grandmother announced.

Diana appreciated their steadfastness, but she was perilously close to tears. Oblivious to the fact that she was not easing Diana's burden, her grandmother continued bluntly, "Dan was too old for you, among other things. Why, what does a forty-two-year-old man want with a twenty-nine-year-old woman, anyway, I ask you?"

"Very little, obviously," Diana said bleakly, "and I'm thirty-one, not twenty-nine."

"You were twenty-nine when you got engaged," her grandmother argued.

"His new wife is eighteen. Maybe that will be his lucky number."

"Diana," Mrs. Foster interceded gently, "I don't know if this is the time to be philosophical or not, but I always wondered if the two of you were right for each other."

"Mom, please. You were very much in favor of Dan for a son-in-law when we got engaged."

"Yes, I was. But I began to have my doubts when you kept him dangling for two years."

"Dangling!" Diana's grandmother put in. "I'd like to see that young man dangling from the end of a rope for what he's done!"

"The point I was trying to make," Mrs. Foster said, "is that if two people truly love each other—if everything is really 'right' and there are no obstacles to getting married, it seems to me they should be in a little more of a hurry to be married than Diana was. I married your father within weeks of meeting him."

Diana managed a wan smile. "That's because he didn't give you a choice."

She sat at her place at the table, shaking her head as dinner courses were served. Her stomach was churning, and the others seemed to understand. "I wish I could just go away for a month until all this dies down," she said when dessert was over.

"Well, you can't," said Gram with unintentional ruthlessness. "That scoundrel pulled this trick only a few days from the Orchid Ball. It's a ritual that we all attend, and if you don't go, people will say you didn't show up because you were heartbroken!"

Diana felt physically ill at the thought of being subjected to public scrutiny at Houston's biggest, most lavish social event. "They'll think that no matter what I do!"

"A pity you couldn't arrive at the ball on the arm of a new fiancé!" said her grandfather with uncharacteristic impracticality. "That would stop the tongues from wagging!"

"Why don't I just show up with a new husband," Diana said, choking on an anguished laugh, "and make them all think I jilted Dan." Sliding her chair back, she said, "I'm going to change clothes and go for a swim. I think I'll spend the night here."

Corey's husband, Spence, was out of town, and Corey joined her in her after-dinner swim. Later, as they reclined in a pair of chaise longues beside the pool, Corey watched Diana's profile as her expression grew increasingly pensive. "I didn't expect you to get over today's news in a few hours, but you look as if Dan's defection is upsetting you more now than it did earlier."

"Actually," Diana admitted without shifting her gaze from the starry sky, "I was worrying about business, not my personal life. More correctly, I was worrying about the damaging effect of my *personal* life on our *business.*"

Shifting onto her side, Corey propped her head on her hand. "What do you mean?"

"I haven't wanted to worry you with company economics when we agreed, at the outset, that you'd handle the artistic end and I'd handle the money side. . . ."

"What's wrong—with the money side, I mean?" Corey prompted when Diana fell silent.

"As you know, we've come under fire several times this year because I don't personally live up to the 'Foster Ideal.' Each time it has happened, there's been a minor fall-off in advertisers and our new-subscription rate has flattened out or declined a little. We've rebounded every time, but thanks to Dan, there's going to be much more fallout this time."

"I think you're overestimating the influence and readership of the *Enquirer,*" Corey scoffed, but her voice lacked conviction. Diana was an astute businesswoman, perhaps even a gifted one, and although she was cautious, she never looked for trouble where none was to be found.

"There were several calls on my answering machine tonight. I listened to them while I was changing clothes after dinner. The story made CBS's and NBC's six o'clock news."

Corey's heart sank and she was filled with anger and regret for this assault on her sister's privacy and pride. Avoiding the personal implications for Diana, she tried to focus on the business ones that seemed to be concerning her sister far more at the moment. "And you think all this publicity about your fiancé breaking off your engagement will affect the magazine?"

"He didn't break off our engagement, Corey. He dumped me for someone else. Our readership is almost entirely female, and our entire success has been built on our readership's belief that the Foster way is the right way—that it brings beauty and harmony to the home and tremendous personal gratification to the women who try it."

"Well, it does do those things."

Diana rolled onto her side, finally facing Corey. "Tell me something, if you were a female who wanted to bring new spirit into her family life, would *you* be inclined to put your faith in the promises of a woman who just got jilted for an eighteen-year-old blond Italian model? Our competition is going to toss every sort of fuel onto the fire to keep this little scandal alive. I mean the fact that I am single, childless, and without a home of my own wasn't so inexcusable as long as I was engaged to Dan. The implication was that I *intended* to practice what we preach in *Foster's Beautiful Living.* Now, because of what's happened, we're going to look as if we're trying to put some sort of money-making fantasy over on an unwitting segment of the population, namely women. Our profits are going to dive, you watch."

Corey couldn't begin to try to judge the effect of Diana's personal

loss on the bottom line of the corporation's profit-and-loss statement; her brain rebelled at the effort, and her artistic nature cried
out its artist's protest that beauty and emotion always took a
backseat when accountants got involved. Moreover, she was starting to suspect that Diana was more deeply alarmed about the
magazine than about the loss of the man she supposedly loved.
"Tell me something," Corey said hesitantly. "What worries you
more right now—your unfaithful fiancé or company finances?"

"Right now?"

"Right now."

"I—I'm worried about business," Diana admitted.

"In that case, maybe you were lucky you didn't marry Dan."

"Because he probably would have cheated on me after we were
married?" Diana assumed bleakly.

"No, because I don't think you were really, deeply in love with
him. I've been thinking about Spence and about how I'd feel if he
did to me what Dan just did to you. I'd be demented with pain and
rage, but it wouldn't have anything to do with the business."

She expected Diana to argue or protest, and she didn't feel
reassured when Diana did neither. Instead her sister sat up, drew
her knees against her chest, and wrapped her arms around them as
if she were drawing into a tight, protective ball. "I don't think I'm
capable of loving anyone the way you love Spence."

Corey stared at her with growing concern.

That very first afternoon they'd met—when Diana returned from
Europe to find she'd acquired a stepmother, a stepsister, and a set of
grandparents—she'd responded to Corey's cool greeting with quiet
warmth, instead of the temper tantrum Corey had expected from
what she'd been sure was a "spoiled, rich brat."

Now, as she looked at Diana's beautiful profile, she remembered
the words Diana had said long ago on that very first day. "You come
with a grandma, too?" Diana had asked, after complimenting the
hand-painted sweatshirt that Corey had thought she'd deride. When
Corey described her grandparents, Diana had raised her eyes and
hands skyward and turned in a slow circle. "A sister, and a mom,
and a grandma, and a grandpa! This could be *very* cool!" It had
certainly been "cool" for Corey; Diana had seen to that. Diana, with
her fragile beauty and dazzling smile and innate gentility, had
paved the way for Corey, standing by her at every turn. Diana was

and had always been the most loving, supportive person Corey had ever met.

The idea that Diana's self-confidence and self-esteem were some-how low enough to make her doubt her capacity for loving was more than Corey could stand. It bothered her far more than Dan Penworth's defection or the possible business consequences of it. "Diana," she said very clearly and very firmly, "what you just said is garbage!"

"Maybe not."

"There's no 'maybe' about it! Has it occurred to you that you've been too busy since Dad died to do anything but work? That you haven't actually dated all that many men? That maybe, just maybe, you settled for 'liking' Dan instead of 'loving' someone else?"

Diana lifted her slim shoulders in a shrug. "Whatever I did wrong, it's going to hurt us badly at the magazine now."

"You were going to marry the wrong man; that's what you did wrong."

"I wish I were married to the right one now."

Chapter 15

"D AMMIT, COLE!" CALVIN EXPLODED AS HE SHOVED HIMSELF OUT OF his chair and stomped across the small living room to the fireplace. "You're wastin' my time trying to talk about proxies and shareholders, when the only thing I'm interested in holding is your baby in my arms! I don't think that's asking too much from you—not when you consider all *I've* done for *you.*" With ruthless determination and flawless timing, he switched tactics from coercion to guilt, while Cole listened in impassive silence and growing anger to a genuine tirade that far surpassed all previous discussions on this particular subject.

"Why, if it weren't for me, you'd be living out at your pa's place, just like his pa did and his pa before him, trying to eke out a living chasin' steers. Instead of that, you do your chasin' in a Rolls-Royce and a private jet." Jabbing his forefinger into his chest for emphasis, he continued, *"I'm* the one who always believed in you, Cole. *I'm* the one who encouraged you to go to college. *I'm* the one who went to bat for you with your pa, and when he wouldn't listen, I'm the one who gave you all my money from my wells so you could get a good

115

education!" In the midst of his angry monologue, Cal stopped and headed for the kitchen. "It's time for my medicine," he announced, "but I'm not finished. You stay right where you are until I get back."

Cole watched him pick his way around an old overstuffed chair and a lamp table piled with magazines and said nothing. Cole hadn't had a good day, and so far, the evening wasn't an improvement. He'd finished his business on the West Coast several hours earlier than he'd expected, and in the happy expectation of having extra time with his uncle, he'd phoned one of his pilots and instructed him to fuel the plane and be ready to leave for Texas ahead of schedule. From then on, nothing had gone well.

The air was unstable, the flight was incredibly rough, and air traffic control advised them to go around a massive storm front over Arizona. Their new course took them an hour out of the way, which necessitated an unscheduled fuel stop in El Paso, where unusually heavy air traffic resulted in another hour's delay. Two hours behind schedule, Cole's pilots now began their final approach to Ridgewood Field, and Cole tried for the sixth time to reach Cal so that his uncle could pick him up at the airport. For the sixth time, he got a recording that the phone was out of order.

Since phone service in Cal's area was frustratingly undependable, and since Cal frequently struck back at the phone company by deducting one thirtieth of his monthly charges for each day his phone was unreliable, Cole assumed the phone company had retaliated as it usually did—by cutting off his service.

When he got off the plane, the heat and humidity seemed to plaster around him like plastic wrap, and Cole resigned himself to renting a car at the minuscule airport and driving out to the ranch.

Ridgewood was forty-five miles north of Kingdom City, which, in turn, was forty miles east of Cal's ranch. Built thirty years before and situated in the middle of nowhere, Ridgewood Field was primarily used by drilling companies who flew in special equipment for repairing the oil and gas wells that dotted the landscape. Most of the other planes that jolted down its washboard runway belonged to Texan Airlines, which flew in twice weekly with special air freight and an occasional passenger on board.

In addition to one concrete runway that was in bad repair, Ridgewood Field offered air travelers a white metal building that served as a terminal. Inside the terminal, which was not air-conditioned, amenities were limited to two rest rooms, one coffee counter, and one battered metal desk where stranded passengers could attempt to rent one of Ridgewood Field Car Rental's *two* available cars from a cheerful heavyset woman who was also the waitress and whose name tag identified her as "Roberta."

Roberta wiped her hands on her apron and took a rental agreement out of the desk while she politely inquired as to Cole's choice of rental cars. "Do you want the black one with the bad muffler, or the black one with the bad tires?"

Cole stifled an irate retort and scribbled his name on the rental agreement. "I'll take the one with the bad muffler."

Roberta nodded approvingly. "The air conditioning works in that one, so you won't swelter while you're getting where you're going. Good choice."

It had seemed so to Cole, too, at the time, but not now. When Cal returned to the living room and started pressing his point even harder, Cole began to wish he'd taken the other car and had a nice blowout on the way here to delay him.

"I'll make you a deal," Cal announced as he lowered himself into the chair across from Cole's. "You bring me a wife who's fit and willing to bear your children, and I'll sign those shares over to you on your first wedding anniversary. Otherwise, I'm going to leave all my worldly goods to Travis's kids. That's my deal; take it or leave it."

In stony silence, Cole returned his stare and began to slowly tap a rolled-up magazine he'd been reading on his knee. At thirty-six, he controlled a multinational corporation, 125,000 employees, and an estimated twelve billion dollars. Everything in his business and personal life was under his complete control . . . everything except this one seventy-five-year-old man, who was now actually threatening to leave half of Cole's company to Travis, who wasn't capable of running a small subsidiary of it without Cole's constant supervision. Cole didn't actually believe that his uncle would betray him by giving away half the corporation that Cole had slaved to build, but he didn't like the sound of his uncle's threat. He had just convinced himself that Cal was bluffing when he belatedly noticed that the fireplace mantel, which had always held a half-dozen framed family photographs, was now filled to overflowing with another dozen photographs—and all of them were of Travis's family.

"Well?" Cal said, abandoning his anger and leaning forward in his eagerness. "What do you think of the terms of my deal?"

"I think," Cole snapped, "that your terms are not only ridiculous, they're crazy."

"Are you saying that marriage is 'crazy'?" Cal demanded, his expression turning ominous again. "Why, the whole damned country is falling apart because of your generation and its lack of respect for good old 'crazy' notions like marriage and children and responsibility!"

When Cole refused to be lured into that debate, Cal gestured toward the large scarred coffee table, which was cluttered, like every other table in the room, with dozens of magazines that Letty, his housekeeper, fought a losing battle to keep orderly. "If you don't believe me, just look at what's in those magazines. Here," he stated, snatching up a copy of *Reader's Digest* from the pile on the end table beside his chair. *Reader's Digest* was a particular favorite of his. "Look at this!" He waved the small magazine with its blue cover and bright yellow print toward Cole; then he tipped his head back, in order to read through the lower part of his bifocals, and recited the titles of some of the articles: " 'Cheating in Our Schools—A National Scandal.' According to that article," he said, glaring at Cole as if it were his fault, "eight out of ten high school students say they *cheat.* It says in that article that moral standards are so low that many high school children no longer know the difference between right and wrong!"

"I don't see what that has to do with the topic at hand."

"Don't you, now?" Calvin retorted, closing the cover and tipping his head slightly back, peering again at the writing on the cover of the magazine. "Then maybe this article is more to the point. Do you know what it's called?"

The answer being obvious, Cole simply stared at him in resigned expectation.

"The article is called 'What Women Don't Know About Today's Men.'" Tossing the magazine on the table in disgust, he glared at Cole. "What I want to know is what is the matter with you young people that suddenly men don't understand women and women don't understand men, and none of you understand the need to get married and stay married and raise good, god-fearing children?"

Cole continued to tap the magazine on his knee while his anger continued to mount. "As I think I've mentioned to you in the past when you've brought all this up, you are hardly in a position to lecture anyone on the merits of marriage and children, since you've never had a wife or a child!"

"To my everlasting regret," Calvin countered, undeterred as he shoved some magazines aside and pulled out a recent copy of a tabloid. "Now, just look at this," he said, pointing a bony finger at the front page and holding it in front of Cole's face.

Cole glanced at the tabloid, and his expression turned derisive. "The *Enquirer?*" he said. "You're subscribing to the *Enquirer?*"

"Letty likes to read it, but that isn't the point. The point is that your generation has lost its collective mind! Just look at the way you young people do things. Look at this beautiful young woman. She's famous and she's a 'Houston socialite,' which means she's rich."

"So what?" Cole said, his angry gaze fastened on his uncle's face and not the newspaper.

"So, her fiancé—this Dan Penworth—just dumped her for an eighteen-year-old Italian girl who's lyin' on a beach with him, half-naked." When Cole continued to ignore the tabloid, Cal let it drop to his side, but he wasn't ready to drop his argument. "He dumped her without telling her, while the poor thing was planning her wedding."

"Is there a point to all this?" Cole demanded.

"You're damned right there is. The point is that Penworth is a Houston boy, born and raised, and so's the girl he jilted. Now, when Texans start mistreating women and stomping all over traditional values, the whole damned country is as good as down the toilet."

Cole reached behind his head and wearily massaged the muscles in the back of his neck. This discussion was going nowhere, and he had a critical business issue to discuss and settle with Cal, if he could only sidetrack him from his absurd obsession with Cole's marital state. In the past, Cole had always managed to accomplish that, but Cal was far more determined today than ever before, and Cole had an uneasy premonition that this time he was going to fail.

It occurred to him then that Cal might actually be getting senile, but he rejected that almost at once. Cal's personality wasn't changing. He'd always been as stubborn and as tenacious as the proverbial bulldog. As Cole had explained to John Nederly earlier in the week, nothing had ever swayed Cal from his course. When oil was first found on his land, he'd announced that money wasn't going to change his life, and, by God, it hadn't—not one bit. He still pinched pennies like a pauper, he still drove a twenty-year-old truck with a stick shift, and he still wore faded jeans and plaid shirts every day of the week except Sunday, when he went to church; he still pored over the Sears Roebuck circulars and still insisted that cable television was an expensive fad that was destined to fail.

"Look," Cole said, "I'm not going to argue with you—"

"Good."

"What I mean is, I'm not going to argue with you about the decline of American civilization, the value of marriage, or the desirability of having children—"

"Good!" Cal interrupted, heaving himself out of the threadbare rocker-recliner. "Then get married and get your wife pregnant, so I can give you the other half of your company. Marry that Broadway dancer you brought home two years ago—the one who had red fingernails two inches long—or marry the schoolteacher you liked in the seventh grade, but marry somebody. And you'd better do it quick, because we're both running out of time!"

"What the hell does that mean?"

"It means we've been having this discussion for two years and you're still single, and I'm still without a baby to dandle on my knee, so I'm settin' a time limit. I'll give you three months to get engaged and three more months to get married. If you haven't brought me a wife home by then, I'm going to put my fifty-percent share of your company into an irrevocable trust in the names of young Ted and Donna Jean. I'll name Travis as administrator of the trust, which will make him your unofficial business partner, then when Ted and Donna Jean come of age, they can help you run the company themselves. That's assuming you still *have* a company left after Travis tries to help you run it." Cal tossed the *Enquirer* on the table and another warning into the charged atmosphere. "I wouldn't take all six months to get the thing done if I were you, Cole. My heart could give out at any time, and I'm changing my will next week so that if I die before you're married, my fifty-percent share of the company goes to Ted and Donna Jean."

Cole was so incensed that he actually considered trying to have the old man declared incompetent. Failing that, he decided he could try to have the will overturned . . . but that would take years after Cal's death and the outcome wouldn't be certain.

His thoughts were interrupted by Letty, his uncle's cook-housekeeper, who appeared in the kitchen doorway. "Supper's ready," she said.

Both men heard her, but neither acknowledged her presence. Cole had risen to face his uncle, and the two men stood in the center of the room, their gazes clashing—two tall, rugged, unyielding men separated by three feet, one generation, and a decision that one couldn't fight and the other wouldn't retract. "Are you capable of understanding that I may not be able to find a woman and marry her in six months?" Cole said between his teeth.

In reply, Cal jerked his thumb toward the stacks of magazines beside his chair. "According to the surveys in those magazines, you have five of the seven most important qualities that women want in a husband. You're rich," he said, listing the qualities in the order he remembered them, "you're intelligent, you're well-educated, you have a bright future, and Donna Jean says you're a 'hunk,' which I guess qualifies you as handsome."

Satisfied that he'd won the battle, Cal endured Cole's icy silence for a moment, then made an effort to discharge some of the animosity that he'd created. "Aren't you just a little bit curious about the two qualities you lack?"

"No," Cole snapped, so furious that he almost couldn't trust himself to speak.

Cal supplied the information anyway: "You lack a desire for children, and I'm afraid that even I would have trouble describing you as 'tender and understanding.'" When his half-hearted attempt at humor failed to evoke any reaction from his enraged nephew, Cal turned toward the kitchen and his shoulders slumped a little. "Letty has supper on the table," he said quietly.

With a feeling of utter unreality, Cole stared after him, so filled with bitterness and a sense of betrayal that he was actually able to observe his uncle's thinner frame and bent shoulders without feeling the shocked alarm that such a sight would normally have evoked. Cal looked far less frail a minute later when Cole strode into the kitchen, carrying a tablet and a gold fountain pen from his briefcase. Cole sat down across from him and slapped the tablet on the table in front of his uncle. "Write it down," he ordered icily while Letty stood at the stove, looking apprehensively from one to the other, a ladle full of chili forgotten in her hand.

Calvin automatically took the pen that was thrust toward him, but his brow wrinkled in confusion. "Write what down?"

"Write down the terms of the agreement and include any specific 'requirements' you may have for the woman I marry. I don't want any surprises if I bring someone home—no last-minute rejections because she doesn't meet some criterion you're forgetting to mention at the moment."

His uncle looked genuinely hurt. "I'm not tryin' to choose a wife for you, Cole. I'll leave all that to you."

"That's damned big of you."

"I want you to be happy."

"And does it look to you like all this is making me happy?"

"Not now. Not right now, but that's because you're riled."

"I'm not riled," Cole retorted with scathing contempt. "I'm disgusted!"

His uncle winced as the verbal thrust found its mark, but it didn't sway the stubborn old man from the course he'd set. He tried to shove the tablet back to Cole, but Cole slapped his flattened palm on it. "I want it in writing," he stated.

In a desperate attempt to soothe the situation before it erupted again into a battle, Letty rushed to the table with a steaming bowl of chili in each hand and plunked them down in front of the men. "Eat while it is hot!" she urged.

"You want what in writing?" Cal demanded, looking stunned and furious.

"Eat now," Letty interjected. "Write later."

"I want you to write down that you will turn over your fifty percent of the company to me if I bring home a wife within six months."

"Since when isn't my word good enough for you?"

"Since you stooped to extortion."

"Now, see here!" Cal exploded, but he looked a little guilty. "I have the right to decide who gets my fifty-percent share in the company. I have the right to want to know that someday your son will benefit from my money and my holdings."

"A son?" Cole countered in a dangerously low voice. "Is that part of the deal? A new condition? I'll tell you what, why don't I marry a woman who already has a little boy so you won't have to wait and you won't have to worry?"

Calvin glowered at him, then hastily scribbled out what Cole wanted written and shoved the tablet across the table with an indignant grunt. "There it is, in writing. No stipulations."

Cole would have left at that point, but he was held back by lack of knowledge of his pilots' whereabouts and by his own inability to believe Cal would actually betray him by carrying out his threat. Cole's mind easily provided him with dozens of examples of Cal's temperamental intractability that indicated he might indeed do the unforgivable, but Cole's heart rejected them just as swiftly.

They ate in uneasy silence, finishing quickly; then Cole returned to the living room, turned on the television set, and opened his briefcase. Working, he reasoned, was safer and far more rewarding than getting embroiled in another argument, and the television set made the silence between them seem less ominous.

Despite the agreement he'd made his uncle write out, Cole was still far from willing to yield to his uncle's bizarre demands as a way of regaining permanent control of his own damned businesses. At the moment he had no idea what he was going to do. All he knew was that his temper was still simmering and that thus far his options where Cal was concerned ranged from civil court battles to mental competency hearings to a hasty marriage he didn't want to some woman he didn't know. All of them were distasteful in the extreme, not to mention grotesque and even painful.

Across from him, his uncle lowered the newspaper he was reading and regarded Cole over the top of the *Houston Chronicle's* front page, his expression innocently thoughtful, as if everything were happily settled to both their satisfaction. "According to what I've been reading, a lot of young women are deciding not to have children nowadays. They'd rather raise 'designer pigs' and chase after careers. Be careful you don't pick a woman like that."

Cole pointedly ignored him and continued writing notes.

"And watch out that you don't pick some gold digger who pretends she wants you and only wants your money."

Cole's simmering temper rolled to a full boil. "How the hell do you expect me to find out what a woman's true motives are in six months?"

"I figured you must be an expert on women by now. Wasn't there some sort of princess who traipsed after you all over Europe a couple of years ago?"

Cole stared at him in frigid silence, and Calvin finally shrugged. "You don't have to know a woman inside and out to be sure she's not interested in marrying your money instead of you."

"Really?" Cole drawled with deliberate insolence. "And based on your own vast experience with women and matrimony, how do *you* propose I find out what motives some future wife may have?"

"If I were you, I guess I'd figure the best way to avoid being trapped by some gold digger is to look for a woman who already has money of her own." Having said that, he raised his brows and waited, as if he honestly expected Cole to applaud his solution, but Cole ignored him and returned his attention to the notepad.

For the next quarter hour the silence in the room was uninterrupted except for the occasional rustling of newspaper pages being turned and folded; then Cal spoke again, on the last subject Cole wanted to discuss. From behind the pages of his newspaper barrier, Cal remarked in a desultory voice, "It says here in Maxine Messenger's column that you're attending the White Orchid Ball on Saturday night, and that you donated the most expensive item to be sold at the auction. Maxine says the ball is 'Houston society's most glittering social event.' You won't have to worry about latching on to a gold digger at a thing like that. Why don't you take a look around, find a woman who appeals to you, and bring her right back here so I can have a look at her, *and,*" he put in slyly, "at the marriage certificate. On your first wedding anniversary, I'll sign over my half of your company to you, just like I said I'd do on that piece of paper."

Cole didn't reply, and a short time later, Calvin yawned. "Guess I'll finish the newspaper in bed," he announced as he stood up. "It's ten o'clock. Are you going to work late?"

Cole was studying a letter of intent that John Nederly had drafted at his request. "I've worked late for the last fourteen years," he said shortly. *"That's* why you and Travis are as wealthy as you are."

For a moment Cal stood looking at him, but he couldn't argue the truth of that, so he started slowly out of the room.

Chapter 16

COLE DID NOT LOOK UP UNTIL HE HEARD HIS UNCLE'S BEDROOM DOOR close, and then he tossed the documents he'd been reading onto the coffee table with a sharp flick of his wrist that was eloquent of his black mood.

The sheets of paper landed on top of the *National Enquirer*—right beside a picture of the woman who'd been jilted by her fiancé.

Right beside a picture of Diana Foster.

Cole lurched forward, picked up the paper, and read the short article with a feeling of grim sympathy for its victim; then he tossed it back where he found it, and his thoughts returned to Cal.

Cole was moodily contemplating his alternatives when a movement on his left drew his attention and he looked toward the kitchen doorway, where Letty was standing with a mug in her hand and a hesitant smile on her face.

For as long as Cole could remember, whenever he disagreed with his uncle, Letty Girandez, who was a terrible cook, had appeared soon afterward with something for Cole to eat and drink—a gesture of comfort from a kindly woman who knew she was a bad cook. In her early sixties, Letty had a plain, round face that managed to convey her inner gentleness and a soft, Spanish-accented voice that lent her an aura of quaint gentility. Cole's expression softened as she made her way across the living room and put the steaming mug on the coffee table.

"Hot chocolate?" he guessed. Letty's prescription for a bad mood was always the same: hot chocolate for evening and lemonade for daytime. And cake. Chocolate cake. "Where's my cake?" he teased, reaching for the mug, knowing he was going to have to drink the entire cup to avoid hurting her feelings. The hot chocolate was traditional, and since Cole had experienced precious little family tradition in his life, he held it in particular reverence.

What familial warmth he'd known, he had mostly found here, with his grandfather's brother and his housekeeper. Letty turned and headed for the kitchen. "There is some chocolate cake left over from yesterday. I bought it at the store."

Although that last information made the cake more, not less, desirable, Cole wasn't hungry. "If you didn't bake it, it isn't worth eating," he teased, and she beamed at the compliment, then turned and started back to the kitchen. "Stay and talk to me for a while," he said.

Letty sat down on the chair his uncle had occupied earlier, but she did it rather gingerly, perching on the edge of the seat, as if she felt she shouldn't be there. "You should not argue with your uncle," she said at last.

"You've been telling me that for twenty years."

"Does your uncle's desire to see you married very soon seem unreasonable to you?"

"That's one way of describing it," Cole said, struggling to keep the bite from his voice.

"I think he believes if he does not force you to marry, then you never will."

"Which is none of his business."

Letty lifted her face to his. "He loves you."

Cole took another swallow of his hot chocolate and set down the cup with angry force. "Which is no consolation."

"But it is true, even so."

126

"Love is not an excuse for blackmail, even if he's bluffing."

"I do not think he is bluffing. I think your uncle will leave his half of your company to Travis's two children if you do not marry."

A fresh surge of fury rocketed through Cole at that. "I don't know how he could possibly justify that to himself, or to me!"

The remark was rhetorical and he hadn't expected an answer, but Letty had one, and he realized that she was absolutely right, that she had seen through all the bluster and excuses, straight through to Calvin's real motivation: "Your uncle is not concerned with money now; he is concerned only with immortality," Letty said as she straightened a precariously high stack of reading material on the end table. "He desires immortality, and he realizes that immortality can only be his through his son."

"I am not his son," Cole pointed out impatiently.

Letty gave him one of her sweet smiles, but her reply was quietly emphatic. "He thinks of you as such."

"If immortality is what he's after, then Travis's two kids have already provided it for him. Travis and I are both his great-nephews. Even if I had children, they'd be related to him in exactly the same way that Travis's are."

Letty bit back a smile. "Travis's son is lazy and sullen. Perhaps he will outgrow that someday, but for now your uncle does not desire to risk his immortality on such as Ted. Donna Jean is shy and timid. Perhaps someday she will show spirit and courage, but for now . . ." she trailed off, leaving Cole to conclude the obvious—that his uncle did not wish to "risk" his immortality on Donna Jean, either.

"Do you have any idea what brought on his sudden obsession with immortality?" Cole asked.

She hesitated and then she nodded. "His heart is growing weaker. Dr. Wilmeth comes often now. He says there is nothing more that can be done."

Cole went from shock to denial in the space of moments. He already knew it was futile to try to get Cal to go to Dallas to see other doctors. Once before, after months of arguing, Cole had finally accomplished that, only to have them all concur with Wilmeth. From then on, Cal had refused to even discuss having another consultation.

Across from Cole, Letty drew a deep, unsteady breath and looked at him with her brown eyes filled with tears. "Dr. Wilmeth says it is only a matter of time before . . ." She broke off, then got up and rushed from the room.

Leaning forward, Cole braced his elbows on his knees, overwhelmed by a terrible sense of fear and foreboding. With his shoulders hunched and his hands loosely linked, he gazed at his uncle's vacant chair while memories of the cozy nights and animated discussions they'd shared over the past three decades drifted through his mind. It seemed as if the only domestic warmth and happiness he'd ever known had been contained in this one shabby-cozy room. All of that would die when Cal died.

If Letty was correct, that time was not far away. His mind went black when he tried to contemplate a life without trips here to see his uncle. This man, this ranch, they were the original fabric of Cole's life. He had discarded the cowboy boots and jeans of his youth for supple loafers of Italian leather, custom-made suits tailored in England, and handmade shirts of Egyptian cotton, but underneath all that exterior polish, he was still as rough and rugged as the denim jeans and scarred leather boots he had worn. In his youth, Cole had hated his roots. From the day he went to Houston to college, he'd worked diligently to banish all traces of the "cowboy" he'd been. He'd changed the way he walked and the way he spoke, until there was no trace of the horseman's loping gait or a west Texas drawl.

Now fate was threatening to take away the last link he had to his roots, and the adult that Cole had become wanted desperately to preserve everything that was left.

Cal's threat to leave his half of the company to Travis and his family was forgotten as Cole tried desperately to think of some action that would forestall the inevitable, that would breathe life into his uncle and brighten his last remaining years. Or months. Or days. Cole's thoughts revolved in an unbroken circle of futility and helplessness. There was only one thing he could do for Cal that would make his remaining days happy.

"Son of a bitch," Cole said aloud, but the curse was one of resignation not defiance. He *was* going to have to marry someone, and marriage in a community-property state like Texas brought with it a whole new set of financial risks for him. Whoever the "lucky" woman was, Cole decided sarcastically, a sense of humor and docile disposition were at the top of his list of requirements for her. Otherwise, he could envision a somewhat heated scene when she realized she was going to be required to sign a prenuptial agreement.

He considered hiring an actress to play the part, but his uncle was too clever and too suspicious to fall for that. No doubt, that had been why he was insisting on seeing the marriage certificate. Luckily, the old man wasn't also insisting on the birth of a boy child before he turned over his share of a company that was rightfully Cole's in the first place. The fact that he hadn't made that a stipulation, too, was proof he wasn't as sharp as he used to be.

He wasn't as well as he used to be, either.

Swearing under his breath, Cole straightened and reached for the mug of now cold chocolate, intending to take it into the kitchen. His gaze fell on the folded newspaper on the top of the pile. Diana Foster's face smiled back at him. She'd had all the promise of beauty to come when she was sixteen, but the longer he looked at her stunning features and confident smile, the harder it became for him to reconcile this glamorous businesswoman or the one he'd watched on CNN with the endearingly prim and quietly poised teenager he remembered. In his mind, Cole envisioned the loyal, intelligent, entrancing adolescent who'd perched on a bale of hay, either watching him in silence or chatting with him about everything, from puppies to politics.

Tonight, when his uncle first commented on the fact that a woman from Houston had been "dumped" by her fiancé, Cole hadn't realized who she was. After he'd read the story in the tabloid, the reality of Diana's embarrassing plight registered on him. Now he again felt a pang of sympathy and indignation for the girl he had known. With her looks and wealth, her kindness and intelligence, he had assumed that she'd enjoy all the best life had to offer. She'd deserved that. She had *not* deserved to be made a national laughing-stock by Dan Penworth.

With a weary sigh, Cole dismissed that subject from his mind and stood up, no longer able to suppress his own concerns by concentrating on the fortunes of a beguiling teenager with unforgettable green eyes who'd become the head of a major company and the subject of an embarrassing scandal instead of the pampered fairy-tale princess he'd hoped she'd become.

Life, as Cole well knew, rarely turned out the way one wanted it to or hoped it would. Not his life, or Diana Foster's . . . or his uncle's.

He picked up the mug of cold chocolate and carried it into the kitchen; then he carefully poured out the remnants and rinsed the mug so that Letty wouldn't discover how he felt about hot chocolate and be hurt by the truth.

The truth was that he hated hot chocolate.

He also hated marshmallows.

He particularly hated illness and doctors who diagnosed problems without offering a cure.

For that matter, he wasn't particularly enthusiastic about a sham marriage that was doomed to failure before it began.

It had occurred to Cole that the most likely, and most agreeable, candidate for his wife was not the "princess" whom his uncle had referred to earlier that night, but Michelle. Besides genuinely caring for Cole, she had no problem with his hectic work and travel schedule. In fact, she'd been very eager to adapt to it—and that was going to be far more important to Cole in this "marriage." Considering his circumstances, his pressing need, and the haste required of him, Cole decided he was damned lucky to have such a viable candidate.

He didn't feel lucky, though, as he headed down the hall to the bedroom he'd used since he was a boy whenever he spent the night at his uncle's. He felt depressed. He was so depressed, he actually felt sorry for Michelle, because he knew damned well she'd agree to the bargain. He knew it just as he knew that she'd be making a mistake, because she'd be settling for what little of himself he had to offer, and that wasn't very much.

His last relationship, with Vicky Kellogg, had failed for exactly that reason, and he hadn't changed since then, nor did he intend to. He was still married to his business, just as Vicky had accused him of being. He was still contemptuous of the aimless thrill-seeking that Vicky and her friends had enjoyed. He still traveled a great deal, which had annoyed her, and he was still incapable of prolonged periods of unbroken laziness. No doubt, he was still the "cold, callous, unfeeling son of a bitch" she'd called him when she moved out. The point that she hadn't understood was that Cole was directly or indirectly responsible for the job security and investment security of more than a hundred thousand of Unified Industries' employees.

The bed beneath him felt lumpy and narrow as he shoved the old chenille bedspread aside and stretched out between fresh white sheets that smelled of sunlight and summer breezes. Against his bare skin, the thin cloth felt weightless and baby soft from Letty's countless washings.

Linking his hands behind his head, Cole stared at the ceiling fan revolving slowly above him. Slowly, his depression began to recede, along with all thoughts of marrying Michelle or anyone else. The idea wasn't just obscene; it was absurd. So was the notion that his uncle might not live until the end of the year.

Cole had been working eighteen hours a day for months; he'd taken a rare day off today to fly down here from Los Angeles only to have weather problems. The stress and weariness from all that, combined with the discovery of his uncle's worsening health, had all combined to warp his thinking, Cole decided, as his eyes drifted closed and an odd sense of confidence and well-being began to assert itself.

Cal was going to live for another ten years, at least. True, he hadn't looked robust tonight, but as Cole tried to assess the individual changes that age and illness had wrought by comparing the Cal he remembered to the man he was now, the changes weren't nearly so alarming as they'd seemed at first. He thought back to bygone days when he'd watched Cal mending fences in the blazing sun or cantering into the corral behind dusty steers he'd rounded up and driven in from the pasture. With his Stetson and boots adding inches to his height, he'd seemed like a giant to Cole when he was little, but when Cole reached his full height of six foot two, he'd been at least three inches taller than Cal.

The reality was that Cal had never been a big man with a powerful physique like Cole's; he'd been lanky and lean, with a wiry strength and endurance that served as well as bulky muscle for the heavy work around the ranch. He hadn't shrunk six inches and wasted away to a skeleton, as it sometimes seemed to Cole that he had. When his arthritis bothered him, as it obviously had tonight, he shifted his shoulders forward, which distorted his posture and cost him an inch or so from his natural height.

His hair hadn't suddenly turned white; it had been white for as long as Cole could remember—thick and white with close-cropped sideburns that framed a tanned, narrow face with a square chin and pale blue eyes that seemed to look out at the world from a different perspective; sharp eyes that gleamed with intelligence, humor, and hard resolve. His face had lost its tan, and his eyes looked out from behind bifocals now, but they weren't faded and dull, and they missed nothing.

True, his body had lost some of its strength from age and lack of exercise, but his real power had always come from his mind. And as Cole had discovered tonight, his mind was as sharp and fit as ever.

In the next few days, Cole would find solutions that would suit his uncle and himself and solve everything. In the morning he would start a vigorous search for some sort of new or updated treatment for his uncle's condition. New medical treatments were being discovered every day, and old, effective ones that had been discarded were being rediscovered. If he'd known sooner that his uncle's heart condition wasn't staying the same or even improving, he'd have been looking hard for solutions already.

He had always found solutions, Cole remembered.

Finding solutions to seemingly insoluble problems was one of the things he did best. It was a knack that had helped bring him wealth and success beyond even his own wildest dreams.

Sleep pressed down on his eyelids as he lay in the plain, unadorned bedroom where, as a boy, he had dreamed of his life as a man. There was something about the monastic simplicity of the small room that had encouraged him to dream big dreams in his youth. Now, in his adulthood, the room soothed and lifted his spirits. Cole owned homes and apartments all over the world, all of them with spacious bedrooms furnished with large beds in a variety of shapes, but he was already falling asleep more quickly here than he'd been able to do elsewhere in years.

He decided the room itself still had some sort of mystical, uplifting effect on him, much as it always had.

Peace settled over him and followed him into his dreams, just as it always had when he slept here.

The window was open and a sliver of moonlight filtered through the sheer curtains, turning them into shiny silken webs that drifted weightlessly on a flower-scented breeze. The air seemed fresher here, just as it always had.

In the morning, when he was well-rested, he would be better able to think and plan and solve. For now, the walls of the room, with their familiar framed pictures, seemed to surround him and shelter him, just as they always did whenever Cole slept there.

On the nightstand beside the bed, an old alarm clock ticked with the loud, steady rhythm of a heartbeat, lulling him further asleep, reminding him that time was passing and things would look better in the morning, just as they always did whenever Cole slept there.

Sometime later, Cole rolled onto his stomach, and the sheet lifted magically, covering his bare shoulders, just as it always seemed to during the night, whenever Cole slept there.

Beside the bed, Calvin Downing gazed down at his sleeping nephew, frowning at the deep lines of tension and weariness etched at the corners of Cole's eyes and the sides of his mouth. He spoke to the sleeping man, his voice lower than the whisper of the curtains drifting against the window, his words low and soothing, tinged with gruff emotion, just as they always were whenever he came in to check on his nephew and felt the need to tell him in his sleep what he could not say to him while he was awake. "You've already accomplished what most men only dream of doing," Cal whispered. "You've already proved to everyone that you can do anything you set out to do. You don't have to keep pushing yourself anymore, Cole."

The sleeping man stirred and turned his head away, but his breathing remained deep, peaceful.

"Things will look better in the morning," Calvin promised him softly, just as he always did whenever Cole slept there. "I love you, son."

Chapter 17

*T*RAFFIC ON THE INTERSTATE BETWEEN HOUSTON INTERCONTINENTAL Airport and downtown Houston was heavy for five P.M. on a Saturday, but the chauffeur maneuvered the long black Mercedes limousine skillfully from lane to lane in a graceful, daring dance of speed, power, and timing.

Heedless of the driver's efforts on his behalf, Cole sat in the backseat, poring over a thick, detailed analysis of the complexities involved in having Unified participate with other corporations in a collaborative effort with the Russians to put a gas pipeline through to the Black Sea. He did not look up until the car glided to a stop beneath the green canopy at the entrance of the Grand Balmoral Hotel and a uniformed doorman appeared beside his window. Reluctantly, Cole put the report in his briefcase and got out.

Condé Nast Traveler had described the fifteen-story Grand Balmoral as an outstanding example of hushed, old-world opulence on a grand scale combined with impeccable service, but as Cole strode across the vast circular lobby with its dark green marble floors and soaring Grecian columns, his thoughts were on Russian railroads and Russian winters, and not the glittering crystal chandeliers above him or the luxurious gilt-edged sofas upholstered in ivory brocade that were organized into inviting seating groups all around him.

On the right of the lobby was a grand staircase that swept upward to a wide mezzanine that circled and overlooked it. In preparation for the White Orchid Ball's *Camelot* theme, the mezzanine was being turned into a mythical forest by dozens of workers who were scurrying about, draping tiny white lights and artificial snow over what appeared to be hundreds of full-size trees. Diverted from his thoughts by the activity above him, Cole frowned in the general direction of the distraction as he headed for the carved mahogany registration desk.

The hotel's manager spotted Cole and hurried down the steps to introduce himself; then he insisted on escorting Cole to the Regent Suite as soon as he'd finished registering. "If there is anything we can do to make your stay with us more pleasant—anything at all—please let me know, Mr. Harrison," he said as he bowed himself out the door.

"I'll do that," Cole said absently, as unimpressed by this special deferential treatment as he was by the magnificent five-room suite with its mauve-and-gold Louis XV furnishings and spectacular view of the Houston skyline. He spent a good part of his life conducting business in luxury hotels all over the globe, and in little more than a decade, he had come to expect the best—and to take it completely for granted.

Having refused the manager's offer to have a maid unpack for him, Cole handed the departing bellman a tip for carrying up his luggage; then he took off his jacket and tie, loosened the top buttons of his white shirt, and walked over to the bar in the living room, where he fixed himself a gin and tonic. He carried it past the fireplace to a pair of doors that opened out onto a balcony and stepped outside. The outdoor temperature was in the mid-nineties, but the humidity that normally made Houston into a steam bath during the summers was absent, and Cole stood at the railing looking out across the city he had called home during college. He'd been to Houston on business a few times in the intervening years, but he'd never spent the night there, and perhaps for that reason, he was suddenly struck by the enormous difference between the style of his departure from Houston fourteen years ago and that of his "homecoming" today.

He had left Houston by bus the day after he graduated from college, carrying all his worldly possessions in a nylon duffel bag and wearing a pair of faded jeans, a T-shirt, and a pair of worn-out, scuffed boots. He had arrived today by private jet, wearing a $7,000 Brioni suit, $600 Cole-Haan loafers, and carrying a $1,500 briefcase. When his plane taxied to a stop in the hangar, a chauffeur had been waiting beside a limousine with its engine idling, ready to whisk him to the Balmoral. He was as accustomed to VIP treatment wherever he went as he was to private jets, penthouse suites, and come-hither looks from glamorous women.

He thought back to that ten-hour bus ride from Houston to Jeffersonville and remembered it as clearly as if it were last week. The day after his graduation, he'd boarded the first bus north to his uncle's ranch (the bus had been a concession to thrift-minded Cal, who, despite his lucrative oil wells, still regarded plane travel as an inexcusable waste of good money). On the day he boarded that bus, Cole's practically only remaining possessions were the clothes he was wearing.

Beyond that, all he owned were the few items in his duffel bag—and his dreams. The duffel bag was small and plain, but his dreams were big and elaborate. Extremely big. Extraordinarily elaborate. Seated beside an old man who belched at regular intervals, Cole had gazed out the window at the River Oaks mansions parading past, and he had indulged himself with fantasies of returning to Houston someday, rich and powerful.

And now he was.

Lifting the glass to his mouth, Cole took a swallow of his drink, amused by the irony of the situation: today was certainly the ultimate realization of that long-ago fantasy, but it no longer mattered to him. He was so completely absorbed in other more far-reaching, significant issues that it didn't matter to him. He had proven himself, won out against all the odds, and yet he was still striving, still working incredible hours, still driving himself as hard as ever. Harder.

As he gazed out at the haze hanging like a dingy apron around the soaring high-rises, he wondered what all his striving was really for. In Denver, the annual shareholders meeting of Alcane Electronics was taking place, and if Cole's negotiators weren't successful in swaying them, Cole was going to have a proxy fight on his hands to take over that company. In California, his lawyers, top executives, and a team of architects were conducting a series of meetings about several office complexes he was building in northern California and Washington State to house the various companies that made up the technological division of Unified.

And if his uncle's health didn't improve . . . that was unthinkable. After his conversation with Letty he had talked to Cal's doctor, who had told him that while Cal's condition was an unpredictable one, Cole should be prepared for the worst at any time.

Cole glanced at his watch and saw that it was six-thirty. He had to appear downstairs for a television interview at seven-thirty, and the Orchid Ball's charity auction was scheduled to begin at eight P.M. That left him with a full hour in which to shower, shave, and get dressed, which was more than he needed. He decided to phone one of his executives at the attorneys' offices in California and find out how things were progressing.

Chapter 18

WITH BRIGHT, ARTIFICIAL SMILES AFFIXED TO THEIR FACES, DIANA'S family and two of her friends stood off to one side of the Balmoral's crowded lobby, struggling valiantly to appear to everyone as if everything were perfectly normal while they watched the revolving brass doors at the main entrance for a sign of Diana. "The decorations are certainly lovely!" Diana's mother remarked half-heartedly.

The others glanced with forced interest at the Balmoral's lobby, the grand staircase, and the mezzanine. The main lights had been dimmed, and the entire hotel seemed to have been transformed into a dense forest of shadowy trees with tiny twinkling lights glittering among branches covered with artificial snow. Ice sculptures depicting medieval knights and their ladies adorned snow-covered "ponds," and waiters dressed in medieval attire, bearing pewter goblets of wine, skirted snowdrifts and moved among the crowd, while the Houston Symphony Orchestra played "I Wonder What the King Is Doing Tonight."

"It does look a lot like the opening scene from *Camelot,*" Corey put in. She glanced at her husband. "Doesn't it?"

Instead of replying, Spence slid his arm around her waist and gave it a reassuring squeeze. "Don't worry. Everything's going to be fine, honey."

"Diana said she'd be here at seven-fifteen and it's seven-thirty," Corey told him, "and Diana is never late." Corey's mother looked around the lobby and saw that the crowd was beginning to drift toward the mezzanine, where the main events were to take place. "Maybe she decided she just couldn't come, after all," Mary Foster said.

Corey's fixed smile gave way to alarm. "Canceling out at the last minute is the worst thing she could do."

"She'll be here," Spence reassured both women. "Diana's never run away from anything in her life."

"I couldn't blame her if she ran away from this," Corey said. "Diana values her privacy and her dignity above everything, and as a result of what Dan did, her dignity has taken a public flogging. In her place, I don't think I'd have the courage to show up here tonight."

"Yes, you would," Spence said with absolute conviction.

She shot him a startled look. "Why do you think that?"

"Pride," he said. "Outraged pride would force you to appear here and face them all down. Pride is all she has left right now, and her pride will demand that she appear at the ball with her head high."

"She'll be here," Doug Hayward agreed.

"As a matter of fact," Spence said suddenly, "Diana has just arrived." He looked at Corey with a smile and added, "And she's done it in grand style."

Baffled, Corey turned. She saw Diana walking calmly through the crowd with her head high, seemingly unaware of the people who turned to stare at her. Corey was so proud of her sister, and so startled by her appearance, that she temporarily forgot about Dan Penworth and the broken engagement.

Normally, Diana opted for subdued elegance rather than glamour at formal affairs, but not tonight. With a stunned smile of admiration, Corey took in the full impact of Diana's ravishing purple gown. Fashioned like a fitted sarong with a deep slash at the side, the gown fell from narrow straps at the shoulders into panels of purple that clung gently to her graceful hips and ended in a narrow swirl just above her toes. Instead of the sleek chignon she normally wore her hair in, she'd let it fall in a cascade of waves that ended at her shoulders—its lustrous simplicity providing an enticing contrast to the sexy sophistication of the gown. Corey gave Diana a fierce hug. "I was so afraid you'd decide to stay home tonight," she whispered.

"I never considered it," Diana lied, returning Corey's hug and smiling reassuringly at her mother and grandparents. She was so nervous and so unhappy and so touched to see her family and Doug and his date waiting for her like an honor guard to see her through the ordeal that she felt perilously close to tears, and the evening wasn't even underway yet.

"You're gorgeous," Spence decreed gallantly, giving her a brotherly hug, "and so's the gown."

"It's lucky that your meetings in New York ended a day early so you could go with us tonight."

It wasn't luck at all that had brought Spence back to Houston in time for the ball; it was Diana's plight that made him cancel the last day of meetings, but Corey wisely chose not to add to Diana's concerns by telling her that.

Doug Hayward stepped away from his date and studied Diana with unabashed admiration. "You look fantastic," he said. He pressed a kiss to Diana's cheek, then clasped her hands in his and stepped back, his smile giving way to a troubled frown. "Your hands are like ice," he said. "Are you sure you want to face everyone, including the media, in one big group tonight?"

Touched by the depth of his concern, Diana pinned a bright fixed smile on her face. "I'll be fine," she assured her former childhood friend. "These things happen to lots of people. Engagements get broken and people marry other people instead. Although," she added with an attempt at humor, "it usually happens in that order instead of the reverse." Instead of amusing him, her joke made him wince, and she squeezed his fingers in a gesture of profound affection and gratitude. He hadn't intended to go to the Orchid Ball at all since, as the junior senator from Texas, he had his hands quite full, but when he discovered that Diana intended to brave it alone in what was going to be her first public appearance after Dan's defection, he'd insisted on going and being seated with the Fosters at their table. He was doing that, Diana knew, partly to lend her moral support and partly as a way of using his considerable social influence among Houston society to help negate the effect of Dan's humiliating actions. "Thank you for caring so much," Diana said with a catch in her voice. "It seems as if you're forever giving Corey and me advice and bailing us out of one jam after another."

"Most of the time it was my advice that got Corey into a jam in the first place," he teased. "You, on the other hand, rarely asked me for advice and never got into any trouble that I can recall."

The last part of that was true, but Diana refused to let him make light of the value of his friendship. "You are very softhearted and very sweet," she said with simple candor.

He dropped her hands and stepped back with an expression of comic horror. "Are you trying to ruin my carefully constructed tough-guy image? My political opponents will make me look like a wimp if they know how sweet and softhearted I really am."

Corey heard him, but she was worriedly studying Diana's face. At close range, she could see that despite Diana's artfully applied makeup and luminescent complexion, her face was abnormally pale and her eyes lacked any luster. They looked wounded and dull. Spence had evidently noticed it, too, because he waved off a passing waiter and walked over to one of the bars that had been set up. A minute later, he returned with two glasses. "Drink this," he instructed. "It will put some color in your cheeks and give you a little courage."

Diana accepted the glass and took a tiny sip, then shook her head, trying to force herself to face a problem she'd been avoiding. There was no way of knowing what was going to happen an hour from now, when she walked into the ballroom with her family and Doug and his date, Amy. Some of the people at the ball tonight would be friends of hers, and if they asked about Dan, their interest in Diana's plight sprang from genuine concern and affection. That was not going to be true in the majority of cases at the ball, however. There, she would be bound to encounter hundreds of distant acquaintances and curious strangers who would watch her every move, searching for something to gossip about with their friends tomorrow, and some of them would relish her misery.

Diana had tried very hard to avoid making enemies throughout her life, but she knew there were those who envied the Foster family's success, and there were those who simply relished other people's unhappiness.

"The press is going to be swarming all over you tonight," Corey said grimly.

"I know."

"Stay close to Spence and me. We'll shield you the best we can."

Diana gave a wan smile. "Does Spence carry a gun?"

"Not tonight," Corey joked. "It makes a bulge in his tuxedo."

Diana managed another smile, but she lifted her gaze to the mezzanine, surveying the crowd up there with all the enthusiasm of a woman facing a firing squad at the top of the stairs. "I wish I hadn't agreed to model that necklace for the auction, before all this happened," she said. "I'll have to go up there in a few minutes so they can put it on me."

"Oh, God, I forgot all about that!" Corey moaned. "I noticed you weren't wearing any jewelry tonight, but I was so pleased to see how glamorous you looked in that purple gown that I forgot you were scheduled to model those damned amethysts."

For over a hundred years, the White Orchid Ball, known sometimes simply as the Orchid Ball, and the charity auction that was a part of it, had been the most illustrious social event of the year for the Texas aristocracy. It was steeped in traditions that had originated when the invited guests were cattle-and-oil barons and prosperous industrialists who arrived in gleaming carriages and waltzed with their ladies beneath crystal chandeliers ablaze with candles. In its present form, it was no longer restricted to a few dozen of Texas's most fabulously wealthy and socially elite families, but its traditions had remained intact and it was widely acknowledged as one of the most successful and acclaimed charity fundraisers in the world.

Diana had been invited to model one of the donated items to be auctioned, and having previously agreed to do it, that was an honor and ritual that she couldn't now reject without bringing even more gossip down on her head. Diana knew that. So did Spence and Corey.

"Finish your drink," Spence insisted. "Two more swallows."

Diana complied because compliance was easier and she needed to conserve all her strength to face the evening's ordeal.

Knowing how concerned Diana always was for his comfort, her grandfather deliberately tried to divert Diana's attention from her plight by bringing up his own. Running his finger around the starched collar of his tuxedo shirt, he said, "I hate wearing this damned monkey suit, Diana. I feel like a damned fool every time I have to put one on."

Diana's grandmother gave him a reproachful look. "Stop cursing, Henry. And your tuxedo looks very nice on you."

"It makes me look like a damned penguin," he argued.

"All the men are wearing tuxedos tonight."

"And we *all* look like penguins!" he countered grumpily, and to stop her from arguing about that, he turned to a more pleasant subject and looked hopefully at Diana. "I think we should do another issue featuring organic gardening. Organic gardening is always popular. What do you think about that, honey?"

Diana couldn't seem to concentrate on anything except the ordeal that loomed in front of her. "That's fine, Grandpa," she said, even though they'd featured organic gardening twice already that year. "We'll do that," she added absently, which made her mother and her grandmother look at her in amazement. "I'd better go and sign out that necklace," Diana said reluctantly. "It's a good thing I'm not in a spending mood tonight," she added with a lame attempt at humor. "First I forgot my purse and had to go back for it." She lifted up her small, oval Judith Leiber evening bag to illustrate. "Then, when I got here, I couldn't tip the parking attendant because I discovered I forgot to take any money with me. All I have is a driver's license and compact in here. Oh, and I remembered to take lipstick. But I brought the wrong color."

Everyone smiled at her predicament as she turned to leave— everyone except Rose Britton, who continued to stare at Diana's retreating form, her forehead wrinkled in a thoughtful frown. Finally she turned to the others and announced in a dire tone, "I think Diana has finally reached her limits, and I'm worried about her."

"What do you mean?" her husband asked.

"I mean that she has been acting very strangely," Mrs. Britton said in her blunt voice, "and she was doing it *before* Dan dumped her."

"I haven't noticed anything strange, Mother," Mrs. Foster said, wincing at her mother's choice of descriptions for what Dan did.

"Then let me give you some examples. Diana has always been the most organized, methodical, punctual, dependable person on God's green earth. Every Friday, at seven-thirty A.M., she has a massage and then a manicure, and every Thursday afternoon at four P.M., she has a meeting with the production staff." She paused to make certain that everyone was in complete agreement with what she'd said so far, and when she saw that they were all listening attentively, she presented her proof: "Two weeks ago, Diana forgot her massage appointment. The following week, she forgot about the production meeting and forgot to tell her secretary that she'd scheduled an appointment with one of our bankers instead! I know, because her secretary called me at home, looking for her."

Spence suppressed a grin at what he regarded as needless concern. "Everyone forgets an appointment now and then, particularly when they're very busy, Gram," he said reassuringly. "According to what Corey has told me, Diana has been under intense pressure trying to run the magazine and implement expansion plans and still stay ahead of the competition. Given all that, an unimportant thing like a massage and manicure would be easy to forget."

"Two months ago," Gram added doggedly, "she also forgot my birthday party!"

"She was working late at the office," Mrs. Foster reminded her mother. "When I called her there, she rushed right over."

"Yes, but when she got here, she'd forgotten my present!—and then she absolutely insisted on going to her apartment to get it."

"That's not unusual for Diana, Gram," Corey said. "You know how considerate she is and how much thought she puts into the gifts she buys for people. She insisted on going back to get your gift because she was determined to give it to you on the right day."

"Yes, but when she got to her apartment, it took her nearly an hour to find my present because she couldn't remember where she'd put it!"

Doug exchanged a look of masculine amusement with Spence before he said, "That's because she probably bought it for you a year ahead of time, Mrs. Britton. Last August, I bumped into her at Neiman's and she told me she was doing her Christmas shopping."

Corey smiled. "She always makes her Christmas list out in August and finishes her shopping in September. She says everything is picked over after that."

"She always comes up with perfect gifts," Doug put in with a reminiscent smile. "Last year *I* gave her a five-pound box of Godiva chocolates and a bottle of champagne, but she gave me a cashmere scarf that I'd mentioned liking. I'll bet that when she found your birthday gift and brought it over, Mrs. Britton, it was exactly what you wanted."

"It was a box of cigars!" she informed him.

Doug's eyes narrowed in sudden alarm, but Mr. Britton only chuckled and shook his head. "She'd ordered the cigars for *me*, to give me on *my* birthday. She always wraps her gifts as soon as she gets them, and she just grabbed the wrong present because she was in a hurry to get back to your birthday party."

Mrs. Britton shook her head, refusing to be pacified. "A few weeks ago, when Diana got back from that big meeting with our printers in Chicago, she took a cab straight from the airport to the office."

"What's wrong with that?"

"Her car was at the airport. If you ask me, she's been working much too hard for much too long," she said flatly.

"She hasn't had a vacation in at least six years," Mrs. Foster said, feeling guilty and more than a little concerned. "I think we ought to insist that she take a month off."

"Diana is okay, I tell you, but she ought to have a vacation, just on principle," Grandpa pronounced, concluding the worrisome discussion.

Chapter 19

*T*HE OFFICIAL PRESS AREA WAS CORDONED OFF WITH A VELVET ROPE ON the far side of the mezzanine above the lobby, not far from the ballroom where the auction items were on display. In keeping with his promise to Unified's public relations department, Cole presented himself to the members of the press and did his best to look delighted to be there. He said he would grant brief interviews to the local reporters from CBS and ABC, then posed for pictures and answered routine questions for the reporter from the *Houston Chronicle* and the local stringer from *USA Today*.

The ABC interview was the last. Standing beside Kimberly Proctor, with the round light of the Minicam aimed straight at him like an unblinking Cyclops, Cole listened to the attractive blonde enthuse about the one-hundred-year history of the White Orchid Ball and some of the traditions behind the auction; then she waved the microphone in his face. "Mr. Harrison, we've all been told by the committee that you've donated the most valuable of all the items in tonight's auction. Just how much is the Klineman sculpture worth?"

"To whom?" Cole countered dryly. Privately, he'd always thought the modernistic piece was a monstrosity, but he'd bought it at a bargain and now it was worth five times more than he'd paid.

She laughed, "I mean, what is it appraised for?"

"A quarter of a million dollars."

"You're a very generous man!"

"Tell that to the IRS, won't you?" he said wryly; then he terminated the interview himself by giving her a brief smile and a curt nod before he stepped out of the camera's range. The tactic surprised her and she followed him. "Wait—I—I was wondering if we could get together later—for a chat."

"I'm sorry," Cole lied politely, "but you'll have to contact our PR department and schedule an interview."

"I wasn't actually thinking of an interview," she said, gazing directly into his eyes and softening her voice. "I thought perhaps we could have a drink somewhere—"

Cole cut her off with a shake of his head, but he softened the automatic rejection with a politely regretful smile. "I'm afraid I don't have even fifteen minutes to myself before I leave Houston tomorrow."

She was lovely, well-spoken, and intelligent, but none of that mattered to Cole. She was a reporter, and if she'd been the most beautiful, brilliant, desirable woman on earth, with the purest motives in the world, he still would have avoided her like the plague. "Perhaps another time," he added; then he stepped around behind her and out of the area, leaving her to interview more eager candidates who were lined up on the other side of the velvet rope.

"Mr. Harrison!" someone else in the press area called, but Cole ignored that reporter and kept walking as if he'd never heard of anyone by that name, stopping only to accept a glass of champagne from a waiter.

By the time he had made his way around the perimeter of the mezzanine to the opposite side, where the festivities were scheduled to take place, at least a dozen people had nodded greetings at him and he'd returned them without having the slightest idea who any of the people were.

Ironically, when he finally did recognize two faces in the crowd, they belonged to the only two people who tried to *avoid* greeting him— Mr. and Mrs. Charles Hayward II. In fact, they swept past their former stable hand with their heads high and their eyes like shards of ice.

Cole paused outside the doorway of the room where the most expensive of the items to be auctioned were on display, and he heard his name being whispered occasionally as the patrons of the ball identified him, but the name that seemed to be most frequently on everyone's lips was Diana Foster's. Only tonight, she was being generally referred to as "Poor Diana Foster," and by women who occasionally sounded more malicious than empathetic to Cole.

From his point of view, the White Orchid Ball fulfilled three distinct and different needs—the first was to provide an opportunity for the wives and daughters of the very rich to get together in elegant surroundings, to show off their newest jewels and latest gowns, and to gossip about each other while their husbands and fathers talked about their golf games and tennis matches.

The second purpose was to raise money for the American Cancer Society. The third was to offer Houston's financially affluent and socially prominent citizens an opportunity to demonstrate their social consciousness by outbidding one another for dozens of extravagantly expensive items that were donated by other members of the financially affluent and socially prominent.

Tonight's Orchid Ball was bound to be an unparalleled success in all aspects, Cole decided.

Armed security guards were positioned in front of the doors to the room where the auction items were on display, and an argument broke out right beside him as a photographer in a red-and-white-checked shirt tried to sidle past one of the guards. "No one but guests are allowed in here after seven o'clock," the guard warned, crossing his arms over his chest.

"I'm from the *Enquirer*," the photographer explained, trying to keep his voice low and still be heard over the roar of the crowd. "I'm not interested in the stuff they're auctioning off, I'm interested in getting a picture of Diana Foster, and I saw her up here on the balcony a while ago. I think she went in there."

"Sorry. No one but guests for the auction are allowed in there now."

The full realization of Diana's sordid plight filled Cole with a mixture of sympathy and disbelief. He'd seen her on television, and he knew she was a grown woman now, but in his mind, he still thought of her as an ingenuous teenager, sitting Indian fashion on a bale of fresh hay, her head tipped to the side as she listened intently to whatever he was saying.

The doors to the ballroom where the banquet and auction were to take place were still closed, and Cole glanced impatiently at his watch, anxious to get in there and to get the whole thing over with. Since that was impossible, and since he had no desire to strike up a conversation with any of the people who seemed to be trying to catch his eye, he stepped into the shadow of a copse of trees, surrounded and obscured by their glittering branches, and lifted the glass of champagne to his lips.

In the years since he'd worked in Houston and lived in the Haywards' stable, he'd attended hundreds of black-tie affairs all over the world. He was frequently bored at them, but he was never uncomfortable. Houston was the exception. Something about being at a function like this in Houston made him feel like an impostor, a fraud, an interloper.

From his vantage point inside the whimsical forest glade, he idly watched the crowd without consciously admitting to himself that he was watching specifically for a glimpse of Diana. . . . And then the crowd parted and he saw her, standing beside a wide pillar near the elevators about fifteen yards from him.

A sharp jolt of recognition was immediately followed by relief and then pure masculine admiration as his gaze drifted over "Poor Diana Foster."

Instead of the wan, humiliated creature he'd feared he'd see, Diana Foster had lost none of the quiet, regal poise he remembered her having. Draped in a gown of royal purple silk that clung to her full breasts and small waist, she moved serenely through the artificial twilight of a make-believe forest, untouched by the clamor and bustle all around her—a proud young Guinevere with delicate features, a small chin, and large, luminous green eyes beneath thick russet lashes and exotically winged brows. Her coloring was more vivid now, Cole thought, and the tiny cleft in her chin was nearly invisible, but her hair was the same—heavy and lush, glistening like polished mahogany with red highlights beneath the light of the chandeliers. A splendid necklace of large, square-cut, deep purple amethysts, surrounded by diamonds, lay against her throat, a perfect complement to the gown. She belonged in striking gowns and glittering jewels, Cole decided. They suited her far better than the pleated pants and conservative blazers she used to prefer.

He stood in the shadow of the trees, admiring her surface beauty but far more intrigued by the indefinable, but unmistakable "presence" that made Diana stand out so clearly, even in the shifting kaleidoscope of movement and color that swirled around her. It was as if everything and everyone except Diana was in motion, from the twinkling tree limbs shifting in the subtle currents of air conditioning, to the men and women who moved about in a blur of vivid hues and animated voices.

She was listening attentively to a man who was speaking to her—a man who Cole was nearly certain was Spence Addison. Addison moved away from her, and Cole stepped out of the shadow of the trees and stopped, willing her to look his way. He wanted her to recognize him; he wanted her to give him one of her unforgettable smiles and to come over to talk to him. He wanted all that with a surprising amount of anticipation.

It was possible she'd snub him as the Haywards had done a few minutes ago, but somehow he didn't think she would. Until now, Cole's youthful dream of a triumphant return to Houston had seemed meaningless to him, which was why even Cole realized how incongruous it was for him to suddenly want the satisfaction of having Diana Foster take notice of him tonight—or, more correctly, of the man he had become.

Based on the icy stares he'd gotten from Charles and Jessica a few minutes ago, Cole doubted that they'd been eager to tell anyone how successful their former groom had become. In that case, there was a possibility that Diana had no idea whatsoever that Cole the stable hand—who'd enjoyed her girlhood conversations and shared her sandwiches—was the same Cole who had just been named Entrepreneur of the Year by *Newsweek* magazine.

The ballroom doors were thrown open, and the entire crowd seemed to shift in unison, obscuring his view as people began making their way into the ballroom. Rather than have Diana disappear into the crowd or enter the ballroom through the doors closest to her before he could speak privately to her, Cole started toward her, but his progress was hampered by the surge of people moving in the opposite direction toward the ballroom. When he finally cleared the last human obstacle, only a hundred or so people were lingering on the mezzanine, but one of them was talking to Diana, and it was Doug Hayward.

Cole slowed to a stop and stood off to the side; then he raised his glass to his mouth, hoping Hayward would walk away. He had no way of knowing if Charles Hayward's attitude toward Cole was now shared by his son, but Cole didn't want to risk having that mar his first meeting with Diana in more than a decade.

Hayward wanted to escort her into the ballroom, but to Cole's relief, Diana refused. "Go ahead without me," she told him. "I'll be along in a minute. I want to get some fresh air first."

"I'll go with you," Hayward offered.

"No, don't, please," Diana told him. "I just need to be alone for a few moments."

"Okay, if you're sure that's what you want to do," Hayward said, sounding reluctant and frustrated. "Don't be long," he added as he started toward the open ballroom doors.

Diana nodded and turned, walking swiftly toward a door with an Exit sign above it.

Cole had enough experience with women to know when one was on the verge of tears, and since she'd told Hayward she wanted to be alone, he felt he should allow her that privilege. He started to turn toward the ballroom, then stopped, assailed by an old memory— Diana telling him about her fall from the horse: *"I didn't cry. . . . Not when I broke my wrist and not while Dr. Paltrona was setting it."*

"You didn't?"

"Nope, not me."

"Not even one tear?"

"Not even one."

"Good for you," he'd teased.

"Not really." She'd sighed. *"I fainted instead."*

As a child, she'd been able to bravely hold back her tears of pain and fright, but tonight, as a woman, she was apparently hurt beyond all endurance. Cole hesitated, torn between the male's instinctive urge to avoid any scene involving a weeping woman—and a far less understandable impulse to offer her some sort of strength and support.

The latter impulse was slightly stronger, and it won out: Cole headed slowly but purposefully for the doors beneath the Exit sign; then he made a brief detour for champagne, which he felt sure would buoy her up a little.

Chapter 20

OUTSIDE, THE LONG, NARROW STONE BALCONY WAS DESERTED AND poorly lit by a few small, flickering gas lamps that created tiny pools of feeble yellowish light surrounded by dark shadows. In Diana's desolate mood, the lonely gloom of the balcony was infinitely preferable to the romantic excitement of the mythical forest that the decorations committee had created, and she was spared the painful irony of having to listen to the orchestra playing "If Ever I Would Leave You."

Hoping to be out of sight of anyone else who might decide to go outside, Diana turned right and walked as far away from the doors as possible, stopping only when she came to the point where the balcony ended at the corner of the building. Standing at the white stone balustrade, she flattened her palms on the cool white stone and bent her head, staring blindly at her splayed fingers, noticing how blank and plain her left hand looked without Dan's engagement ring on it.

Two stories below, a steady procession of headlights glided along the wide, treelined boulevard in front of the hotel, but Diana was oblivious to everything except the bewildered desolation she felt. In the last few days, her emotions had veered between the lethargic helplessness she felt now and sudden bursts of angry energy that made her into a whirlwind of mindless activity. Either way, she still couldn't seem to absorb the reality that Dan was married. Married. To someone else. Only last month, they had talked about attending tonight's ball together and he'd reminded her repeatedly to arrange for a seat for him at her family's table.

On the boulevard below, the sudden screech of car brakes was accompanied by an ear-splitting symphony of honking horns. Jarred from her thoughts, Diana braced for the sound of clashing metal and breaking glass, but when she looked toward the intersection, there'd been no real accident. She was about to look away when a black Mercedes convertible like Dan's glided toward the hotel, its yellow turn indicators blinking as it neared the entrance. For a heart-stopping second, Diana actually believed it was Dan in that car; and in that magic fraction of time, his arrival seemed plausible. . . . He'd come to explain that there had been some sort of colossal mistake.

Reality crashed down on her as the sports car swooped closer to the green canopy at the hotel's entrance and she saw that the Mercedes was dark blue, not black, and the driver was a silver-haired man.

The swift plunge from soaring, unexpected hope to the grim truth sent Diana spiraling even further into a pit of misery. Through a haze of unshed tears, she watched the car's passenger door open, and a stunning blonde in her mid-twenties swung her long legs out. Diana studied the girl's short, tight dress, noticing her aura of sexy confidence, and she wondered when Dan had also begun to prefer sexy young blondes to conservative thirty-one-year-old brunettes like Diana. Based on the newspaper pictures, she was sickeningly certain his new wife was ten times prettier and more voluptuous than herself. No doubt Christina was also more feminine, more fun, and more adventurous, too. Diana was certain of all that, but she wasn't certain exactly when Dan had begun to feel, to *notice*, that Diana wasn't enough for him.

She wasn't enough. . . .

That had to be true; otherwise, he wouldn't have been able to toss her aside as casually as he'd toss out the trash. She wasn't enough for him, and the crushing humiliation of it made her stomach churn. Before Diana, Dan had always dated women who were glamorous, tall, and curvaceous—sophisticated debutantes in their twenties and thirties who were eternally witty and religiously dedicated to nothing more than looking good and playing hard. Diana, on the other hand, was dedicated to her work and to the growth and prosperity of the family enterprises. In fact, the only thing Diana had in common with Dan's other women was that she'd also been a debutante. Beyond that, the contrast was as glaringly evident as her shortcomings. She was only five feet four inches tall, her hair was an ordinary dark brown, and she was far from voluptuous. In fact, while the scandal was erupting over breast implants, she'd teased Dan about being glad she hadn't had the surgery. Instead of laughing, he'd remarked that some of the implants were safer than others, and that she could still have one of the safer ones if she wanted to.

In her mood of dismal self-loathing, Diana now wished she'd gone through with the surgery. If she were any sort of a woman, she would have concentrated harder on her looks instead of settling for a "natural" look and counting on intellect instead of beauty to keep her man. She should have had her hair streaked, or frosted, or maybe cropped as short as a boy's with shaggy bangs. Instead of a long gown like the one she was wearing, she should have opted for one of those skintight, thigh-high couture dresses that were so in fashion right now.

The bang of a metal door slamming closed made her look around in wary alarm toward a tall man in a tuxedo who had just emerged from the hotel. Her relief that he was apparently one of the ball's guests, rather than a reporter or mugger, was immediately supplanted by irritation that he was moving in her direction, instead of away.

Cloaked in shadow and silence, he kept coming toward her, his step slow, purposeful. His arms were bent at the elbows, and he was holding something in each hand. For a split second her fevered imagination conjured up a pair of revolvers in those hands; then he passed through a pool of gaslight and Diana saw that in his hands he was holding . . .

Two glasses of champagne.

She gaped at them, and then at him as he closed the remaining distance between them. At close range, he was easily six feet two inches tall, with wide shoulders and a hard, stern face defined by a square chin, an iron jaw, and straight, thick dark brows. His shadowy face was darkly tanned, but his eyes were light and disconcertingly amused as they gazed into hers.

"Hello, Diana," he said, in a deep, resonant voice.

Diana tried to smooth her features into a semblance of polite confusion when what she wanted to do was stamp her foot and tell him to go away. Good manners, however, had been fed to her along with baby pabulum and she was incapable of unprovoked rudeness. "I'm sorry," she said, monitoring her voice for signs of impatience, "if we've met, I don't recall it."

"We've definitely met," he assured her dryly. "Many times, in fact." He held out a glass to her. "Champagne?"

Diana refused it with a shake of her head as she studied his face, more convinced by the moment that he was playing some sort of game with her. Although she preferred men with refined features and lithe builds to men like this one who exuded brute strength and overpowering masculinity, she knew she wouldn't have forgotten this man if she'd met him. "I don't think we have," she said with polite firmness, putting an end to the game. "Perhaps you're mistaking me for someone else."

"I'd never mistake you for anyone else," he teased. "I remember those green eyes and that sorrel mane of yours very clearly."

"Sorrel mane?" Diana uttered; then she shook her head, weary of the game. "You definitely have me confused with someone else. I've never met you before—"

"How's your sister?" he asked. The stern line of his mouth relaxed into a lazy smile. "Does Corey still like to ride?"

Diana gave him a long, uncertain glance. Either by accident or design, he was standing just beyond the reach of the gas lamp, but he was beginning to sound—and seem—familiar. "Are you a friend of my sister's, Mr.—?"

He finally stepped forward into the light, and in a burst of shock and delight, Diana recognized him. "That's very formal," he teased, his familiar gray eyes smiling down at her. "You used to call me—"

"Cole!" she breathed. She'd known he was expected to appear at tonight's function, and she'd been very much looking forward to seeing him again until a few days ago, when her life had been torn apart and everything else had faded into the background. Now she couldn't seem to adjust to the shock of seeing him.

Cole saw the pleasure that lit up her face when she recognized him, and it warmed him with astonishing intensity, softening for a few brief moments the cold, hard streak of cynical indifference that was his norm. Regardless of what the Haywards may have told her about the reason for his abrupt departure from their employ, regardless of the intervening years, Diana Foster's friendship for him was still there, unspoiled and unchanged.

"Cole? Is it really you?" Diana said, still reeling from shock and delight.

"In the flesh. More accurately, in the tuxedo," he joked, holding the glass of champagne toward her again. She hadn't wanted it from a stranger, he noted, but she took it from an old friend, and as he gazed down at her lovely, upturned face, he was flattered and pleased. "I think this calls for a toast, Miss Foster."

"Make the toast," she said. "I'm still too shocked to think of one."

He lifted the glass. "Here's to the luckiest woman I know."

Diana's smile faded and she shuddered. "God forbid!" He obviously didn't know what had happened to her, and she quickly tried to pass off her reaction with a casual shrug. "What I meant was that I've been luckier—"

"What could possibly be luckier than narrowly escaping marriage to a spineless son of a bitch?"

That remark was so outrageous and so unquestioningly loyal that Diana felt twin urges to laugh and cry. "You're right," she said instead. To avoid his gaze she took a quick sip of her champagne; then she hastily changed the subject. "When the news got out that you were actually going to appear tonight, people were very excited. Everyone is dying to get a look at you. I have so many questions to ask you—about where you've been and what you've done—that I hardly know where to start—"

"Let's start with the most important question," he interrupted firmly, making Diana feel like a child again, confronting a much older, wiser male. "How are you holding up through all this?"

Diana knew he meant the gossip that was all over the ballroom about her broken engagement. "I'm doing just fine," she said, frustrated by the slight quaver in her voice. She thought she heard the door open further down the balcony, and she lowered her voice in case someone had come out. "Fine."

Cole glanced over his shoulder in the direction of the sound. Illuminated by the Exit sign over the door was a man in a red-and-white-checked shirt who jumped back into the shadows when Cole looked in his direction. Cole's first impulse was to attack the spying reporter; his next impulse was to make use of him. Cole decided on the second alternative for the moment. With his free hand, he reached out and tipped up Diana's chin. "Listen carefully, and don't move."

Her eyes widened in instant alarm.

"There's a tabloid photographer watching us, waiting to grab a picture of you. I suggest we give him a picture worth splashing across the front page of their next issue."

"What?" Diana whispered in panic. "Are you crazy?"

"No, I've simply had more experience than you with negative press and prying photographers. He's not going to leave until he gets some sort of picture of you," Cole continued while, from the corner of his eye, he watched the reporter step out of the shadows and lift his camera again. "You have a choice. You can let the world think of you as a discarded woman, or you can let them see me kissing you, which will make them wonder if you ever cared about Penworth at all and if I've been your lover all along."

Diana's mind was whirling with alarm and horror and glee, as well as the effects of two drinks in less than an hour on an empty stomach. In the brief moment she hesitated, Cole made the decision for her. "Let's make it convincing," he ordered softly as he set down both of their glasses. His free hand then slid around her waist, curving her body into his arms.

It happened too quickly to resist, and then it seemed to happen in slow motion as Diana felt her legs press into his thighs and her breasts against his chest, followed by the sudden shock of his warm lips covering hers.

He lifted his head a fraction, his eyes looking into hers, and she thought he was going to let her go. She had the feeling he intended to let her go. Instead, his hands shifted, one of them drifting upward over her bare back, while the other tightened, and he bent his head again. Diana's heart began to pound in erratic, confused beats as his mouth settled firmly on hers, slowly tracing each soft curve and contour of her lips. His tongue touched the corner of her mouth, and her body jumped in surprise. One part of her brain ordered her to pull free immediately, but some deeper, more compelling voice rebelled at such an unjust reaction to his gallant efforts.

His tender efforts.

His persuasive efforts.

Besides, she realized, the photographer might have missed his first few shots. Diana acted on the side of justice and prudence and slid her hands up his jacket and tentatively, uncertainly kissed him back. The pressure of his mouth increased invitingly as his hand slid up and curved around her nape, his fingers shoving into her hair.

A loud burst of music and thunder of applause inside the ballroom announced that the formal festivities were already under-way in the ballroom and snapped them both back to the present. Diana pulled away with a self-conscious laugh, and he shoved his hands into his trouser pockets, gazing down at her with his dark brows drawn into a slight frown. Cole looked to see if the photographer was still present and was glad to see that he had apparently gotten his shot and left.

"I—I can't believe we did that," Diana said nervously, trying to smooth her hair as they walked toward the door into the hotel.

He shot her a sideways glance that was filled with a meaning she didn't understand. "Actually, I wanted to do that years ago," he said, reaching out and opening the heavy door for her.

"You did not." Diana rolled her eyes in smiling disbelief.

"The hell I didn't," he said with a grin.

Inside, the mezzanine was nearly deserted. Conscious of missing lipstick and mussed hair, Diana stopped when they came to an alcove where the rest rooms were located. "I need to make some repairs," she explained. "Go ahead without me."

"I'll wait," Cole stated irrefutably, and he stationed himself at a nearby pillar.

Startled by his gallant determination to stay near her side, Diana tossed him a hesitant smile and vanished into the ladies' room. Several of the stalls were occupied, and as she walked up to the dressing table to smooth her hair, a lively discussion was underway between two of the occupants: "I don't know why everyone is so surprised," Joelle Marchison told her companion. "Anne Morgan said Dan told her months ago that he wanted to break his engagement to Diana, but Diana wanted to marry him and she kept begging him to stay with her. Anne said that marrying someone else and letting Diana find out about it in the newspapers was probably the only way that Dan could break free of her once and for all."

Rooted to the floor, Diana listened to a chorus of fascinated exclamations from the other stalls and felt tears spring to her eyes. She wanted to shout at all of them that Anne Morgan was a jealous, spiteful liar who'd been in love with Dan herself and had lost him to Diana, but even if she had had the nerve, she was afraid she'd lose control and start to cry. The door to Joelle's stall started to open, and Diana darted into an empty stall and stayed there until everyone left, wounded by the unprovoked malice of women whom she had never harmed in any way; then she walked back to the vanity and tried to dab at her eyes without ruining her makeup.

Outside the ladies' room, Cole was being treated to a recitation of the same information by two of the women who'd been in the ladies' room and who were now imparting the news to their friends: "We just heard that Dan Penworth has wanted to get rid of Diana for ages, but she wouldn't let him go!"

"It serves her right," one of them announced. "The media has always treated her like a princess. Personally, I am sick to death of hearing about how wonderful that magazine is and how successful she is, and how gracious, and all that bullshit."

The other woman was kinder. "I don't care what you say; I pity her, and so do a lot of people."

Partially concealed by the pillars at the side of the alcove, Cole heard every word, and he marveled at the viciousness of the female sex toward their own, and then he wondered which would hurt Diana more—their spite or their pity. He had a feeling she'd prefer their spite.

Chapter 21

COLE KNEW THE INSTANT HE SAW DIANA'S PALE FACE THAT SHE'D heard something of what her "friends" were saying in the ladies' room, and because he couldn't offer any comfort, he offered his arm instead. When they reached the ballroom doors, they were closed and the opening speech was underway.

Frowning, she drew back, loath to draw more notice by entering the ballroom noticeably tardy and with Cole. "I suppose your table is in the front?"

As the donor of the most expensive item to be auctioned that night, Cole was to occupy the seat of honor at the head table, just below and in front of the auctioneer's podium. "Table one," he confirmed. "Front row center."

"Our table is in the third row." She sighed. "Why couldn't at least one of us have been seated at the back of the room? There's no way we can slip in there unnoticed." Anxious to get inside before they were any later, she reached for the big handles on the heavy doors, but he laid his hand on her arm to stop her from pulling them open.

"Why try to be invisible? Why not let them think what everyone who reads the *Enquirer* is going to think in a day or two—that you don't give a damn about Penworth and you're interested in me, not him."

"No one who knows me is going to believe that!" she cried, almost wringing her hands in despair. His whole face tightened. "You're right. How stupid of me. I forgot that this is a gathering of the rich and useless, who would never believe you'd switch from one of their own to an ordinary, common man—"

Diana glared at him, confused and frantic and dumbfounded. "What are you talking about! There's nothing ordinary or common about you."

She meant it, Cole realized with a surprise that was outweighed by self-disgust at his ridiculous outburst. "Thank you," he said with an assessing smile as he studied her flushed, upturned face. "At least anger put the sparkle back in your eyes. Too bad my kiss couldn't have accomplished that."

Diana made the mistake of looking at his mouth, then had to look away before she could concentrate on the issue. "I'm not accustomed to kissing men I hardly know, particularly when someone else is watching me."

"You've gotten awfully finicky," he joked. "You used to kiss stray kittens and mongrel pups all the time."

The analogy was so absurd that Diana laughed. "Yes, but *only* when I thought you weren't watching me."

In the ballroom, polite applause heralded the end of the opening speech. Cole pulled open the heavy doors, put his hand beneath her elbow, and escorted her forward. Murmurs erupted throughout the ballroom as one thousand startled people observed the unexpected arrival of their guest of honor—a notoriously illusive billionaire recently listed by *Cosmopolitan* magazine as one of the World's Fifty Most Eligible Bachelors—who strolled nonchalantly into their midst with his hand possessively cupping the elbow of Diana Foster— Daniel Penworth's recently discarded fiancée.

Cole escorted Diana to her table in the third row and seated her there in the vacant chair between Spence and Diana's grandfather. He nodded politely to everyone, but he winked at Corey, smiled warmly at Diana and briefly touched her shoulder, then strode off to his own table in the front row.

Diana watched him for a moment, impressed and amused by his

supreme indifference to the excited curiosity his appearance was generating. Keeping her expression pleasant and neutral, she looked at Doug and his date, Amy Leeland, who were seated across from her to the left; then she glanced to the right at her mother and grandparents. Corey was one seat away, between Spence and Doug, and her eyes were filled with questions, but her expression was perfectly composed.

They were all dying of curiosity, Diana realized, but they all knew the first rule of social survival—always present a calm, united front. In keeping with that rule, Spence, Corey, and Doug smiled at her as if there were nothing in the least extraordinary about Diana arriving conspicuously late on the arm of a man whom they hadn't seen in over a decade and who treated her with possessive familiarity.

Diana's mother and grandfather had no idea at all who he was, but they followed suit.

Diana's grandmother, who had begun ignoring social rules at approximately the same time she attained the age of seventy, decided to ignore this one, too. She stared at Cole Harrison's back with a perplexed frown, then leaned forward in her chair and demanded of Diana in a loud stage whisper that got the attention of three people seated at the table behind her, *"Who was that man, Diana?"*

Anxious to avoid a discussion that would be heard by others, Diana said hastily, "That's Cole Harrison, Gram. You know—he's the man who donated the Klineman sculpture that you were admiring earlier."

Rose Britton was aghast at that notion, and in her advancing years, she'd also developed a disconcerting desire to state the entire truth, regardless of the consequences. "I did *not* admire it," she protested in an indignant whisper that was overheard by two more people at the table behind her. "I said," she clarified, "that it was hideous."

She glanced at the others in an innocent invitation to argue the merits or lack thereof of the sculpture, but everyone launched into diversionary small talk to avoid doing exactly that. "Well, it is," she told Diana as soon as she looked her way. "It looks like a huge pipe-cleaner doll!"

Diana was anxious to explain to her that Cole Harrison was the same Cole who'd worked at the Haywards' when Diana was a teenager, but she was afraid to do it now, for fear that the elderly lady might then begin reminiscing about the food they'd sent over to him and be overheard. Cole had gallantly come to her rescue tonight, and Diana was determined to protect his pride and his privacy in return.

Chapter 22

To DIANA'S INTENSE RELIEF, THE MINOR FLURRY CREATED BY THEIR late and conspicuous arrival soon died down. Waiters began serving the first course of the dinner that was included in the $1,000 cost of a ticket to the ball, and the events of the last half hour finally began to sink in.

She could hardly believe the forceful, sophisticated male in the elegant black tuxedo who'd materialized out of the shadows on the balcony was actually the same jean-clad youth who'd talked with her while he curried the Haywards' horses . . . and teased her while they played cards . . . and greedily dug into whatever food she brought along.

She reached mechanically for a crusty roll and broke it open, her hands then going still. . . . The Cole she'd known before had always been hungry, Diana remembered fondly. A smile touched her lips—judging from the adult Cole's tall, muscular physique, he'd undoubtedly been hungry because he'd still had some growing and "filling out" to do.

A politely insistent voice near her ear intruded on her reverie as two bottles of excellent wine appeared in her peripheral vision. "Would you prefer red wine or white wine, miss?"

"Yes," she murmured absently.

The confused waiter hesitated, looked helplessly at her and then at Spence, who was on her left and who came to the waiter's aid. "Perhaps both," Spence suggested blandly.

Another waiter followed in his wake and slid a bowl of shrimp bisque in front of her; animated conversations and bursts of laughter swirled around her, blending with the soft clink of flatware against china, but Diana noticed none of that. Cole had changed a great deal, she decided as she absently spread a rosette of butter onto the roll, then laid it on the plate without touching it and reached for a glass of wine instead. She picked up the one closest to her hand, a chardonnay, smooth and mellow.

The years had not mellowed Cole, she thought a little sadly, just the opposite. As a youth, he'd had an aura of hard-bitten strength, but he'd seemed approachable and kind, even gentle at times. Now there was a cynical edge to his voice and a coldness in his eyes— she'd witnessed both when she objected to entering the ballroom with him. He was battle-hardened, toughened. But he was still kind, she reminded herself. When the photographer had appeared on the balcony, he was kind enough to rush to her rescue. He was also quick enough and smart enough to instantly devise a plan that turned a negative situation into one that would work in her favor. To accomplish that, he had kissed her. . . .

Diana's hand shook as she reached for her wineglass again and took another hasty swallow. She should never have let that happen! What a foolish, uncharacteristically impulsive thing for her to do. And what a kiss! Soft at first . . . awkward for her as she came into unexpected closeness with the legs and chest and mouth of a stranger—an old friend, whose mouth had covered hers with casual expertise and then with teasing insistence . . . and then with increasing demand. He'd lifted his head, ended the kiss, stared into her eyes . . . and then he'd kissed her again . . . almost reluctantly, and then almost . . . hungrily.

Diana's cheeks reddened with embarrassed heat, and she drained the rest of the chardonnay, trying to steady her nerves. She shouldn't have let that second kiss happen. Other women got jilted, and *they* didn't throw themselves into the arms of the first available man who offered sympathy.

Or did they?

Now that she thought about it, maybe they did!

In fact, now that she thought about it, she realized she was overreacting to everything and making far too much out of a simple, meaningless kiss enacted purely for the benefit of a spying reporter. While she was obsessing on a kiss, Cole had probably forgotten the entire trivial incident. For all she knew, he had escorted a woman to the ball who was with him now. Either way, he was undoubtedly being showered with attention at the head table and having a perfectly pleasant time.

She tried to resist the impulse to find out for herself and failed. Cole's table was two rows in front of Diana's and a little to the left, directly in front of the auctioneer's podium, which was on a raised platform. By looking slightly to the left or the right, she could see between the shoulders of the group at the next table and see most of the people at Cole's. Casually, she lifted her glass to her lips and looked to the right. The head table was larger and seated more people, two of whom made Diana's heart sink the instant she saw them.

Franklin Mitchell was the chairman of this year's ball, and he and his wife were naturally seated at the head table—but so was their son, Peter, and his wife, Haley, formerly Haley Vincennes. The other couple were friends of Peter and Haley's. The elderly woman with blue-tinted white hair, with her back to Diana, was undoubtedly Mrs. Canfield, whose ancestors had founded the White Orchid Ball. The balding man beside her had to be her son Delbert, a middle-aged bachelor.

Franklin Mitchell said something that got a loud burst of laughter from the others at the table, and Diana shifted her gaze to the left. Conner and Missy Desmond were also at the table, and everyone was laughing except—Diana's searching gaze collided with a pair of piercing gray eyes that locked on to hers, refusing to break the glance. Clearly disinterested in both his meal and the people at his table, he was leaning back in his chair, openly watching her, his expression strangely speculative.

Diana couldn't imagine why he was looking at her that way, but a polite smile seemed appropriate and she gave him one.

He answered with a slow nod and a smile that was as warm as it was bold, but what disturbed Diana was the odd, almost calculating look in his eyes.

Hastily, she yanked her gaze from his and joined the conversation at her own table, but her mind was on Haley Mitchell and what she was likely to say to Cole if she'd seen him arrive with Diana. Haley thrived on vicious gossip; she created it and then used it like a weapon against anyone she didn't like, and there were many she didn't like — nearly all of them women.

She particularly despised Diana because one evening several years earlier, when Peter was still single and particularly drunk, he'd stood up during a wedding reception where he was a groomsman and Diana was a bridesmaid, and instead of proposing a toast to the bride and groom, which everyone thought he was going to do, he proposed marriage to Diana. She had tried to pass it off as a joke, and everyone else let it go at that — except Peter himself and Haley, who'd been in love with him for years.

He'd married Haley soon after that, but Haley never forgot that she was Peter's second choice, and Peter never forgot that Diana had turned him down. Haley despised Diana with a jealous loathing that seemed to grow stronger with each year, as did the rumors that Haley's marriage was in trouble. Diana knew beyond a doubt that if Haley imagined there was anything between Cole and Diana, she'd launch a hate campaign right there at the table in front of him.

That possibility added yet more stress to the evening that lay ahead of her, and Diana couldn't cope with it. Instead, she looked across the table at Doug and Amy and asked what plans they'd made for the rest of Amy's visit in Houston; then she picked up a fresh glass of wine and forced herself to concentrate on every word they said.

She was so determined to participate and distract herself that she didn't notice that Spence, who was on her left, had a clear view of Cole and that he was watching the other man in frowning silence. Corey noticed his grim preoccupation, however, and when the main course was being cleared away, she leaned close to him. "What's wrong?" she whispered.

He waited until a waiter had finished filling his coffee cup, then tipped his head toward the head table. "Harrison's looked over at Diana several times tonight, and I don't like it."

Corey was surprised but far from displeased. In Diana's present predicament, Corey thought that a little flattering attention from a highly desirable male couldn't do anything but help lift her status and bolster her pride tonight. "Why don't you like it?"

"Because I don't like Harrison."

"Why not?" Corey asked, stunned.

He hesitated for a suspiciously long time, then tried to dismiss the matter with a shrug. "Among other things, he has a reputation for being devious and single-minded. Diana is in a very vulnerable state right now, and her guard is down."

"Spence, Cole is an old friend, and you're being overprotective!"

Laying his hand over hers, he gave it a reassuring squeeze. "You're right."

Corey would have pursued the subject, but she was prevented from doing that by the auctioneer, who'd walked onto the stage to open the auction. He rapped his gavel on the podium, and excitement surged through the huge ballroom, silencing conversations and causing everyone to turn and look in his direction.

"Ladies and gentlemen," he proclaimed, "when we're through here, you'll have an additional half hour to enter your final written bids on those items being offered at the silent auction in the Empire Ballroom. That brings us to the moment you've all been waiting for. Without further delay or further comment, I invite you to open your hearts and your checkbooks, and to remember that every dollar of the proceeds from this auction will go directly to cancer research. Now, if you will refer to the individual catalogs at your table, you will find a complete listing of the items being auctioned off, along with a description of each."

There was a general rustling as people reached for their catalogs. "I know many of you are eager to get to the Klineman sculpture," he said, and jokingly added, "in an effort to minimize your wait and heighten your tension and desire, we have placed that article partway down the list at number ten."

Laughter rippled around the room, and he waited until he had everyone's complete attention, before he spoke again. "Item one," he proclaimed. "This is a small pencil sketch by Pablo Picasso. Who will open the bidding at forty thousand dollars?" An instant later, he nodded with satisfaction. "Mr. Certillo has offered forty thousand dollars. Do I have forty-one thousand dollars?" Within a few minutes, the sketch was sold for $66,000, and the next item was introduced.

"Item two is a splendid Tiffany lamp, circa 1904. Who will offer fifty thousand dollars? . . ."

Chapter 23

THE "HONOR" OF BEING SEATED AT THE HEAD TABLE WAS ONE THAT Cole would have gladly forgone. His official host was a tall, distinguished-looking, gray-haired man named Franklin Mitchell, who was the vice chairman of a family-owned oil company and a conceited, superficial pain in the ass. Mitchell's guests were his wife, his son and daughter-in-law, and a young couple named Jenkins, who appeared to be close friends of the son's. The six of them represented the sort of arrogant superciliousness that Cole most despised.

The other two couples at the table were a portly bachelor in his fifties named Delbert Canfield and his ancient mother, whom he dutifully referred to as "Mama," and Conner and Missy Desmond. The Desmonds were an attractive, middle-aged couple who made a brief, valiant effort to find some sort of common ground with Cole. Unfortunately their personal interests seemed to be limited almost exclusively to their golf handicaps, their tennis games, and their friends. Since Cole was neither interested in nor conversant in those three topics, conversation lagged and then collapsed.

Rather than waste an evening listening to idle gossip and mean-ingless small talk, Cole simply ignored his table companions and put his time to better use. For a while he thought about Cal's illness and his outrageous demand that Cole marry within six months, and occasionally he allowed himself a glimpse of Diana to see how she was holding up; then he turned his thoughts to problems he could actually solve.

By the time the first course was being cleared away, he had mentally outlined his agenda for the annual meeting of his board of directors and had decided to declare a stock dividend in advance of the meeting to ensure his proposals were ratified.

During dessert, while Mitchell boasted about his strategy for getting himself elected president of River Pines Country Club, Cole silently mapped out his own strategy for putting Cushman Electron-ics at the top of the computer-chip industry.

The auction was well underway, and Cole was working out alternative uses for his newly acquired subsidiary, in the event their new chip didn't live up to its promise, when he realized that Franklin Mitchell was talking to him. Having failed to engage Cole in conversations on topics ranging from Cole's ancestry and person-al background to his opinion about the Houston Oilers' chances of making it to the Super Bowl next year, Mitchell had evidently decided to introduce hunting as his next subject. "Have you done any shooting, Cole?"

"Some," Cole replied, stealing a glance at Diana and then reluc-tantly turning his attention to Mitchell. For some reason, she looked far more tense now than she had an hour ago.

"I ought to invite you to our ranch to hunt deer. Splendid place — fifty thousand acres."

He lifted white brows as wide as Cole's thumb in expectation of a reply to an invitation that hadn't actually been one. It was a subtle verbal trap that Cole had witnessed before, and it was invariably used by narcissistic asses like Mitchell who had to constantly prove their social superiority in any gathering that included a newcomer. Since he hadn't actually invited Cole to the "splendid" ranch to hunt deer, any form of polite, positive response that Cole made would immediately reduce him to the status of a hopeful supplicant. In view of all that, Cole had no qualms about expressing his real opinion. "Frankly, I don't see any point in freezing my ass off in the woods at dawn, hoping against hope that a deer will pass by."

"No, no, no. We don't do that. We have feeders all over the ranch—the deer go there to be fed every day."

"You mean, you just hang around the feeders until the deer come to eat," Cole speculated straight-faced, "then while they're peacefully munching their grain, you jump out and blow a hole through them, and afterwards, you cut off their heads and hang them over the fireplace?"

Mitchell looked irate. "It's not the way you make it sound."

"Really, how is it, then?"

"Are you against shooting?" he retaliated, growing angry at the implied criticism of his sport and casting a look over Cole that clearly questioned his masculinity.

"Not at all. But I eat what I shoot."

Mitchell relaxed a little. "Good, good; so do we. Always. So, what do you shoot?"

"Skeet," Cole replied, and was instantly annoyed with himself for taking out his disdain for the rich and lazy on a man who wasn't worth his time. Mitchell's wife and daughter-in-law were surprisingly amused by Mitchell's obvious discomfiture, but Delbert Canfield and his mother regarded Cole in wary, awkward silence after that. The Desmonds had been talking to each other about the sailing lessons they were taking and were unaware that anything unusual had transpired.

The ninth item had sold for $190,000, and the auctioneer's voice suddenly rose with excitement, providing a welcome diversion for the occupants of the head table. "This next item needs no further description," he said, beaming with anticipation as he strode to the center of the low stage. He swept the velvet draperies back, exposing the Klineman sculpture that Cole had donated, and a sigh of admiration and expectation rippled through the audience. Conversations broke off as would-be owners gazed at the huge bronze figure and decided how high they were willing to go.

"This is the moment many of you have been waiting for, a once-in-a-lifetime opportunity to own this magnificent sculpture from a master who is lost to the world now. Bidding," he said, "will begin at two hundred thousand dollars, and bids will be taken in five-thousand-dollar increments only." His brows lifted, and a self-assured smile crossed his face as he gazed out upon the audience, letting the excitement build for a few moments; then he said crisply, "Who would like to open the bid—" A hand lifted somewhere in the audience and he nodded instantly. "Mr. Selfer has opened the bidding at two hundred thousand dollars. Do I have—yes, two hundred five thousand dollars from Mr. Higgins. And two hundred ten thousand dollars from Mr. Altour, thank you—"

"Two hundred and fifty," Franklin Mitchell called out.

Cole suppressed a smirk at the idiocy that prompted an offer of $250,000 for a four-foot-tall hunk of metal that looked like bronzed bananas and body parts to him.

"Two hundred and seventy," someone else shouted.

The auctioneer began to beam. He looked inquiringly to Mitchell.

"Three hundred," Mitchell said, thereby sinking to new depths in Cole's personal estimation.

"Three hundred thousand dollars, and we've only just begun!" the auctioneer enthused, gauging the heightened tremors of determination in the room with the accuracy of a human seismograph. "Don't forget, this is for charity, ladies and gentlemen—"

"Three hundred and ten," someone else bid.

"Mr. Lacey has bid three hundred ten thousand dollars," he announced, then quickly added, "and Mr. Selfer has reentered the bidding." He paused for the signal and nodded approvingly, "at four hundred thousand dollars! Mr. Selfer has bid four hundred thousand dollars! Do I have four hundred ten thousand dollars? Four hundred ten thousand dollars?" He searched the room. "Fair warning, ladies and—" He interrupted himself with another quick nod and smile to say, "We now have four hundred ten thousand dollars. We're at four hundred ten thousand dollars. Do I have four hundred twenty thousand dollars?"

In the end, the Klineman went for $470,000. While the audience cheered, the delighted new owner wrote out his check and handed it to one of the auctioneer's assistants; then he got up and went to the head table to shake Cole's hand. The handshake was more than a mere gesture of gratitude; it was one of several traditions left over from long-ago White Orchid Balls, and it symbolized an acceptable transfer of ownership and responsibility at that moment from the item's donor to its new owner.

As the new owner walked proudly away, the former owner

looked at his watch and tried to hide his bored impatience by perusing the colorful brochure that cataloged the items being auctioned. There were four more major art items left, Cole noted, plus a dozen pieces of expensive jewelry and furs that were listed under the category "For the Ladies." On the inside cover was a two-page explanation of the history and traditions of the hundred-year-old White Orchid Charity Ball, and Cole read the enthusiastic narrative with growing amusement.

According to the brochure, the early balls were never open to the public, but limited only to prominent Texas families. Among the interesting little insights included was the information that from the inception of the auction to the present day, those items meant specifically for the feminine gender, such as jewelry and furs, were always modeled by the ladies, for the ladies.

In an effort to atone for upsetting Mrs. Canfield and Delbert earlier, Cole laid down the brochure and gestured toward it with a forefinger. "Based on what I read in here, you have an interesting set of customs associated with this ball, Mrs. Canfield."

Delbert's mama looked wary but hopeful at his sudden change in attitude. She was at least eighty, with bluish white hair, the complexion of a china doll, and a bosom that was weighted down with ropes of pearls. "Many of them go back a hundred years," she said.

Cole nodded encouragingly. "According to the brochure, items of special interest to women, such as jewelry and furs, are always modeled by other women who attend the auction, rather than simply being put on display."

"There's a delightful logic behind that tradition," she told him, warming to her subject with girlish delight. "You see, in the early days of the ball, it was assumed that whatever jewelry or fur a lady chose to 'model' was something that she—and therefore the others at the ball—expected her husband to buy for her."

"It sounds like a sort of gentle extortion," Cole suggested with a trace of a grin.

"That's exactly what it was!" she confirmed with shameless glee. "Oh, and it did run the prices of things up wonderfully for charity's sake. Why, when Delbert's father and I were first married, I chose an enormous ruby brooch to wear. Naturally, I assumed Harold would know the tradition, but he didn't, and I didn't get the brooch that night. I was ever so disappointed, and embarrassed, too."

"I'm sorry," Cole said because he couldn't think of anything else to say.

"Not as sorry as Harold was the next day," she countered with a gruff smile. "Why, I couldn't hold my head up around my friends for an entire week."

"That long?" Cole joked.

She nodded. "That's how long it took Harold to find another ruby brooch in New York and have it sent here."

"I see."

With that, Cole ran out of small talk. He opened the brochure and scanned the remaining items, trying to calculate how much longer it would be before he could leave the ballroom and return to the pile of pressing work spread out on a coffee table in his suite upstairs. Under the heading "For the Ladies," he counted twelve items, all jewelry and furs. Next to each item were the words "Shown by . . ."

The last item in that category captured his attention. It was donated by a local jeweler and was being "shown by" Miss Diana Foster. According to the brochure, the item was *"A splendid necklace and earrings of perfectly matched deep purple amethysts surrounded by 15 carats of fine white diamonds and set in 18-karat gold. From the collection of the late Countess Vandermill, circa 1910."*

Cole lifted his gaze from the brochure and looked at Diana. She was talking to Corey and looked perfectly composed, but she was noticeably paler than she'd been earlier. He knew how miserable she'd felt about making a conspicuous entrance, and he knew how much she must be dreading having to model that necklace.

Missy Desmond was looking at her own brochure and evidently reached the same conclusion. "Poor Diana Foster!" she exclaimed. "I wonder why she didn't ask them to find someone else to model that necklace."

Cole thought the answer to that was obvious: since Diana's name was already in the printed brochure, she wouldn't have been able to withdraw without calling it to the attention of one thousand people.

Across the table, Haley Mitchell, who had felt more than a little slighted that Cole Harrison had apparently recognized Diana Foster from their teenage acquaintance but not herself, watched his gaze stray yet again to Diana, and so did her husband, who'd been drinking steadily from the moment the meal began. Leaning sideways, Peter whispered, "Diana seems to have made a new conquest. Harrison can't keep his eyes off of her."

"Just like you can't," Haley snapped back, incensed that her husband had dared to mention Diana's name to her and even more enraged because what he said about Cole Harrison was true. Turning to Missy Desmond, she said, "The reason Diana Foster didn't let someone else model that necklace is because she couldn't bear to pass up being in the spotlight, not even for five minutes." She leaned forward and included her friend, Marilee Jenkins, in the conversation. "Have you noticed that tonight she's playing the martyr? Just look at that brave little smile she's wearing."

"I feel rather sorry for her," Mrs. Canfield admitted. "What Daniel Penworth did to her was inexcusable."

"No, it was *unavoidable*," Haley argued. "Diana was like a noose around his neck. He didn't love her, and he tried to let her down gently, but Diana wouldn't give up. People think that Diana is sweet and kind, but the truth is she doesn't care about anybody or anything except herself and that stupid arts-and-crafts magazine that she runs."

Marilee Jenkins seconded all that with a nod. "I don't blame Dan one bit!"

Cole waited for someone else at the table to come to Diana's defense. Mrs. Canfield looked uneasy and Missy Desmond looked bewildered, but no one spoke a word in Diana's behalf. The auctioneer announced that the first of the ladies' items was about to be auctioned, and Cole deliberately turned his shoulder to his dinner partners.

A few tables away, a slender redhead arose to applause and began to model a magnificent diamond necklace she was wearing. She carried the whole thing off with the ease and aplomb of someone who knew she was born to be admired and "on display," smiling as she moved about the crowd, and her husband opened the bidding. As soon as her husband bid, another man at their table instantly topped his bid, grinning as he deliberately forced the husband to go higher. After that the bidding was rapid, frequently accompanied by bursts of laughter around the room, which made Cole correctly assume that the husband's friends were cheerfully forcing the husband to pay more and more.

Cole rather enjoyed watching the game, which was played with gusto as each wife and girlfriend arose to model her desired auction item, and each man involved bore the expense forced on him by his friends, who bid against him with blasé humor. His gaze kept straying to Diana's table, wondering how she was reacting, but as each item was awarded to the lady who was already wearing it, he noticed that her expression grew subtly more somber and tense.

When the time was finally nearing to auction off the necklace she was wearing, she began to fidget with it, her long fingers curling around it and then slowly flattening over it as if she wanted either to hide it or tear it off. Her entire body seemed to freeze as the auctioneer proclaimed, "Ladies and gentlemen, the next item to be auctioned off is an extraordinary example of the workmanship of a bygone era—a remarkably fine amethyst-and-diamond necklace, being shown by Miss Diana Foster."

Cole understood why she would naturally dread being the focal point of so many fascinated gossips, but not until she actually slid back her chair to stand up, did he belatedly realize that her embarrassment was going to be compounded a hundred times by the conspicuous absence of Dan Penworth, who should have been bidding on that necklace. He watched her rally and manufacture a smile as she arose, and at the same time he heard whispers erupt around the room.

At the table behind him, a man jokingly remarked that Dan had probably married his Italian girl to avoid the cost of Diana Foster's necklace, and everyone laughed.

Cole felt anger and protectiveness begin to simmer inside him— emotions that leapt into steady flame as the clueless auctioneer beamed at Diana and then at the crowd in obvious expectation that her own man would open the bidding. "Opening bid will be fifteen thousand dollars. Do I have fifteen thousand dollars?" He paused, bewildered by the awkward silence. "This necklace is a bargain at twice that amount. "Will someone give me ten thousand dollars?" His expression cleared and he nodded. "Yes, thank you, Mr. Dickson. . . ."

The bidding paused at $13,000 so that a prospective purchaser could have a closer look at it. "Poor Diana," Mrs. Canfield said, addressing her remarks to Cole. "I knew her papa very well. He'd have bought her that necklace just to put an end to this."

"Diana needed to be knocked down a peg or two, and everyone knows it," Haley Mitchell argued. "She's a conceited bitch."

Franklin Mitchell had the grace to look a little embarrassed at his daughter-in-law's language, if not her venom. He glanced at his inebriated son as if he expected him to say something, but when Peter spoke, it wasn't to contradict his wife. "Diana has always had a very high opinion of herself," he informed Cole.

"It's the truth," the senior Mrs. Mitchell said coldly.

Unaware of the very personal reasons the people at his table had for disliking Diana and relishing her plight, Cole mistakenly assumed everyone else in the ballroom was just as heartless and just as vengeful.

In his mind he saw a lovely, dainty teenager holding out a sack filled with food, her smile sunny and soft as she contrived to give him food and simultaneously spare his pride. *"Could you possibly find some room for some of these canned peaches, Cole? My grandmother loves cooking and canning, but we're running out of storage space in the pantry. . . . I hope you can help us eat some of Gram's potato salad and chicken; she made enough for an army last night!"* He remembered other things, such as how perfectly neat and clean she always seemed to be, from the tips of her polished loafers to the tips of her fingers, their nails neatly filed but never polished.

Interlaced with his reverie was the auctioneer's voice: "I have thirteen thousand dollars—Do I have fourteen thousand dollars? I have thirteen thousand dollars."

"Peter," Haley said suddenly, her voice filled with excited malice. "Buy that necklace for me. I want it."

"Final warning, ladies and gentlemen," the auctioneer intoned.

Peter Mitchell looked at Diana, who was two tables away "modeling" her necklace, and he called out in a loud, slurred voice, "Wait— we'd like a closer look!"

Cole watched Diana turn and move obediently toward their table. He already knew that Diana had originally believed her faithless fiancé would be buying the necklace for her tonight. Now it suddenly occurred to him that she'd undoubtedly bought the purple gown she was wearing because it set the amethysts off to perfection.

He watched Diana's smile wobble as she paused across from him and subjected herself to Mitchell's leering at her breasts; he saw her fingers lift to the largest stone at the bottom of the necklace to show it to him—the long, slender, womanly fingers that had once been a girl's hand holding out offerings to him.

Mitchell reached for it, deliberately brushing his knuckles over the soft skin above her bodice. In a swift but subtle countermove, she stepped back, reached behind her nape, unclasped the necklace, and held it out to him in her hand.

Her fixed smile never wavered, but as Mitchell reached for the necklace, her gaze recoiled from his hand, bounced to Cole's face, then quickly darted away. In that one brief, unguarded moment while her gaze encountered his, Cole saw something that drove him to an instant and monumental decision.

Maybe he had a latent and heretofore unrecognized urge to play the knight in shining armor for some damsel in distress, or maybe his next action was merely the civilized version of a prehistoric male swinging his club at an adversary to prove his superiority. Maybe he was subconsciously aware that fate was offering him an opportunity to solve not only Diana's problems but his own. Perhaps it was a combination of all three.

But whatever his motives, the outcome was a foregone conclusion, even before Mitchell looked over at the auctioneer and announced, "I'll make it fifteen thousand dollars."

"Twenty-five," Cole snapped before the other man had drawn a breath.

The auctioneer looked stunned but ecstatic. "Ah-ha! We have a new and serious bidder in the competition," he informed the audience with a triumphant smile. "Mr. Harrison has just jumped the bid by ten thousand dollars," he continued, attracting the attention of people who hadn't been particularly interested in the necklace until then, "and *he* hasn't yet had a close-up view of this unique piece! Miss Foster," he said to Diana, "will you please allow Mr. Harrison a moment to inspect the extraordinary quality and color of the stones, as well as the superior craftsmanship of the necklace itself."

With a smile that clearly showed relief, Diana hastily obeyed the suggestion to move around the table to Cole. When she reached his chair, she held the glittering necklace out to him in her hand, but

Cole ignored it completely and looked at her face instead. With a warm, teasing smile, he said, "Do you like it?"

Diana saw the amusement glinting in his silvery eyes, and she sensed instinctively that he was *deliberately* prolonging the moment and playing to their audience, but she was desperately anxious to get *out* of the spotlight, rather than share in the increased glare that came as another hundred pairs of eyes swiveled toward Cole Harrison. Diana didn't care who bought it; she only wanted the ordeal to end. "It's beautiful," she proclaimed with an emphatic nod.

Cole leaned back in his chair, shoved his hands into his pants pockets, and his smile turned lazy, as if he had all the time in the world to ponder his purchase and was actually enjoying the audience's attention. "Yes, but do *you* like it?"

"Yes, honestly! It's splendid." In the sudden hush of curiosity stealing over the ballroom, Diana's breathlessly emphatic declaration rang loudly enough to cause a ripple of good-natured laughter.

"Then, *you* think I should buy it?"

"Of course, if you have someone to give it to."

The auctioneer sensed instinctively that the audience's interest had peaked and would soon begin to ebb. "Mr. Harrison," he asked, "are you satisfied with your inspection, sir?"

Cole's smile turned openly admiring as he studied Diana's face. "Extremely satisfied," he said, plainly referring to Diana and not the necklace.

"Then the bidding will continue," he told the audience. "Mr. Harrison has offered twenty-five thousand dollars. Do I have thirty thousand dollars?" He looked expectantly to Peter Mitchell, who nodded.

He looked around the room to see if anyone else signaled, and when they didn't, he looked to Cole. "Mr. Harrison?"

If Diana hadn't been so unhappy and so tense, she'd have laughed at Cole's infectious grin as he casually held up four fingers, jumping the bid to $40,000 as nonchalantly as if it were forty cents.

"Forty thousand dollars!" The auctioneer crowed. "Mr. Harrison had bid forty thousand dollars, and all of it is destined for charity. Mr. Mitchell?" he urged. "Will you make it forty-five?"

Haley Mitchell nodded yes to her husband, but Peter Mitchell hesitated, glowering at Cole. In response, Cole relaxed further back in his chair and quirked a challenging brow at him. "No," Mitchell bit out.

"Fair warning," the auctioneer called. "Sold!" he proclaimed. "For forty thousand dollars to Mr. Cole Harrison!" Turning toward Cole, he added, "I know I speak for all the patrons of the White Orchid Ball when I say that we are deeply grateful for your extraordinary generosity to our very worthy cause tonight, Mr. Harrison. And may I also say," he joked, "that I sincerely hope the lucky lady who receives that necklace not only appreciates your generosity but also your excellent taste!"

"I hope she does, too!" Cole replied, evoking a burst of laughter as he grinned with a relaxed affability that was in complete opposition to the chilly indifference he'd displayed all night. Then he added, "Let's see what she thinks—"

The audience warmed instantly to this fascinatingly intimate glimpse of the enigmatic tycoon whom one columnist had described as having a circuit board for a brain and a computer for a heart. They watched, captivated, as he slid his chair back and slowly stood up.

Diana was so upset at being kept in the limelight that she tried to step backward as soon as he lifted the ends of the necklace from her outstretched palm. Cole prevented her escape by stepping forward, draping the necklace around her throat, and reaching behind her neck to close the heavy clasp.

Diana stared at him in wide-eyed confusion.

He looked back at her in expectant silence.

The audience erupted with laughter and applause, and in the back of the room, cameras lit up like a swarm of startled lightning bugs.

"Well?" Cole teased, thereby confirming to everyone within hearing that *she* was definitely the lucky lady. "What do *you* think about my taste?"

Diana suddenly concluded that he was *pretending* to give her the necklace, just as he'd pretended to kiss her outside on the terrace earlier that night to fool the photographer. Presenting her with the necklace was merely a very clever—and very kind—public ploy to help her save face. "I think you have wonderful taste," she assured him with belated enthusiasm. *I think you are a magnificent fake!* she thought with amused admiration.

"Are you impressed enough to dance with me?" he challenged, positively exuding sophisticated charm. "I hear music in the next room." Without waiting for an answer, he took her elbow and propelled her past a maze of tables and delighted guests, toward the adjoining ballroom. Their audience realized the show was over and began a slow exodus to the next room.

They were halfway across the ballroom when Diana stopped short. "Wait," she said with a sheepish smile, "I want to introduce you to the rest of my family! After what just happened, they'll be dying to meet you." She turned around and began slowly wending her way through the emerging crowd.

Chapter 24

IN THE TIME IT TOOK TO REACH HER FAMILY'S TABLE, DIANA BEGAN TO feel distinctly lightheaded and a little giddy. For days, she'd faced the world at work and at home, and had hidden her private pain over Dan. On top of that, she'd had to brace herself to face the nightmare of this auction . . . but the auction was suddenly *over*, and it *hadn't* been a nightmare because Cole had turned it into an entertaining drama with a Hollywood happy ending.

The abrupt, unexpected release of so much pressure and stress came as a shock to her entire nervous system. She felt weightless without the heavy emotional armor she'd had to wear for nearly a week. Buoyant.

A few hours ago, she'd been Daniel Penworth's cast-off fiancée, the object of pity and ridicule. A few hours from now, the press was going to portray her in a new role with Cole Harrison— probably as his lover. That was so incredible that she felt a sudden urge to giggle.

Somehow she managed to keep her face straight and introduce Cole to her grandparents and mother, but the feeling of giddy mirth was swelling inside her as she watched them react in their own individual ways to what Cole had done:

Corey's greeting was filled with laughing approval, and she gave him a quick hug. Mrs. Foster was less effusive but very friendly. Spence and Grandpa smiled politely and shook Cole's hand. Grandma stared into his eyes as if she were trying to assess his soul. Amy Leeland actually blushed when Cole smiled at her.

Doug Hayward was not only antagonistic, he was openly insulting. He stood up and shoved his hands into his pants pockets to avoid shaking Cole's hand. Without taking his contemptuous gaze from Cole, he explained to Amy, "Harrison used to work at our stable, mucking out stalls. Now he donates artwork at charity balls." To Cole he added, "It's amazing how far a man can actually climb in America, isn't it, Harrison?"

Cole's jaw hardened and his eyes turned cold.

The inexplicable hostility between the two men was palpable, and Diana's family automatically turned to her to intercede. No matter how awkward or volatile the social situation, Diana could always be counted on to step in and defuse it with her special gifts of diplomacy, sensitivity, and humor.

This time, however, Diana seemed unwilling or unable to do that. Instead, she beamed a bright smile at the two men, who were glaring at each other like silent duelists awaiting the signal to begin pacing off, and she gaily announced, "I can see how anxious you both are to catch up on old times, but you'll just have to wait because Cole and I are leaving." With that, she swept up a plain black handbag from the table, linked her hand through Cole's arm, and turned with enough momentum to partially pull Cole with her.

Feeling that courtesy required some form of parting remark from him, Cole looked over his shoulder and saw Hayward stalking away. "Diana has agreed to take her life in her hands and dance with me," he explained to her family.

The group at the table watched with a variety of reactions as the couple departed. With the exception of Diana's grandmother, everyone seemed to think the evening was a triumph that would mark a complete turning point in Diana's unhappy personal life. "Mr. Harrison was exactly what Diana needed tonight to help her get over Dan. She has her pride back now, and she looks happy again."

"Diana is a survivor," Spencer put in.

"Diana is practical," Grandpa added. "She knows Dan wasn't the man for her, and she's putting him behind her already."

"Diana is a fighter and she's brave," Corey agreed.

"Diana," Grandma contradicted flatly, "is at the end of her rope!"

"Nonsense, Gram," Corey said, partly because she didn't want to believe that. "She's always been independent and self-sufficient. She's calm . . . she's grace under pressure, and . . ."

"*And,*" Grandma interrupted triumphantly as she produced the ultimate proof of Diana's mental state, "she's just walked off with my black purse!"

That particular revelation caused the entire group to turn in alarmed unison and gape at the departing Diana. As all of them knew, Diana's fastidious attention to detail was unflagging; her flair for style was as legendary as her ability to be perfectly groomed and coordinated no matter how difficult the circumstances. Lying on the table was Diana's little purse—a glittering Judith Leiber evening clutch shaped like a jeweled sugarplum, with a silver stem and green leaves. The fact that she had actually walked away in a glamorous purple gown with a matronly black handbag dangling over her forearm was so completely out of character that the entire family felt deep tremors of genuine alarm.

"As you can see," Grandma sadly declared, "Diana has finally reached her limits. There's the proof."

Chapter 25

"IF YOU'RE REALLY GOING TO DANCE WITH ME," COLE JOKED WHEN they neared the entry to the adjoining ballroom, "I suggest you have something to drink first." He stopped at a banquet table with an untouched place setting, lifted a bottle of champagne from the cooler in the center of the table, and poured some champagne into an unused glass. "Alcohol acts as an anesthetic," he told Diana with a grin as he handed her the glass, "and dancing with me could be a painful and dangerous experience."

Diana took the glass, so relieved that her personal ordeal was over and so grateful for his kindness and ingenuity that she would have danced with him if her feet were bare and he was wearing golf cleats. No longer were women eyeing her with pity or disdain. In fact, she noted with amusement, they weren't looking at her at all — they were looking at Cole, and Diana couldn't blame them. With his thick black hair, piercing gray eyes, and tall, athletic physique, Cole Harrison was magnificent.

The same male qualities that had made all the girls fantasize about him long ago were even more pronounced now. There had always been a rugged strength and latent sexuality about him, but now it was enhanced by an aura of cool sophistication and indomitable power.

Walking into the adjoining ballroom, she sipped the champagne, enjoying the looks of confusion on the faces of the same acquaintances who earlier had eyed her with pity or satisfaction.

The orchestra was playing a popular slow song as they neared the dance floor, but when Diana started to put the glass of champagne down on a table, he shook his head. "Finish it."

"Are you really that worried about stepping on my feet?" she asked, her smile filled with a mixture of gratitude, relief, and laughter.

"Certainly not," he teased. "I'm worried that you'll be so tense and stiff that *you'll* step on *my* feet."

With a laugh, she drained the glass and tucked her hand through his arm, drawing him close in an unconscious gesture that seemed a little possessive to Cole and pleased immensely. He was about to negotiate one of the most important "business deals" of his life with a lovely, unsuspecting woman who needed to trust him enough to accept his bizarre offer.

When he slid his arm around her on the dance floor, Diana gazed up at him, her features soft and warm with gratitude. "Cole?"

He returned her smile, but the gray eyes that regarded her from beneath half-lowered lids seemed preoccupied, thoughtful. *"Hmmm?"*

"Has anyone ever told you that you are very sweet and very gallant?"

"Certainly not. Generally, I'm described as cold, calculating, and ruthless."

Diana was aghast at the injustice of that. With her heart filled with gratitude and her head swimming from all the wine and champagne she'd drunk to reinforce her courage, Cole Harrison seemed completely wonderful and omnipotent—a mighty defender who'd charged to her rescue, vanquished her foes, and saved her from humiliation. He was gallantry and daring in a world filled with cowardice and malice. "How could people possibly *think* such awful things about you?"

"Because they're completely true," he stated with calm finality.

Diana's reply was an irrepressible giggle. "Liar."

He looked stung. "Now, that is one thing I am not."

"Oh." Trying unsuccessfully to bite back a smile, she decided he was joking because he was embarrassed by her praise, and she switched the topic. "Who did you *really* buy this necklace for?"

Instead of answering, he gazed at her in speculative silence for so long that Diana began to wonder uneasily if he'd had a recipient in mind, or if he'd actually spent $40,000 on a necklace merely to bolster her status tonight. His next words relieved her mind. "The necklace is a wedding gift for my future wife."

"How wonderful! When are you getting married?"

"Immediately after I propose."

He sounded so matter-of-fact that Diana couldn't resist teasing him. "Either you're very certain she'll say yes, or else you're hoping to sway her with this necklace. Which is it?"

"I'd say it's a little of both. I'm hoping to sway her with this necklace, and I'm *fairly* certain she'll say yes, once I explain the wisdom and benefits associated with such an arrangement."

"You sound as if you're proposing a business merger," Diana advised him with a surprised smile.

Cole quickly reviewed the plan he'd conceived in the last half hour and made his final decision. In a deceptively casual tone, he said, "The last time I asked someone to marry me, we were both sixteen. Obviously, I need to practice my technique, Kitten."

Diana was a little disconcerted to discover that Cole Harrison hadn't been nearly as decisive and knowledgeable about women as she'd thought he was when she was sixteen and crazy about him. Most of all, she was touched by the name he'd called her. *Kitten.* The old nickname he'd occasionally used for her seemed poignantly familiar at that moment—a reminder of a time when she chatted with him while he worked in the Haywards' stable surrounded by the sweet smell of fresh hay and oiled leather, their desultory conversation punctuated by the muted shuffling of horses' hooves. Her life had been so simple then; her future had seemed so bright and full of exciting possibilities. "Kitten . . . " she whispered softly, her eyes shadowed with the realization that those old promises of a bright future hadn't worked out at all the way she'd imagined.

Sensing the sudden dipping of her mood, Cole maneuvered her

smoothly off the dance floor. "Let's go somewhere else and work on my proposal technique. Our audience is too big in here."

"I thought you wanted an audience for us."

"They've seen all they need to see."

He pronounced that with the arrogance of a royal decree, and with his hand beneath her elbow, he maneuvered her off the dance floor and out of the crowded, noisy room.

Chapter 26

WHERE ARE WE GOING?" DIANA ASKED, LAUGHING AS HE LED HER toward the elevators. It felt better and better to laugh. Tomorrow, reality would crush her again like a boulder, but for tonight, Cole and the wine and the necklace were all combining to provide an unexpected respite from the misery, and she was determined to enjoy it. "How about Lake Tahoe?" Cole suggested as he pressed the elevator button. "We could get married, go for a swim, and be back here in time for brunch tomorrow."

Diana assumed he was practicing his proposal on her again, and she took pains to hide her amusement at his blunt haste and his unromantic attitude. "Tahoe's a little too far," she said breezily. "Besides I'm not dressed for it."

She glanced down ruefully at her gown, and Cole's eyes followed her gaze, drifting over the creamy gentle swell of her breasts above the bodice of her gown, then dipping to her narrow waist. "In that case, there's only one other place that offers the sort of atmosphere and privacy required for what I have in mind."

"Where is that?"

"My suite," he said as he ushered her into the crowded elevator and slid a key into the slot beside the top button marked Penthouse.

Diana fired him a glance of real concern, but there were people from the ball in the elevator and she couldn't possibly argue in front of them. When the last elderly couple got off on the floor beneath his, however, she turned to him and shook her head. "I really shouldn't disappear from the ball like this, particularly not with you, not with—"

"Why not with me, *in particular?*" he asked coolly.

The elevator stopped and the doors opened into the penthouse's black marble foyer. Instead of getting out, Cole braced his hand against the door to prevent it from closing. A little dizzy from the champagne and the elevator's swift ascent, Diana felt an inappropriate urge to giggle, not cower, at his forbidding expression. "You've been so busy helping me save my reputation that I'm not sure you've realized the jeopardy you've put your own in. What I meant before was that I shouldn't have disappeared with you without first telling my family why you really bought this necklace. Furthermore, if any of those pictures of us make the news, and people know you're about to be married, you're going to look like a man without integrity."

Cole felt a sudden urge to laugh. "*You* are worried about *my* reputation?"

"Of course I am," Diana said primly, stepping out of the elevator and into the private vestibule of his suite.

"Now, that," Cole said with a grin, "is a first. In fact," he added, as they entered the suite's living room and he switched on the tiny lights concealed in the cove of the ceiling, "I have a feeling tonight is going to be a night of several firsts."

He glanced over his shoulder at Diana, who had stopped near the coffee table in the middle of the living room. She was watching him, her head tipped to one side, her expression more puzzled than wary. Puzzled was good, Cole decided. Wary was bad. He walked over to the bar and removed a bottle of champagne from the refrigerator. Alcohol in the bloodstream of a woman who was already delightfully rosy from gratitude and relief would help keep her wariness under control.

"'Firsts'?" she repeated. "What is there that you haven't done until tonight?"

191

"For starters," he said lightly, "I've never stood outside on the balcony of this suite with a woman." He popped the cork on the champagne and plunged the bottle into the ice bucket on the bar. "Shall we make that another first?"

Diana watched him unbutton his tuxedo jacket and loosen his bow tie; then he tucked the ice bucket into the crook of his elbow and, with a champagne flute in each hand, paused to flip a wall switch with his elbow, which made the heavy draperies in front of the balcony doors glide apart. Superimposed over that image was a memory of him in faded jeans and shirt, currying a horse with one hand and reaching for a bridle with the other while he carried on a conversation with her about her schoolwork. Even then, he'd always seemed to be doing several things at once. He stepped aside, waiting for her to precede him onto the balcony, then handed her the drink he'd poured.

He'd noticed her smile as he opened the balcony doors. "Have I done something amusing?"

Diana shook her head. "I was just thinking that, even in the old days, you always seemed to be able to do several things at the same time and completely effortlessly. I always admired that."

The compliment was so surprising to Cole, and so pleasing, that he couldn't think of a reply, and so he watched in silence as she stepped past him onto the tiny patio.

Walking over to the railing, Diana gazed out at the glittering carpet of Houston lights far below while soft music drifted from the stereo in the living room and her mind drifted inexorably to Dan.

Cole joined her, but angled his body so that he was facing her, with his elbow propped on the railing. "I hope you're thinking of Penworth, and not me, with that woebegone expression on your face."

Chafed at having been described as woebegone, Diana proudly lifted her chin. "We haven't spent much time together in the last year, and I've practically forgotten him already."

Instead of replying, Cole merely raised his brows and regarded her in skeptical silence, managing to convey not only his disbelief but also his disappointment in her obvious unwillingness to confide in him. After the way he'd come to her rescue tonight, Diana knew he deserved more than a brush-off for an answer. "That was a lie," she conceded with a shaky sigh. "The truth is that I've accepted what happened as being final, but I feel . . . furious. I feel furious and humiliated."

"Of course you do," Cole said with amused sympathy. "After all, you've just been dumped by the scum of the earth."

Diana's jaw dropped. She stared at him in angry shock. And then she burst out laughing.

Cole's answering chuckle was rich and deep as he slid his arm around her, pulling her close to his side. The soft, fine fabric of his jacket brushed her bare skin as he curved his arm around her shoulders, his fingers sliding warmly up and down her arm. Even though she was merely a stand-in for his soon-to-be fiancée, it was still nice to know that someone—someone tall and handsome and very special—seemed to find her appealing enough to want to spend time with her tonight. Appealing and worthwhile. Not like Dan who'd— She lifted the glass to her mouth and took a long swallow to chase away the thoughts of Dan.

She remembered that Cole wanted to perfect his proposal technique, and that reminded Diana that she was still wearing the necklace. "I'd better take this off before I forget and leave with it," she said, reaching behind her neck for the clasp.

"Leave the necklace alone," he instructed. "I bought it for you."

Her hands stilled at his tone. "No, you bought it for the woman you intend to marry—"

"That's what I just said."

Diana gave her head a shake to clear it. Turning so that she could see his face, she shoved her hair back off her forehead and ruefully admitted, "I've had much more to drink tonight than I normally would have, and I seem to be having trouble following the thread of our conversation. It's as if you're talking in riddles."

"In that case, I'll make it clearer. I want you to marry me, Diana. Tonight."

She grabbed the high railing and gave a shriek of laughter. "Cole Harrison, are you drunk?"

"Certainly not."

She studied him in adorable confusion. "Then . . . am *I* drunk?"

"No, but I wish you were."

Finally, she loosened her grip and turned to him with a wobbly smile. "You can't really be serious."

"I am *very* serious."

193

"I don't want to s-seem ungrateful or critical," she said in a laughing voice, "but I f-feel I ought to warn you that you're now carrying gallantry too far."

"Gallantry has nothing to do with it."

With unemotional objectivity, Cole observed Diana's struggle to regain control over her hilarity. She was so damned lovely, he thought. The newspaper picture of her had probably come from a magazine press kit, and it hadn't done her justice. It had been a moderately glamorous business photo of a smiling, confident woman, but the real-life Diana was far more arresting. The photo hadn't even hinted at the entrancing warmth of her sudden smile, or the red highlights in her glossy hair, or the jeweled sparkle of her thick-lashed green eyes. As far as he could recall, the tiny cleft in the center of her chin had been completely missing.

She could hardly keep her face straight as she said, "Either you are carrying pity for me to an unbelievable extreme, Mr. Harrison, or else you're not playing with a full deck."

"I am neither dim-witted nor crazy," he stated, "and pity has nothing to do with my reasons for wanting this marriage."

Diana searched his shadowy face for some indication that he was joking, but his expression was completely unemotional. "Am I *honestly* supposed to take you—I mean, this proposal—seriously?"

"I assure you, I'm completely serious."

"Then, do you mind if I ask you a few questions?"

He held out his arms in a gesture of complete cooperation. "Ask me anything you like."

She tipped her head to the side, her face a mirror of confusion and disbelief overlaid with amusement. "Do you happen to be under the influence of any mind-altering drugs?"

"Absolutely not."

"Am I supposed to believe that—*um*—you fell in love with me when I was a teenager, and you've—*ah*—carried a torch all this time, and that's why you want to marry me now?"

"That scenario is as ludicrous as the one before it."

"I see." She was absurdly disappointed that he hadn't had even a tiny crush on her when she had been insane about him.

"Would you rather I'd lied about having a crush on you?"

"No. I'd rather *you* tell *me* your reason for wanting to marry me," she said flatly.

"There are two reasons: I need a wife, and you need a husband."

"And that," Diana speculated dryly, "makes us perfect for each other?"

Cole looked down at her glowing eyes and smiling mouth and had an impulse to bend his head and slowly kiss the smile from her lips. "I think it does."

"I don't know why you need to get married," Diana said tightly, "but believe me, marriage is the *last* thing *I* need."

"You're wrong. Marriage is *exactly* what you need. You've been publicly jilted in the world press by a jerk, and according to what I read in the *Enquirer,* your magazine has been under a competitor-driven media attack for nearly a year over your personal state of 'unwedded bliss.' Now that's going to escalate. What did the headline in the *Enquirer* say . . . ?" He paused, then quoted, " 'Trouble in Paradise—Diana Foster Is Jilted by Fiancé.' " Shaking his head, he said bluntly, "That's bad press, Diana. Very bad. And extremely damaging for business. By marrying me, you could save your pride and also save your company from the negative effects of those headlines."

She gazed up at him as if she'd just suffered a mortal blow from the last person she expected to hurt her. "How pathetic and desperate I must seem to you if you could even suggest such a thing and believe I'd go along with it."

She shoved away from the railing and started to turn toward the doors into his suite, but Cole caught her arm in a gentle but unbreakable grip. "*I'm* the desperate one, Diana," he said flatly.

Diana stared at him dubiously. "Just exactly what makes you so 'desperate' for a wife that any woman will do?"

Instinct and experience told Cole that a little tender persuasion could vastly further his cause, and he was prepared to resort to that, but only if logic and complete honesty weren't enough to persuade her. In the first place, she was vulnerable right now, and he didn't want to do or say anything that might make her ultimately regard him as a possible substitute for the love, and lover, she'd lost. Second, he had no intention of complicating their marriage with any messy emotional or physical intimacy.

And so Cole ignored the instinct to reach up and brush back a wayward lock of shiny dark hair from her soft cheek, and he squelched the temptation to tell her that she was a long way from

195

being just "any" woman to him or that she was as close to his ideal of femininity as any female could be.

He was not, however, morally opposed to diluting her resistance with as much alcohol as he could pour down her. "Finish your champagne, and then I'll explain."

Diana almost started to argue but decided to compromise and took a sip, instead.

"My problem," he explained calmly, "is an old man named Calvin Downing, who is my mother's uncle. When I wanted to leave the ranch and go to college, it was Calvin who tried to convince my father I wasn't thumbing my nose at him and everything he represented. When my father couldn't be persuaded to see things that way, it was Cal who loaned me the money for tuition. Just before my senior year of college, a drilling company ran a test well on Cal's ranch and it came in. It wasn't a gusher, but it made him about twenty-six thousand dollars a month. And when I graduated and went to Cal with a wild scheme for making money that no banker would agree to finance for me, it was Cal who handed over all his savings to help me get started. From the time I was a kid, Cal believed in me. When I started dreaming of making it really big and getting rich—it was Cal who listened to my dreams and believed in them."

Fascinated by his candor and unable to see how such a kind and caring old man could now be the source of Cole's unnamed "problem," Diana sipped her champagne waiting for him to continue, but he seemed content to watch her instead. "Go on," she urged. "So far he sounds like the last man in the world to cause a 'problem' for you."

"He *thinks* he's solving a problem, not creating one."

"I don't understand. Even if I hadn't had so much wine and champagne tonight, I don't think I'd understand."

"You don't understand because I haven't told you that part, which is this: After I graduated, my uncle gave me all his savings from the well on his land, and then he borrowed another two hundred thousand dollars against it, so that I could start my own company. Naturally, I insisted on signing a legal note for the money and on making him a full partner in the business."

To the best of her recollection, the article in *Time* magazine about Cole Harrison's spectacular business successes placed his net worth at over five billion dollars. "I assume you repaid the loan?" she prompted.

He nodded. "I repaid it—along with interest calculated at the rate in effect at the time, as agreed in the note." A wry smile softened his granite features. "Among my uncle's eccentricities is a streak of stinginess a mile wide, which made his willingness to hand over all his money to finance my business plan even more meaningful. To illustrate my point, despite Cal's wealth, he still clips coupons from the newspaper, he still fights with all the utility companies about his bills, and he still buys his clothes at Montgomery Ward. He is so bad that if his phone service goes out for a few hours, which happens several times a year, Cal deducts one day's charges from his bill."

"I didn't know you could do that," Diana said, impressed.

"You can," Cole said dryly. "But they'll turn your phone off until you pay up."

Diana smiled at the colorful description he'd provided of a stubborn, elderly man with a big heart and a tight fist. "I still don't understand how your problem is connected with him."

"The connection is that Cal was a full partner in my original business, and I—who owe my current success to his past moral and financial support—could never bring myself to hurt or offend him by asking him to sign papers dissolving the partnership, not even after I repaid his loan with full interest. Besides, I would have trusted him with my life, and so it never occurred to me that he would balk at turning over his stock when I asked him to do it, let alone consider signing it over to someone else."

Diana was astute enough as a businesswoman to immediately grasp the devastating impact of such an action, but she couldn't quite believe that the man Cole had described would be capable of such treachery. "Have you formally asked him to sign over his shares to you?"

"I have."

"And?"

A grim smile twisted Cole's lips. "And he's perfectly willing to do that, except for one small problem that he feels I'm obliged to solve for him before he can justify giving my company's stock back to me."

He paused and Diana, who was helplessly enthralled, said, "What problem?"

"Immortality."

She gaped at him, caught between laughter and confusion. "Immortality?"

"Exactly. It seems that in the last six or seven years, about the time he turned seventy and his health began to fail badly, Uncle Calvin acquired a strong desire to immortalize himself by leaving behind a brood of descendants. The problem is that besides me, he has only one other blood relative, my cousin. Travis is married to a woman named Elaine and they are both very nice but far from brilliant, and they have two children who are neither nice, nor brilliant, and Cal can't stand either one of them. Because of that, Cal now wants to see *me* married so that I can produce clever babies to carry on the family line."

Still unable to believe she understood what he was trying to tell her, Diana said, "And if you don't do that, then what?"

"Then he will leave his share of my corporation to Elaine and Travis's children, Donna Jean and Ted, who are both in college." He paused to take a swallow of his drink as if he wanted to wash away the bad taste of the words. "In that event, Elaine and Travis would become my business partners with enough shares between them to control the company on behalf of their children until Donna Jean and Ted come of age. Travis already works for me, as the head of Unified's research and development division. He's loyal and he does his best, but he doesn't have the brains or imagination to run Unified, even if I were willing to hand it over to him, which I assuredly am not! His kids lack his loyalty and their mother's common sense and kindness. In fact, they're greedy, egotistical schemers who are already planning how to spend my money when they get their hands on it."

Diana bit back a helpless grin at his plight: Cole Harrison, the invincible wheeler-dealer, the lion of Wall Street, was being held over the proverbial barrel by a frail, elderly uncle—an uncle who was probably getting senile. "Poor Cal," she said on a smothered laugh. "What a dilemma. One great-nephew has no business acumen, but he has a wife and children. The other great-nephew is a brilliant entrepreneur, without a wife *or* children—"

"And without the slightest desire to ever have either," Cole added, summarizing his own attitude. Satisfied that she'd grasped the full situation, he lifted his glass in a sardonic toast to her insight.

His unequivocal wish to remain not only single but childless was obscured for the moment by Diana's helpless amusement at his disgruntled tone. "You do seem to be in a remarkable fix," she said with a wayward smile.

"Which, I gather you find entertaining?"

"Well, you have to admit it *is* just a little . . . *er* . . . gothic," Diana managed unsteadily.

"At the very least," he agreed grimly.

"Although," she continued with an irrepressible grin, "in gothic romances, it's the *heroine* who gets coerced into a marriage she doesn't want. I've never heard of a hero who got himself into such a position."

"If your intention is to cheer me up, you're not succeeding," he said bitterly.

In fact, he looked so chagrined by her description of his "unhero-like" predicament that Diana had to look away to hide her laughter. She was so amused that it took several moments before she realized how presumptuous and offensive his proposed solution actually was. "And so," she concluded, trying to sound as calm and detached as he had earlier, "when you saw me tonight, you remembered I'd been jilted, and decided I'd be eager to marry you and help solve your problem—particularly if you bought me a necklace to help me save face."

"I'm not that selfish—or that vain, Diana. I know damned well you'd throw my proposition in my face, except for one thing."

"And that is?"

"By marrying you, I'd be offering *myself* as a solution to *your* problems."

"I see," Diana said, though she didn't see at all. "Do you mind explaining how?"

"Simple logic. Even though you've been publicly jilted, you can save your pride if you marry me immediately. Tomorrow, the newspapers will be filled with pictures of us kissing on the balcony tonight and the story of my buying you this necklace. If our marriage is announced the next day, people are going to assume that we've had something going all along and that you probably did the jilting, not Penworth."

Diana shrugged to hide the sharp stab of anger and hurt she felt at his callous summation of her own predicament. "I don't have that much pride to save, not if it requires anything as outrageous and rash as what you're suggesting."

"No, but you *do* have a business to save. The shield of being engaged for the last two years was already wearing thin. Now that that is gone," Cole finished, "your competitors will double their attacks and the media will collaborate in publicizing all the furor and hype for their own benefit."

Anguish and anger turned her green eyes stormy an instant before her long lashes swept down, concealing her emotions from Cole's view—but not in time to prevent him from noting that her reaction to the mention of Penworth's defection wasn't nearly as violent as her reaction to this very viable threat to her company.

Despite her delicate features and fragile, feminine beauty, Diana Foster was apparently a woman who put business first. If nothing else, Cole decided as he watched the breeze ruffle her dark auburn hair, they certainly had that in common.

While he gave Diana time to consider what he'd said, he tried to put together what little he knew about the business that meant so much to her, but there wasn't much. Based on the bits and pieces he'd read or seen on the news this week, all he knew was that the company was founded by the Foster family.

The business had apparently begun as a Houston catering service for the very rich—one that specialized in "natural" foods presented in lavish ways, but using only handmade or homegrown ornamentation. Somewhere along the way, that practice had been dubbed the Foster Ideal, and it had ultimately resulted in a magazine called *Foster's Beautiful Living.* He'd seen a copy at the airport magazine stand earlier that week, shortly after he'd seen Diana on CNN, and he'd leafed through it. Amid all the glossy photographs of brightly painted furniture, stenciled walls, and tables covered with hand-decorated linens and laden with gorgeous food and stunning homemade centerpieces, the philosophy of the magazine—and the basis for the Foster Ideal—seemed to be that by returning to basics, a woman could and would achieve personal satisfaction, a sense of vast accomplishment, *and* domestic tranquillity. Beyond that, all he noticed was that the photography had been superb, and that Corey Foster Addison was responsible for it.

That hadn't surprised him, since his every recollection of Corey as a young girl included a camera. He had, however, felt a certain amused irony over the fact that the founder and publisher of that homey, back-to-basics magazine was, in reality, a pampered Houston debutante—one who had once admitted to him, while seated on a bale of hay and grimacing at a smudge on her hand, that she'd never been a tomboy because she didn't like getting dirty.

He glanced sideways at her moonlit profile, and he marveled at the stupidity that had prompted Penworth to prefer an eighteen-year-old Italian model over Diana Foster. Even when she was a teenager, Diana had sparkled and glowed with wit, intelligence, and gentleness. As a woman, her vivid coloring, lovely figure, and innate poise made her stand out like a queen among peasants.

Cole had been with enough models to know that they were boringly obsessive about every molecule of their skin and hair, and that the bodies that looked so beautiful in designer clothes and magazine centerfolds felt like skin stretched over a skeleton in a man's bed.

Penworth was a fool, and he had blown his chance.

Cole Harrison was not a fool, and he was not going to blow his.

Chapter 27

*D*ECIDING THAT DIANA HAD NOW HAD AMPLE TIME TO FACE REALITY as he'd portrayed it, Cole said quietly, "I wasn't trying to hurt or embarrass you, I was only trying to describe your situation as it actually exists."

She swallowed audibly and looked down at her hands; one held her champagne glass but the fingers of the other one were clutching the railing so tightly that her knuckles were white, and when she realized Cole had noticed that, she automatically loosened her grip. She didn't like having her emotions exposed to anyone's eyes, even his, Cole realized. That was something else they had in common, and it pleased him because what he wanted from her was a completely impersonal partnership, a businesslike arrangement with no emotions to deal with while it existed, or while it was being dissolved.

On the other hand, her continued silence was not what he wanted, and he deliberately forced her out of it. "Diana, if you're blaming me for something, then blame me for being blunt, but not for creating your unhappiness."

She drew a deep, steadying breath, but there were angry tears in her voice. "Why should I blame you for stating the problem in all its ugly reality?"

"I didn't merely state the problem," Cole pointed out gently. "I also offered you a perfect solution. Me."

"Yes, you did, and I do appreciate the offer—honestly I do . . ."

She trailed off, and Cole realized that although his solution still struck her as bizarre and impossible, she was being careful not to hurt his feelings. The knowledge made her seem very sweet in his estimation, and very naïve, because his feelings were not involved in this bargain. He preferred to live his life in a permanent state of unemotional objectivity.

"The problem is," she began again in that same soft, gentle voice, "I can't quite see the logic in exchanging a fiancé I loved but who didn't love me for a husband I don't love and who doesn't love me either."

"That's what makes it so perfect!" Cole said, putting his hand on her arm as he pressed his point. "Our marriage won't be complicated by messy emotions."

She put down her glass and wrapped her arms around herself as if she were chilled by his attitude, dislodging his hand in the process. "Are you really as cold and unfeeling as you sound?"

Gazing into her beautiful, upturned face with her breasts only inches from him, Cole felt anything but cold. For the first time since he'd conceived his hasty plan tonight, it occurred to him that sexual desire for her could actually become a complication. He circumvented the obstacle by silently vowing to avoid all serious intimacy with her. "I'm not cold," he said aloud. "I'm being practical. I have a pressing problem that acquiring a spouse would solve for me, and you're in exactly the same predicament. Our marriage won't be complicated by messy emotions; it will be a friendly business arrangement, terminated at the end of a year by a quiet, congenial divorce. We're the perfect solution for each other. If you were superstitious, you could say this was fate."

"I don't trust fate. I used to believe Dan and I were fated for each other."

"There's a major difference between Penworth and me," Cole said with a bite in his voice. "I don't break my word when I give it."

It was at that moment, with his steely eyes boring into hers and his deep voice resounding with conviction, that Diana truly accepted that he was in absolute, dead earnest about all this. She was still reeling from the shock of that when he took her chin between his thumb and forefinger; he forced her to meet his compelling gaze. "During the year we're married," he stated, "I give you my word that I will conduct myself publicly as if I were the most devoted and faithful of husbands. I will not knowingly do anything to cause you even a moment of the humiliation or anger that Penworth has brought you. In fact, I will do everything in my power to ensure you never regret our bargain in any way," he finished and then set down his champagne glass.

There is no bargain, Diana's mind warned her in a whisper, but the silent argument was being overturned by the effect of a somber handsome face, a deep, hypnotic voice, and a powerful male body that loomed before her, tall and strong—a man who was offering to shield her from the world with a pair of broad shoulders that looked as if they could shoulder all her burdens. The combination of all that was becoming dangerously, sweetly appealing, particularly because he wasn't talking about love or even affection.

"In the eyes of everyone," he continued, his low voice gaining force, "you will appear to be my cherished wife, and during the year we're married, you *will* be that."

Cherished . . . An antiquated word . . . sensitive and sentimental . . . unlike anything Dan had ever said to her. And totally unlike anything she'd have expected Cole to say.

His hands slid up her arms then down, velvet manacles pulling her closer to him, deeper into the sensual spell he was weaving with the help of a great deal of French champagne and wine laced with romantic Texas moonlight. "Naturally," he continued with gentle firmness, "I will expect the same promises from you. Is that agreeable?"

Diana couldn't believe she was seriously considering going through with this, not even when she felt herself nod slightly.

"I haven't agreed to the whole plan," she warned shakily, "only to the conditions."

His right hand left her arm and came to rest lightly against the side of her face, tipping it up to his. "Yes, Diana," he said with a knowing smile, his fingers spreading over her cheek, "you have. You just haven't said the words yet." His eyes and his voice were casting a spell. "By tomorrow, all your worries and all of mine can be over. All you have to do is say you agree, and I'll have my plane ready to take off for Nevada in an hour."

If he'd kissed her then, she would have bolted; if he'd released her from the gentle hold of his hands, she'd have run for her life. But when he slid his hand around the back of her nape and pressed her face against his chest in a strangely paternal gesture, Diana's remaining resistance suddenly collapsed. He was offering her, personally and professionally, a safe haven for a year . . . He was offering her his protection . . . He was offering to rescue her from humiliation, anxiety, and stress.

He was offering all that to Diana, who had been exhausted, disillusioned, and angry earlier, but who was now beginning to enjoy the increasingly delicious mindless languor induced by more alcohol than she normally consumed in an average month and by a man who made everything seem simple and easy. Cole was offering to rescue her and cherish her this very night. All she had to do was nod her head and it would be over.

Above her, his voice was a whisper lightly stirring her hair. "We can leave in an hour and be back here in time for breakfast."

Diana swallowed and closed her eyes, blinking back sudden tears that turned the small gold studs on his shirt into blurry little knots. She tried to say something, but the words lodged in her throat behind a huge lump of fear and hope and relief.

"All you have to do is give me your word that for a period of one year, you will do exactly what I'm offering to do—which is to give a convincing performance for all the world to see that we are truly and happily married."

Diana finally dragged sound through the giant constriction that seemed to start in the pit of her stomach and reach to her chin. "We don't even live in the same city," she protested weakly.

"Which makes our pretense that much easier to maintain. Our separate business interests require me to maintain a Dallas residence, while yours require you to keep your residence in Houston. Since the two cities are only a forty-five minute commute by plane, people will simply assume we're commuting."

Diana smiled a little, her cheek pressed against the starched pleats of his shirt. "You make everything sound so simple."

"Because it *is* simple. All we have to do is maintain a spirit of friendly collaboration. During the year we're married, you'll occasionally need me to escort you to some function or another, and I'll arrange my schedule to be there for you. Just give me as much notice as you can."

Diana thought that over as best she could; then she leaned her head back and studied him with a hazy smile. "No matter where it is, and even if it involves the press? I know you hate reporters, but the media is important to our business."

Despite her unsteady condition and the bizarre offer he was coercing her into accepting, Cole noted with amused admiration that his intelligent future wife was warily trying to close up loopholes before she agreed. He nodded. "No matter where it is," he agreed, "and I'll expect the same from you. Fair enough?" Cole waited expectantly for her to agree.

Instead she lifted her head and peered hard at his face, obviously trying to compensate for the poor light and the dulling effect of the champagne on her senses. "Do you have any other terms?"

The last thing Cole wanted to do was get mired down in details and lose the forward momentum he'd been steadily gaining. "We can talk about all the little details tomorrow. Do we have a deal?" Again he waited for her to agree.

His future wife bit her lip, considered that for a moment, and ruefully shook her head. "I think now would be better," she stated; then she gave him a tiny smile, as if to apologize for putting him to so much trouble. "That way, we won't have any miscon— misunderstandings," she amended when the right word eluded her.

Cole couldn't suppress his admiring grin. Even when she was under extraordinary pressure, Diana Foster was neither a fool nor incautious. He was beginning to understand how she had become such a formidable force within her own industry. "All right," he conceded, "here are the only major terms we need to agree upon: First, at the end of one year, we will obtain a quick, quiet divorce with neither of us making any sort of financial claims against the other. Agreed?"

She winced at the word divorce, and Cole felt a tiny pang of guilt for making her first marriage one that was a sham. On the other hand, she had as much to gain from this marriage as he did, and far less to lose. Since Texas was a community-property state, and since Cole was far wealthier than she, he had much more to lose if she tried to renege on the postnuptial agreement that would have to be drawn up immediately after their marriage.

"Agreed," she whispered solemnly.

Cole's voice gained force and his mind shifted to travel arrangements. "Beyond that, I'll only ask for two other concessions. First, neither of us will ever reveal to *anyone* that this marriage was merely a convenient business arrangement. Second—"

"No."

"What?" He stared at her in disbelief. "Why not?"

"Because I'll have to tell my family. I'll have to tell my sister. You know—Corey?" she provided helpfully, and Cole suddenly suspected that she was either far more tipsy, or far more nervous, than he'd supposed a few minutes ago.

"I know Corey," he gravely assured her.

Behind her back, he lifted his wrist and tipped the face of his watch to the light from the doorway. It was ten minutes past eleven. The pilots of his Gulfstream jet were staying at a motel near the airport and they both carried pagers. His limousine was on twenty-four-hour call. If the wedding chapels in Lake Tahoe didn't stay open all night, he knew they did in Las Vegas. The logistics were not a problem. Diana was.

"I'll have to tell my whole family. And Spence, too. He's part of the family."

"What if I refuse to agree?"

She rolled her eyes at him in amused superiority. "We can't very well expect them to believe we took one look at each other tonight, fell in love, and eloped, now can we?"

"They can't prove it isn't true. Let's stick with that story, anyway."

She stepped away from him and lifted her chin to its haughtiest and most obstinate angle. "I will not upset my family with a lie, and I will not knowingly make a promise I can't keep."

She meant every word, Cole realized. Obviously, Texas's Businesswoman of the Year hadn't sacrificed her scruples or her youthful idealism during her climb up the ladder of success, and his voice was gruff with pleasure and something that felt like pride. "In that case, I concede."

"You—do?" Diana was feeling more dazed by the moment at everything he said and did. One moment, he was offering her marriage as coolly as he'd offer to hold the door open for a stranger, and the next, he was yielding a point to her with a distinct warmth in his eyes. Trying to shake off the heady effect of the alcohol and his silvery gaze, she said, "You said there were two other concessions—"

"The second concession is that you agree to accompany me to my uncle's ranch sometime during the next week or two and spend a few days there, allaying any suspicions or fears he may have about our sudden marriage."

"I probably have some meetings." She frowned, a troubled goddess with the summer breeze blowing her hair and ruffling her gown. "I *always* have meetings. I suppose I could rearrange my schedule and either visit your uncle next week or the week after."

"That settles it then," Cole said briskly.

She was so nervous, her voice actually shook. "I—Shouldn't I have terms?"

"Tell me what they are as you think of them. I've already promised to do everything I reasonably can to cooperate." Convinced that the moment was now exactly right to stop talking and put the plan into action, Cole walked into the suite, phoned his pilots at their motel, and then ordered his limo to be brought to the front of the hotel. After that he dialed his secretary's number in Dallas and gave the sleepy but stalwart woman a set of instructions that snapped her awake and made her stammer.

"Everything is arranged," he said as he walked back out on the balcony. He lifted the bottle of champagne out of its icy nest and refilled both glasses. "The limo is waiting downstairs, and my plane is being refueled. This definitely calls for a toast," he added, holding a glass toward her.

Diana looked at the glass in his hand and her faltering courage collapsed. "I can't!" she cried, crossing her arms protectively over her chest. She'd spent the time while he made phone calls trying desperately to decide whether her misgivings were based on good judgment or whether her panic was the result of the same cowardly, conservative streak within her that she hated and that frequently paralyzed her and caused her to pass up unique business opportunities.

Wordlessly, he put both glasses on the table with an ominous little clink, then took a step toward her. "What do you mean, you 'can't'?" he demanded.

Diana jumped backward out of his reach. "I can't! Not tonight." Her voice was shaking so hard that she scarcely recognized it, and she bumped into the railing in her desperation to escape from what she perceived to be a threat. "I need time!"

He was blocking the path into the suite, and Diana started to sidle behind one of the balcony's chairs, but the urgency and regret in his deep voice checked her in midstep and made her fear of him absurd. "Time is the *only* thing I can't afford to give you, Diana."

Diana heard all sorts of confusing signals in that sentence—from a desperate attempt at bribery, to an effort to salvage his pride by impressing her with his wealth. "With everything you have to offer," she assured him as she reached behind her neck and unclasped the heavy necklace he'd bought earlier, "you'll find lots of women who will jump at your suggestion in the hope it might lead to permanence—including some in the ballroom downstairs."

"I imagine you're right," he said, his voice suddenly flat. "Possibly I was reaching far above myself, but I would have liked the wife in this scheme to be a woman I'm proud to have share my name, which happens to limit my choices to one—you."

He said it so coolly that it took a moment for Diana to hear the meaning behind the words. "Why me?"

"A variety of reasons," he said with a shrug. "Not the least of which is that despite your lofty social status, you also knew me when I was paid to muck out horse stalls, and you don't seem to find that repellent."

His blunt reference to his lack of social status, combined with his earlier attempt to bribe her, made Diana's chest ache. Tears stung her eyes as she gazed at the powerful, dynamic man before her who, for some reason, was oblivious to his own worth. His face was almost too rugged to be handsome, and yet it was one of the most attractive faces she'd ever seen. Masculine pride and granite determination were sculpted into every hard angle and plane on his

209

face. Cynicism had etched lines at the corners of his eyes and mouth, but in the strength of his features, Diana saw the mark of battles fought and won, of lessons learned the hard way. And there was no overlooking the sensuality in the mold of his mouth, not even when it had a sardonic twist, as it did now. If he hadn't had money, women would still have thrown themselves at him—and yet, for some unfathomable reason he was willing to settle for an empty marriage and a life without children.

She herself had been little more than a child when she first started visiting him at the Haywards', and he'd seemed to enjoy her company very much. He'd even gotten her a stuffed toy kitten for her sixteenth birthday, she suddenly remembered, and while she'd been melting with joy, he'd leapt to the conclusion that it wasn't good enough. *"You've probably had dozens of really exotic stuffed animals."*

Cole had been her friend, her fantasy lover, her mentor. Tonight he had been her knight in shining armor.

How foolish she was being now, to mistrust him and turn down an opportunity that was heaven-sent.

Guilt swelled in her chest and she wondered when *she* had become jaded and cynical. "Cole," she whispered, and watched his expression soften at the sound of her voice. "I'm sorry—" She held out her hand in a gesture of conciliation, but his gaze riveted on the forgotten necklace in her palm, and his expression turned to stone.

"Keep it!" he said shortly. "I bought it for you."

"No—" she began awkwardly; then she wished she'd had that other glass of champagne for courage when she saw the ominous expression in his eyes. "What I mean is, could you possibly repeat all those excellent reasons you gave me earlier?"

Cole saw the yielding softness in her eyes, and somewhere deep within him, he felt the faint stirrings of an emotion so long dead, or so foreign to him, that he didn't recognize it. And even so, it made him smile.

It made him reach out and lay his palm against the side of her cheek and tenderly smooth a lock of gleaming russet hair off her warm cheek.

"I can't decide," she told him a little shakily.

"Diana," he whispered, "you've already decided."

210

Diana's senses were beginning to reel with the shock of her decision and the touch of his hand. She tried to make a joke of it. "I have? What did I decide?"

His eyes gleamed with laughter, but his tone remained solemn. "You decided you'll marry me in Nevada tonight."

"I will?"

"You will."

Chapter 28

I will. . . . I will. . . ." Diana turned her head on the pillow, but the words followed her, echoing as if from the distant end of a long tunnel, combining with odd images that tumbled around in her brain in a shifting kaleidoscope of disjointed events and unrelated noises. *I will. . . . I will. . . .* In her dream, the two words were overlaid by the incessant drone of jet engines, the muted ringing of a telephone, and the shadowy, indefinable presence of dark male, a looming, powerful figure that she sensed in her dream but could not see. His presence gave her twin sensations of being in grave danger and of being safe; the voice she heard was not his voice, and yet he seemed to control her answers.

"Will you?" Now the voice was hers—a whisper in the dim glow of a soft light near an unearthly bed that seemed to float as she lay upon it. He was standing beside the bed, leaning over her, his hands braced on the pillow beside her head, resisting her. *"No."*

Her hands were on his shoulders, and she pulled him closer, watching his eyes begin to smolder. Roaring engines drowned his voice as his sensual lips formed a soundless word. *"No."*

She slid her hand around his nape, and the banked fires in his eyes leapt into flames. She was in control now, she knew it, she gloried in it. "*Yes . . .*" she whispered, and his scorching gaze dropped to her lips.

She was in control as his mouth covered hers, exploring . . . tantalizing, then slowly opening on hers, urging her lips to part, his tongue probing between them, forcing entrance.

He was demanding control, taking it away from her, and she moaned in protest even while she crushed her lips to his and fought to subdue his tongue with her own. Large hands covered her breasts, fondling them possessively; then his mouth seized her nipples, drawing them taut, and she cried out. She couldn't lose control, wouldn't, *must not!* He knew she wanted to hold back, he knew it, but he shoved his hands into the sides of hair, turning it into a tangled mess. His ravenous mouth left her breasts, only to invade her mouth again while his body moved on top of hers and his hips began to move sensuously.

She tried to resist the erotic demands, the heat, the pressure of him, but he wouldn't let her, and her legs parted as his hands lifted her buttocks and his rigid erection unerringly found the wet warmth at the entrance to her body. He thrust into her, his mouth devouring hers . . . and then it began—the slow, demanding thrusts that steadily increased in power and force, driving her to a terrifying precipice. She fought it, tried to recoil from it.

He knew she was fighting her own desire, but he wouldn't leave her alone. Wrapping his arms around her, he rolled onto his back, his body still joined fiercely to hers. He curved his hands around her hips, forcing her into a tempo that made her forget that her hair was a tangled mess and her breasts were too small and her hip had a scar on the side of it.

She rode him and rode him because he wouldn't let her stop. Because she couldn't stop. Didn't want to stop. Wild now. She was wild and sobbing with need, and his hips were moving with hers, hands caressing her breasts, fingers squeezing her taut nipples. She cried out as explosions racked her body, and he arched his back while deep spasms drove him higher and deeper into her. Engines screamed and the bed crashed to earth, rocking her violently off him; his arms wrapped tightly around her, holding her, while blue lights flew past the windows with dizzying speed. Eerie lights.

Blue lights . . . revolving around and around . . . spinning past.

Diana tossed her head on the pillow, afraid of the lights, trying to escape the clutches of the demon lover who had taken much more than she meant to offer.

She tried to turn and run, but an entity was guarding her, preventing her from moving—a terrifying, four-legged beast as black as the hounds from hell. Its fangs were huge; its ears were pointed and stiff; its body was gaunt from starvation. Satan from *Rosemary's Baby. She* was Rosemary!

In her dream, Diana screamed with fear, but the actual sound was only a parched whisper: *"No!"*

Propelled by terror, Diana broke free of the nightmare and opened her eyes. Pain stabbed through the sockets of her eyes and embedded itself in her brain as she blinked dazedly at a spacious, but wholly unfamiliar bedroom. The sound of a door opening made her jerk her chin in that direction, which caused the pain to worsen, the room to revolve, and her stomach to lurch alarmingly. A man whom she suddenly identified as Cole Harrison was strolling into her bedroom as casually as if he had a right to be there. "Easy now," he told her in an amused voice as he moved toward her with a tray in his hand. "Don't make any sudden movement."

Diana couldn't seem to think beyond the misery of her entire body. She tried to speak, but all that came out was a small croak. She swallowed and tried again. "What—happened . . . to me?"

"It's only a theory, but your nervous system is probably under assault by a buildup of acetaldehyde," he provided with cheerful sympathy as he put the tray on the nightstand. "In severe cases, that causes blurred vision, headache, nausea, trembling, and dry mouth. At least that's the theory we're working on at Unified's pharmaceutical division. In layman's terms, you have a colossal hangover."

"Why?" Diana whispered, closing her eyes against the glare of bright orange liquid in a tall glass on the nightstand.

"Too much champagne."

"Why?" she said again. She wanted to know why she was here, why he was here, and why she'd made herself sick, but her brain and her mouth refused to function properly.

Instead of answering, he sat down on the bed, causing her to moan aloud when the mattress shifted and she rolled a little sideways. "Don't try to talk," he said with stern authority that contrasted with the gentleness in his movements as he slid his left arm beneath her shoulders, lifting her slightly upright. "This is buffered aspirin," he said, giving her two white tablets. Diana's hand shook as she took them from him and pressed them awkwardly between her lips. "And this," he added as he lifted the glass of orange liquid from the tray and held it toward her lips, tipping it carefully so she could drink, "is orange juice with a little 'hair-of-the-dog.' "

Diana's stomach lurched violently at the thought of dog hairs in her orange juice, but before she could react, he tipped it up, forcing her to swallow; then he eased her back down onto the pillows. "Go back to sleep," he said gently as her eyes closed. "You'll feel much better when I wake you up later."

Something cold and soothing was pressed against her forehead. A washcloth.

Cole Harrison was a kind, caring man, she thought. She needed to tell him that. "Thank you for helping me," she murmured as his weight lifted from the mattress and he stood up.

"As your husband, I consider it my duty to nurse you through any and all hangovers."

"You're very nice."

"I was hoping you'd still think so this morning, but I had some doubts."

The carpet muffled his footsteps as he walked away, and she heard the door close softly behind him as she lay there, waiting for the anesthesia of sleep. For several moments, his parting remarks were merely a baffling joke she tried to ignore, but they'd evoked stubborn images that began marching insistently behind her aching eyes. She remembered being at the Orchid Ball and drinking wine and champagne . . . and an amethyst necklace, and more champagne. She remembered going up to Cole's suite . . . and more champagne . . . and a limousine ride to Intercontinental Airport . . . and the cabin of a private jet, where she drank more champagne. She remembered another limo ride through a city ablaze with lights . . .

The images slowed and sharpened into better focus. She'd gotten out of the car and walked into a place with an arched trellis covered with fake flowers. A short, bald, smiling man had talked to her while she leaned her head back and mentally removed those awful flowers, replacing them with fresh ivy vines.

Swallowing against a surge of nausea, Diana tried not to think about the bald man and the flowered trellis, but the tableau seemed to be etched into her aching brain, a foggy, strangely ominous vignette—and yet, he'd seemed a pleasant enough man. . . . He'd walked Cole and her to the door when they left. He'd waved to them and called out something to her as the limousine started to roll away from the curb. She'd leaned out of the window and waved back at him as he stood in the doorway beneath a pink-and-green neon trellis, with blinking neon bells above it and some words below it.

Words below it.

Words . . .

Words, in scrolling pink-and-green neon letters.

WEDDING CHAPEL

The man in the doorway had been calling out, *"Good luck, Mrs. Harrison!"*

Reality struck Diana with enough force to set off fresh explosions of pain in her head and a holocaust in her stomach. "Oh, my God!" she moaned aloud, and she rolled over, pressing her face into the pillow, trying to blot everything from her mind.

Chapter 29

WHEN DIANA AWAKENED AGAIN, SOMEONE HAD OPENED THE HEAVY draperies, letting filtered sunlight into the room through the filmy sheers, and a telephone was ringing somewhere in the suite.

For several moments, she lay perfectly still, her eyes closed, taking cautious mental inventory of her body's condition, afraid to move lest her nerves begin to jangle and her head pound as it had earlier. She still felt shaky and her head still ached, but her skull no longer felt as if it were going to split in half.

Having dealt with the physical side of her situation, she reluctantly allowed herself to contemplate the outcome of her first true bout with inebriation.

She had married Cole Harrison.

Her heart began to hammer as the reality of that reckless, irrational act clamored in her brain. She was married to a stranger! He was a heartless opportunist who'd taken advantage of her state of mind last night and convinced her that marrying him would also benefit her, not just him.

She was clearly insane. So was he.

She was a fool. He was a monster.

She needed to be locked up in an asylum.

He needed to be shot!

Somehow, Diana forced herself to break off her unjustified mental tirade and block out the guilt and panic that were causing it.

She had *not* been completely irrational last night, and Cole had *not* coerced or forced her into marriage. As calmly as she could, Diana reviewed everything she could remember about his reasoning and her reactions.

In the bright light of day, without the lulling effects of champagne, it was obvious that Cole had amazing powers of persuasion. It was equally obvious that she'd let emotion and sentimentality drive her to do something that was incredibly impulsive. But the more she thought about it, the more Diana realized that the logic behind their agreement was still sound.

Last night, Cole had been the pawn of a well-meaning old man named Calvin, who was jeopardizing the business empire Cole had built. This morning, Cole was victor, not victim, and the uncle he loved was going to be a very happy man.

Last night, the credibility and the financial future of Foster Enterprises had been in jeopardy, and Diana had been the object of scorn and pity—the discarded fiancée of a wealthy Houston socialite. This morning, Foster Enterprises was secure and Diana was the "cherished wife" of a handsome billionaire tycoon.

Diana felt vastly better, though she was not looking forward to trying to convince her family that Cole wasn't some sort of manipulative monster and that she hadn't lost her senses.

To escape thinking of that scene, she tried to remember more about what had happened after Cole's plane took off from Las Vegas, but her memory was fuzzy. She remembered being impressed when she first saw the interior of his plane, and she remembered asking Cole if they could go to Las Vegas instead of Lake Tahoe, because she'd already been to Lake Tahoe. From then on, things began to blur and meld with her dreams. She wasn't certain whether her disjointed memories were real or only part of the vivid dreams that had pursued her while she slept, and she wasn't up to thinking hard enough to solve the mystery.

Rolling over, she shoved back the sheets and was surprised to discover that she was naked. Considering how inebriated she'd been last night, it was amazing that she'd managed to unfasten her gown and get undressed herself. It occurred to her that Cole might have had to undress her, but that mortifying possibility was more than she could bear to contemplate at the moment. It was then that Diana realized she had nothing to wear except the purple silk gown she'd worn last night. The dining room at the Grand Balmoral was a favorite for Sunday afternoon dinner, and the prospect of walking through the hotel lobby in that gown, added to everything else that lay ahead, was enough to make her lie back for a moment in exhausted dread. She couldn't phone her family and ask them to bring clothes to the hotel, because she didn't want to explain about this whole escapade while she was in Cole's suite. With a sigh of resignation, Diana climbed out of bed.

Chapter 30

Cole LOOKED UP WHEN SHE EMERGED FROM THE BEDROOM WITH HER hair still wet from her shower and her slender body completely engulfed in one of the hotel's thick terry-cloth robes. Her bare toes peeped from beneath the hem of the robe, which should have stopped at mid-calf, and the shoulder seams fell to her elbows. Last night, Cole had thought she couldn't possibly look more desirable than she had in that provocative purple gown, but he'd been wrong. Wrapped in an oversize robe, with her face scrubbed free of makeup and her thick russet hair falling damply at her neck, Diana Foster had the dewy freshness of a rose at dawn.

He laid the Sunday *Houston Chronicle* on the coffee table and stood up. "You're looking better," he told her.

She gave him a weak smile. "I've decided to be very brave and try to go on living."

Chuckling at her quip, he gestured toward a linen-covered table laden with platters of food. "When I heard you turn on the shower, I phoned room service and had them send up some food."

She looked at the eggs and bacon and pancakes and shuddered. "I'm not *that* brave."

Ignoring her protest, Cole walked over to the table and pulled out a chair for her. "You have to eat."

She sighed, but she padded over to the table, slid into the chair, and unfolded her napkin.

"How do you feel?" Cole inquired, sitting down across from her.

"The same way I look." As she spoke, the oversize robe slipped off her left shoulder, leaving it bare, and she pulled it back in place.

"*That* good?" he said,

The warmth in his deep voice and the bold admiration in his eyes did astonishing things to Diana's heartbeat, a reaction that was so unexpected and so strong that her cheeks grew hot. With a faint smile, she quickly dropped her gaze from his and reminded herself that he was merely playing a part, living up to his promise to make her happy during the tenure of their bargain. A bargain—that was all it was to him, and to her. The problem was, she didn't know how she could possibly make her family understand that.

She reached for a slice of dry toast and lapsed into silence, trying to anticipate the scene with her family later. Cole had insisted on being with her when she told them they were married, and she appreciated his honorable desire to buffer, or share, the results of an action he had instigated. She didn't expect them to make any sort of angry scene, but Grandma in particular was likely to have some strong opinions and she wasn't likely to withhold them on Cole's account or Diana's.

Cole watched her expression grow increasingly somber as each minute passed. "Can I help?" he offered finally.

She glanced up with a guilty start. "I'm afraid not." When he continued to regard her in waiting silence, Diana conceded to his silent instruction and told him what was worrying her. "I just don't know how to explain to my family that I married a virtual stranger on an impulse and for purely practical reasons. I mean, once they calm down, they'll begin to understand. Not agree probably, but understand."

"Then what's the problem?"

"The problem is that I'm dreading their reaction when they discover what we did. I'm going to give them the shock of a lifetime."

221

"Not necessarily."

"What do you mean?"

"You made some phone calls from my plane."

Diana gaped at him. "Who did I call?"

"Marge Crumbaker."

Relief restored a little color to her cheeks. "Marge is an old family friend." In case he'd forgotten, she added, "Marge used to be the society columnist for the *Houston Post,* but the *Post* went out of business. So in this instance, that's good."

"When you finished telling her the news, you called Maxine Messenger."

"That's bad." Diana's heart sank at the mention of the *Houston Chronicle*'s society columnist; then she brightened. "Did I ask Maxine to keep it confidential?"

"I'm afraid not," Cole replied, intrigued by the play of emotions across her expressive face. "There wouldn't have been much point in asking her to keep it confidential, anyway."

"Please don't tell me I called anyone else."

"Okay."

She stared at him through suspicion-narrowed eyes "I did call someone else, didn't I?"

"Eat something. You'll feel better."

She picked up her spoon, nudged a red cherry off the top of a half grapefruit, and lifted a bite toward her lips.

"Who else did I call?"

"Larry King."

Denial and self-disgust reduced her voice to a choked whisper. "Are you telling me," she enunciated in dire tones, "that I actually called CNN in the middle of the night and asked to talk to Larry King?"

"I'm afraid so. He wasn't there, however."

"Thank God!"

"So you talked to some man in the newsroom instead."

She shook her head, groping desperately for a reason to be optimistic, and she hit on a lame one. "I have a common name, and besides, my grandfather is the one who's popular with men. I'm associated with the magazine and most of our readers are women. There's no way that newsman at CNN would have recognized little old me by name or reputation."

"Possibly not," Cole said. "But he recognized 'little old me' by name and reputation."

"You should have stopped me!" she moaned. "You should have taken the phone away. No, you should have pushed me out of the plane. At least if I were dead, my body wouldn't feel as bad as it does."

Unable to suppress a grin, he nodded at the plate of food in front of her and refused to say another word until she complied with his order. "Finish your grapefruit and have some more orange juice and a little of that egg."

She gazed at the three items and shuddered a little. "Everything looks so . . . so *yellow*. The grapefruit, the egg, the orange juice. The color is hurting my eyes."

"That's what happens when you drink too much."

"Thank you for that unnecessary lecture on a subject for which I can now qualify for a Ph.D."

"You're welcome," Cole said with unshakable good humor. "Eat some toast. It's brown, so it shouldn't hurt your eyes."

"It has butter on it, and that's yellow."

"Stop it, Diana," he said on a chuckle. "I don't feel so great either, but I refuse to get sick on my first morning as your husband."

"I'm sorry." She picked up a piece of toast and looked at him, her expression so troubled that Cole felt genuinely sorry for treating her concerns lightly and for trying to avoid more questions. "What's wrong?" he said gently.

"Tell me the truth—when I was calling those people, did I sound happy? Or intoxicated?"

"You sounded happy *and* like you'd possibly had a little to drink," Cole said diplomatically, "but I doubt they'd think much about that. Brides frequently have a little too much champagne on their wedding night."

"A *little* too much?" Diana repeated with shame. "I was disgustingly drunk—"

"You weren't disgusting," Cole argued with a tiny smile tugging at the left corner of his mouth.

Somewhat reassured, but undeterred, Diana added, "I was insensible—!"

"Not entirely," he gallantly contradicted.

"I drank so much I must have passed out in the plane." She

nibbled tentatively at the toast, then took a full bite before putting the slice back down.

"No," he argued reassuringly, "you fell *asleep* after a long, stressful evening."

"Why, it's a miracle I didn't throw up—!" Unconsciously, Diana paused, expecting him to deny that as well.

Instead, he quirked a brow at her. Silence. Assent.

"Oh, I didn't!" she breathed, dropping her face into her hands.

"You felt better afterward," he pointed out kindly.

She let her hands fall away and drew in a deep breath. "Did I do anything else?"

"You told me a few very funny jokes." He helped himself to some eggs.

"I had strange dreams all night—they were so vivid they were more like hallucinations—but I can't remember all of them, and I'm not sure if what I *do* remember actually happened, or if it was part of those dreams. What I mean is, have I forgotten anything else that's important?" She picked up the slice of toast, but instead of taking a bite she looked directly at Cole.

Define 'important,' Cole thought, remembering the way she had ensconced herself in his lap shortly after takeoff on the way back to Houston. While the jet hurtled skyward, she had laughingly told him nursery rhymes with silly, altered endings that made the rhymes seem hilarious.

He remembered the way she had pressed her lips to his for a small kiss, and later when he deepened the kiss, she had slid her hand beneath his tuxedo jacket and curved it around his neck, tentative at first, and then yielding, and then holding his mouth locked to hers. While the plane streaked through the predawn sky at cruising altitude, he had struggled to keep things from getting too far out of hand, while his delectable wife engaged in playful, inebriated, and astonishingly effective tactics aimed at seeing how far his control could be stretched before it broke.

He lost a little of it at thirty-two thousand feet, and stretched out on the sofa, bringing her down on top of him. This morning, he was having problems trying to forget things that she couldn't remember at all. On the other hand, her lack of recall was for the best, since there would never be a repetition of that. "Nothing worth remembering," Cole said.

"I know I did something else. I remember watching the casinos go by from the car and thinking how brilliant the lights were and how exciting it all seemed." She took another bite of the toast and realized she was feeling a little bit better.

She saw Cole's expression shift from gravity to poorly concealed amusement, and in her anxiety, she crossed her arms on the table and leaned forward. "I did something while we were there, didn't I?" she demanded. Her fevered imagination conjured up an image of an inebriated woman in a purple gown trying to climb on stage and dance with the showgirls. Or, dear God, were they *strippers?* "Whatever I did, it was awful, wasn't it?" she said weakly.

"That depends. Are you morally or religiously opposed to gambling?"

"No."

"Then it wasn't awful."

Diana threw up her hands in joyous relief and cast her eyes heavenward. "I *gambled!*" she cried.

In the space of a few hours Cole had seen her switch from solemnity to panic to relief to humor, and it occurred to him that no matter her mood, he thoroughly enjoyed her company. He always had. With a sideways smile, she picked up her fork and took a bite of scrambled egg. "How did I do?"

"Not bad."

"I lost," she concluded with a muffled laugh, her happiness and her appetite remarkably unspoiled by that discovery. When Cole nodded, she reached for the orange juice and drank a little. "How much did I lose?"

"At the roulette table? Or at baccarat? Or at the slot machine?"

She put the glass down, nonplussed. "I lost at all three?"

"Yes, but I stopped you before you got into a high-stakes poker game," he added as he picked up his coffee cup and took a sip.

"How long were we at the casino?"

"Not long—a half hour."

"Then I couldn't have lost very much," Diana said, but something in his carefully noncommittal expression made her pause. "How much did I lose?"

"About three thousand dollars."

She was appalled, but she nodded and said very formally, "I'll write you a check."

225

"That's not necessary."

"I insist. A lady must always pay her own gambling debts," she quoted with humorous finality, as if she'd learned it in finishing school.

She wasn't merely beautiful and intelligent and witty, she was obstinate as hell, Cole realized. But then, so was he. "And a gentleman always pays for the honeymoon," he countered firmly.

Unfortunately, by referring to a thirty-minute stop in a casino as a "honeymoon," he had inadvertently made a mockery of the word and a mockery of the abrupt, unromantic wedding that preceded it. He realized this as soon as he'd said it, and so did Diana. Her smile faded, but he noted that she didn't grow angry or hurt. She simply . . . readjusted to reality.

"I wish you hadn't let me make those phone calls from the plane," she said instead.

"I didn't stop you because it was to your benefit and to your company's benefit for the public to find out as soon as possible that you'd married me." He hadn't stopped her because of that and also because her phone calls to the media had eliminated any possibility that she could back out of their bargain this morning. On this point, however, he wisely kept his thoughts to himself, and she cooperated by changing the subject to something more neutral.

"At least I understand now why I kept dreaming of slot machines. Except that in my dream, the slot machine was gigantic—taller than you and at least five feet wide."

"That wasn't a dream."

"Really?" she said with well-bred interest, but it wasn't a question, it was a courteous statement. She had retreated behind a wall of pleasant reserve, which was her norm, and Cole switched his thoughts to business details, which was his.

"We have some practical details to discuss, but we can do it on the way to see your family."

She nodded, looked at her watch, and got up. "It will be five o'clock by the time we get there. Corey had to retake some shots for the magazine, so the crew should be wrapping up when we get there."

With her hand on the bedroom door she stopped and turned. "Last night I walked off with my grandmother's purse instead of my own. Since I didn't have any identification with me, how did we get married?"

Cole was pouring coffee into his cup and he glanced up, his expression wry. "Actually that caused a minor problem for a few minutes, but the wedding chapel belongs to a man and his wife. She recognized you, and with the help of an extra hundred dollars, her husband agreed that was proof enough of your true identity."

Diana accepted that with a nod, her thoughts turning to the problem of clothing. "It's a good thing I left my car with the valet last night, or I wouldn't be able to get into my apartment to change clothes."

Chapter 31

A HALF HOUR LATER, SHE'D CHANGED INTO A PAIR OF WHITE LINEN slacks, white sandals, and a lilac silk shirt that she'd knotted in the front at the waist, and they were on the way to the family house on Inwood Drive.

Because she still was feeling a tad under the weather, Cole took the wheel of her car, and as he drove along familiar boulevards lined with gracious mansions set back among the trees, he felt a strong sense of déjà vu combined with a feeling of total unreality. Of all the bizarre, unpredictable twists and turns his life had taken in the years since he'd last driven down these streets, the oddest by far was to return here with Diana Foster sitting beside him—as his wife.

Oblivious to the direction of his thoughts, Diana was concentrating on the best way to break the news to her family. Somehow, she had to portray an optimism she didn't completely feel and simultaneously convince them that last night's marriage was not only sane but ideal.

She was working out her strategy, rehearsing her opening speech, and deciding on the right location to give it when Cole reached into the inside pocket of his navy blazer and extracted a folded sheet of hotel stationery. As he handed it across to her, he said in a businesslike voice, "While you were sleeping this morning, I wrote out a summary of the terms of our verbal agreement. Basically, it sets out that our marriage will last for one year. At the end of that period, we will obtain a quiet, amicable divorce with neither of us making any financial claims against the other."

A bicyclist was in the middle of their lane when they rounded a curve, and Cole paused as he went around her; then he continued, "Naturally, any gifts we give each other, such as our wedding rings or the necklace I bought you last night, will remain the property of the recipient."

"Wedding rings?" Diana echoed blankly. "What wedding rings?"

He reached into the outside pocket of his jacket and extracted two plain, wide gold bands, holding them toward her in his palm. "These wedding rings."

"When did you get those?"

"The Silver Bells Wedding Chapel is a fully equipped, full-service establishment. I bought them there from the owner, and we exchanged them during the ceremony." With a sigh of mock dismay he chided, "How quickly some of us forget the tender, poignant moments in life."

Diana took the smaller of the two rings from his palm and held it between thumb and forefinger, puzzled by his description of the event as poignant and tender. "*Was* it a tender moment?" she asked, peering at his profile.

A smile quirked his lips. "You seemed to think it was. You cried during most of the ceremony."

"I always cry a little bit at weddings," Diana admitted ruefully.

"At your own wedding," he ungallantly said, "you cried so hard you had to stop twice to blow your nose."

Diana's initial horror gave way to a sudden burst of hilarity at the picture of a drunken bride in a purple gown bawling her heart out and blowing her nose. She slumped down in her seat, her body quaking with laughter. "Before the ceremony, you were deeply distressed about the decor." Diana laughed harder.

A few moments later, however, Cole's brisk words made her

sober and straighten. "Look over my list, and see if you have any questions or comments," he instructed.

Diana unfolded the sheet of paper and read what he'd written. His handwriting was a bold scrawl, and yet it was remarkably legible.

"It's pretty straightforward."

"Very," Diana murmured.

"Your attorney can use it to draw up the formal document. As soon as it's drafted, have it faxed to me at my home in Dallas."

With his left palm on the steering wheel, he took a slender wallet out of his pocket and extracted a white business card from it. He handed his card to her, and Diana realized with a twinge of alarm that she'd actually married a man whose phone number and address she did not know.

"Do you have an attorney whom you can trust to handle your end of this discreetly and quickly?"

Diana couldn't possibly turn this over to the sedate law firm that represented Foster Enterprises. Lawyers gossiped among themselves, and even if she had the nerve to confess what she'd done to one of those lawyers, she couldn't trust them to keep the titillating information completely confidential. The only attorney she could trust, personally and professionally, was Doug Hayward. Doug had given up law for politics and in a real legal battle, he'd be no match for the kind of attorneys Cole was likely to have, but this wasn't a battle, this was a simple agreement.

Postnuptial agreements had become fairly common, she knew, though she was pretty certain they were usually preceded by prenuptials. According to what she'd read and heard, wealthy middle-aged people with children from an earlier marriage, or charitable bequests to protect, frequently used them when they remarried because they held up much better than prenuptials in court.

Charles Hayward, Doug's father, would probably know lots of friends who'd used them, and he'd have good advice to offer Diana and Doug. His advice and help had been invaluable to Diana after her father died.

"I know someone," she said after a prolonged moment.

Cole turned off Inwood onto the long treelined drive that led to the house Diana had lived in when he knew her as a young girl, and

230

he saw several cars in front of the house. "It looks like your family has a lot of company."

"The Explorer is Corey's and the BMW is Spence's. Spence is here because we try to have Sunday dinner as a family when we can. The other cars belong to Corey's assistants. Corey's redoing a shoot she wasn't happy with."

Chapter 32

*T*HE FOSTER'S HOME WAS A STATELY PLACE, MUCH LIKE MANY OTHERS Cole had been in that were built in the late fifties and early sixties, but the rooms he glimpsed as she led him across the foyer and down a hall toward the rear of the house had a subtly different ambience. Some of the rooms were formal and beautiful, some were casual and cozy, but *all* of them were inviting.

The kitchen was huge and had obviously been redesigned for very serious cooking projects, with two commercial stoves, two sinks, an oversize refrigerator and freezer, and an abundance of copper pots and pans hanging overhead.

A middle-aged woman who Cole assumed was either cook or housekeeper or both was slicing summer squash at a chopping block, and she nodded toward the back door. "Everyone is still working in the back," she told Diana, and then in a mildly irritated voice she added, "Your grandpa told me his new organic fertilizer is producing much bigger squash. Why does he keep growing squash, squash, and more squash? We don't have enough space or enough recipes for more squash. The freezers are full of squash casseroles

232

and squash-everything-else. Unless your mother and grandma can come up with a recipe for squash ice cream, we can't use any more squash!"

"We can always paint it," Diana replied imperturbably.

Cole was still trying to adjust to the idea of painting squash when he followed her outside into another world. The back lawn was at least three acres in size, and every segment of it was charmingly designed to please the eye and yet be of use in the family business. People were everywhere.

While two photo assistants waited on the sidelines with lights and reflectors, Corey was in the middle of a vast vegetable garden, posing her grandmother, who was dressed in a parka and holding a huge pumpkin in her hands. Piles of dried oak leaves were spread about her feet. Mary Foster, with a jar of paint in one hand and brush in the other, was touching up the face of a scarecrow. All three women seemed startled to see Cole with Diana, but not displeased, he noted. Which meant they hadn't heard the news yet.

"We'll be finished in two minutes," Corey called. "I just want one more shot."

Spence was standing beside a blanket, dividing his attention between his wife and the identical twins who were working their way to the blanket's edge in pursuit of a huge ball. He turned and smiled at Diana. Then he looked at Cole and nodded, but he did not smile.

"We're working on the October issue right now," Diana explained, nodding toward the garden.

"Your grandmother must be roasting in that parka," Cole observed.

Tables had been set out on the right side of the lawn near a workshop that looked more like a storybook cottage. At one of the tables, two women were putting down wreaths and centerpieces made of pinecones, berries, and what looked to Cole liked painted vegetables. Vegetables, he realized with some amusement, actually were very attractive when painted.

At another table a young man and woman were vigorously removing tarnish from a pile of large, old, brass door knockers. Three doors in various stages of refinishing were leaning against the side of the workshop. "We're doing a feature on 'Giving Doors a Personality,'" Diana provided. As she spoke, two more young men with paint-stained clothes emerged from the workshop and began carrying the doors inside.

"Be careful with those doors, boys," Henry Britton called out from his worktable in front of the cottage workshop. The space on top of the table and below it was covered with drawings anchored against the breeze by wooden boxes of various shapes and sizes with no particular use that Cole could discern.

When Henry saw Diana and Cole, he called to them to come over. He wiped off his hand to shake Cole's; then he turned to his granddaughter, his weathered face and light brown eyes intent on what he had to tell her. "I've been thinking about this for weeks, Diana, and I'm certain I'm right. Take a look."

Diana peered at the drawings and then at the small wooden boxes he was making. "What are they?" she asked, trying very hard to concentrate.

"They're birdhouses! Birdhouses would be a big hit!" Henry predicted. "Not just ordinary ones, Diana, but birdhouses that look like little castles and cottages with thatched roofs and miniature barns and Southern plantation houses. I could fix up some modern-looking ones, too, that look like town houses and apartment buildings."

Corey and her mother and grandmother had finished in the garden and were close enough to hear the last of his words. "Henry Britton," his wife exclaimed, "did I just hear you actually say you intend to build apartment buildings for birds?"

"I said no such thing. I was talking to Diana about drawing up a bunch of designs for birdhouses."

"We already featured birdhouses two years ago, Dad," Diana's mother said, sounding a little stressed-out by the constant need for originality.

"These aren't birdhouses for birds, Mary," he said, sounding a little frustrated himself. "These would look like birdhouses, only they're ornamental. You set them in your garden for decoration. Hell's bells," he said, slapping his leg in enthusiasm. "They'd be cute as the dickens all lined up in a row in a garden—"

His wife was unimpressed. "Sort of like a suburb for birds, you mean?"

He gave her a testy look. "Corey could set them around in just the right way, with some of my pink and orange impatiens behind them and little green shrubs here and there. Corey could get some great photographs for the magazine out of a setup like that."

"I just don't think miniature birdhouses that birds can't use would go over very well with Diana's subscribers."

"Yes, they would. Every Christmas, you spend two days under the Christmas tree, lining up miniature ceramic houses so they look like one of those Norman Rockwell towns, but nobody's going to live in those either. I can't see why my little houses wouldn't look just as nice outdoors in the summertime."

Everyone paused and looked at Diana for a deciding opinion.

Although Corey was responsible for the artistic presentation of the magazine, and the others were responsible for coming up with the projects that were featured in it, it was Diana who carried the full weight of responsibility for satisfying their subscribers, which, in turn, directly affected the ultimate financial success or failure of the magazine, ergo the family business.

Diana had to force herself to concentrate on this instead of the announcement of her marriage. "Actually," she said after a pause, "I think Grandpa is right. We might even want to use garden ornaments and decorations as the main feature in one of the issues."

Satisfied with that, Henry returned to a more pleasant subject and looked hopefully at Diana. "Last night you and I talked about doing another issue featuring organic gardening. Organic gardening is always popular. Maybe we could combine my birdhouses and some other garden ornaments, like you suggested, with organic gardening.

"Well," her grandfather said, interrupting her mental wanderings, "if you like the idea, I'll start putting together a list of article ideas tomorrow."

Diana was trying to decide where to assemble the family for the meeting. "That sounds good, Grandpa," she said. "Let's do that," she added, which made her mother and her grandmother and Corey all stop and gaze at her in amazement. "But we already featured organic gardening not long ago."

"Oh, that's right. I forgot," Diana said absently. "That was for vegetables and fruits. We can do this one on flowers." She looked at the group and plunged in. "I'd like to talk to all of you in the living room for a few minutes."

Corey glanced up at the angle of the sun. "I've been waiting all afternoon to catch the sunlight coming through those branches the way it is now. Give me ten minutes to get Spence and the twins under the tree on a blanket. This shot is for me."

"Take thirty minutes," Diana said, realizing that it would be that long before the crew left and her family had time to get cleaned up.

"By the way," Corey added as she headed off toward her camera and tripod, "Cindy Bertrillo called and Glenna took the message. Cindy said to call her as soon as you can. She has to confirm something with you. She didn't say what it was."

Cindy was in charge of the magazine's public relations department. She was the person the press called whenever they wanted to confirm something, and Diana was very certain what it was that Cindy was being asked to confirm. "I'll call her later," Diana said.

Cole had stopped to watch the controlled bustle on the lawn as the crew from the magazine began putting the equipment away. "I've heard the terms 'family business' and 'cottage industry' before," he said with quiet admiration, "but I've never seen or imagined anything like this. You should be very proud of what you've created."

"I capitalized on it and marketed it," Diana corrected him, "but I didn't create it." She tipped her head toward her family. *"They* created it."

He didn't believe her, Diana knew, and it would take too long to explain to him that long before Diana's father had married Henry Britton's daughter and whisked her and his new stepdaughter off to his white-pillared mansion in Houston, the entire Britton family had been the consummate do-it-yourselfers.

Chapter 33

A LL RIGHT," DIANA SAID WITH A NERVOUS SMILE AS SHE LED THE small contingent into a formal living room with a grand piano at one end and a large fireplace with a raised marble hearth at the other. "Everyone get nice and comfortable."

In the middle of the room, separated by a carved mahogany coffee table, stood two long sofas upholstered in a rich burgundy and gold stripe, strewn with an assortment of plump pillows covered in jewel-toned plaids that made the sofas, and the room, seem more inviting and warm. With an expansive wave of her arm, Diana gestured toward the sofas and the pair of chairs beside them that faced the piano; then she walked over and stood near the keyboard.

Cole positioned himself at the opposite end of the piano, where he could participate in the proceedings if necessary without actually being in the middle of them; then he watched with amusement as Diana leaned against the piano for support, nervously rubbed her palms together, and generally behaved as if she genuinely dreaded the effect of her announcement on her family. From Cole's point of view, which was based on his own upbringing and adult experiences, Diana was a grown woman who had weighed the risks, made her decision, and shouldn't expect either support or even any real interest from her family.

Diana's mother and grandmother sat on one of the sofas, and Corey and Spencer Addison seated themselves on the opposite one. Diana's grandfather elected to remain standing, however, and rested his hands on the back of one of the chairs facing Diana. "No, no, Grandpa—please sit," she said.

"I'd rather stand."

"You'd better be sitting when you hear this," Diana mumbled.

"This must be one great big surprise you have in store for us," Henry teased her as he sat on the chair. Having followed her wishes, he beamed an expectant smile at her, clearly harboring the mistaken belief that Diana's visible nervousness came from excitement and that whatever she had to say couldn't possibly be anything but pleasing. "Okay, we're all here, and we're all sitting down," he pointed out. "Fire away."

Diana looked around at the attentive faces of her assembled family, rubbed her palms against her thighs, and admitted with a choked laugh, "I haven't felt this nervous since I was sixteen and had to stand here and tell everyone that I'd wrecked the new car Dad had just given me for my birthday."

Corey realized that Diana's normally unshakable composure was failing her badly, and she made a quick effort to give her more time to compose herself. "Actually, Diana didn't wreck the car," she confessed with an impenitent smile. "I wrecked it that time."

Diverted, the family turned and gaped at her in confused disbelief, but Diana's grandmother was more interested in the present. Trying to make a connection between wrecked cars and family meetings in the living room called by Diana, she furrowed her brow and said, "Is your car wrecked again, Diana? Is that why you've called us in here?"

"My car is fine," Diana said. *My life is a wreck,* she amended silently, then glanced sideways at Cole. He lifted his brows in a challenge to her to get down to business, and Diana automatically obeyed. "Okay, here goes," she said, directing her full attention to her mother and grandparents. "Last night, after the auction, I introduced Cole to you for the first time, remember?"

Her mother and grandparents nodded in unison.

"However, even though you hadn't met Cole before, the fact is that Corey and Spence and I have known him for a long time. A long, long time," Diana emphasized in a lame attempt to lessen the implausibility of her hasty marriage by emphasizing the length of time she'd actually known him. "To us—to Corey and me at least—Cole is actually an old family friend!"

"We know all about that, dear," Diana's mother said. Turning to Cole with a pleasant smile, she said, "Last night, on our way home, Corey told us all about who you are. Who you were, I mean. She told us you used to work for the Hayward family, and that she and Diana and Spence all used to see you there when they visited."

Cole noted that she discreetly avoided connecting him with the Haywards' stable, but Diana's grandmother evidently saw no reason for half-truths or evasions: "Diana used to talk about you when she was a teenager," she added enthusiastically. "She told us you lived in the Haywards' stable and took care of their horses, and that you didn't have enough food to eat and were always hungry. I used to help Diana pack up those bags of food she brought you whenever she went to the Haywards'."

To Cole's amusement, the other occupants of the room were so distressed by her tactlessness that they all leapt to his rescue in a rushed flurry of compliments and justifications that flew around the room like a volleyball during a tournament, with Corey making the opening serve: "Gram, the Haywards' stable is much grander than most peoples' homes!" She looked expectantly at her husband.

Spence fielded Corey's conversational ball: "When I was in college," Spence said, "I used to come over here and stuff myself on whatever they were having for dinner. I think an enormous appetite goes along with being male and under twenty, don't you, Henry?" Spencer asked, slapping the ball to his wife's grandfather.

Henry was older and a little clumsy, but he lunged manfully for the ball and managed to keep it in play: "No doubt about it. I've never been able to resist Rose's cooking myself. Not only that, but I've slept in our barn with a horse, too. When our old mare got sick and stopped eating, Corey and I slept out there together one night, because we didn't want Pearl to die alone. Rose brought our dinner down to us, and we shared some of our dessert with Pearl. The taste of that baked apple must have given her a reason to go on living, because after she ate it, she got to her feet and stayed there.

"After that, she was so partial to apples that she'd start nickering the moment she saw one, and she lived to be twenty-two!"

Greatly satisfied with his effort, he slapped his knee and beamed at his unsuspecting daughter, sending the conversational ball flying straight at her. "Well, Mary?" he prodded when she looked flustered. "Remember how partial Robert was to whatever Mother cooked or canned? He just couldn't eat enough of whatever it was."

"That's true!" Mrs. Foster said, belatedly rushing forward to assist the home team. "My husband gained twenty pounds after we came to live here with him. He used to have a big dinner and then sneak down for midnight snacks, even though he wasn't truly hungry. Diana knew that, and I'm sure that's why she wanted to bring you all that extra food, Cole."

Having made her successful play in the verbal volleyball game, she looked about for someone who hadn't participated yet, realized her mother was the only possibility, and quickly decided it was wiser to send the ball out of bounds instead. She aimed it straight at Cole on the sidelines. "You know how fanciful teenage girls can be," she told him with a smile. "You were probably stuffed to your ears and wishing Diana would stop bringing those bags of food, while Diana was convinced she was rescuing you from starvation. You were being polite and Diana was being . . . an overimaginative teenage girl."

Everyone looked expectantly at Cole, as if waiting for an official decision on the success of the game. When he realized it, he quickly declared an end to the match and issued his ruling: "Diana was very kind, and I appreciated her kindness."

Until then, Rose Britton, had observed the entire scene with the innocent impartiality of an uninvolved spectator, but she shook her head in amused disagreement with Cole's verdict. "Diana has always been thoughtful and kind, but the truth is, she had a crush on you! That's why she lugged all those sacks of groceries and leftovers to you all the time. We all knew how she felt about you. Although," she confided with a reminiscent smile as she leaned a little forward, "Diana wasn't nearly as obvious as Corey was about Spencer. By the time Corey was sixteen, she'd wallpapered her bedroom with Spencer's pictures and turned the place into a shrine!

Diana was much more secretive, but it was my opinion that she was probably as crazy about you as Corey was about Spencer. She had all the symptoms of a girl in love, and we thought—"

"Mother!" Mrs. Foster said in a low, imploring voice. "This isn't the time or place for that."

"The truth's the truth, right occasion or not," Rose Britton said; then she looked to Diana, of all unlikely people, for support. "Was I mistaken, dear?"

Diana's initial dismay over her grandmother's commentary had already given way to relief. She'd been trying for hours to think of something to say to make her abrupt marriage to Cole seem less unjustifiably impulsive, and she seized on the fragile excuse Gram had just inadvertently provided her. "No, you were absolutely right, Gram!" she exclaimed in a voice that sounded too eagerly enthusiastic for what was, after all, ancient history. "In fact I had a tremendous crush on him!" she added, stealing a quick glance at Cole to see how he was reacting to that piece of news, but his expression hadn't altered by so much as a flicker. Completely impervious, he stood with his arms loosely folded over his chest, his feet planted slightly apart, watching her. A little startled by his lack of response, she returned to the main issue. "Now that you all remember how I felt about Cole when I was young, then what I have to tell you might not come as such a—a gigantic surprise. . . ." The people she loved most in the world gazed at her in happy expectation of hearing something nice, and Diana faltered.

"Go ahead," Spence urged with an encouraging grin. "What's your surprise?"

Diana drew a steadying breath and plunged in. "Well, last night, after the auction, Cole and I danced for a little while. And then . . . and then . . ."

"And then?" Grandpa prodded when she seemed to choke on the end of the sentence.

"And then we went up to Cole's suite, and we had a drink, and . . . we talked . . . about things." Diana glanced at the coffee table between the sofas, wishing it would rise up on end on its legs and rush forward to shield her.

"And then what happened?" Gram prodded, looking expectantly from Diana to Cole.

Diana confessed the rest in a halting torrent of words: "And then we . . . left the hotel . . . and we . . . flew to Las Vegas . . . and we . . . got married!"

The taut silence that followed her announcement tore through Diana's nervous system like nails scraping over a chalkboard. "I know you're all a little shocked right now," she told the five faces that were staring at her in incredulous horror.

Her grandfather was the first to recover and react. Aiming a look of pure, undiluted loathing at Cole, he said bitterly, "Mister, you must be some great talker. Especially when you get a lady alone in your hotel room. Especially if the lady's heart's just been broken and if she's had more to drink than she's used to having."

"No, now wait!" Diana interrupted, stunned by her mild grandfather's unprecedented anger and determined to take matters in hand. "It wasn't like that at all, Grandpa. Cole and I made a business arrangement that will benefit both of us personally as well as benefiting Foster Enterprises. By marrying Cole, I salvaged a little of my personal pride, but more important, I salvaged our magazine's public image. Cole has a problem, too, that being married to me will solve. He realized how beneficial a quick marriage would be for both of us, and then we discussed the terms and agreed on a temporary arrangement that would suit us both."

"What sort of 'temporary arrangement'?" Spence demanded of Cole in a hostile voice.

"Marriage for one year—in name only—for business purposes," Cole retorted, matching Spence's tone.

"That's it?" Spence said, sounding more confused now than angry.

"That's it," Cole said.

"Just exactly what is your problem that marriage to Diana is supposed to solve?" Spence asked.

"It's none of your damned business."

"Maybe not," Grandpa said tersely, "but it is *my* business, young man."

Diana had never imagined things would go this badly, and she opened her mouth to plead for calm, but to her surprise, Cole capitulated to her grandfather with glacial courtesy, but courtesy nonetheless. "To put it succinctly, I have an elderly uncle—a surrogate father, actually—who is seriously ill and desperately, obsessively, determined to see me become a husband and father before he dies."

"And just how do you intend to become a father in a name-only-for-business-purposes marriage?"

"I don't," Cole stated flatly. "But he doesn't need to know that, and unfortunately, he won't live long enough to discover it on his own."

"You've got everything all figured out, haven't you?" Grandpa said with biting disdain; then he looked at Diana. "What I can't understand is how you let this conniving schemer talk you into going along with all this."

"He didn't talk me into anything, Grandpa. I told you, I agreed to marry Cole because it will solve some very difficult problems—his problems, and mine, and ours," she emphasized, lifting her hand and gesturing toward all of them.

"Having you marry some conniving, smooth-talking cad you haven't seen in years isn't going to benefit your family one damn bit!" Grandpa fired back.

"Yes it will!" Diana insisted, so caught up in her explanation that she failed to notice she was inadvertently agreeing that Cole was a "conniving, smooth-talking cad." "Anything that benefits Foster Enterprises benefits all of us, because we *are* Foster Enterprises. That's the way the public sees it, too. We've all had so much media exposure that the public feels like they know all of us. They watch you and Gram and Mom and Corey on cable television on *The Foster Way,* and they love not only what you do, but who you are. Their letters prove it. They write about how much they enjoy seeing you tease Gram and call her 'Rosie.' They love seeing Mom work with you and the affection you all have for each other. And their favorite program of all time was when Corey brought the twins on the show to demonstrate techniques for photographing babies. They enjoyed the demonstration and learned some tricks, but they loved it when Molly reached out her arms for Gram to be held, and when little Mary made a grab for one of Mom's cookies. However, if you suddenly gave Gram a black eye, or Corey got arrested for drunkenness, or Mom got busted for shoplifting—and the media found out and turned it into a circus—then your program's ratings would fall like a rock. For the same reason, when Dan jilted me and it hit the news media, it made me, and everything I represent, look pathetic and foolish. Do you understand now?"

"No, I don't!" Grandpa retorted impatiently.

"Then let me make it clearer: the public associates the four of you mostly with *The Foster Way*, but they associate me almost exclusively with the magazine, and no matter how you look at it, the theme behind every article in *Foster's Beautiful Living* magazine, and every one of Corey's wonderful photographs in it, is always the same: domestic beauty and harmony. And that's where the problem lies for me. As the magazine's publisher and spokesperson, I should believe in that theme and live up to it, but I don't have a husband or a baby and, as one reporter discovered somehow last year, I spend more time at our offices than at my apartment. If you'll remember, at the end of that newspaper piece, the reporter remarked that I'd make a better representative for *Working Woman* or *Vogue* or *Bazaar* than for *Foster's Beautiful Living*. And that's while I was still engaged to Dan. Once he jilted me—and for an eighteen-year-old—for an Italian heiress, my credibility and prestige with the public took an enormous blow, aided of course by a whole lot of humiliating media conjecture, and that would have directly affected the magazine. First we'd lose subscribers and, soon after, we'd lose advertisers." Finished, she looked at her grandfather, who didn't hesitate to voice his personal opinion about that possibility.

"If we've got subscribers and advertisers who are fickle enough to drop the magazine just because you picked the wrong man to trust and love, then the heck with them. There's plenty more out there where they came from. Just let the old ones go and get some new ones!"

"Let them go? Get some new ones?" Diana sputtered in disbelief as frustration and turmoil finally drove her to tell them things she'd hidden from them for nearly a decade: "None of you realize how hard it's been for me to keep Foster Enterprises thriving and growing, because I didn't want you to know. My God, I've invested my entire adult life in that company. I was only twenty-two and right out of college when Daddy died." She looked up at the ceiling for a long moment to keep herself from crying. "I didn't know anything about anything, except that, somehow, I had to find a way to maintain our standard of living and keep us all together. I know all of you thought I was brilliant and capable and confident when I convinced you that we could handle a catering business and then branch out into related businesses right away, but I wasn't. I was scared and I was desperate!"

Diana was so intent on making them understand what led up to her decision to marry Cole that she didn't notice the growing sorrow and regret in her family's expressions. Gentling her voice, she held out her hands as if asking for understanding. "I know you've always assumed that because Daddy and his friends were all wealthy and successful, and because I grew up among them, that I had inherited some sort of instinctive ability to start up a successful business, but I didn't."

When she paused for a moment, her grandmother reminded her in a quiet, gentle voice, "And yet, that's exactly what you did."

Diana's overwrought emotions veered from near-tears to near-laughter. "It was a fluke!" she said. "What I 'inherited' from my upbringing was a healthy fear of poverty. That, and a firsthand knowledge of how callous and cold wealthy people can become when one of their own goes broke. There's a stigma associated with it, and I didn't want Corey to discover it the hard way. I didn't want any of you to experience it. I wasn't some sort of daring entrepreneur, I was scared of the alternative, and so I took a risk, an enormous risk. All we had was this house, and I was so scared when I mortgaged it to start up the business that I threw up when I got home. I just couldn't think of any other way to keep us together and go on living as we had."

She paused and took a deep breath before she confessed the true extent of her youthful incompetence. "I made some costly mistakes, particularly in the beginning, that I will always regret. In order to raise money from private investors, I sold them stock in the company, stock that's now worth a fortune in comparison to the money I got for us. I've made other mistakes, too, like holding us back out of fear several times when I should have pushed forward."

Finished with the worst of her admissions, she said ruefully, "Everything I've achieved with Foster Enterprises hasn't been the result of genius; it's been the result of endless worry and work, combined with a whole lot of luck!"

The only person who didn't look completely taken aback by Diana's revelations was Cole, yet he was the most stunned of all. He'd assumed that *Foster's Beautiful Living* magazine had started out as a hobby, a whim when Robert Foster was still alive—a self-published vanity magazine that the Foster family had originally used to show off the family's unusual living style, showcase Corey's exceptional photographic ability, and give Diana a chance to dabble at being a publisher when she graduated from college. Never, ever, would he have imagined that the magazine had been created out of financial necessity and daring, not boredom and unlimited wealth. Until that moment, he'd also assumed that Diana was probably Foster Enterprises' figurehead, not its founder.

What astonished him most of all was that she'd undertaken the enormous risk and responsibility when she was only twenty-two. Twenty-two. He'd been the same age when he struck out on his own, but he'd already led a hard life by then; he was used to scandal and hardship and opposition. Diana, on the other hand, had always struck him as being delicate and sheltered and endearingly prim.

In the uneasy silence that occurred while the family came to terms with the second major shock of a decade, they seemed to have forgotten that Cole was there, and normally he would have preferred not to be. He knew he could put an end to the discussion by either excusing himself or politely reminding them that such personal family matters were better discussed with family and not outsiders. He had, in fact, perfected that tactic and used it often, whenever a woman he was seeing attempted to draw him into a discussion about her children, her parents, or her ex-husband and his family. Discussions among family members or about family members invariably made him feel like an alien being who had sprung from a rock in a cave and had spent his first two decades on some uninhabited planet.

His own youth hadn't given him the slightest insight into normal family dynamics nor even a glimpse of how members of a loving family interacted.

Henry Britton finally spoke, his words springing from guilt and hurt. "Diana, you didn't need to put yourself through all that for our sakes. We weren't your dependents, after all. Your grandmother and mother and I could have gone back to Long Valley and lived as we used to live. Corey could have gone to college nights and worked for a photographer during the day."

Cole expected Diana to indulge in some sort of righteous outburst at having her efforts and sacrifices treated as unnecessary, but although her voice was teary, she smiled softly and shook her head. "You don't understand, Grandpa. I couldn't let that happen without at least putting up a fight. Corey has a rare gift, but she had to have a chance to show it off, and she might never have gotten that chance if she'd had to support herself by taking candid wedding shots for some local photographer who'd take all the credit and pay her peanuts in return."

Diana transferred her gaze to her mother and grandparents, and her voice grew heavy with emotion. "None of you realize how remarkably talented you are. You all have such amazing gifts that millions of people have fallen in love with you and everything you represent. The three of you still think of what you do as sort of a hobby, as 'puttering' in the gardens or in the workshop or in the kitchen, but it's much more than that. You see beauty in simple things and show other people how to see it, too. You prove to people that there's pleasure and harmony to be found in the creative act. You've reminded people that the job of a true hostess isn't to show off her home or her possessions, but rather to make each and every one of her guests feel special and important. People watch you on television, working together and laughing together, and they believe in you."

Diana's voice shook with feeling as she added, "The four of you have made a *real difference* in the attitudes and priorities of a huge number of people—men and women, young and old. The politicians all talk about a return to traditional values and getting back to basics, but you have shown people a lovely, simple route that will take them there."

Finished with every explanation and argument she could think of, she returned to the original reason for the meeting: "Whether or not you believe all that, you *have* to believe me when I tell you that Cole did not coerce me into marrying him. In my opinion, marrying him was the best of all possible alternatives, and I'm glad he trusted me enough to ask me. I know he'll live up to his part of the bargain, and I intend to live up to mine."

Diana sensed instinctively that the best thing to do for now was to let her family discuss the matter among themselves and come to terms with it. She looked at Cole and said, "We'd better go now."

Still grappling with his surprise over Diana's gentle but emphatic support of him in opposition to her family, Cole followed right behind her, but when they neared the doorway, Diana's grandmother issued an invitation in the form of a gruff challenge: "Do you intend to at least stay for Sunday dinner, young man?"

Diana refused in an attempt to spare Cole any more of an ordeal. "Not today," she said. "Another time, maybe," but to her surprise, Cole turned to Gram with an equally challenging smile and said, "I wasn't aware that I'd been invited."

"You are now," she announced.

Mary Foster seconded the invitation with quiet firmness. "Please have dinner with us."

Henry made it unanimous, though his voice was gruff. "You haven't had any of Rose's cooking in a long time."

"Thank you," Cole said to all of them. He glanced at Corey, and he thought he saw in her eyes a tentative offer of friendship. "In that case, I'll be happy to stay."

Diana decided it was still best to take Cole outside so that her family could talk freely among themselves and come to terms with her unorthodox marriage. They had already begun to change their attitude in the living room and the proof was their invitation to Cole to stay for dinner. She had every reason to think that the meal would be a pleasant one for Cole, but since he had had no way of knowing that, she'd been both surprised and pleased when he accepted their invitation.

Chapter 34

OUTSIDE, THE WORKTABLES AND EQUIPMENT HAD ALL BEEN PUT AWAY, and without their presence to distract the eye, the back lawn had been restored to its normal state of manicured, semitropical splendor.

Palm trees surrounded by fragrant gardenias leaned gracefully over chaise longues at poolside, their giant fronds rustling softly in the breeze. Stately clumps of crepe myrtle dripping with blossoms added dignified splashes of light pink and white, while the pink and red asters covered themselves in exuberant glory and the hibiscus bushes flaunted exotic flowers the size of salad plates in colors ranging from tangerine to yellow to red.

Since Diana knew that men were usually enthralled by her grandfather's workshop, with its array of tools, equipment, mill-work, and fine woods, she took Cole there first. He pretended to be interested in everything she showed him, but she could tell that he wasn't, so she invited him to stroll through the greenhouse and then the cutting gardens tucked into the back corners of the lawn.

When he still seemed distracted, she decided that the scene in the living room had darkened his mood far more than he'd let show. In view of some of the things that had been said, she couldn't blame him. Deciding to bring it out in the open, Diana stopped on the lawn near the pool. Leaning her shoulders against a palm's smooth, thick trunk she said simply, "I'm sorry about what was said inside. Please try to make allowances for my grandfather's age."

"I did," he said dryly.

"But you're still embarrassed," Diana surmised.

He shook his head. "I'm not embarrassed, Diana."

"Are you angry?" she asked, studying his features for a clue.

"No."

"Then what are you?"

"I'm impressed."

"By what?" Diana asked, taken aback.

"By you," he said solemnly.

She rolled her eyes in laughing disbelief. "For a man who's impressed, you've been looking awfully grim."

"Probably because it doesn't happen very often, and I'm not used to the feeling."

He was serious, Diana realized, and she was momentarily speechless with pleasure and surprise.

"By the way," he added, "that isn't my 'grim' look."

"It isn't?" she said, still glowing from the compliment. "What's your 'grim look' like?"

"I don't think you want to know."

"Oh, go ahead. Let me see it—"

Cole was so unaccustomed to being treated with teasing impertinence that it startled a shout of laughter from him, and Diana thought there was a rusty quality to it.

"You haven't asked me what about you impressed me. . . ."

She pretended to ponder that. "Well, I know it wasn't Grandpa's workshop. You called a beautiful piece of mahogany 'a board.' And I don't think you know a hybrid rose from a hibiscus either."

"You're right on both counts. But I do know a little bit about business. I realized your magazine was a success, but I had no idea you'd managed to create national personalities out of your stepmother and her parents. At the very least, that's an amazing feat!"

"I didn't create personalities for them," Diana said with a shake of her head and a wry, affectionate smile. "They were unique when I met them, and they haven't changed a bit. They were forerunners of a coming trend."

"What do you mean by that?"

"About a month after my father and stepmother were married, they took Corey and me to Long Valley, and I met my grandparents for the first time. Although I wasn't familiar with the term at the time, they were the consummate 'do-it-yourselfers.' During the day, my grandfather was a surveyor for a town with a population of about seven thousand. But he spent his evenings and weekends in his garden, where he experimented with ways to grow the biggest and best flowers and vegetables in west Texas without resorting to chemical fertilizers or insecticides.

"When he wasn't poring over seed catalogs or searching through books for new or ancient methods of controlling garden insects and diseases, he spent his time in the little workshop behind their house, where he built everything from dollhouses and scaled-down furniture for Corey, to wooden jewelry boxes and rocking chairs for my grandmother. I loved everything about my grandfather's workshop, from the wood shavings on the floor to the smell of the wood stains he used. I remember on that first visit, I stepped on a little piece of wood about an inch square lying beside his workbench. I picked it up and started to toss it into a trash can beside his workbench. He laughed and stopped me and asked me why I wanted to throw away a kiss. I was fourteen at the time and although he was only in his late fifties, he seemed very old to me. So when he described a little chunk of soft wood as a kiss, I was horribly afraid that he was old and—" With her forefinger Diana made a circular motion near her ear, a child's pantomime for *crazy*.

"But he wasn't," Cole ventured with a smile, enjoying her tale and the way the sun glistened in her hair and the way her eyes glowed when she spoke of the people she loved. She was part of America's aristocracy, but there was a wholesomeness and gentleness about her that had always appealed to him—now more than ever, because he realized how rare that combination really was.

"No, he wasn't crazy. He picked up a little carving knife and whittled it into a rounded triangle; then he reached on the shelf and tore off a piece of old silver foil. He wrapped it in the foil and

251

dropped it into my palm. And there it was—a Hershey's 'kiss.' One with no calories, he told me, laughing. There was a bowl of them, I later realized, on a coffee table in the living room."

"How did your grandmother and mother fit into the picture?" Cole asked when Diana turned aside to study a large gardenia bush beside them.

She glanced at him, then returned her attention to the fragrant bush. "My mother worked as a secretary for a manufacturing company when my father met her, but she spent her free time as my grandmother did—cooking and canning and baking to her heart's content."

She snapped off a stem from the bush and turned back to him, her hands cupped around a mound of glossy, dark green leaves with one perfect blossom in the center that looked as soft and white as whipped cream.

"Go on," Cole urged, watching her lift the blossom to her nose.

"My grandmother used the fruits and vegetables that my grandfather grew, and she experimented with recipes that had been handed down in her family from mother to daughter for generations. Every recipe had a name that conjured up friendly ancestors and bygone events along with wonderful tastes and delicious smells. There was Grandma Sarah's three-bean salad and Great-grandmother Cornelia's cherry cinnamon pie. There was harvest-moon cake and wheat-threshers ham biscuits."

Ruefully, she admitted, "Until my first trip to Long Valley, I actually thought strawberries grew on trees and that 'canned goods' meant tin cans with labels on them that said Libby and Green Giant, and that the cans belonged out of sight in a pantry. You can imagine, then, how I reacted to the sight of bright yellow peaches in a glass jar with a label on it depicting a peach tree with a baby sitting beneath it on a blanket, framed in a border of peach blossoms and leaves. To me, it was more than wonderful, it was positively exotic."

He eyed her with amused fascination. "Did you really believe strawberries grew on trees?"

"Why wouldn't I?" she replied, batting her lashes in a comic imitation of a dopey femme fatale. "I thought chicken was created in a carton with plastic wrap. Actually," she admitted sheepishly, "I still prefer to think of it that way"; then she finished her tale: "I thought my grandparents' house was magical. When they came to live with us in Houston, our house began to change in the same wonderful ways, from the back lawn, which had only had a swimming pool and some palm trees when they got there, to the rooms in the house."

Finished, she lifted her hands and offered the flower to him, cradling it in her palms as if it were a priceless treasure. "It's exquisite, isn't it?" she said softly.

You're exquisite, Cole thought, and he shoved his hands into his pockets to avoid the temptation to cradle her hands in his and lift the flower to his face, and then see how her fingers would taste against his lips. Lack of control over his sexual urges had never been a problem for him. Neither had sentimentality, lack of concentration, or the urge to protect a member of the opposite sex beneath the age of sixty. Annoyed with himself for his unprecedented failings in all three of those areas in the last twenty-four hours, he said curtly, "And so you managed to create a market for their talent and philosophy. You were very clever."

She looked a little taken aback by his brusque tone, but she shook her head and her voice remained soft yet firm. Like her body, Cole decided, and glowered at the tree trunk in self-disgust for the direction of his thoughts. "I didn't need to create a market; it was already there and growing bigger each year, though no one seemed to recognize it at the time."

"What do you mean the market was there and growing?"

"We live in a time when Americans are feeling more and more rootless and more separated from each other and their natural surroundings. We live in an impersonal world; we come home to huge subdivisions filled with near-identical houses that are filled with mass-produced everything, from furniture to accessories. Nothing seems to give us a sense of timelessness, of stability, of roots, of real self-expression. People feel a desire to personalize their immediate surroundings, even though they can't personalize the world beyond. The Foster Ideal is about rediscovering the pleasure of, and depth of, one's own creativity."

"I thought women were more interested these days in discovering how high they can climb on the corporate ladder."

"We are, but unlike men, we're learning early that we can't define ourselves by our success or lack of it at work. We want more from life than that, and we have more to give than that."

Cole frowned in confusion. "Are you implying that career-oriented women make up a significant part of your magazine's readership?"

She nodded, clearly enjoying his misguided notions. "The demographics are going to surprise you. Based on our market surveys, sixty-five percent of our readers are college-educated women who have, or have had, successful careers. There's been a growing trend among American career women to postpone having children until they're in their thirties, then to take a hiatus and stay home during their children's formative years. Once they stay home, they throw themselves into raising children with the same dedication and zeal they brought to their former careers. They're high achievers, used to taking charge and making a difference. Some of them worked in creative areas, others in business and finance. They bring all that creative and organizational ability with them to their new roles, except they don't have any outlet for it—other than their homes. They start looking at ways to improve on their homes, to personalize them, and make them more functional or more beautiful. Their need for self-expression combines with a natural desire to conserve money, and presto—they discover *Foster's Beautiful Living.* And through us, they discover themselves."

"That's a pretty tall order for one magazine," Cole said, annoyed with himself for noticing how beautifully she spoke. And moved. And looked.

"Foster Enterprises does much more than publish a monthly magazine. We also publish coffee-table books and market a line of environment-friendly, all-natural cleaning products. We also market do-it-yourself 'kits'—those usually are created either by my grandfather or under his supervision. We started out doing seasonal television specials around the holidays on CBS, and the ratings were so high that CBS wanted to sign us to an exclusive contract for six specials a year. I turned it down because I think we're better off financially, and from an exposure standpoint, doing a weekly program and syndicating it. Our production costs are relatively low, so CBS's offer to underwrite them in return for an exclusive contract didn't appeal as much to me as it would to someone with a more costly show, such as a sitcom or even a talk show."

"It sounds like you've got it made."

"That's how it *sounds,* but that's not how it is. The truth is, we're under tremendous pressure all the time, not only because competitors have been springing up everywhere, trying to carve out a piece of our reputation and our profits for themselves, but because the public seems to hold us to higher standards than our competition, and we have to live up to that. The pressure is intense to constantly come up with newer and better ideas for every issue, every book, every television program than we've done before. We have to look better, be fresher, and offer more than everyone else. That was a lot easier to do before, when we were virtually the only game in town, than it is now. We've actually fired two 'spies' who were planted by competitors."

Cole stared at her in shock. "Somehow, I always associate corporate spying with the areas of electronics or defense."

"I know, so did I—until that happened. The other problem is our public image," Diana said, bringing up Dan without actually referring to him, "and keeping that intact can be a public relations nightmare, not just for me, but for all of us. We have to be careful about everything we say and do, no matter where we are or who we're with."

"All of you?" Cole repeated. "I thought *you* had the biggest problem in that area because you're primarily identified with the magazine."

"I gave you that impression in the living room, but it wasn't completely accurate. We're all identified with it. The thing that made *Foster's Beautiful Living* unique from the very beginning is that it was, and is, a family endeavor, and the public has always been attracted by that. So, unfortunately, has the press, which means we can't even disagree on some minor point when we're filming a program without later reading in some gossip column that 'There's trouble in the Foster paradise' or some other idiotic catchphrase.

"My mother writes a column for the magazine that's one of its most popular features. In it, she reminisces about her girlhood recollections of holidays at her grandparents' homes, the things her mother taught her, and jokes about some of her fears when she gave early parties. She tells stories about Grandma and Grandpa and Corey and me when we were young. All of us have appeared in the photo layouts from time to time, and our readership has come to feel that they know us. The public who buys our magazine, regards all of us as friends. When Corey married Spence, handmade congratulatory cards arrived by the truckload. When the twins were born, readers sent thousands of baby gifts, all handmade. We ended up featuring some of them in a baby issue. When Grandpa broke his leg, more gifts and get-well cards arrived. To the public, we have to remain one big, happy family, living the good life that we expound upon in our issues."

While he listened, Cole was reassessing the extent of her achievements. It truly bothered him that someone who'd accomplished what she had, with very little help, and not much money behind her, thought so little of her accomplishments.

Cole moved forward and braced his hand on the tree trunk above her head. "Tell me something," he said sternly. "Why do you think your mistakes are so enormous that they override your incredible success? In the living room, you downplayed all your own talent and achievements and made your successes seem like nothing more than dumb luck."

She flinched and looked away. "You don't realize how damaging my mistakes have been, or how many I've made."

"Tell me what they were and let me be the judge of that. I promise to be impartial."

Diana was glad of the opportunity to spend time with him, getting reacquainted, but she wished he weren't so insistent about this topic. With a reluctant sigh, she leaned her shoulders against the trunk and gave in. "You got the gist of it in there. I passed up some wonderful opportunities over the years because I didn't want to take a chance—I was afraid of growing too fast."

Cole gazed down at her upturned face, marveling that Diana seemed as genuine and unaffected now as she had been when she was sixteen, and almost wishing that she wasn't. This marriage of theirs was not foolproof, and he didn't want to succeed in what Penworth had failed to do—turn her into a cold cynic.

"I think," she joked, "I'm seeing your grim look right now."

"No," he replied with a half-smile. "That was my impressed look again." Before she could question him about its cause, he replied to her earlier comment. "Businesses fail all the time because someone lets their dreams outpace their financial resources. It's much wiser to err on the side of conservatism."

"I erred on the side of foolishness. The largest of my mistakes was waiting until two years ago to market our own line of gardening and crafts products. When we finally did that, they sold like we were giving them away."

"You must have had reasons for waiting, reasons that seemed sound at the time," Cole pointed out.

"I did. Basically, I was concerned about quality control and start-up and warehousing costs. When we finally launched the product line, it was a huge success, which means we lost a lot of revenue while I was dragging my feet."

"That's hindsight," Cole scoffed.

Diana refused to be patronized. Crossing her arms over her chest, she countered tartly, "Would *you* have waited and deliberated while all the competition was getting a head start?"

At the beginning of the discussion Cole had promised to be truthful. He kept that promise. "No," he admitted.

"There, you see? You have daring and foresight."

"No, I don't 'see.' There's one major difference between my circumstances and yours. When I started Unified Industries, I had sufficient money behind me and more available if I needed it."

She brightened, but just a little. "I did other things I wish to heaven I could undo."

"Like what?" Cole persisted, reacting to some inner need to give her honest consolation even though he knew he was prying.

"As I said in the living room, I practically gave away shares in our new company to raise money to get us started, and later to keep us going."

Cole felt a sudden desire to reach out and touch her cheek, and when he answered her, his voice was unaccustomedly gentle. "I'm amazed that at twenty-two you could talk a bank into investing in your scheme, let alone round up individual investors."

Diana shrugged. "The bank wasn't taking much of a risk, because we put this house up as collateral."

Refusing to let her denigrate her accomplishments, Cole said, "Really? Then how did you get private investors to put up their hard-earned cash on a high-risk, no-potential-profit deal?"

"Oh, that," she said with a rueful laugh. "I packed up my briefcase with official business plans and projections and called on my father's friends. They all thought we were probably going to fail, but they felt sorry for me, so they patted my head and gave me five thousand or ten thousand—figuring all along that they'd at least end up with a tax loss they could use to offset profits on their income taxes. In return for that, I gave them stock certificates in the new company." She sighed and looked away. "In short, I gave away so many pieces of our business that when they were added up, we were down to fifty percent for ourselves."

"Diana, did you have any other choice?"

"If I had dreamed how profitable and successful we'd be now—"

"I'm talking about before, when you were starting up," he said sternly. "Did you have any other way to raise the money you needed?"

She hesitated and then shook her head. "None."

"Then stop blaming yourself for not being psychic and give yourself credit for overcoming hundreds of hurdles all by yourself— hurdles that would eliminate all but the most gifted and flexible entrepreneurs!"

Diana gazed up at his stern, handsome face and realized he was completely serious. "Coming from you, that's high praise indeed."

He grinned then. "Just remember that. I can't have my wife going around belittling her accomplishments. It might reflect badly on my judgment," he joked, "and cause Unified's stock to drop."

"And Wall Street to collapse," Diana put in, her spirits lifting crazily beneath the warmth of his sudden smile.

Chapter 35

STANDING AT THE KITCHEN SINK, WHERE SHE WAS TEARING RED LEAF lettuce into small pieces, Corey studied the couple in the backyard. She was so absorbed with the scene and its possibilities that she jumped when her husband came up behind her and put his arms around her waist. "Where is everyone?" Spence asked.

"I suggested they relax before dinner. Glenna and I have everything under control in here."

"I tucked the girls into bed and gave them a kiss from Mommy. That's where I'd like to be—" he whispered as he nuzzled the side of her neck, "—in bed. With you."

Corey turned her face up for his kiss just as the housekeeper bustled into the kitchen, and they automatically moved apart like guilty teenagers. "Go ahead with what you were doing," Glenna said. "Don't let me interrupt. I'm just trying to get a six-course meal for seven people on the table."

Scowling, Spence watched her bustle off. "Why does she always say something that makes me feel guilty?" Automatically, he picked up a knife and began slicing green peppers into thin strips. "She's been doing that for fifteen years."

Corey smothered a laugh, but her attention was on the scene beyond the window. "She does it because it works so well. You're helping with the salad, aren't you?" She handed him a clean dish towel. "If you tuck this into your waistband, you won't get anything on you."

The former star quarterback from Southern Methodist University eyed the towel askance. "Real men don't wear aprons," he joked.

"Think of it as a loincloth," she suggested.

They worked in companionable silence for several moments, both of them watching the couple in the backyard. Diana was leaning against a palm tree and Cole was in front of her, with his hand on the trunk above her head. Whatever she was saying to him made him laugh. "When we were teenagers," Corey said with a reminiscent smile, "I was so completely infatuated with you that I didn't understand why all the other girls thought Cole Harrison was so incredibly sexy."

"But now you do?"

Corey nodded. "I'd love to photograph him someday. He has a marvelous face—it's all hard planes and tough angles."

"He doesn't look like *GQ* or Brooks Brothers material to me."

"Oh, he isn't! There's way too much raw masculinity about him for a men's clothing model. There's almost a . . . a predatory quality about him."

She dropped a fistful of curly lettuce into the bowl and picked up some long, damp spinach leaves, shredding those as she continued thoughtfully. "I'd photograph him in a setting that suits his looks."

Spence scowled out the window, piqued by Corey's fascination and lavish praise of another man's face. "What sort of setting?" he asked as he began slicing a red onion.

"I think I'd choose some sort of rugged terrain. A desert in the hot sun, maybe, with barren mountains in the background."

Mountains without trees or snow struck Spence as ugly. He nodded agreeably. "That'd work. Suits him perfectly."

Blithely unaware of the negative reason behind his affirmative comment, Corey stopped tearing spinach for a moment and continued studying her subject.

"Tell me something," Spence challenged. "How would you hide his eyes?"

"Why would I want to hide his eyes?" she asked, looking over at her husband.

"Because they are as cold and hard as granite. I watched him in the living room this afternoon, and I don't think there's an ounce of warmth or feeling in him."

"He does seem a lot harder than I remember him being," Corey admitted, "but I don't think he's cold. Think of the way he bought her that necklace at the auction and made everybody think it was love at first sight for him. Now look at the two of them together out there. When I do that, I see Prince Charming who rushed forward at the ball to rescue Cinderella."

In skeptical silence, Spence gazed out the window. Realizing his lack of response was disagreement, Corey said, "What do *you* see when you look at them?"

"I see Little Red Riding Hood smiling at the Big Bad Wolf."

She laughed at the storybook images, but her smile faded as he continued, "Based on everything I've read and heard, I can tell you that the man you're rhapsodizing about is probably the most unfeeling son of a bitch you've ever encountered, as well as being the most ruthless entrepreneur of this decade."

Corey forgot the greens she was shredding. Although she wasn't nearly as astute about the stock market as Spence was, she certainly kept up on national news. "I don't understand why you would say that. Not long ago, it was all over the news that he'd 'masterminded' some sort of buyout of a computer company and they kept calling it 'a major coup.' They didn't say he'd done anything illegal."

"He bought Cushman Electronics, Corey," Spence said flatly. "They called it a coup because, just before Harrison bought it, there were rumors all over Wall Street that Cushman's new computer chip had problems in the testing phase, and Cushman's stock plunged from twenty-eight dollars a share to fourteen dollars. As soon as it fell to fourteen dollars, Unified Industries moved in and Harrison got himself a company worth three hundred million dollars for half that much."

"What's wrong with that? Aren't you supposed to buy stock when it's low, in hopes it will go higher?"

"Who do you think *started* the rumors? And guess who is said to own the independent testing facility that Cushman used to test their chip?"

Corey's jaw dropped. "Has anyone proved that Cole's people falsified test results or started the rumors?"

"If someone can prove either thing, he'll go to jail."

Corey felt a shiver of apprehension, but it was offset somehow by her memory of Cole at the Haywards' stable, gently soothing a sick colt, and the way he seemed to soften now when he looked at Diana in the backyard. "Until someone proves it, it's really nothing but an ugly rumor," she announced.

"Rumors seem to follow him everywhere," Spence pointed out sarcastically. "Whatever Harrison does, he always has some sort of intricate hidden agenda in mind. Last night," he said, "he was in need of a suitable wife to pacify his uncle. He saw the perfect opportunity with Diana, so he played Sir Galahad at the auction—with the press there to record his performance—and while she was glowing with champagne and gratitude, he flew her to Nevada and married her—another 'major coup' for his record. In less than twelve hours, he coerced his way into this family, and now he's driving all of *us* crazy trying to second-guess him."

Corey smiled at the last part of what he'd said and started putting everything they'd sliced, shredded, or chopped into a beautiful wooden bowl, burnished from years of use. "Besides being handsome and sexy, Cole's a billionaire, and he's been seen with lots of beautiful women. Believe me, Spence, Cole didn't have to go to all that trouble last night, just to get a beautiful wife."

"Harrison didn't just get himself a beautiful *wife* when he married Diana," Spence scoffed bitterly. "Last night, Cole Harrison also accomplished the nearly impossible: he got himself a shiny, new public image."

"How?"

"When those pictures from last night hit the news, the public is going to believe Cole Harrison took one look at the woman Dan Penworth discarded—a woman who also happens to be one of America's sweethearts—and in true fairy-tale style, he rescued their beautiful damsel in distress, showered her with jewels, whisked her off in his private jet, and married her that same night. By the end of this week, Cole Harrison will become the most noble, romantic hero of the decade."

"I just can't believe he's that bad. He was always so *nice* when he worked at the Haywards'."

Spence leaned forward, rinsed off his hands, and wiped them on a towel, his expression grim. "I doubt that he was all that 'nice' even then."

"Why do you say that?"

"Because among his many enemies are Charles and Doug Hayward. They hate him thoroughly."

Corey's hands went still over the salad bowl. "Doug's never given any indication of that."

"He gave you one last night. When the auction was over, Diana brought Harrison over to the table. Do you remember what happened?"

"Yes, of course. Doug said something that I thought was tactless and unlike him, but he'd seemed strange all during dinner."

"He was perfectly normal until Diana walked into the ballroom with Cole Harrison. Later, he deliberately avoided shaking Harrison's hand."

"But—"

"Listen to me, honey. Last night you were so euphoric because Harrison had 'charged to Diana's rescue' that I didn't want to spoil it for you, but the truth is that Doug and Charles Hayward thoroughly *despise* him. I'm only telling you now so you don't set yourself or Diana up for a fall by dreaming that this marriage might turn into anything more than it is."

"Despise him?" she whispered. "Why? What could Cole possibly have done?"

"I've told you everything I know, and the only reason I know that much is because Doug visited me in Newport several years ago right after he'd gone to visit Barbara in the hospital in New York. He was upset because she wasn't doing any better, and I took him sailing and then out to dinner, hoping to cheer him up." Spence walked over to one of the cabinets and retrieved bottles of white wine vinegar and extra virgin olive oil, which he opened and began pouring into measuring cups. "We'd had some wine, and we decided to spend the rest of the evening at my house. We went into the library to watch the news, and the latest issue of *Newsweek* was on the coffee table. Harrison's picture was on the cover and when Doug saw it, he launched into a diatribe against Harrison that was so filled with malice you wouldn't have believed Doug was doing the talking."

Spence looked up from whisking the oil and vinegar together. "He ranted about revenge and how long he and his father have been waiting for the right chance. Somehow Barbara came up, and then I thought the man was going to break down and cry. The next thing I knew he'd gotten himself under control and he went to bed. The next morning he apologized and said he'd had too much to drink the night before, and that I shouldn't pay any attention to his 'drunken ramblings.'"

"Maybe that's all they were," Corey said hopefully as she gave a final toss to the undressed salad. "Doug has never been able to drink."

"Believe me, I know," Spence said with a reminiscent smile. "When I was at SMU, he used to stay with me at the fraternity house whenever he came to Dallas. To this day, I've never seen anyone but Doug turn into Superman and try to leap tall buildings in a single bound—on three rum and Cokes."

Corey nodded, but her attention had returned to the couple on the lawn. She watched Cole closely as he listened intently to whatever Diana was telling him. Beside her, Spence observed the same scene. Without meaning to, Corey spoke her thought aloud. "I just don't believe it."

Spence wisely refrained from reminding Corey that she hadn't believed a carpenter's assistant was stealing tools from their garage a month ago, even when she saw a wrench sticking out of his back pocket.

Corey refrained from pointing out to Spence that *he* had liked Dan Penworth, who had turned out to be a world-class rat. That wouldn't have done any good anyway, because the whole family had liked Dan. "Can you at least try to give Cole the benefit of the doubt? It would make everything so much easier."

Spence looked at her worried face and gave in with a deliberately suggestive leer. "Okay, beautiful, but it'll cost you," he said; then he turned to leave. Corey caught his arm. "Cute loincloth," she teased, reaching around his waist to free the towel.

Spence returned the compliment by turning toward her, reaching behind her, and playfully cupping her derriere. "Cute butt," he said and nipped her ear.

To their left, Glenna marched in on her silent, rubber-soled, orthopedic shoes. "I'll just get the duck off the grill before it turns into a chunk of charcoal," she volunteered in a long-suffering voice.

Corey stiffened and Spence froze; then he pulled her tighter to him and, laughing, kissed her anyway.

Chapter 36

WHEN COLE WALKED INTO THE FORMAL DINING ROOM BESIDE DIANA, he assumed from what he saw that her family had decided to try to pretend Diana's sudden marriage was a reason for celebration instead of homicide.

A large bowl of yellow roses in the center of the dining room table was flanked by candelabra aglow with tapers; the table was laid with formal china and gleaming silver flatware. A large china platter contained succulent slices of roasted duck breast, a large plate was piled high with fluffy buttermilk biscuits, and two serving bowls held new potatoes roasted with olive oil and rosemary, and steamed young asparagus.

The ladies made gallant attempts to smile at him, and even Grandpa managed a polite nod as he took his place at the head of the table and indicated Cole should take the seat at his right. Diana's grandmother sat on her husband's left, directly across from Cole, but when Diana started around the table to sit beside Cole, Gram said, "Corey, dear, why don't you sit next to Mr. Harrison and let

Spence sit next to me so we can all have a chance to get to know each other."

Mrs. Foster took her place at the foot of the table and Diana sat between her mother and Spence. Cole saw Mrs. Foster register confusion at the peculiar emphasis on an even more peculiar seating arrangement, but one glance at the lineup Gram had neatly arranged showed him that Gram had managed to put him squarely in the "hot seat." Grandpa was on his left, Gram and Addison were directly across from him, Corey was on his right, and Diana—his only ally—was well removed.

Nothing could have made Cole feel like a bigger hypocrite than thanking an imaginary God he didn't believe in for things He hadn't accomplished in the first place, and then compounding the idiocy by asking for favors He had neither the power—or perhaps the inclination—to grant. Hypocrisy was not one of Cole's many faults, and so he bent his head less than an inch and studied the hand-embroidered yellow rose on his napkin while he waited for the official inquisition to begin.

Henry Britton was not a man given to procrastination. He finished the prayer and said, "Amen. Cole, what are your plans?"

Before Cole could phrase an answer, Diana looked squarely at Corey and said, "Corey's dying to hear about the wedding, and I made her wait until now, when I could tell all of you at once."

Corey unhesitatingly picked up her cue. "Let's hear about the wedding first, Grandpa. After we catch up on the present, Cole and Diana can tell us all about the future." To Cole she added, "Will that be all right?"

In those few moments, Cole arrived at several meaningful conclusions: Gram was not, as he had earlier supposed, merely *elderly, outspoken, and endearingly eccentric,* she was *elderly, outspoken, possibly eccentric, and probably wily as hell.*

Corey was an unswerving ally of Diana's, and possibly neutral where he was concerned, while Diana—Diana with her lovely features and soft voice—was skilled enough in diplomacy to be a tremendous asset at any table, be it dinner table or boardroom table.

He watched her give an enthusiastic accounting of an abrupt, unromantic wedding she barely remembered and flavor it with the sort of details guaranteed to interest both sexes.

"We left the hotel in Cole's limousine and went to the airport. Cole's plane is a Gulfstream, Grandpa, and much larger than a little Learjet. You could add it to the model airplane mobile you've designed for boys' bedrooms. Anyway, there was a magnum of champagne in a cooler when we got on board, and one of the pilots was already in the cockpit doing—whatever pilots do before the plane takes off," she said, dismissing the preflight ritual with a wave of her graceful fingertips. "A few minutes later, the other pilot, whose name is Jerry Wade, arrived. Oh, and, Gram—" she added, turning to include that lady in the conversation, who had been frowning intently at Cole until then, "In the dark, he's a dead ringer for your favorite movie star! I told him he has to drop by and visit you some evening."

Fascinated by the way that remark pulled Rose Britton's attention away from him, Cole waited to discover who her favorite movie star was. "He does! Really?" Grandma said with a mixture of doubt and delight. "He looks like Clint Eastwood?"

"Clint Eastwood is practically bald," Grandpa put in irritably, "and he whispers when he talks!"

Corey leaned sideways and answered Cole's unspoken question as she handed him the platter of asparagus, "Gram is crazy about Eastwood, and it makes Grandpa jealous. It's so cute."

"Mom, you'd love what Cole has done to the inside of the plane. You feel as if you're walking into a beautiful living room, furnished in platinum leather, with touches of brass and gold. There were two curving sofas that faced each other, with an antique coffee table between them, a matching buffet with brass hinges, and several chairs."

She'd neatly captured her artistic family's attention, and as Cole listened to her colorful descriptions of everything from the Waterford crystal lamps to the oriental carpet in the plane's main cabin, he made two more interesting observations about Diana: first, she had an indisputable talent for using words to create a vivid picture, and second, she was not mentioning the plane's second-most important feature—its bedroom.

In his mind, he could still see her startling beauty as she lay across the bed's gleaming silver satin comforter, propped up on an elbow, draped in a vivid purple silk gown that provided him with an erotic glimpse of her full breasts above her bodice. Her face had been turned up to his, inviting his kiss, but as he'd bent over the bed, he'd hesitated. Cold reason and hard logic went to battle against his desire, and they won out over everything else, just as they always did with Cole. Regretfully but resolutely, he'd whispered, "No"; then he'd started to draw back.

Her hand lifted, sliding over his shoulder and behind his nape, her fingers gliding into the short hair above his open shirt collar, and he'd looked into eyes as green as wet jade and as vulnerable as a hurt child's. "No," he repeated, but he heard the hesitation and regret in his voice. So had Diana.

Diana switched to a description of the plane's cockpit, and he wondered whether she'd not mentioned the bedroom out of delicacy, embarrassment, or actual lack of memory. It was hard to believe she could remember that the interior of the plane was upholstered in pale gray leather and forget that one-third of the plane's cabin was a bedroom. On the other hand, she hadn't seen the bedroom until *after* they were married . . . after the stress of a ceremony in a garish, neon-lit chapel, a stop at a casino, and more champagne provided by him to eliminate the stress. She'd forgotten much about the wedding ceremony and the casino; Cole supposed it was equally possible she'd forgotten about the time they'd spent in the plane's bedroom.

Diana paused in her story to serve herself some of the roasted duck that had just been passed to her, and Diana's grandmother seized the opportunity to proceed where her husband had left off: "Tell us about yourself, Mr. Harrison," she said.

"Please call me Cole, Mrs. Britton," he said politely.

"Tell us about yourself, Cole," she corrected, though he noticed she did not suggest he call her by anything other than Mrs. Britton.

Cole deliberately referred to his present, not his past. "I live in Dallas, but I travel a great deal on business. In fact, I'm gone about two weeks out of every four."

She dismissed that, peered at him intently above the rim of her glasses, and bluntly inquired, "Do you go to church on Sunday?"

"No, I do not," he informed her without hesitation or apology.

A disappointed look creased her brows, but she persevered. "I see. Well, then, what about your family?"

"They don't go to church either," he retorted with cool finality.

She looked completely taken aback. "I was asking about your

family, not whether they went to church." She broke off a small piece of buttermilk biscuit and buttered it. "Won't you tell us a little about your background?" she invited quietly. "Tell us about where you're from and about your family."

The suggestion that he do so was so impossible, so abhorrent that Cole stalled for time by taking a bite of his salad while he glanced at the people gathered around the table—nice people who believed there was nothing unusual about sharing Sunday dinner or sitting at a gleaming wood table or having knives and forks that matched or a carpet beneath their feet instead of filth.

He glanced at Diana, who looked as fresh and perfect as an American Beauty Rose, at Addison, who'd never done anything more "demeaning" than lose a tennis game at the country club, and at Mary Foster, who subtly managed to exemplify dignity and grace and unaffected kindness.

On his left, Diana's grandfather smelled of fresh soap and Old Spice, instead of sweat. Across from him, Diana's grandmother gazed at him with alert, hazel eyes, her brows slightly raised in hopeful expectation, her face set off by wavy, white hair cropped jauntily and sensibly short, and gold wire-rimmed glasses that looked very nice on her. She looked proper and decent.

Cole would have found it easier and kinder to describe to her the lurid details of his most erotic sexual encounter than to tell her the truth about his early life and origins. Rather than spoil her illusions about her temporary grandson-in-law, he answered the questions with the same evasions that always served his purpose: "I'm from a small town in west Texas called Kingdom City. I had two older brothers, who are dead now, and a few cousins, who eventually moved away and with whom I've lost touch—except for one of them. My only other living relative is my great-uncle, who I told you about earlier. My father expected me to stay and work the ranch. Cal believed I had the brains to make it through college, and he badgered me until I began to believe it. He'll like Diana very much. I'm eager for him to meet her next week."

"I'm eager to meet him, too," Diana put in, but she had picked up on the sudden chill, the aloof reluctance in Cole's entire demeanor at the questions involving his background, and she remembered that years ago, he'd been exasperatingly vague when she tried to find out more about him.

"My uncle lives west of Kingdom City, which is about one hundred eighty miles from San Larosa. It's not quite the hill country, but it's beautiful and unspoiled." Cole paused and ate a bite of duck.

"San Larosa," Rose Britton said to her daughter. "Wasn't that one of your stopping places when you and Robert took the girls on their first camping trip to Yellowstone?"

"It's a popular place for campers," Cole said, anxious to change the subject. "Although, I understand that much of the area's only suitable for experienced hikers and campers."

For some reason that comment evoked laughter from the entire family.

"We weren't exactly 'experienced,'" Mrs. Foster explained. "Corey and I had camped out a few times, and Robert had been a Boy Scout. His only other 'camping experience' was limited to 'tennis camp' in Scottsdale. But the girls and I thought it would be fun, so off we went on a three-week trip, each of us confident we knew all there was to know about 'roughing it.'"

Cole found it hard to imagine Diana as an avid camper when, even as a fourteen-year-old, she had seemed to be very fastidious about everything from her white tennis shoes to her short, neatly filed fingernails. "Somehow, I never thought of you as someone who would like roughing it, even when you were young."

"We all had a great time. I loved it," Diana lied, straight-faced.

Something about that didn't ring true, and then a hazy memory snapped into focus. "Didn't we once have a conversation at the Haywards' stable about things we disliked the most?"

Because Diana had been so infatuated with him at the time, each of their conversations had seemed like earthshaking events to her, and she realized almost at once what he was referring to. Surprised that he remembered it, she took advantage of an unexpected opportunity for lighthearted banter. "Did we?" she asked with a look of innocent bewilderment, before taking a bite of roasted potato.

Cole wasn't fooled "You *know* we did," he countered with a lazy smile. "Your top two least-favorites were dirt and camping."

"No, they were *snakes* and camping," Diana corrected him, her eyes sparkling with merriment. "Dirt was third on my list." She looked at Corey and jokingly said, "Even so, we were very well organized and prepared for every eventuality, weren't we?"

Corey realized immediately what Diana wanted her to do, and she complied at once, eager to help Diana lighten the mood at the table. "Our father wanted the trip to be a joint family effort, so before the trip, we all had assignments. Dad was in charge of transportation and finances; Mom was in charge of food and beverages; Diana was in charge of safety manuals and safety items. I was in charge of first aid and photography. And we were both supposed to have whatever items we felt we needed to be comfortable and safe. I figured Band-Aids and some sunblock would cover first aid, so I started reading up on wildlife photography, but Diana had a much different approach to preparedness. Weeks before we left, she began poring over *The Camper's Guide to Survival in the Wilderness,* and *The Camper's Companion.*"

"And," Diana emphasized laughingly, "the L.L. Bean catalogs, from which I had selected and ordered what I felt were absolute necessities for Corey and me."

Cole's gaze shifted to her the moment she spoke, and Corey saw his smile grow warm before he turned his attention back to Corey, who continued, "The day before we left, Dad went to get the motor home he'd rented, and Diana and I started carrying down the rest of our 'personal provisions' that she'd been storing in the attic as they arrived. Then we started with her 'campers' safety essentials' that the guidebooks had recommended, and then with the first-aid stuff."

Gram joined in the story with a smile. "The girls had to make at least fifteen trips to get it all downstairs," she told Cole.

"And then," Grandpa added, chuckling, "Robert had to hitch a U-Haul trailer onto the camper to get it to Yellowstone. The problem was—" he continued, his shoulders starting to shake with laughter, "Robert had never driven anything longer than his daddy's Cadillac in the fifties. When he pulled out of the driveway, he knocked over his mailbox with the trailer, and he drove off down the street, dragging the pole and box behind him—"

"Henry and I laughed so hard we could hardly chase after the mail."

Cole was so entertained by the story and this additional glimpse into Diana's past that he forgot he was in hostile territory. "What did Diana take along that took up so much room?" he asked, but Corey hesitated.

"Go ahead and tell him," Diana told her with a laughing look. "He's part of the family now, so, technically, he has a right to know."

"It wasn't all Diana's stuff, it was for me, too," Corey loyally pointed out before she went on. "If she hadn't planned for both of us, I'd have left on a two-week trip with a torn sleeping bag, a couple pairs of shorts and T-shirts, my camera equipment, twenty rolls of film, and some Band-Aids. Period. Anyway," she continued, "Diana had an entirely different sense of what we needed in order to camp out in comfort and safety. She'd ordered a white tent for us with a red, white, and blue awning over the flap; then she'd coordinated our sleeping bags, our clothes, and even our lanterns and flashlights with the trim on the tent. Diana's were blue. Mine were red. We even had red, white, and blue plastic bottles filled with lotion and aspirin and everything."

Uneasy about making fun of Diana's preparations, Corey stopped and poured herself more iced tea.

"You forgot the repellents," Diana prompted, laughing. "To be on the safe side, I'd brought a dozen cans each of mosquito repellent, wasp repellent, crawling-insect repellent, and flying-insect repellent. I also had several jumbo containers of snake repellent, which I diligently sprinkled around the outside perimeter of our tent every time we put it in a new place."

"*Snake repellent?*" Cole said to Diana with a choked laugh. "What did you think of Yellowstone?"

"It depends on who you ask," Diana said dryly, and the rest of the family burst out laughing. Mrs. Foster wiped her eyes and said, "The first day in Yellowstone, we all went hiking. Corey got pictures of mountain goats, and I got some lovely sketches. Diana got poison ivy and Robert got an allergy attack."

"The nights were fun though," Corey argued. "We cooked out and roasted marshmallows and sang songs."

"And after we went to bed, the raccoons raided our trash containers and the bears waited for a chance to dine on us," Diana put in as she cut a bite-sized piece of duck. "I don't think there was a raccoon within ten miles of our camp that went to bed hungry while we were there."

"Looking back," Corey said with an impenitent grin, "it was a very one-sided vacation. While I hiked through the woods, oblivious to everything except getting a perfect photograph, Diana trooped behind me lugging a first-aid kit and reading in her manual about the danger of surprising elk in rutting season and what to do if you encountered an unfriendly bear."

"You were lucky she did," Mary Foster pointed out, sobering a little.

"That's true," Corey told Cole. "You see, on the day we were supposed to leave to come home, I sneaked out of camp with my camera and tripod just before dawn—strictly against Daddy's orders, which were that no one left camp alone. The thing was, I wanted to enter a photography contest in the Youth/Outdoors category, but I hadn't gotten anything that I felt was really outstanding. Then, on the last day in Yellowstone, I saw something that I just knew would be a winning shot. We were about a mile and a half from camp, hiking, when I spotted several elk crossing a stream near a waterfall that was streaming out of a steep wooded hill. I knew if I could get that shot, with the sun rising over the hill in the background, I'd have a chance to win that contest. I asked Daddy to go with me, but by then his allergies were so bad that he said my elk would hear him wheezing and coughing and they'd take off before we could get close enough for a photograph. So I decided to go alone."

"You didn't ask your mother to go, instead?" Cole asked.

"Mom spent most of the evening cooking dinner and packing up, and she said she was exhausted."

"What about Diana?"

"I didn't have the heart to ask Diana. She was covered with poison ivy, sunburn, and pink calamine lotion. Besides, she'd twisted her ankle the day before. Anyway, she heard me sneaking out of the tent before dawn, and she started itemizing all the dire things that can happen to an inexperienced camper alone in the wilds, but I headed off anyway with only a flashlight and my camera gear.

"A few minutes later, I heard something crashing through the woods behind me, and I smelled the calamine lotion, so I figured it had to be Diana. Sure enough, there she was, limping down the trail with her ankle wrapped in an elastic bandage, carrying her trusty emergency kit in one hand and her blue flashlight in the other. What a morning," Corey finished with a reminiscent laugh. "When we got to the spot I'd picked out, I realized the angle of the light was going to be all wrong on this side of the stream, so we had to find a shallow place to cross the stream, work our way through the woods on the side of the hill above the waterfall, and then back down."

"Did you get your picture of the elk at sunrise?"

"No, I got lost instead. The light wasn't very good yet, and I didn't know we'd ended up on the bank of another stream near a different hill, so I set up my tripod and attached my telephoto lens. The sky was turning bright pink, and there still weren't any elk, so I left Diana with the camera, in case the elk showed up, while I walked a few yards to the edge of the clearing. I crouched down on my hands and knees so I wouldn't be at the elk's eye level, and crawled out of the woods onto the bank, waiting for my eyes to adjust from the gray shadows to the pink light reflecting off the water. With the sun where it was, I couldn't see the waterfall at all yet, so I sat down and dug out of my pocket the bag of leftover marshmallows I'd brought for breakfast. And then I saw it—he was coming out of the water and heading straight at me."

"The elk?" Cole ventured, while passing the plate of biscuits to Diana's grandfather.

"No, the *bear*. He was quite young, several inches shorter than I, which I didn't realize because he was running on all fours. I thought he was charging me, and I jumped to my hands and knees, but before I could stand up, he was there. I screamed, he stopped, and we stared at each other, eyeball to eyeball, both of us startled and frightened. He came up on his hind legs and I sprang to my feet and threw my marshmallows at him; then I ran as fast as I could in one direction, while he fled in the other.

"To top everything off," she said, laughing, "when we started back, we realized we were lost, and the further we walked, the more lost we became. Diana kept insisting that her books on camping safety said we should stay put, but I wouldn't listen, until she finally pretended she couldn't walk any further on her ankle. At nightfall, she used the matches in her emergency kit to build a little fire to help the searchers find us.

"I'd forgotten to change the battery in my flashlight, and it gave out before I heard what I thought were wolves howling. Diana wouldn't let me use her flashlight, even though it had a fresh battery. She said we needed it to signal search planes if any flew close, and I knew she was right. Instead, I built a bigger fire for

275

more light, but every time I heard that howling sound, I got closer to hysteria," Corey admitted and took a sip of iced tea. "I was shivering so hard I could hardly talk, and I had to keep my face turned away so Diana wouldn't see the tears running down my face. I felt like such a fool, particularly because I'd teased Diana about being afraid of snakes and picking a bouquet of poison ivy and lugging that emergency kit with us everywhere—and there I was, crying like a baby while she calmly took care of all the practical matters of survival. I'd ignored all the camping manuals, but Diana had read them from cover to cover, which was why she was able to make me laugh about the threat of wolves. Finally we went to sleep by the fire. Even after we were rescued the next morning, she never teased me about being so stupid. In fact, we never discussed those imaginary wolves again, until now."

When Corey showed no indication of explaining her last sentence, Cole said, "Imaginary wolves? I don't understand."

"Obviously," Corey informed him, "you haven't read the *Yellowstone Camping Manual* either." She smiled infectiously. "You see, there *weren't* any wolves in that part of Yellowstone back then. The park service had corralled them in a distant part of the park, far from the campers. Those were the ones we were hearing."

Cole thought that seemed virtually impossible, as well as counter to the wildlife philosophy of the national parks. "Do you mean that the park authorities rounded up all the wolves in that gigantic parkland and then put them behind fences?" He looked at Diana for an answer, but she seemed to be engrossed with tracing the pattern on the handle of her knife with her forefinger.

"No, of course not!" Corey explained. "The wildlife commission realized that the wolf population was out of control in Yellowstone because the wolf's natural predator, the Rocky Mountain black ocelot, was almost extinct there, so they imported them from California. The ocelots hunted the wolves and ran them deep into the mountains."

Diana could feel Cole's gaze leveled on her, and when she couldn't avoid it any longer, she finally lifted her eyes from her silverware and saw the knowing amusement in his expression. "Very tidy explanation," he said dryly.

"I thought so," Diana said, swallowing a giggle.

Corey looked from one to the other of them, her own thoughts on

276

the long-ago explanation she'd accepted without question at the time. Now that she'd repeated it aloud, it sounded very odd. "Diana—" she said suspiciously. "It was a total lie, wasn't it?"

"It was a whopper!" Henry Britton hooted. "Surprised you bought it, Corey girl."

Privately, Cole thought Diana's solution had been ingenious, but as a new and temporary family member, he didn't feel entitled to voice a dissenting opinion. Instead, he concluded, "So you spent a terrifying night alone and never got to enter the photography contest, after all?"

"On the contrary, I won second place in the Candid Series division," Corey informed him with a grin.

"Congratulations," Cole said.

"Don't congratulate me," she countered wryly. "I didn't take them, I was *in* them."

"Who took them?"

"Diana did. When I saw the bear and tried to scramble up on my hands and knees, she thought I'd seen the elk and was trying to stay out of the frame, so she pressed the shutter release as I'd told her to do, and the automatic camera started shooting in rapid sequence. After we got back, I tossed the roll of film out, but Diana retrieved it for laughs. When it was developed, she selected three shots—as required by the contest—and sent them in."

"Yes," Mary Foster said with a reminiscent smile, "and *National Photographic* magazine even used the captions Diana had sent in when they featured the pictures."

"What were your captions?" Cole asked.

"The first picture was when the bear and I first met, nose to nose. Both of us were crouched on all fours, staring at each other, startled and scared." Corey laughed. "Under that one, Diana had written 'On your mark—' The second picture was of the bear and me rearing up on our feet, ready to run. Beneath that, Diana had written 'Get set—' The last picture was the funniest of all, because we were both fleeing for our lives in opposite directions. Diana called that one 'Go!' "

Chapter 37

*D*IANA AND COREY HAD SET THE TONE WITH THEIR CAMPING STORY, and by the time dessert was over, each person at the table had become the subject of an amusing and sometimes revealing anecdote, including Spencer Addison. And somewhere, midway through the meal, Cole began to be treated as a welcome audience, rather than a mistrusted intruder.

The last tale concerned Rose Britton's irate response to a fan on Oprah Winfrey's show who gushed about how much she'd like to be married to Henry. At the end of the good-natured laughter that followed the recounting, Mary Foster looked at Cole with a smile. "I'm afraid you're discovering all our dark family secrets," she told him.

"They're safe with me," Cole assured her with an answering smile, but privately he found a certain grim amusement in the comparison of this family's "dark secrets" to those of his own. Nevertheless, he was grateful and surprised that the meal had gone off so smoothly, that no more prying questions were directed at

278

him, and that everyone seemed to have accepted him for the time being as a new family friend.

Everyone except Addison.

Addison wasn't neutral. Every instinct Cole possessed warned him that Addison was solidly opposed to Diana's marriage. Not that he made it obvious. Addison was much too well-bred to disturb his wife's family with any sort of unpleasant coldness at their table. In Cole's experience, men like Addison invariably sided with their own kind, no matter how stupid or shortsighted or evil their socially prominent friends might be. By virtue of birth and upbringing, Addison was already a natural foe of Cole's in any situation that pitted Cole against another member of "the privileged class," and Cole knew it. He understood it. In business, Cole always made it a practice to force adversaries like Addison out into the open, where they couldn't hide their feelings and intentions beneath the nearly impenetrable layers of social custom and ritual. Cole did that because it made them feel awkward, exposed, and uncomfortable, which made any contest of wits more equal.

In this case, Cole saw no reason to force Addison from his position of passive opposition into one of open enmity. Diana had already married him, and for some reason, Cole knew she would not back out of the agreement she'd made with him.

He trusted her, Cole realized, as he watched her talking to Corey.

He trusted her, and this realization was profoundly disturbing. And then he pictured her trooping through the woods after Corey with an emergency kit and a bandaged ankle, and his alarm turned to mirth.

Despite the harmony and gaiety during dinner, the farewells in the foyer were understandably awkward.

Normally newlyweds left the bride's home under a shower of rice, with family and friends shouting good wishes. Since that was inappropriate, Diana's family tried to improvise, and to Cole, the results were as endearing as the family itself.

Diana's mother held out her hand to her new son-in-law, hesitated, and then blurted uneasily, "It was very nice to meet you after all these years, Cole. Will we see you again?"

"I'm sure you will."

279

Grandpa shook his hand. "Welcome to the—You're welcome here anytime."

"Thank you."

Spencer Addison did not pretend this was a meaningful occasion, but he seemed more amused than hostile. "I never knew Diana hated dirt and snakes. What did you do about the big blacksnake that lived in the Haywards' stable?"

Anxious for the opportunity to show Spence how kind Cole had been, even then, Diana answered before Cole could. "Cole trained him to stay away when I was there so I wouldn't be afraid."

"Really?" Spence said to Cole, his brows raised in amused challenge as he reached out to shake Cole's hand. "How did you manage that?"

"I brought in a Rocky Mountain black ocelot to drive him up into the rafters," Cole replied drolly.

"You *lied* to me?" Diana demanded, laughing.

Corey gave Cole a hug.

Grandma gave him a dozen cookies and a loaf of freshly baked bread.

Chapter 38

$\mathcal{T}$HE AWKWARDNESS IN THE FOYER GREW STRONGER IN THE CAR AS Diana wondered how she and Cole could part on some sort of appropriate and, preferably, uplifting note. Cole had checked out of the Balmoral when they left, his luggage was in her trunk, and his pilots were waiting for Cole to call them with a departure time.

If the local television stations hadn't already run the news clips of Cole giving her the necklace, the story and pictures would surely hit the Monday morning paper and the announcement of their marriage would have to follow immediately. In Diana's exhausted state, the immediate future seemed perilous and overwhelming.

The clock on her dashboard showed 7:15, and the prospect of being alone in her apartment with nothing to do but anticipate tomorrow's siege of phone calls, comments, and stares from friends, associates, employees, and newspeople was depressing and overwhelming.

She turned onto San Felipe and decided to ask Cole up to her apartment for a drink. There were probably many details they needed to go over.

Beside her, Cole watched her expression go from thoughtful to somber to unhappy, and he guessed the reason. "Why don't you invite me up for a drink?" he suggested.

That startled a laugh from her. "I was just going to do that."

Diana's high-rise apartment had glass exterior walls that provided a beautiful view, and the spacious interior was clearly the work of a good designer. Filmy white draperies with graceful swags and valances complemented the thick white carpeting and inviting groupings of white sofas and chairs. Silk flower centerpieces and throw pillows provided splashes of mauve, light green, and white. Earlier, Cole had thought her apartment luxurious and well done, but now he noticed it lacked the profusion of homey touches that had been so much in evidence at the River Oaks house, and that surprised him.

On a table beside the sofa her pager was beeping and the light on her answering machine was flashing. She went directly to the pager. "Make yourself comfortable," she said, dialing the telephone with one hand and holding her pager in the other. "There's a call on here from Cindy Bertrillo, who handles public relations for us," she explained.

"Why don't I make the drinks," Cole suggested.

She sent him a brief smile of gratitude, listening to the phone ringing. Tipping her head toward the right, she said, "There's a liquor cabinet in the island in the kitchen. Plain Coke for me, please." No one answered at Cindy's house, so she hung up the phone and pressed the playback button on the answering machine.

She had eleven messages, ten of which were from friends and acquaintances wanting to ask her about Cole Harrison. The last few calls referred to a newscast at six PM that showed a videotape of Cole Harrison presenting her with the forty-thousand-dollar necklace. She skipped through those as soon as she got the gist of the call.

The last one was from Cindy Bertrillo, twenty minutes ago: "Diana, this is Cindy. I just got back from my sister's in Austin, and I had some really weird calls from the media on my machine. I tried to reach you at your folks' house, and they said you were on your way home. I need to give you the press release on the new Holidays by Hand kits we'll be offering soon, so I'll run over there now and tell you about the messages in person. I didn't say anything to your parents," she added with a smothered laugh, "but wait until you hear the stories that are going around! If you aren't there, I'll leave the press release with the doorman. Bye."

The buzzer at the door sounded before Diana could touch the rewind button, and Diana braced herself. Cindy and she traveled together whenever Diana did television or radio appearances, and they had more than a formal employer-employee relationship; they had become friends over the years. Cindy knew perfectly well that Diana had been engaged to Dan for two years; she also knew the names of most of the men Diana had gone out with before that, and Cole Harrison hadn't been one of them.

Cindy rushed in like a fresh breeze, tanned, smiling, and brimming with inexhaustible energy. "The rumor mill has out-done itself," she announced cheerfully, shoving her sunglasses up onto her head and following Diana over to the sofa. Diana was too tense to sit, and Cindy was clearly too wound up to sit, so they faced each other across the cocktail table as Cindy burst out with her news: "You are *not* going to believe this!" she began. "What did you do last night—dance with Cole Harrison, or did you just smile at him?"

"Yes," Diana said weakly, unable to summon the courage to make her announcement a moment sooner than she had to. "I mean, I did both."

"Well, wait until you hear what the press is making out of that!" she said, choking back a laugh so she could go on. "The business editor at the *Chronicle,* an Associated Press reporter, and a produc-er at the Financial News Network all left messages on my machine wanting confirmation of the rumor that Foster Enterprises wants to merge with Unified Industries!" She threw her hands up in laughing disbelief. "That's as absurd as a guppy trying to merge with a shark!"

She saw Diana's gaze shift toward the kitchen. "Wait, you haven't heard the best part," she said. Diana's attention returned to her, and she announced with a laugh, "Some woman, who said she was *you,* called CNN and Maxine Messenger and said she'd just married *Cole Harrison!* Can you *believe* it?"

"No," Diana admitted truthfully. "Not yet."

"The producer at CNN said the woman sounded like she might have been drinking. Also, all four of our local stations want the true story. Now, what shall I say when I call them back?"

In the doorway, Cole watched with amused admiration as a becoming pink blush tinted Diana's porcelain cheeks, then deepened when Cindy said, "Shall I call the rumors of your marriage to Harrison 'ludicrous' or 'simply ridiculous'? Or do you want to take a softer approach?"

A deep baritone voice made Cindy's head jerk toward the doorway as a dark-haired man raised his glass to his mouth and suggested blandly. "Personally, I'd take the softer approach."

Shock momentarily overcame her manners. "You'd what? Who are you?"

The glass lowered, revealing a very familiar face. "I am the shark who married the guppy last night," he said drolly.

Cindy sank down on the arm of the sofa. "Hanging is too good for me," she murmured in a small, meek voice.

She recovered and stood up as he came to stand beside Diana and slid his arm around her waist. "I'm Cindy Bertrillo," she said gravely, offering her hand across the table. "I used to be public relations director for Foster Enterprises."

Cole had expected Diana to voice some sort of sharp reprimand, which was what he would have done in similar circumstances, but as he silently shook the publicist's hand, he wasn't completely indifferent to her misery or her humor.

Diana and Cole spent a few minutes bringing Cindy up to date with the fact of their marriage, after which the publicist turned her considerable talents toward dealing with a public announcement. It soon became apparent that the best method for all concerned was to give a short press conference midmorning the following day. Although the publicist never said it, Cole sensed that, from a public relations standpoint, she was delighted to have Diana free of the stigma of Penworth's desertion, and she positively lit up when she realized that Diana and Cole had known each other for years.

When the meeting was concluded, Diana showed her out. Then Diana walked into the kitchen, where Cole was filling a water glass from the faucet. "Where would you like to sleep tonight?" she asked.

His gaze swerved to her. "What are my choices?"

"Here," Diana said innocently, "or the Balmoral."

"Here."

She nodded. "Why don't you call your pilots and tell them of the change of plans and then bring your suitcase up, and I'll get the guest bedroom ready."

Chapter 39

FOR SOME REASON, MEMORIES OF LAST NIGHT'S DREAM BEGAN TO PLAY through Diana's mind as soon as she went to work putting fresh sheets on the bed in the guest bedroom. It had seemed so real, and yet . . . not. That strange, floating bed, the demon lover who made her behave in ways she never normally would. Insistent mouth—gentle hands . . . tender . . . rough.

She shook her head and reached for a pillowcase, embarrassed by the direction of her thoughts, but as she shoved a pillow into the case, the memories came back again, hovering at the edges of her mind. Blue lights. Small room, low ceiling, filled with steam or smoke or something that made everything look gray. Gray.

Behind her, Cole strode silently into the room, carrying a black garment bag in his right hand and a briefcase in his left. "Could I—"

With a stifled cry, Diana whirled around, her hand clutching a fistful of silk shirt over her heart, then she laughed. "Oh, it's you . . ."

He eyed her worriedly as he put his briefcase down at the foot of the bed. "Who were you expecting—Jack the Ripper?"

"Something like that," she said dryly, pulling the spread up and then folding a corner back.

"Am *I* making you nervous?" he asked.

She turned and watched him slowly strip off his jacket, hypnotized by the unexpected intimacy of the ordinary act. "No, of course not," she untruthfully assured him. His eyes held hers as he dropped the jacket over a chair, loosened his tie, and pulled it free of his shirt collar. For one anxiety-filled moment, Diana thought he was going to undress right in front of her.

A knowing smile tugged at the corners of his mouth as he loosened the top button of his white shirt. "I *am* making you nervous."

She thought quickly for something to blame her reaction on, and came up with a partial truth. "It has nothing to do with you, really. While you were getting your luggage out of the car, I started thinking of a dream I had last night. It was—well—a very *um* . . . graphic . . . dream in some ways. It seemed so real."

He unbuttoned the second button on his shirt, an odd gleam lighting his eyes. "What sort of a dream was it?"

"Do you remember an early thriller movie called *Rosemary's Baby?*"

Cole thought back and remembered something about demonic possession, and then he nodded. "The woman in it was drugged and then forced to have sex with the devil."

Diana nodded and turned away, snapping on the lamp beside the bed. "Well," she explained as she turned and headed toward the door, "last night, *I* was that woman."

Cole's fingers froze on the third button of his shirt.

Blithely unaware of the verbal blow she had just delivered, she sailed out of the room, turning in the doorway with her hand on the light switch. "Your bathroom is right through there. Can I get you anything before I go to bed?"

"A large bandage might be nice," he said sardonically.

Diana's eyes widened, sweeping quickly down the length of him, from his broad shoulders and white shirt to his black trousers and black loafers. "For what?"

"For my ego, Diana."

Diana's brain simply shut down. It blocked the pathways between

287

hearing and logic. She nodded and backed out of the room. "Well. Good night."

Safe behind the door of her own bedroom, Diana, like an automated machine, went about the routine of getting ready for bed. In the shower, she mentally recited the names of all the articles in the last three issues of *Beautiful Living*. As she blew her hair dry, she felt a compulsion to remember all the names of the students in her seventh-grade class. As she put on her pajamas, she began preparing her Christmas list.

As she walked over to her dresser to change the wake-up time on her clock radio, she burst into tears.

Snatching a handful of tissues from a box beside her bed, she marched over to the chaise longue at the far end of the room, flopped onto it, and gave free rein to the tears that had been building up inside her for days. For the first time since she'd picked up the *Enquirer* and read about Dan's marriage, she gave in to self-pity. She wallowed in it. With her hands over her face and the tissues pressed to her eyes, she drew her knees up against her chest and rocked back and forth, sobbing.

She thought about the way Dan had complimented her mind and her looks and used silence to criticize her body and her performance in bed. "Bastard," she whispered, crying harder.

She thought of the years she'd wasted, trying to juggle her schedule to suit his, only to have him marry a child bride. "Monster!" she wept, rocking back and forth.

She thought of her insane marriage to Cole Harrison, and she cried harder. "Lunatic."

She thought of herself during her own wedding, swaying drunkenly on her feet and leaning back trying to mentally redecorate an arched trellis, and she moaned. "Idiot!"

She thought of Cole this morning, gallantly nursing her through a hangover and grinning good-naturedly as he recounted her drunken antics of the night before.

She thought of the dream that wasn't a dream, of a bedroom in shades of misty gray aboard a private jet as it hurtled through the sky and finally slammed onto a runway, racing past blue lights.

She thought of a man who tried to refuse her idiotic attempt at seduction. And didn't. He'd made it very clear, and she'd agreed, that sexual and emotional intimacy were not to be part of their agreement. Then at the first possible moment, she'd thrown herself at him, and because Cole had always been kind, he'd overridden his personal aversion to the idea and made love to her.

In return for his kindness, his thoughtfulness, his self-sacrifice, *she* had just delivered the ultimate insult by likening his lovemaking to a terrifying scene out of *Rosemary's Baby*. He had so much pride and he was so sensitive to the disparity between their backgrounds that he must have been twice as much hurt by her remark as he'd been by her having forgotten the incident.

A fresh stream of guilty tears poured from her eyes, and Diana leaned her forehead on her knees, her shoulders shaking with shame and sorrow.

She wept until her head ached and the well of tears and regret finally ran dry; then she wiped her eyes and blew her nose. The minutes ticked past as she stared thoughtfully at the picture on the wall across the room, reevaluating the past and considering new plans for the future. She was going to hire more management personnel, delegate responsibility, and take time for herself— beginning with a long, relaxing vacation of about eight weeks. She'd go to Greece, she decided, take a luxury cruise around the islands, visit friends in Paris, explore Rome, see Egypt. She might even have a meaningless sexual fling. Maybe two. By contemporary standards, she was practically a nun. She was entitled to all of that, more than entitled. She would be careful not to violate her agreement with Cole by embarrassing him in any way.

Cole. She thought through that situation for another minute, then got off the chaise longue and resolutely went to her closet for a robe. She owed Cole the most abject, sincere apology.

With his shoulder propped against the wall and his jaw clenched, Cole listened to the heartbroken sobs coming from the next room, punishing himself with the sound of her weeping. He was a pariah, Cole thought with a blaze of self-loathing, a devil who destroyed anyone he touched. He was a Harrison; he wasn't fit to be around decent people. He'd had no right to think he could climb higher than any of the other Harrisons. He could make money, buy better clothes, clean himself up, get rid of his accent, but he couldn't get rid of the filth of Kingdom City that was stuck to his soul—it thrived in his genes.

There were any number of women he could have made his bargain with, actresses, waitresses, or one of the bored, brittle socialites who were as morally and spiritually bankrupt as he was. Diana Foster wasn't one of them; she was special. Exquisite. Alluring. Untouchable.

Irresistible . . .

He'd had no right to go near her last night, let alone convince her to marry him, and he'd been a filthy bastard to have sexual intercourse with her. He'd never meant for that to happen. He'd convinced himself it wouldn't happen. His convictions and self-control had lasted less than one damned day! He'd said she'd hurt his ego. He had no right to an ego where she was concerned.

He thought of her accomplishments and he was so damned proud of her it made his chest ache. He looked around at the sound of a soft knock on the door. "Cole, may I speak to you for a minute?"

He told her to come in, and she entered his room wearing a simple white silk robe with her monogram in navy blue on the pocket, a handkerchief clutched in her hand, and Cole's long-dead conscience reared up with a vengeance. Twenty-four hours ago, she walked into a hotel with the proud carriage of a queen. After one day of marriage to Cole Harrison, she looked like a woebegone waif. A year from now, if she stayed married to him, she'd probably look as bedraggled and hopeless as his mother.

"Diana—" he said, his voice carefully expressionless.

She shook her head to silence him and her hair glowed like copper in the lamplight. "Please sit down," she said shakily, walking over to a pair of overstuffed chairs angled toward each other with a reading lamp between them. "I have some things I need to tell you," she said, waiting until he'd sat down beside her.

She was going to try to call the whole deal off. "I think I already know what you want to say," he said, leaning forward and propping his elbows on his knees.

"First of all, I want to apologize for the childish way I've behaved about this whole thing. I've been absurdly concerned about what people will think, and I'm ashamed of that. I'm very proud of being married to you, and beginning tomorrow, no one will have reason to ever think otherwise."

Cole stared at her pale face, his dark brows drawn into a frown of utter disbelief.

She lowered her eyes to her lap and studied her folded hands; then she looked up and met his gaze directly. "Next, I want to tell you how much I regret what happened in the plane last night."

"I don't want to run the risk of looking too far afield for explanations," he said wryly, "but is it possible that last night happened because we are attracted to each other? I sure as hell wanted you. And I know you wanted me." The sudden glamour of his lazy smile was almost as effective as his admission. "In fact," he said softly, "I have it from an unimpeachable source that you used to want me, a long time ago."

She stood up slowly and so did he. "I refuse to regret or apologize for what happened last night," he said. "We wanted each other. It was as simple as that. We're about to spend a week together. We're married."

Diana felt herself falling under the spell of that rich baritone voice.

"More importantly, we like each other, and we're friends. Is there any part of that you don't agree with?"

"No," she said, searching his somber face. "What are you suggesting?"

"I'm suggesting that you consider having a real honeymoon with me when we're at the ranch. Don't answer me now," he said. "Think about it. Will you?"

Diana hesitated. "Yes."

"In that case," he said, pressing a brotherly kiss to her forehead, "I suggest you get out of here, before I decide to try to rush you into another major step in your life."

Chapter 40

COLE HAD BECOME ACCUSTOMED TO BEING WATCHED BY MEMBERS OF both sexes if they recognized him when he walked into an office building, but he had never been subjected to a frank scrutiny anything like the one he was treated to when he arrived at Foster Enterprises that morning. Within minutes, it became obvious that Diana had a much freer relationship with her staff than he had with his own, and it was also apparent that she was far better liked by the people who worked for her than was usual. Particularly in his case.

Cole was used to being treated with awe, with fear, and even with veiled hostility, but he was always treated with respect, and he was never, ever treated with relaxed cordiality, let alone impertinence. Diana introduced him to everyone in all the departments, where Cole was subjected to everything from stern admonitions to take care of Diana to smiling remarks about the difference in their height ensuring that he would be head of the family to flagrant comments about his physical attributes. At first he was astonished, and then he found it amusing. A perky twenty-year-old in the layout department complimented his tie, and a wheelchair-bound artist asked him how long he had to work out each day to stay in such great shape. When they left the sales department, another woman made a remark about his build that made him glance at Diana in disbelief.

"What did she just say?" he demanded in a whisper.

Diana kept her laughing face lowered. "She said you have 'great buns.'"

"That's what I thought she said." After a moment he glanced at her. "The woman in the last department—the one with the ink on her hands—liked my tie. Thank you for loaning it to me."

That morning he'd realized the only tie he'd brought along as a spare had a black background, not dark blue, as he'd thought. Diana solved the problem by going into her bedroom and emerging with a tie box. "I loved this when I saw it," she explained, "so I bought it for—someone."

Cole assumed from her pause that she'd bought it for Penworth, and even though it was a little brighter than the conservative ones he normally wore, he was glad to have it.

"It isn't a loan, it's a gift," Diana said simply. "And it wasn't for Dan. When I see things I like, I buy them to have on hand."

The press conference was scheduled to take place in Diana's large office, where thirty reporters and photographers had already crowded. Outside the door, Diana stopped and turned, straightening the knot in his tie in an ordinary wifely gesture that seemed so much more intimate under their unusual circumstances. "Perfect," she announced.

Cole thought she looked "perfect" in her lemon silk dress with its jaunty white collar and wide white cuffs, and the bold admiration in his gaze told her that. The unspoken compliment made her fingers curl inside his handclasp as she stepped forward and opened the door to her noisy, crowded office.

The first thing Cole noticed was that Diana's grandparents, her mother, and Corey were near the front by her desk. It was a show of family solidarity that shocked and touched Cole as he walked to the front of the room while cameras flashed and Minicams whirred.

The next thing he noticed was that the atmosphere at this press conference was vastly different from that of any other of his experience. There was no hostility or suspicion in evidence. Instead of shouting loaded questions at him that were filled with innuendo, they joked about his long-standing bachelorhood and teased Diana about a woman's right to change her mind—a remarkably gallant way of ignoring Penworth's defection that surprised and pleased Cole. Diana bore it with unflappable serenity, her smile never wavering.

"How long have you known each other?" someone called.

"We first met when Cole was in college," Diana replied, each of them taking a turn with an answer, as Cindy had suggested they do.

"When's the honeymoon?"

"Later this week, when we can both clear our schedules," Cole answered, referring to their trip to visit Cal.

"Where are you going?"

Diana opened her mouth to reply, but Cole interceded. "You are the last people on earth we'd tell," he replied with a joking affability that was in complete opposition to his hostile reputation with the press.

The whole thing went off without a hitch until the very last question was called out to Cole by a thin, bespectacled man in the first row. "Mr. Harrison, would you care to comment on the rumor that the Securities and Exchange Commission is preparing an investigation into possible improprieties in connection with the Cushman deal?"

He felt, rather than saw, Diana stiffen, and Cole had an almost uncontrollable impulse to yank the little weasel off his feet and throw him through the window. To everyone's astonishment, particularly Cole's, it was Diana's grandmother who waded in with her verbal fists raised. "Young man," she warned the forty-year-old journalist in an irate voice, "I can tell you've been eating chemical fertilizers on your food and they're affecting your disposition!"

The entire room erupted with laughter that lingered as the news people filed out of Diana's office. Cole's limousine was waiting outside to take him to the airport so that he could be at his Dallas office for a meeting in an hour and a half. He was furious with the reporter and touched by the presence of his temporary relatives, particularly Diana's grandmother. He looked at the Fosters and was at an utter loss for what to say. For lack of knowing any other way to handle it, he sent a general smile in their direction; then he leaned down and pressed a brotherly kiss to Diana's cheek. "I'll see you on Thursday."

He closed the door behind him, leaving the family alone in

Diana's office. Henry Britton was the first to speak. "I wonder," he said, staring thoughtfully at the closed door, "how long it's been since anyone spoke up for that boy."

Corey stayed behind to help Diana straighten up her office. Spence's negative remarks about Cole's allegedly questionable business practices revolved in her mind in tandem with the reporter's alarming reference to an SEC investigation.

She picked up a gum wrapper and a scrap of paper from the pale blue carpet. As she pushed four chairs back into place at the far end of the room, Diana walked over to her desk and perched a hip on the edge of it, watching her. "Corey?"

Corey looked up with a bright smile as she carefully lifted one of the pieces of Steuben crystal from Diana's collection, a beautiful peacock, off a bookshelf and returned it to its rightful place in the exact center of a small conference table. "Hmm?"

"What's wrong?"

Corey stepped back to check the position of the peacock in relation to the crystal candy bowl and moved the bowl two inches to the left. "Nothing's wrong. Why do you ask?"

"Because I'm the compulsive organizer, remember? You're the gerbil who likes clutter."

Corey jerked her hand away from the pieces of glass candy she'd been about to sort by shapes and swung around. "It's just that reporters always make me feel uneasy."

"Particularly," Diana speculated with a knowing smile, "when they make insulting innuendoes about your new brother-in-law?"

"Particularly then," Corey admitted with a sigh. She couldn't bear to tell Diana that Spence had his own doubts about Cole's integrity, but she couldn't leave Diana without some sort of warning either. "Spence said yesterday that Cole has made a lot of enemies over the years."

"Of course he has," Diana replied without concern. "The only way to avoid making enemies is not to succeed in anything."

That made perfect sense, but what impressed Corey most, as she looked at Diana, was her sister's ability to be calm and logical at such a time. Perched on the edge of her desk with every shining hair neatly in place and her trim figure set off by a bright silk dress, she looked more like a fashion model than a CEO.

She had founded a thriving corporation and she managed to run it without losing any of her femininity or humanity.

Corey smiled and spoke her thought aloud. "You do us women proud, Sis," she said softly, then she vanished with a cheerful salute.

When she left, Diana stared dreamily into space, remembering the tender, unforgettable things Cole had said last night and thinking of the honeymoon that would begin on Thursday. By the time she surfaced to reality and glanced at her watch, she realized she wouldn't have time to call Doug until after the production meeting. She didn't want him to hear about her marriage on the news; she wanted to tell him herself.

Doug was pacing back and forth in her office when she returned from her meeting, and judging from the ominous look on his face, he was not happy for her. As a precaution, Diana closed her office door, and the instant the latch clicked into place, he exploded in a low, incensed voice, "Of all the stupid, irrational—I can't believe you actually married that—that piece of slime! You've lost your mind! God, I could shake you!"

Diana had intended to try to reason with him, but she was so annoyed by his description of Cole that she walked behind her desk instead. In angry silence, she stood there while Doug paced back and forth in front of her, raking his hands through the sides of his hair like a man demented. "You have to unload him, now. Today. Make an announcement that he drugged you, do anything, but get away from him and stay away from him. He's not fit to be in the same room with you. Shoveling manure is all he's fit to do!"

"Why, you *snob!*" Diana burst out.

"If despising a corporate mobster makes me a snob, then I guess I am one."

"How dare you talk like this!" Diana burst out. "Who do you think you are, anyway?"

Instead of quieting him down, her obstinance sent him over the edge. Slapping both hands on her desk, he leaned across it, his teeth clenched. "I am your friend. Now, do this for me—get rid of that sonofabitch!"

"You're being completely irrational."

He started pacing again. "What does it take to make you understand?" He stopped and turned to her again. "His days of wheeling and dealing on the stock exchange are over! The SEC is going to shut him down, and that's only the beginning. When the federal government is done with him, he'll go to jail where he belongs, just like Ivan Boesky and Michael Milken. The state of Texas will shut him down here, too. When everyone is finished with him, he's going to be a broke ex-convict!"

Diana was shaken, but she managed to sound reasonably calm. "Why do you say that?"

"Because the Cushman deal was dirty. He's a cheat and a manipulator. He's an animal!"

"Tell me why you're saying this. Give me one piece of evidence, instead of just gossip."

"I can't!" he bit out.

"Then, please," she said softly, holding out her hand to him, "don't start believing in rumors. Trust my judgment. Be happy for me."

At last, he calmed down, but his sudden sadness was worse than his anger. "Diana, I would have walked in front of a truck for you if you'd asked me to do it, but I cannot be happy for you, and I cannot help you if you stay married to him."

"I intend to stay married to him," she said with a quiet conviction that surprised even her.

His face paled as if she had slapped him. "That bastard really has a way with females of all ages, doesn't he? Even you. He can get you to do anything."

Diana assumed Doug had known that all of Diana's teenage girlfriends had crushes on Cole, and she refused to respond to that or his parting shot. Her throat hurt with tears as her lifelong friend stalked to the door of her office.

"Doug?" she said, her voice strained with hurt.

He turned, his face set. "Yes."

"Good-bye," she whispered achingly.

Chapter 41

COLE COULD HARDLY BELIEVE IT HAD BEEN ONLY A FEW DAYS SINCE he'd walked through the doors of Unified's executive office building. He had married Diana Foster. He had actually done that. The thought made him smile as he walked past the startled receptionist.

To add to his feeling of unreality, everything seemed to have changed since he last was here. When he drove onto the grounds a few minutes ago, the manicured grass suddenly reminded him of emerald velvet, and the lake, shimmering blue crystals. He'd commented on the remarkably fine day and unusually bright sky to his chauffeur, and although the driver agreed at once, he had been shocked that his normally silent employer had taken a moment for idle conversation.

They didn't really notice the difference in the surroundings, Cole knew.

Because *they* hadn't just married Diana Foster. They didn't know how sweet she was, or how funny, or how brave and beautiful. Their wives had probably never packed up snake repellent to take on a camping trip or sobbed during their own wedding and then sat on their lap and told them jokes in a plane. Their wives had probably never worn a royal purple silk gown and walked through a ballroom like a queen, then gotten tipsy on champagne and called CNN to announce their marriage. . . .

An executive staff meeting was just breaking up as Cole walked past secretarial cubicles and neared his office. A dozen of his executives filed out of the conference room, including Dick Rowse and Gloria Quigley from public relations, and Allan Underwood, the vice president of human resources. They looked at him with uncertain smiles, and finally Allan Underwood broke the ice. "What a surprise!" he said to Cole, referring, Cole knew, to his marriage to Diana. The others immediately chimed in with a chorus of remarks.

"Congratulations, Cole."

"It's great!"

"So nice!"

"Terrific!"

"Wonderful."

Cole was in a hopelessly lighthearted mood. "Oh—so you all like my new tie that well?"

"Your new what?" Gloria said blankly.

"My tie," Cole said, but he couldn't quite control the smile that lifted a corner of his mouth or gleamed in his eyes. "It's brighter than the ones I usually wear."

"I meant your new—"

"Yes?"

"Wife."

"Oh, yes," Cole replied, losing the battle to hide his smile. "She gave me the tie."

He turned and headed off to his office.

Behind him the executives gaped at each other. "Was he serious about the tie?" Underwood asked the others.

Gloria rolled her eyes at him. "No, it was a *joke!*"

"Cole never jokes," Dick Rowse said.

"He does now," Gloria said and sauntered down the hall to her own office.

"Congratulations, Mr. Harrison," Cole's secretary said with a formal smile as she followed him into his office, notepad in hand.

"I'm a great fan of the whole Foster family," Shirley Forbes confided.

"So am I," Cole said with an answering smile as he opened his briefcase on the desk and began removing the files he'd taken with him. Unable to dwell any longer on Diana, he turned his attention to pressing business matters. "Tell John Nederly I want to see him."

Shirley nodded. "He's called twice already, asking to see you."

"Congratulations on your marriage, Cole," Nederly said as he walked in. "My wife called me with the news an hour ago. She's excited about the prospect of meeting Miss Foster someday. She's a big fan."

Cole wasted no time on niceties. "Close the door," he replied curtly. "Now, what the hell is going on?" he demanded, leaning back in his chair and studying one of Harvard Law School's most gifted graduates with a frown of extreme displeasure. "This morning a reporter informed me during a press conference that I'm under investigation by the Securities and Exchange Commission."

Nederly shook his head. "You're not."

Cole's frown cleared, but only for a moment.

"The SEC has asked the New York Stock Exchange to investigate the Cushman buyout, which is the first step, and that's what's happening now."

"Then what?"

"The SEC reports directly to Congress so they have oversight powers, which means that regardless of what the NYSE finds, the SEC will review it and make their own decision.

"If they think there's evidence of probable wrongdoing, you'll be subpoenaed to appear at a hearing before an administrative law judge of the SEC. If the SEC judge rules against you, he'll turn it over to the federal courts, and you'll probably be subpoenaed to appear before a grand jury. There's no way of knowing what they'll try to charge you with—*stock manipulation* is a sure thing, so is *general fraud.* They won't hit you with *providing false information* unless they can prove we falsified the testing information."

"Tell me something," Cole said in a low, furious voice, "don't you think the last part of that recitation is a little premature?"

Nederly looked down at his suit and flicked a speck off his trouser leg. "Maybe I was showing off my superior knowledge," he tried to joke.

"Or?" Cole snapped.

Nederly sighed. "Or maybe I don't have a good feeling about this, Cole. The NYSE investigation is moving forward at an unusually fast pace, and I've already heard a rumor from a semireliable source that the NYSE investigation is just a routine formality. The SEC already thinks there's reasonable cause to subpoena you before their own judge."

"What 'reasonable cause'?" Cole said scornfully.

"One week, Cushman's stock is selling at twenty-eight dollars a share and rising because they're working on a new microprocessor. The next week rumors start circulating all over Wall Street and the media that the new chip is unreliable. The stock drops to fourteen dollars, and you offer to buy the whole company. It looks suspicious as hell!"

"Let's not forget I paid nineteen dollars a share, not fourteen dollars."

"Which you had to do in order to buy the entire company. I'm not denying that Cushman's shareholders got a good deal when you exchanged their stock for ours. They got an even better deal because you arranged a tax-free exchange."

"Then what the hell are they bitching about?"

"I said, it looks bad on the surface."

"I don't give a damn about how things look—"

John shook his head, his expression solemn. "I think you'd better start."

"Is that your best legal advice?"

"There's nothing else you can do right now."

"Like hell," Cole said in a savage voice; then he pushed his intercom button. "Shirley, get me Carrothers and Fineberg in Washington on the phone. I'll talk to either one of them."

The name of the most expensive and most influential law firm in Washington made John smile a little. "I've already got them working on your behalf. Maybe they can persuade the SEC in advance that they're acting recklessly."

Cole instructed his secretary to cancel the call. Satisfied that a combination of expensive legal talent and lack of proof would cause the SEC to drop the whole thing, he leaned back in his chair again and subjected Nederly to a thoughtful scrutiny.

"Anything else you want to talk about?" the lawyer asked.

"Your tie," Cole said blandly.

Nederly seemed to be as alarmed by the potential slur on his perfect appearance as he'd been by the various threats to Cole and Unified that they'd just discussed. "What's wrong with my tie?"

"It's very conservative."

"You always wear conservative ties, too."

"Not anymore," Cole said, amused by the discovery that the immaculately groomed lawyer had apparently been imitating him.

Chapter 42

$\mathcal{A}$LTHOUGH IT WAS NEARLY SEVEN-THIRTY, SEVERAL OF UNIFIED'S executives were working late, and Cole could hear them moving around outside his office door. He still had another hour's work, and he wanted to call Diana, but from his house, where he could talk to her at leisure. He'd left her less than eight hours ago and he was already looking forward to talking to her again. The fact that he reminded himself of an infatuated teenager was amusing to him, rather than disturbing.

Cal had called early that afternoon, when he heard about Cole's marriage on the news, and demanded that Cole's secretary get him out of a meeting to talk to him. Instead of being thrilled, Cal had been furious that Cole had "actually gone right out and married just anybody" so he could get Cal's signature on the stock transfer. To Cole's amused astonishment, the elderly man had announced that such an act was a violation of their agreement, since the intent of it—in his mind—was to see Cole settle down with a mate. It had taken several minutes to calm him down and make him understand who Diana actually was.

On the coming Wednesday morning, Cal had an appointment with his heart specialist in Austin, and Cole intended to fly him there and hear what the doctor had to say himself. He'd hoped to be able to pick Diana up in Houston after the appointment, but she had an impossible schedule that day and couldn't leave until Thursday, which meant he had to wait another day to see her—another day before they could be together. In bed. Thinking of taking her to bed—sober and willing—was enough to make him rigid, and he forced his attention back to the contract he was reading.

He'd just signed his name on the bottom line when Travis walked into his office wearing a polo shirt and a pair of casual pants. "You're here!" Travis burst out, closing Cole's door. "Thank God!"

In his early forties, Travis had a face that was pleasant when he didn't look worried—which was not often—and the athletic body of a man who exorcised his anxieties by running six miles every morning before dawn. He was a hard worker, and although he wasn't the intellectual giant that many of the scientists who reported to him were, he was a good choice for head of research and development. He had common sense and a tight fist, usually at appropriate times, when it came to spending the corporation's assets, and he was extremely loyal. For that reason, Cole trusted him more than anyone else who worked at Unified.

"I'm here," Cole agreed with a wry smile and watched Travis walk restlessly over to the bar. "But if you have to thank something for that fact, then thank the preparer of this contract, because it's taken me nearly an hour to wade through it."

Travis stared blankly at him as he splashed bourbon into a glass. "Oh, that's a joke, right?"

"Evidently not a good one," Cole replied dryly, tossing his pen aside. "Now, what's wrong?"

"I don't know. That's why I'm here, and that's why I'm having a drink."

Even for Travis, this degree of uneasiness was unusual. "I thought maybe you were celebrating my marriage."

Travis turned with the glass in his hand and walked over to Cole's desk looking like he'd been punched. "You got married and you didn't even *tell* Elaine and me? You didn't even *invite* us?"

Touched that Travis was actually hurt by that, Cole shook his head. "It was completely unplanned. We decided to do it on

Saturday evening, and we flew to Las Vegas—before she could change her mind," he added truthfully. "Now, what has driven you to drink?"

He took two deep swallows of the bourbon. "I'm being followed."

Even though logic told Cole that was extremely unlikely, he couldn't suppress the vague feeling of disquiet that trickled through him. "What makes you think such a thing?"

"I don't think it, I know it. I noticed the guy yesterday when I left the house. He was parked down the street in a black Chevrolet, and he followed me all the way here. When I left tonight to go home for dinner, I spotted the car parked on the side of the highway outside our main gates. He followed me home. So I changed clothes tonight and ran over here on foot, cross-country, so he couldn't follow me. He tried, though. I saw him."

Cole studied him closely. "You aren't, by any wild chance, having an affair, are you?"

"I don't have the time or inclination for one, and besides, Elaine would kill me."

The last part of that was essentially true, so Cole accepted it. "Is it possible thieves are planning to break into your house and trying to learn your habits first?"

Travis finished his drink in two more gulps. "Not unless they're looking for a challenge instead of loot. We have two guard dogs, a state-of-the-art security system with cameras watching the place, electric gates—the works."

"Then why else would anyone be following you?"

Travis sank into a chair. "Could it have anything to do with the investigation by the NYSE?"

The feeling of dread Cole had felt earlier solidified into anger. "If that's the case, they're wasting their time."

Cole watched the rearview mirror when he left the office that night. A dark blue, late-model Ford followed him almost to the gates of his estate; then it disappeared around a curve.

Cole's phone was ringing when he walked into the house. The voice on the other end was a trembling whisper, scarcely recognizable as Travis's. "We've got trouble, Cole. Something's going on."

"What are you talking about?" Cole said, frowning. "Where are you? Why are you whispering?"

"I'm in my office, but I'm not sure I'm alone up here."

Frustrated, Cole shrugged out of his suit coat. "What do you mean, you aren't sure?" Travis's office was in the research and development building, on the same floor as the main laboratory, and he had a clear view of the area.

On the other end of the line, Travis drew a long, audible breath, and his voice sounded a little more normal, though still panicky. "After I left you, I was too keyed up to go home, so I decided to come over here and do some paperwork. I turned on the main ceiling lights in the lab, and while they were coming on, I thought I saw a shadow moving around the corner; then it disappeared. I ran to my office and out into the hall behind it, but I didn't see anyone. He must have gone down the exit stairs on the south end of the building."

Cole paused in the act of loosening the tie Diana had given him. "Are you sure you actually saw someone?"

"No."

Relieved, Cole started to reach for the messages his housekeeper had left for him beside the telephone.

"—But I'm damned sure I locked my file cabinets, and one of them is open."

"I'll take care of it," Cole said shortly. Corporate espionage was always a possibility, but Unified had considerable security precautions in place as a safeguard. "Was there anything in the cabinet that a competitor would find especially enlightening?"

"No, not really."

"Good. Then go on home. I'll handle it."

When Travis hung up, Cole called Unified's chief of security, Joe Murray, and waited impatiently while Murray's wife called him away from the ball game on television. In his mid-fifties, Murray was a balding ex-marine and built like a halfback, with a deep gravelly voice that suited his physical image perfectly. He chewed gum and guffawed over his own jokes while he ambled around peering over everyone's shoulder, managing to give the impression of being an ordinary ex-security guard who'd somehow been promoted to a desk job that was way beyond his capabilities.

In truth, he was a former FBI undercover agent with a list of major criminal arrests that were owed to his ability to look innocuous and not too bright while he insinuated himself into the inner circles of his prey. His salary was $225,000 a year, plus stock options and a benefits package.

When he answered Cole's call, the deceptive jocularity was absent from his manner. "Do we have a problem?"

"A little over a half hour ago, we had an intruder on the sixth floor of R and D," Cole told him. "Travis had left for the day and decided to go back to his office to do some work. He found a file cabinet that was unlocked. Nothing in it was vital to us, even if it was taken."

"Did he see anyone?"

"He thought he saw a shadow move around the corner before the lights came on all the way."

"Could he have forgotten to lock the cabinet before he left?"

"Travis is unlikely to forget something like that."

"You're right. I'll go over there right away and check it out. If the security guard at the desk on the main floor saw anything, or if I find out anything, I'll get back to you right away."

"Do that," Cole said. "And starting tomorrow, I want a regular security guard posted at the main entrance around the clock."

"I told you we should have put electric gates up there, instead of that cutesy little gatehouse."

During the day the gatehouse was manned by an elderly man wearing a blazer with the company insignia on the pocket. He was there primarily to give directions to visitors. The actual security was handled by men in similar blazers who sat at reception desks on the ground floor of each of the buildings on campus. The executive office building was the exception. In keeping with the illusion of elegance and luxury, the receptionist in Cole's building was a woman, but there was always a man in a blazer unobtrusively present in the area.

Cole reconsidered the philosophy behind all that and overruled Murray again. "I spent a fortune to make Unified's property one of the most beautiful in the world. I'm not going to gate it off, put uniformed guards with guns down there, and make it look like a minimum-security prison instead."

"It's your call, Cole," he said, but he was already distracted, eager to get going while the trail of the intruder was still fresh. "Anything else?"

"Yes—Travis and I are both being tailed. A black Chevrolet is on him. Mine's a dark blue Ford."

"Any idea why or who?"

"None," Cole said, because it didn't make sense that the SEC would resort to that. Abduction for ransom was a possibility, but too far-fetched to take seriously. That left only one other possibility, and Cole wasn't willing to discuss that, even with Murray. "They're wasting their time, whoever they are. They won't find out anything useful or incriminating by tailing me."

"Do you know how to shake them if you need to?"

"I watch the movies," Cole said sardonically. "I can figure it out."

After he hung up, Cole fixed himself a drink and carried it into the living room, where glass walls overlooked a gigantic free-form swimming pool with a gazebo and arched bridge that spanned it in the center. At the far end, a rock waterfall was created by two thousand strands of colored fiber-optic lights that were inserted into long tubes the diameter of plastic straws. Water flowed through the tubes and tumbled over the rocks like colorful fireworks tumbling down to earth.

Cole propped his feet up on the coffee table and dialed Diana's number. She answered on the second ring, her soft, musical voice soothing and cheering him. "How was your day?" he asked her.

Diana refused to think about Doug's visit. "It was lovely. How was yours?"

Cole discounted annoyances like SEC investigations, the threat of subpoenas, an intruder, and being tailed by someone in a dark blue Ford. "Great. Everybody liked my new tie."

Chapter 43

*T*HE BLUE FORD WAS STILL FIVE CARS BEHIND WHEN COLE'S CHAUFFEUR swung the limo into Unified's entrance the next morning. As it drove past, Cole got the license number. Whoever was following him obviously didn't want to press his luck by following Cole onto Unified's campus. "Be here at five o'clock, Bert," he told his chauffeur, who also shared household tasks with his wife, Laurel. "If I'm not out by five-thirty, go directly back home."

"Right, Mr. Harrison."

Murray was already waiting outside Cole's office, entertaining Shirley and Gloria with some sort of story about his days as a Little League baseball "hero." He followed Cole into his office, and when the door was closed, he observed casually, "Gloria Quigley is secretly convinced you walk on water, and Shirley would testify to it, to uphold your image."

"Really?" Cole was mildly surprised by that since he'd never cultivated their good opinion or any sort of personal relationship, with either woman. "I wonder why."

"Loyalty," Murray stated flatly. "They give it unconditionally to people they respect. Identical personality types, by the way."

Instead of answering, Cole scribbled something on a notepad and tore off the sheet. "This is the license number of the blue Ford."

"I'll check it out right away," Murray said, tucking it into the pocket of his nondescript charcoal gray suit jacket. "Speaking of personality types," he continued, idly studying his fingernails, "your cousin seems unusually jumpy. Do you know any reason why that might be?"

"I can think of several reasons," Cole said with mild sarcasm. "The New York Stock Exchange is investigating us at the request of the SEC, he's being followed wherever he goes, and last night, somebody was trying to go through his files."

"I see what you mean. By the way, as you've probably guessed, the security guard at R and D saw nothing unusual last night. No one entered the building after six P.M., and the people he saw leaving it after that time were all employees known to him by sight. We turn on alarms at the stairwell entrances from the inside at seven, which means no one can leave the building that way without using a security card or setting off alarms, and no one at all can get in."

"Then how did he get inside?"

"He could have slipped past the guard at the reception desk when the employees were coming back from lunch and then whiled away the afternoon in the building without a visitor's badge, which I doubt. On the other hand, he couldn't have gotten onto Travis's floor without a security card to open the door, which makes me think he was already on the floor."

Cole drew the obvious conclusion. "An employee?"

"Possibly. It could also have been a woman, since Travis isn't certain what he saw. Or it could have been an illusion, a trick of the lights going on, and when Travis realized a file cabinet was unlocked, he jumped to conclusions. As I said earlier, he's jumpy. I've dusted the file cabinet and desk for fingerprints, and I'm running a check on them right now. I'll follow up on this license number as soon as I get upstairs, but it may take a day or two to get a make on it."

He started for the door and stopped when Cole said irritably, "Why a day or two? Why not an hour or two?" Murray's slight, uneasy hesitation had already set off warning bells in Cole's brain

310

before the security chief answered. "You and Travis spotted the Ford and Chevrolet without much trouble. In both cases, the cars were parked down the street from your homes, but pretty much in plain view, right?"

"Right."

"Unfortunately," he said with an apologetic sigh, "that sort of amazingly clumsy technique is usually limited to law enforcement officials—either state or local. They always seem to think they're invisible."

Cole's brows snapped together over eyes like shards of ice. "Are you telling me," he enunciated in a low, incensed voice, "that the *police* are tailing us?"

"That's my hunch. I'll confirm it as soon as I can check this out."

When he left, Cole made three phone calls in rapid succession. The first was to a car-rental agency, who promised to deliver a plain, four-door sedan to his office by noon.

The second call was to a private, unlisted phone number in Fairfax, Virginia, belonging to a senior member of the United States Senate who had the ear of the president, a seat on the Appropriations Committee, and a great deal of political clout. He had also received three hundred thousand dollars in campaign contributions from a fund-raiser held by Cole Harrison and was hoping for another such event before the next election.

According to his wife, Edna, Senator Samuel Byers was attending a meeting of the Appropriations Committee that morning. Cole left word with her, but he had to wait until she finished exclaiming over how much she loved *Foster's Beautiful Living* magazine and had extracted a promise from him to bring Diana to Fairfax for their annual Christmas party.

His next call was to a number that only Cole knew existed. He drummed his fingers impatiently on the desk, and when Willard Bretling answered, Cole said simply, "I'll be there tonight at six."

"Who is this, please?" Bretling asked, his voice distracted and scratchy from lack of use.

"Who the hell do you think it is?" Cole snapped.

"Oh, of course, I am sorry. I have been playing with our toy all night," the seventy-year-old said in a gleeful voice.

Senator Byers called on Cole's direct line at four o'clock, just after Cole hung up from Diana. "I'm sorry to hear about your trouble,

Cole," Sam said, and he sounded sincere. "I'm sure it will all blow over in a week or two."

"I am not so sure," Cole countered.

"What can I do?"

"You can find out who the hell is behind it and how far it's already gone."

"I'll find out what I can," Sam promised, but before he hung up, he added awkwardly, "Until this little tempest in a teapot blows over, it might be best if you don't call me at the office or at home, son. I'll call you. Oh, and give your new wife a great big hello from me," he added.

Cole swore in disgust at that last piece of hypocrisy, then leaned back in his chair and closed his eyes. He tried to conjure an image of Diana to calm the chaos of the day, and she appeared in his mind, walking with him in the backyard just after they'd announced their marriage to her family.

"For a man who's impressed, you've been looking awfully grim," she'd said.

"That isn't my 'grim' look."

"It isn't? What's your 'grim look' like?"

"I don't think you want to know."

"Oh, go ahead," she'd teased. *"Let me see it—"*

The memory made Cole chuckle out loud.

Chapter 44

COREY POINTED TO THE EIGHT-BY-TEN GLOSSY PHOTOGRAPHS SHE'D arranged across the conference table in Diana's office. "What do you think? Should we use this one or that one?"

"What?" Diana said, staring out the window and watching a big jet make a slow turn and begin heading west.

Leaning forward, Corey put her hand on her sister's arm. "Diana, your mind isn't on any of this, and if you're not going to be able to concentrate, why don't you join Cole at his uncle's today instead of waiting until tomorrow?"

Diana shook her head. "No, I told him I couldn't leave today. I've taken next week off, but I have too many things to do before I can leave. He's going to fly in and pick me up tomorrow."

"Don't you think he'd be happier if you went today instead?"

"I know he would," Diana said with a quiet smile. Cole had been disappointed that she couldn't join him until tomorrow, but he'd understood. "Anyway, he's on his way to Austin with his uncle right now. Even if Cole's secretary could reach him and tell him that I could leave today, I doubt his uncle would be up to the flight here and then all the way back to where he lives."

Corey could tell Diana was wavering, and it made her happy. All her instincts told her that Cole Harrison was exactly the man for her sister. "You could find out Cal's address from Cole's secretary, fly there yourself, and call Cole to come and get you when you land."

"Don't tempt me," Diana warned. She got up and wandered over to the window, so distracted by the desire to leave right now for Jeffersonville that at first she didn't pay any attention to the black Mercedes convertible pulling up in front of the building. When she did notice it, the young woman who got out of the car captured her attention first. In her late teens or early twenties, she was wearing a thigh-high pink skirt that displayed long, beautiful legs, and a pink strapless knit top stretched taut over full breasts. Everything about her was voluptuous, from her clothing to her full lips, flowing hair, and pouty expression. The man who was driving reached across from inside, tugged her hand, and drew her back into the car, as if he didn't want her to go inside with him, then got out himself.

Diana's voice dropped to a dazed whisper. "Dan's here. And he's brought his bride."

"What!" Corey said, racing to the window. The new wife got out of the car again, in obvious defiance of his wishes, and while Dan laughed and tucked her back into the car, Corey got a good look at her. "Can you *believe* that!" she exploded. "She looks like a—an oversexed teenager."

Diana felt a stab of jealousy and hurt that vanished in moments. "She's perfect for him," she decided aloud. "She's obviously jealous and insecure about him coming up here, and he *loved* it! He was laughing."

"He's a pig!" Corey said angrily. "He obviously needs constant reassurance of his virility. What can he possibly talk to her about?"

Diana thought back to her relationship with him and realized that while he had *said* he was proud of everything Diana had achieved in her career, he had always given her the subtle feeling that she was lacking in other areas. *"Your career takes so much out of you, Diana."* He'd said that a thousand times. On the other hand, even without a career, she'd never have had his new wife's breasts or long legs. And if she had had them, Diana wouldn't have been caught dead in that outfit. "How could I have been so blind?" she murmured. Then she turned from the windows and walked over to her desk.

"Are you going to see him?"

"Just for a moment," Diana said, pressing the intercom button that buzzed on her secretary's desk.

"Do you want me to stay?" Corey asked.

"It's up to you. He wants to absolve himself of guilt by creating some sort of friendly relationship with me." Sally answered the intercom, and Diana asked her to call Cole's secretary and get specific information about Cal's address and phone number. Sally was also to ask her to tell Cole that Diana was on her way, and then to make the flight arrangements for today. As soon as she was finished, Sally's voice dropped to an apprehensive whisper. "Mr. Penworth is walking down the hall," she warned.

"Diana!" he exclaimed a moment later, looking windblown and suntanned and charmingly embarrassed. "I got back yesterday, and I came straight here as soon as I could."

Diana leaned back against her desk and folded her arms over her chest. "I see that," she said mildly, filled by the strangest feeling of relief mixed with disgust. She hadn't lost someone wonderful. He was weak and selfish, and he was a coward. Cole had been right when he made that toast the first time she encountered him on the balcony.

"I wish you'd say something to make this a little easier," Dan said, looking genuinely disappointed in her lack of helpfulness. "Look, I know you were hit hard by what happened between us."

"Of course I was," Diana said. He actually looked flattered and pleased by her admission. "After all," she added with an irrepressible smile as she quoted Cole, "I was jilted by 'the scum of the earth.' "

In a fit of righteous indignation, he turned on his heel and stormed out of her office. After a moment, Diana looked over at Corey, who was leaning against the wall opposite Diana's desk. Her face alive with mirth, Corey shoved away from the wall. Very slowly and very loudly, she clapped.

Chapter 45

DIANA HAD TO CHANGE PLANES IN AUSTIN AND AGAIN IN SAN Larosa. She wasn't naïve enough to expect the flight from San Larosa to Ridgewood Field near Kingdom City to be aboard a 747, but neither had she anticipated that she would have to hike a half mile in high heels across the tarmac to board a miniature plane that she might have thought was "cute" if it had a solid coat of paint in one color and jet engines instead of old-fashioned propellers.

The closer she got, the smaller the Texan Airline plane looked. She picked up her pace to a near run, trying to keep up with the baggage handler, who had also taken her ticket and checked her in at the gate.

Evidently, the young man noticed the rapid clicking of her high heels, because he stopped and turned. "Right this way, Miss Foster—or is it Mrs. Harrison?" he said with a grin. "I saw you and your husband on the news."

Diana's attention was riveted on the small dilapidated aircraft she was expected to board. "Is that fit to fly?"

"I trust it," he said with a smile.

"Yes, but would you *fly* in it?"

"I do it all the time."

The interior of the plane was shabby and dirty. Her seat tipped from side to side when she sat in it, so she felt around on the floor, located both ends of the seat belt and buckled it snugly in place, using it to anchor herself and the wobbly seat to the floor of the plane. The ticket agent–baggage attendant winked at her as he bent in half and squeezed into the cockpit; then he slid a pair of aviator sunglasses onto his nose, and assumed a new role. Pilot.

The plane lumbered down the runway, bumping, and clanking, engines straining, swaying from left to right with enough force to jar Diana's seat partially loose from its seat belt mooring; then at the last moment the plane heaved itself into the air with an audible groan and began straining toward the sun.

Satisfied that having made it up, the old plane could make it down, she opened the envelope to look over the instructions to Cal's ranch. Unfortunately she made the mistake of glancing into the cockpit just as the pilot raised his hand to shade his eyes and *he* began scanning the horizon. Right to left. Left to right. No radar.

Diana could not believe it! Gripping the sides of her little seat, she watched the pilot's head make its slow, constant swivel, and without realizing it, she began to help him. Leaning forward, she peered out through the tiny windshield, compulsively scanning the horizon with her heart in her mouth . . . left to right . . . right to left . . . left to right.

An hour later the aircraft slammed onto the landing strip at Ridgewood Field and galloped to the terminal. The pilot smiled at her as he unbuckled his seat belt, opened the plane's door, and put down the steps. Then he turned to offer her a hand. "Did you enjoy your flight?" he asked.

Diana stepped onto hot solid pavement and drew her first easy breath of the past hour. "If you're taking up a collection for radar, I'd like to contribute," she said wryly. He laughed and nodded over his shoulder. At the end of the airstrip, surrounded by an assortment of small planes, Cole's jet gleamed in the sun, a sultan among peasants.

"After you've flown in that, everything else is a letdown. Is your husband going to pick you up?" he added.

"I have to call him first."

Inside, the little metal terminal building was hot and stuffy. Across from a desk with a Car Rental sign on it was a vending machine. A woman in a waitress uniform whose name tag said "Roberta" was chatting with two elderly men who were drinking coffee from paper cups at a small lunch counter. On the opposite wall between two restrooms was a pay phone.

After twenty minutes of busy signals, Diana had the operator check the line and was informed there was no one on the line. Diana assumed Cole's uncle's phone was out of order and decided to rent a car.

"I'm sorry, miss," Roberta said, looking as if she truly was, "but we only have two rental cars. The one with the bad muffler was rented this morning by a drilling company man who came in on that red plane. The car with the bad tires got wrecked last week and it's being fixed."

"In that case, where can I find a taxi?"

That brought a guffaw from one of the elderly men at the lunch counter. "Girlie, this ain't St. Louis, Missouri, nor even San Angelo. We ain't got no taxicabs standin' around here."

Diana was frustrated but undeterred. "When's the next bus into Kingdom City?"

"Tomorrow morning."

She decided to appeal to the gallantry of the male native Texan. "I'm here to meet my husband. We were married last weekend, and this is our honeymoon."

A honeymoon touched a responsive chord in Roberta's heart. "Ernest," she pleaded, "you could take the lady to Kingdom City, couldn't you? It's only a few minutes out of your way. Do it and I'll give you free coffee every time you come by for the next two weeks!"

The man named Ernest chewed thoughtfully on his toothpick and then nodded. "Make it three weeks and you got yourself a deal, Bobbie."

"Okay, three weeks."

"Let's go then," said Ernest, shifting off a stool at the counter and sauntering toward the front door.

"Thank you very much," Diana said, relieved. She held out her hand to the man. "My name is Diana Foster." He gave her outstretched hand a quick shake and introduced himself as Ernest

318

Taylor. His gallantry clearly didn't extend to suitcases, because he glanced over his shoulder at her luggage and said, "I'll meet you at the curb so you don't have to lug them things out to the parking lot."

"That's very kind of you," Diana said with concealed sarcasm as she turned to get the first of the three cases. She'd nearly completed her third and final trip when she shoved the hair out of her eyes and saw the vehicle that was going to take her into town, and if she hadn't been so tired and frustrated, she'd have sat down on the nearest piece of Louis Vuitton luggage and laughed till she cried. Gliding up to the curb was a dusty dark blue pickup truck with a Ronald Reagan bumper sticker and a mountain of oil drums, fishing gear, toolboxes, and cable piled in the bed. "The latch on the tailgate is broke. Just hoist them suitcases over the top of it into the back," Ernest suggested from the corner of his mouth that wasn't clamped on the toothpick.

Diana knew there was no way she could lift the heavy luggage over the tailgate, into the back of the truck. "I wonder if you could possibly give me a hand?" she asked.

Ernest opened his door, but stopped with one booted foot on the ground. "You thinking of giving me something for my trouble?" he asked. "Like five bucks, maybe?"

She'd intended to give him twenty dollars for the ride, but she was no longer feeling quite so charitable. "Fine."

Ernest swung down from the truck and proceeded to toss five thousand dollars' worth of Louis Vuitton luggage on top of dirty toolboxes and filthy rags, but when he aimed the third piece for the oil drums, Diana's voice burst out in a desperate cry. "Could you handle that a little more carefully? Those suitcases are very expensive."

"What, this thing?" he said with a disdainful expression as he held the suitcase at arm's length as if it were weightless. "Can't see why. Looks to me like it ain't nothing but canvas with a plastic coating on it—"

Knowing it would be futile to try to debate this point with a man who willingly drove such a filthy vehicle, Diana chose not to comment. Unfortunately, Ernest misconstrued her speechlessness as sudden recognition of the truth, which drove him to press his point. "Nasty-lookin' color combination—brown with kinda greenish tan letters all over it saying 'LV.'" That said, he tossed the last case onto the oil cans, then slid behind the steering wheel and waited, watching Diana clear a stack of road maps, fishing tackle, and a can of WD-40 off her seat. "'LV,'" he pointed out, "ain't even a word."

Since he seemed unwilling to put the truck into gear until she said something, Diana reluctantly replied, "They are initials."

"Secondhand stuff, huh?" he concluded sagely as the truck's gears cranked and they headed down the short gravel driveway toward the highway. "You know how I figured that out?"

Diana's mood went from mild irritation to mirth. "No, how did you guess?"

"'Cause your initials ain't *LV*. Right?"

"Right."

"Who'd that ugly stuff belong to before it got foisted off on you?"

"Louis Vuitton," Diana said straight-faced.

"No kidding?"

"No kidding."

He slammed the brake pedal to the floor along with the pedal beside it and shifted gears at the stop sign. "He a boyfriend of yours?"

Perhaps it was the exhilarating effect of the mountains and Cole's nearness, but Diana suddenly felt in complete charity with everything. "No, he's not."

"Sure glad to hear it."

She turned her head and gazed in fascination at Ernest's profile. He had skin the color and texture of dried leather, brown eyes, hollow cheeks, and a toothpick hanging out of the side of his mouth. "Really, why are you glad?"

"'Cause there ain't no red-blooded American male alive who'd be caught dead carrying suitcases with his initials pasted all over them, and that's a fact."

Diana tried to remember details about the men she'd seen in the Louis Vuitton store making purchases for themselves. After a moment she stifled a smile and nodded. "You're right."

Chapter 46

$\mathcal{H}$ERE WE ARE. KINGDOM CITY ON THE LEFT," ERNEST SAID AS HE stuck his arm out the window, giving a hand signal for a left turn. "This is Main Street."

A thrill went through Diana. This was Cole's home, and she tried to absorb everything about it. The downtown district comprised ten blocks of businesses and stores, including the Capitol Theater in the center, which was flanked by a drugstore and a hardware store. Across the street was The Hard Luck Café, a Farmers Insurance agency, the Kingdom City Bank, a bakery, and three variety stores that seemed to carry everything from tape recorders to horse saddles.

Ernest let her off at The Hard Luck Café to use their pay phone, but to Diana's disappointment, Cal's line was still busy. She'd already ascertained that Kingdom City had a taxi service, so she resigned herself to that.

As they pulled up at a stop sign in front of Wilson's Feed and Grain, however, Ernest shifted his toothpick to the other side of his jaw. "You got any other ideas about how to get where you're going?"

"Yes, I'm going to take a taxi."

"It's busted." As proof, he nodded meaningfully toward the parking lot in front of Gus's Repair Shop, which was nearly blockaded by vehicles waiting to be repaired. In the front row, parked parallel to the curb, Diana saw a white Mercury sedan with its hood up and the word *TAXI* printed in black on the door.

Ernest had already made it clear that he wasn't available to take her to Jeffersonville, so at the moment, Diana's choices seemed to be limited to hitchhiking or standing on a corner with a fistful of money in her hand, asking passing vehicles to give her a ride. Neither one seemed safe. "Ernest," she said in a voice of helpless femininity, "I'm really desperate, and I just *know* you can think of something. Is there someone around here who would rent their car to me?"

"Nope."

"I'd be willing to pay very generously."

Until then, Ernest had not seemed to fully comprehend the magnitude of the problem or to be personally concerned with finding a solution, but at the words "pay" and "generously," his entire demeanor underwent a distinct change. "How much does a regular rented car cost you?" he asked, slanting her a speculative sideways glance.

Diana remembered signing a charge slip for a Lincoln Town Car she'd rented in Dallas for several days. "Two or three hundred dollars, I think. Why? Have you thought of a car I could rent?"

"I know just the ticket!" he announced with startling enthusiasm as he slammed down on the clutch and brake pedals, and swung the old truck into Gus's repair yard, stopping behind the taxi and blocking part of the driveway with his back fender. "I'll go see what kind of deal I can make for you."

Diana was so grateful she nearly patted his arm as he slid out of the truck, leaving the door swinging on its hinge.

In a gratifyingly short time, a man emerged from the cinder-block building. He was wearing a light blue shirt and dark blue work pants with a grimy rag dangling out of a back pocket. The oval patch on his shirt pocket proclaimed in red letters that he was "Gus." As he walked, he pulled the rag from his pants and began wiping his hands. "Pleased to meet you, miss," Gus said a little uneasily. "Ernest says you're interested in the Ford, and he's bringing it around."

From the rear of the building, Diana heard an engine crank followed by a mechanical cough and sputter, then silence. Another attempt to start it brought success, and Diana opened her purse, hoping Gus took credit cards. "There he is," Gus said.

Laughter and horror left Diana gaping at a rusted orange pickup truck that was, if possible, in even worse shape than the blue truck she'd ridden in to Kingdom City. It was coated in a thick layer of dirt, with the front bumper tied on with a rope and the passenger window held together with duct tape. Speechless, she watched Ernest climb out of the truck, his expression pleased. "You're joking," she told him. "What am I supposed to do with that?"

"You buy it!" Ernest exclaimed as if that should have been obvious as well as exciting. Stretching his arms out, he lifted his hands palms up in a gesture of absolute jubilation. "You buy it for five hundred bucks; then you keep it or sell it back when you leave."

Diana knew she was trapped, but she couldn't believe this was her only solution, and the idea of paying five hundred hard-earned dollars for a rusty, filthy, disreputable pile of orange junk was almost more than she could bear. "I can't believe that thing is worth five hundred dollars."

"She's solid as a rock," Ernest said, displaying a remarkable ability to overlook details such as loose bumpers, a headlight that was hanging by its electrical wires, and the taped-together glass.

Diana had no choice and she knew it. "I'll take it," she said in a small, miserable voice, reaching into her purse for her credit card. Still silent, Gus took the card and walked into the shop. He returned a few minutes later with a charge slip for her to sign and a handful of cash. While Diana signed the ticket, Ernest pitched her suitcases into the back of the orange derelict in the driveway; then he came around to make certain the proceedings were successfully concluded. "That does it, then," he said, and to Diana's confusion, she saw him hold out his hand to Gus, who then counted out $490 in bills into it.

"Where's my other ten bucks?" Ernest said, scowling.

"You still owed me for that tire."

Belatedly sensing a scam, Diana rounded on both men. Since Gus had never urged her to buy the damned truck in any way, she put the blame solely on Ernest and shifted her narrowed gaze to his impenitent, leathery face. "Do you mean to tell me," she said in a low, indignant voice, "that you just managed to foist your own car off on me?"

"*Sure* did," he said with a grin. Then he added insult to injury by nudging her in the side and confiding, "I'd have taken two hundred and fifty dollars and been glad to get it."

Inwardly humbled, Diana looked him straight in the eye and told the larcenous old man a lie she hoped would keep him awake nights. "Yes, but I'd have *paid* a thousand dollars." The expression of dismay on his face was so comical and so satisfying that Diana's temper cooled considerably even before she heard Gus's choked laugh.

Ernest followed her around to the driver's door and held it open while Diana climbed gingerly onto a filthy, torn, vinyl seat; then he closed the door for her. The steering wheel seemed enormous, but Diana got a good grip on it; then she felt for the brake pedal with her toe and the gearshift with her hand. Her foot encountered three pedals, not two, and when she looked at the gear lever, she saw a diagram instead of nice little letters indicating *Drive, Park,* and *Reverse.* A stick shift. Her heart sank.

"Betcha can't handle a standard transmission, can you?"

"Certainly," Diana lied, looking over her shoulder while her heart bumped nervously. The only way out of the crowded lot was to back down the driveway, which sloped downward to the street. Pretending to wait for two mothers carrying babies to walk behind and past her, Diana glanced at the diagram and tried to remember the trick associated with using the clutch and the brake that Doug had taught her when she was sixteen.

Satisfied that no one was behind her, she shoved at the clutch and yanked on the gearshift, wincing at the metallic screech of gears; then she released the clutch with a jolt that made the truck shake and she slammed down on the accelerator. As the truck careened backward and gathered speed, Diana steered frantically, and Gus yelled a warning over Ernest's roar of laughter, but somehow the truck landed safely on the street, pointed in the opposite direction. Pride and common sense made Diana decide to circle the block, rather than turn it around.

Chapter 47

WHEN THE TRUCK ACTUALLY HELD TOGETHER FOR FIVE FULL MILES, Diana relaxed enough to take note of the scenery. This was a part of Texas she rarely saw but that everyone who watched westerns automatically identified with the state. Behind miles of fencing that separated vast pastures from winding county roads, newborn calves frolicked beside their mothers and gangly foals with flying tails scampered in short bursts on unsteady legs while watchful mares looked on.

She could imagine how it would look in springtime, when the bluebonnets and buttercups and Indian paintbrush would burst into bloom, spreading their blossoms like a fluffy patchwork quilt over the rumpled hills and shallow valleys.

She had to stop once at a filling station to make certain she hadn't passed the turnoff to Cal's house, because the addresses were usually painted on rural mailboxes that were partially covered by tall grass.

Up ahead, she saw what had to be the right place, and she gingerly slowed the truck, praying it wouldn't die when she navigated the turn. It backfired when she slowed down, and the gears screeched horribly when she tried to shift into a different gear, but she made the turn. Once she had done that, she was confronted with a new series of problems in the form of a hilly gravel drive a mile long that twisted in and out among trees that no one had wanted to cut down apparently, and then rose sharply again.

"She should be here any minute," Cole told Cal, glancing at his watch. "If she's not, I'm going to go look for her." He'd called his office, learned that Diana was on her way, armed only with Cal's address, and he'd phoned the airfield immediately. The woman who worked there said Diana had arrived and gotten a ride with a local man who, she assured Cole, was "pretty respectable."

"You should have gone after her," Cal told him worriedly. "You can't have a wife wandering over the countryside, lost and alone. That's no way to treat a wife."

"If I knew which road the man she's with had taken, I would try to intercept her," Cole explained patiently, surprised by the signs of unprecedented nervousness his uncle had been exhibiting ever since he realized Diana was on her way.

Cal's next words were interrupted by a loud boom that cracked like thunder from the direction of the driveway. "What the hell is that?" he said, following quickly after Cole, who was already heading for the front porch.

"I assume it's Diana's ride," Cole said, staring in disbelief at an orange pickup truck with a loose bumper and a drooping headlight that was slowly lurching its way toward them, accompanied by the rhythmic screech of grinding gears and deafening backfires.

Cal watched for a moment, but he was more concerned with making a good first impression on his new niece. He smoothed his hair back carefully at the temples with both hands, squared his shoulders, and checked his tie. "Cole," he said with a strange hesitation in his voice, "do you think Diana will like me?"

Surprised and touched by his uncle's unprecedented nervous uncertainty, Cole said with absolute certainty, "Diana will love you."

Satisfied, Cal directed his attention to the approaching vehicle just as it gave one more earsplitting screech and then shot forward in a burst of speed. "Looks like he *finally* found second gear." Squinting, he added, "Can you tell if Diana's with him?"

Cole was younger and his eyes were better. As the truck reached the level spot that led directly to the front door, Cole stared with widened eyes at the face of his wife. "It's Diana," he uttered, hurrying down the porch steps to the drive with Cal right at his heels.

When they stepped out in front of her, Diana was so glad to see them that she mixed up the clutch with the brake and stepped down on the accelerator.

"Look out!" Cole shouted, jumping out of her path and dragging Cal with him. The truck missed them by inches, rolled to a stop, backfired, and died.

Shaking with fear at having nearly run over both men, Diana dropped her forehead on the steering wheel while Cole ran around the truck to help her out. She straightened just as he grabbed the handle to open her door. "Who owns this pile of sh—junk?" Cole demanded. The door handle came off in his hand, and he reached through the open window, groping for the handle on the interior.

He got hold of it, yanked the door open, and held his hand out to Diana to help her down. Like the elegant young woman she was, his wife accepted his hand, daintily removed her derriere from a tear in the vinyl seat as deep as a canyon, and then gracefully alighted.

Pausing for a brief moment to brush the dirt off her clothes, she flashed a warm smile at Cal, who was standing at Cole's elbow; then she looked at Cole with a sheepish smile. "We do."

Cal gave a sharp bark of laughter.

"This is my house," Cal explained, ushering her in the front door and insisting that she sit on his chair because it was the most comfortable; then he rushed off to the kitchen to get her a glass of fresh lemonade. Neat stacks of magazines and books on a vast array of topics were everywhere, and on the coffee table, in plain view, he had carefully placed the latest copy of *Foster's Beautiful Living*.

Diana could hardly believe that the gallant, endearing man who beamed at her as if she were the sunshine of his life was the same ferociously determined man who had forced his powerful nephew into marriage by blackmailing him with half of his own corporation—albeit for "Cole's own good."

327

"We'll just stay here for a little while," he explained, handing her a glass of lemonade and then standing in front of her as if she might need help drinking it. Finally, apparently satisfied that she could handle it, he sat down across from her on the sofa beside Cole and continued with the schedule for the day. "In a little bit, we'll go over to the other house. We'll eat supper there, and then you and Cole will stay there and I'll come back here."

Diana had come to adore him in less than five minutes. "Oh, but I thought we were going to stay with you," she said, shooting a confused look at Cole, "so we could get to know each other while I'm here."

"The other house is right here on the ranch," Cal assured her, positively beaming with pleasure that she wanted to see more of him.

After showing her around his home, he decreed that it was time to leave.

Cal's house was on flat ground in a wide clearing, situated for convenience not the view, but the other house, a mile further down the road and around a sharp bend, was positioned for view and setting, and it had both. "How beautiful!" Diana exclaimed as she slid out of Cole's station wagon.

Perched on the edge of a wooded hilltop that faced out across a shallow valley was a cozy house of stone and rough-cut cedar surrounded on three sides by a huge cantilevered deck that hung suspended in midair over the edge of the hill. Inside, it was rustic, with a huge fireplace at one end and rows of sliding doors at the other that opened onto the deck. Two large bedrooms opened off the living room, and the kitchen looked out over the hills in the opposite direction from Cal's house.

"This is Letty," Cole said fondly, leading a plump woman with her hair pulled back in a bun out of the kitchen and into the living room. Letty seemed almost as happy to know Diana as Cal was.

"Supper will be at six," she said, already retreating back into the kitchen. "It is nothing fancy. And nothing like the beautiful pictures in your magazine, either."

"I'm not much of a cook," Diana admitted.

"Good," she replied with a twinkle in her eyes.

Diana turned around and through the doorway saw Cole putting her suitcases at the foot of a king-size bed. He turned and caught her watching him, and a bolt of electricity seemed to shoot from his body straight into hers. He'd put his arm around her shoulders in a casually possessive gesture when he'd introduced her to Cal. But nothing in that gesture, or anything else he'd done, indicated what he felt about whether this was going to be a honeymoon or not.

She wasn't certain if that meant he took for granted that it was, or that he wasn't overly concerned one way or another.

All that began to change when dinner was over.

Chapter 48

*S*UNSET HAD PAINTED THE SKY IN WILD STREAKS OF LAVENDER, PURPLE, and red by the time they'd finished dinner and Letty had cleared away the plates.

The initial nervousness that Cal had displayed when she first got there had vanished. In its place was the assumption that she was part of the family and always would be. Besides making Diana feel like a fraud, it led to several questions about motherhood, such as how she would run her company and still have a baby. To make matters worse, she had the distinct feeling that Cal was aware that she'd not considered any of that and was suspicious about why not.

Annoyingly, Cole didn't seem to suffer any of her guilt or self-consciousness. In fact, *he* was making her uncomfortable, and she had a feeling he was doing it deliberately. While appearing to pay attention to the conversation, his heavy-lidded dark silver eyes were making a leisurely appraisal of her features that made Diana self-consciously reach up to lift a strand of hair off her cheek.

He was leaning back in his chair with his long legs stretched out in front of him and his feet crossed at the ankles, ignoring the sunset in favor of her. Without moving a muscle or saying a word, he was emanating an aura of predatory virility that was tangible enough to cut with a knife.

And to cap everything off, both men were completely unself-conscious about other things that made Diana acutely uneasy, things that seemed to creep into the conversation with nerve-racking regularity. Diana's simple compliment about the hand-wrought-iron table they were sitting at led Cal to provide her with the information that Cole had actually had a king-size bed shipped down four days ago to replace the double-size one that had been in the bedroom. And then he remarked that among other new furniture that had arrived by truck was the big L-shaped sofa in the living room, which had more pillows on it than any three beds he'd ever seen.

When she said that she thought the landscaping around the house was very pretty, she discovered that Cole had had an army of workmen up there manicuring the place until an hour before she arrived. "It wasn't fit to bring a bride to," Cal informed her. Then he tipped his head to a double chaise longue on the deck a few yards away. "Cole had that sent down from Dallas for your stay," he confided. "I've never seen the likes of it, have you?"

She turned and looked at the double chaise and nodded with a smile. "Once before."

"Shows you what I know. Looked to me like he was putting a bed right there on the front porch! I've seen beds on porches before," he joked, "but they usually have box springs tossed out beside them, along with an old wringer-washer."

Diana's heart jumped. Maybe it did look like a bed.

"Cal," Cole said mildly.

Diana thought his objection to the topic of beds too late and too little.

If she agreed to "honeymooning" here, which she had rather expected to do, she'd envisioned something that started a little later and progressed a little slower.

At exactly 8:30 Cole looked at Cal and Cal looked at his watch, quickly stood up, and announced, "Well, it's time I get back to work." Since he didn't have work, and since it was only now fully dark, Diana leapt to the obvious conclusion that Cole thought it was time to use one of the many new, fully padded, horizontal surfaces in the house, and Cal wanted them to get busy making him a great-great-nephew.

Diana stood up almost as abruptly as he did. "I think I'll take a shower and change into something . . . cleaner!"

Cole watched her back through the door, puzzled by her reaction to being alone with him. He was certain she intended to go to bed with him. He was *fairly* certain . . .

He wasn't certain at all.

A few minutes later, he went into the kitchen for a glass of iced tea and noticed his bedroom door was open. One of her suitcases was missing and the bathroom she was using was the one in the second bedroom. He tipped the pitcher up, considering the ramifications of that. Separate bathrooms in Diana's circle, and his own now, were a practical and convenient accoutrement. She was being civilized and sophisticated. Or shy. Or evasive.

Normally, Cole could size up the most complex situations in a matter of minutes. Tonight, he couldn't seem to second-guess the intentions of his own wife. Frowning, he went into his bedroom, intending to take a shower. He pulled off his shirt and belatedly remembered he'd taken a shower an hour before she got here. Now he was acting like a nervous bride.

He went back to the kitchen, dumped out the iced tea, and decided to have a drink instead. He carried it onto the porch and stretched out on the double chaise.

He knew damned well Diana wanted him.

They were attracted to each other. Wildly attracted.

He'd offered to let her make the decision. She was either having a hard time making one — or she'd made one he wasn't going to like and was trying to avoid telling him.

The stars came out, one by one, and the sky darkened until they twinkled like bright jeweled paths across the sky.

In the guest bedroom, Diana finished brushing her hair at the dresser and debated over what to wear. It was really too early to be in a robe, not to mention transparently suggestive. She decided to put on a pair of white shorts and a bright green silk shirt instead. Cole was probably expecting her to appear in something filmy and revealing. A negligee. Something fragile and lacy.

She put on a touch of lipstick and thought of Cole expecting a replay of their wedding night, only much more so, and her hand trembled so hard she dropped the lipstick tube. She'd been so intoxicated then that she hadn't known where, or who, she was, but she knew now, and her stomach cramped with nervous uncertainty.

What was she *doing*, letting herself in for this! She picked up the brush and brushed her hair again. Husband or not, Cole was a stranger. An unknown entity who stepped over barriers the size of mountains without qualm or difficulty and showed no concern for repercussions.

She was concerned enough for both of them. There was no point in denying that after he had left Houston, she had thought of him a thousand times a day, and every thought was sweeter than the last one. And there was no denying that the idea of "honeymooning" here with him had made her knees weak and still did. But now that she was here, there was something wrong with the picture. Although they were legally married, it was clearly understood between them that was *temporary*. So what Cole had actually suggested in Houston was that they compound and complicate the farce by indulging in an orgy of sex for a week.

When he presented the idea, he had offered it as a suggestion and left the decision to her. She had decided to do it.

Now that she was here, it was obvious he'd made assumptions, acted on them, and intended to have things his way. She decided not to do it. At least, certainly not tonight.

She was not going to relinquish control. She liked being in control of her life, her present, her future, and she normally handled it very well. Except when Cole got involved, and then he turned everything upside down. It was a pattern that needed to stop. It was a lesson he needed to learn.

Emboldened by that resolve, Diana put the hairbrush on the dresser and left the guest bedroom.

The rest of the house was dark, but the light was on in Cole's room, and she assumed he was showering, so she decided to wait for him on the porch.

She walked outside and closed the door behind her; then she walked over to the railing, looking out at the hills bathed in moonlight. She'd been standing there a full minute when a low-pitched, seductive voice said, "Would you like to join me?"

Diana whirled around. He was stretched out on the longue,

wearing loafers and pants, but his chest was bare, and in her state of mind, the fact that he'd taken off his shirt struck Diana as a deliberately provocative maneuver.

Her gaze riveted on the bronzed skin that covered an acre of muscled chest and sinewed shoulders; then it shifted nervously to his eyes. He wanted her to join him on the chaise. He'd been out here waiting for her. Her treacherous heart began to beat a little faster.

Very firmly, Diana reminded herself of her decision. "I don't think so," she said with a smile that made her refusal seem, unintentionally but distinctly, flippant and blasé. Unable to fix that, she stayed with it. "I think I'll get a glass of lemonade, though."

As she walked past Cole's chaise, he caught her hand and forced her to stop and turn. In silence, he studied her face as if he were searching for an answer, and while she was distracted by that, he was slowly pulling her forward. His tone was so gentle that it disturbed her balance as much as his action. "Don't play games with me, Kitten." He took her other arm and tugged.

Diana landed on top of him, her forehead at his chin, his left hand on her upper arm. Bracing her palms beside his shoulders, she levered her chest off of his and stared at him in irate disbelief. His right hand lifted, and his knuckles stroked softly up her bare arm in a patient caress while his gaze held hers. The message in those compelling gray eyes was as clear as if he were whispering it: *Make up your mind.*

Diana gazed at the sensual mouth only inches from hers. Inviting mouth. Tender smile. *Make up your mind.*

Without volition, her lips moved closer to his, and her heart began to race with excitement. *Decide.*

Her eyes drifted closed, and her breath came out in a sigh. She kissed him softly and felt his lips answer, moving on hers, moving with them, while his hands slid up her arms and tightened. She broke the kiss, and he let her, but the body beneath hers was hardening and the gray eyes were beginning to smolder. He laid his palm against her cheek, slowing running it back, curving it around her nape, urging her closer. *Again.*

Her arms went weak, and her breasts flattened against his hard chest as his mouth opened on hers in a deep, hungry kiss. His fingers shoved into her hair, holding her mouth imprisoned, while his arm slanted over her hips and he rolled her onto her side, leaning over her.

His tongue tasted and urged and slowly drove into her mouth while his thighs pressed into her. Rigid thighs. Demanding.

Her hands pressed him closer; her body strained nearer. He tore his mouth from hers long enough to unbutton her shirt and spread it open, and what he saw nudged him another step closer to the edge. Pert nipples hardened to tight buds tipped two exquisite pale globes that were in perfect proportion to the rest of her.

He touched the nipple and it tightened more. He bent his head and kissed it, and she moaned aloud and arched her back in a burst of pleasure that startled him with its intensity. Trying to slow himself down, he kissed the other nipple, drawing it into his mouth, and her fingers tightened reflexively in his hair, her back arching higher.

Stimulated by the expression of *her* pleasure, his body surged in an urgent desire to do more. With an effort, he made himself slow down and rolled her back on top of him. To his surprise, she pulled her shirt closed and started to get up. He stopped her at the exact moment when she was straddling his erection.

Diana thought she knew exactly why he'd slowed down. She bent her head to avoid his gaze and self-consciously started to button her shirt over her small breasts.

A hoarse word stilled her fingers. "Don't!"

Her gaze snapped to his, her hands holding the edges of her shirt closed. Cole pulled her hands away so that he could see. "Beautiful," he whispered, spreading her shirt all the way off her shoulders. He cupped his palms over her breasts, caressing them.

Diana's heart began to thunder with a mixture of shock, embarrassment, and exquisite pleasure.

Cole was so attuned to her that his own heart began to hammer, and he suddenly realized that he was actually feeling *her* reactions in his body. He rubbed his thumbs over her nipples and his own nipples hardened. "Touch me," he whispered to her, half afraid of what would happen when she did.

The shaken sound of his voice made Diana's hands tremble as she bent low over him and covered his nipple with her lips, teasing it with her tongue. When he drew in his breath sharply, Diana felt the sudden jerk of his hips beneath her as if he were inside her, and suddenly she was yanked forward onto the chaise and immediately was pinned beneath him. Together they were caressing hands and eager mouths and urgent limbs shedding clothes to give more pleasure.

Her breasts were beautiful, his body a sculpture, he was master, he was enslaved. His groan was her music and her sigh his benediction. They clung together unmoving, while her body welcomed the slow thrusting heat of him, and what began as a gentle rocking became fierce, demanding thrusts. She strained toward him in trembling need and he drove into her again and again in a desperate desire to take her with him all the way. She cried out and held him when she found it, and he joined her there.

Afterward, as she lay crushed tightly in his arms, the tears falling softly on his chest were hers. He felt them there as he stared beyond, where stars once bright and clear wavered and shimmered before gray eyes now strangely blurry.

He closed his eyes and knelt beneath the heavens, head bowed.

He offered bargains, bribes, and promises.

And when no answer came, he whispered fiercely, *"Please."*

He laid his hand against her wet cheek; she turned her face into his palm. "I love you," she whispered.

He was blessed.

Lying in the king-size bed with her head resting on his chest, Diana smiled in the darkness as she waited for Cole to say something. She had a very strong suspicion he was, at that very moment, calmly reinventing the rest of her life, and probably with the same forcefulness and speed he had handled matters thus far.

She was intensely curious as to how he would try to navigate around some of the obstacles to their fledgling marriage. He loved her and she loved him, which was all that truly mattered, but there *were* some little complications. She counted them off in her mind:

She lived in Houston and ran a big business there.

He lived in Dallas and ran an even bigger business there.

She wanted to bear his children.

He didn't want children.

Obviously, she decided as she traced the line of a hard muscle over his rib cage, this was going to take more than navigation; it was going to take a miracle.

Closing her eyes, she decided to count on one more of those. She dozed, and when she awoke a few minutes later, the little lamp on the night table was on. His fingers were threaded through hers and he was holding her hand. "I've been thinking," he said tenderly, "and I've arrived at some conclusions."

She smiled to herself at that unsurprising announcement. She could not seem to stop smiling. Turning her face up to his, she braced herself to find out how far he'd taken the decision-making process without consulting her.

"We have a logistics problem," Cole began. He saw her eyes begin to shine with laughter, and he cuddled her closer. He could not be close enough to her. "I think you'll have to move to Dallas, darling. I can't move Unified to Houston. It's a bad idea for several reasons, not to mention fiscally suicidal."

She feigned a sigh. "Under the terms of our original agreement, we're to maintain separate residences in the two cities. That was the deal."

Cole thought she was serious. "That's impossible."

"That was our agreement. We had an iron-clad verbal agreement."

He brushed that aside with amused male arrogance. "You can't have an iron-clad verbal agreement. It's a complete contradiction in terms."

"So all bets are off?"

Cole looked down sharply, studying the deceptive innocence of wide jade eyes fringed in long russet lashes beneath gracefully winged brows. "Diana," he whispered, "you are beautiful. And you are getting at something. What is it?"

"I would be willing to move the administrative and business divisions of Foster Enterprises to Dallas and leave the art and production staff in Houston under Corey."

"Then that settles everything," he said with satisfaction, bending his head to kiss her. His body was already thrilling to the idea of making love to her again.

She splayed her fingers and ran her hand down the plane of his stomach, her eyes turning hopeful and full of appeal.

"Whatever it is you're asking for with that look in your eyes," Cole said mildly, "the answer is yes."

"I'm asking for babies. Your babies."

He tipped his chin down, frowning warily. "How many?"

Her smile dawned like sunshine, her eyes sparkled like the eight-carat oval diamond he'd slipped on her finger while she dozed. He'd brought the ring here, hoping this would happen. No, he'd never dared to hope *this* would happen.

"I'd like three children," she replied.

"One," he countered sternly.

She looked at him. "I'll give you Park Place and Boardwalk and all my rental properties if I can have two."

"Done!" he said with a chuckle.

Chapter 49

C AL'S FRONT DOOR WAS OPEN, SO DIANA WENT ON INSIDE. COLE HAD
let her sleep late and had left her a note to come down to Cal's when
she was up. She could hear Cal talking to Cole in the kitchen while
Letty served breakfast. "Was I wrong not to tell you before?"

"No," Cole said flatly. "And now that you've told me, I couldn't
care less."

Cal sounded relieved. "Do you mind doing those errands for me?
You could stop by the old place and see if there's anything you
want. It's on your way."

Diana walked into the kitchen, just as Cole added in a chilly
voice, "I remember where it is."

They were sitting at the table, and Cal gave her a quick smile of
greeting; then he returned his full attention to the discussion under
way. Diana moved around the table to help Letty carry plates of
scrambled eggs and biscuits smothered with white country gravy to
the table. "You remember where what is?" she asked.

"My ancestral home." There was a snide, toneless quality to his
voice when he said that, and Diana noticed it as she put one hand on

his shoulder and leaned around him with his plate. "I'll go with you. I'd love to see it."

"No!" he said so sharply that Diana paused as she put the plate in front of him. He apologized for his tone by reaching up and catching her hand, pressing it to his shoulder for a moment.

The two men waited until Diana slid into her chair; then Cal picked up his cause again, and Diana had a glimpse of where Cole had gotten his tenacity. "If you'd read something besides financial statements and stock prospectuses once in a while, you'd know about grieving and getting resolution after a loss. Deal with it now or deal with it later, that's what the psychologists say. It's right there in the living room in books and magazine articles written by the experts."

"Last year," Cole said wryly to Diana, "he was on a campaign to have me 'get in touch with my feminine side.'"

Diana choked on her coffee.

She had already gathered that someone who lived in the general area had died, but since Cole seemed completely indifferent to the person's death, she didn't pursue the subject. Moreover, when Cal tried to return to the topic again, Cole said tersely, "I do not want this subject discussed in front of Diana."

Cole left right after breakfast to do a series of errands for Cal in town that he expected to take two hours at most, but he insisted that Diana stay with Cal. When he got up from the table, he rumpled her hair, leaned down, and pressed a kiss to her cheek, then walked forward . . . without letting go of her wrist. Laughing, Diana was hauled out of the house onto the porch, soundly kissed, then sent back inside.

Cal observed the little vignette with an expression that struck Diana as somber at best and disapproving at worst. Feeling a little hurt and a little self-conscious, she walked over to the fireplace mantel, where framed pictures, mostly quite old, were lined up in rows. With her hands linked behind her back, she studied each one, while Cal's gaze bored through her from behind.

"Is this Cole?" She lifted a frame off the mantel, brought it over to the sofa, and sat down beside him.

He flicked a glance at the picture and then pinned her with a look that was disturbing and was meant to be. "Why don't you and I have a little talk about something besides pictures," he said in a no-

nonsense tone that proved two things very clearly: Calvin Downing was far more astute than he seemed, and he was no pushover.

"What," Diana said warily, "do you want to talk about?"

"You and Cole. That all right with you?"

She nodded, and he said, "Good, because we were going to do it anyway."

Diana was not a pushover either. "Mr. Downing, maybe we'll wait until Cole comes back."

Oddly her tart retort did not offend him. "You got more than looks. You got spunk, too, and that's good. Now, do you have a heart?"

"What!"

"And if you do have one, who does it belong to?"

Diana stared at him, riveted by the topic if not his tone. "I don't understand."

"Well, I'll grant you, it's a little complicated to me, too. Because less than two weeks ago, I picked up the *Enquirer,* and there was your picture, smack dab on the front page, with a story that says you got jilted by your fancy beau. A week later, you're married to my nephew, Cole."

Five days ago, she'd have been humiliated by the mere mention of that article. Instead a wayward smile curved her lips. "Well, yes," she admitted, "I can see how that would look a little odd."

"That's the *only* part makes sense," he contradicted bluntly. "Cole was mad and I showed him the picture to make a point, and I figured he made a point right back by marrying you to get his stock back. But then he told me you're the little girl he used to talk about when he was in college, and I remembered your name was Diana Foster, so I know it's really you. Are you following me?"

"So far, yes."

"Okay. So I figured the two of you are old friends, and you just got jilted, and Cole needed a wife to get his stock back—so you two struck a deal. How am I doing so far?"

Diana eyed him askance. "Pretty well," she admitted with a trembling smile.

"Now, I also know Cole worries about my heart. So after he got over being boiling mad over the bargain I stuck him with, he decided it would be better, for my sake, if the two of you pretended you actually give a damn about each other. Are you with me?"

She nodded warily.

"Good, because now we're coming to the part that scares the hell out of me."

"What's that?"

"Yesterday he was up at the house driving everybody crazy about every little detail so it would be as nice for you as it could be. He was giving a damned good imitation of a man who thought a whole lot of his wife. I got real excited to meet you. Last night, he couldn't keep his eyes off you. But I've gotta tell you straight out, Diana, I didn't get the idea you shared his feelings. Yet, this morning, he's wearing his heart on his sleeve, so I figure you had something to do with that last night."

He paused for emphasis, his voice turning insistent as he reached the real issue: "Don't go playing around with his heart, girl. Either take all of it or leave it alone. Don't go taking little bits and pieces, when it suits you—and if it suits you. I don't think it's in you to be mean or cruel, but sometimes, if a woman doesn't know how a man feels, that could happen."

Diana collapsed back against the sofa, laughing softly, hugging Cole's picture to her chest. She turned her face to the elderly man who loved her husband, too, and said, without shame or pretense, "Cole isn't wearing *his* heart on his sleeve. That is *my* heart."

He looked fifteen years younger . . . and belatedly embarrassed. Looking around for some way out of the situation he'd brought on himself, he got up and went over to the fireplace. "That picture you have is Cole when he was sixteen. Here's two others."

He presented them to her with great care, and Diana held them that way, but her smile began to fade and her heart began to ache. She'd looked at enough photographs at the magazine to notice things quickly, and the dark-haired little boy with his fingers shoved into the heavy coat of a mixed-breed collie at his side was looking at the camera with a very solemn expression. Much too solemnly for a six- or seven-year-old. She took the other picture.

"He was nine there," Cal said. The collie was on one side of him, and another mixed-breed dog was on his left. Diana scarcely noticed the dogs; she noticed that although he was trying to smile, he didn't look happy. And his pants were several inches above his ankles in both pictures. He was standing beside an old tire swing in one shot and in front of a shack of some sort in the other.

342

She forgot about all that when she suddenly realized that Cal could give her tidbits of information about Cole. "Even when I knew him before," she confided with a smile, "he was frustratingly secretive about his past." She patted the seat beside her. "Tell me everything. Tell me what he was like when he was little and what his mother was like and—everything."

"What's he told you?" Cal asked warily.

"Nothing! I know he had a brother who was two years older than he and another brother who was three years older, and they both died in an accident right after Cole went to college. I know his mother died of cancer when he was in his first year of college. He never told me when his father died. He's had so much tragedy," she added quietly.

She waited for Cal to talk after he sat down, but he seemed deeply troubled and genuinely at a loss. He kept looking over at the piles of reading material. "I like psychology," he said, seemingly apropos of nothing. "Do you believe in it?"

"Of course."

"Do you believe it's good for a person to keep bad things bottled up inside of him, and to hide those things from the woman who loves him—And go on doing so for as long as he lives?"

Diana knew with absolute certainty and grave foreboding they were talking about Cole. She wanted to help, but she didn't want to pry.

"I—I wouldn't want him to feel I pried into anything."

"I'd call it lancing a wound, not prying."

"I don't like wounds that don't heal," Diana said. "The question is, can I help them heal?"

"You couldn't hurt."

She looked at the picture she was holding and thought about lying in Cole's arms last night. He had so much love to give, and she wanted it all. She didn't want to risk losing any of it. "If what you're going to tell me is really bad, then how will Cole feel if he knows I know it?"

"He won't have to worry that you'd change if you found out. He won't have to wonder how you really feel. Dr. Richenblau calls it 'cathartic.' It won't take long to tell. What you do about it is up to you."

Diana drew a deep breath and nodded. "Tell me."

343

"Well, you said he's had a lot of tragedy in his life. The biggest tragedy was that he was born with the name Harrison."

That was the last thing Diana expected him to say. "Why?"

"Because in Kingdom City, where Cole grew up, that name is a curse. For as long as anyone can remember, the Harrisons have been wild and worthless. They're drunkards and cheats and hell-raisers, the whole worthless lot of 'em, and Cole grew up with that stigma. When Cole's mama eloped with Tom Harrison, my brother cried. He couldn't believe his baby girl had done it. Turned out Tom had gotten her pregnant, and in that day and age, in these parts, girls who got pregnant had to get married. No two ways about it."

Diana watched him bend down and straighten magazines and generally stall; then he straightened and said, "Cole's two brothers got killed the year after Cole went away to college. They were in Amarillo, and they were drunk, and they wanted to get even drunker, but they didn't have any money. So they beat an old lady half to death for her purse; then they jumped in their car and took off. They ran a red light, and the cops went after them. They were going over a hundred miles an hour when their car hit a lamppost. Good riddance to 'em, I said then and I say it now, too.

"Cole's daddy liked those two boys of his, though. They were chips off the old block."

When he paused, Diana said flatly, "But Cole wasn't."

"Never was. Never could be. He was smarter than all three of them put together, and they knew it. They hated him for it. About the only friends Cole had in those days were his dogs. Dogs and horses and cats—Animals just loved that boy and he loved them right back. They understood each other. Guess maybe it was because they all knew how it felt to be helpless with no one to turn to."

"So Cole was the only one who went to college," Diana said aloud.

Cal gave a mirthless laugh. "He was the only one to make it past the tenth grade." Tipping his head back, he said, "You know the collie that was with Cole in the picture?"

"Yes."

"About a week before Cole left for college, his brothers gave him a little going-away present."

Diana knew it wasn't going to be good, but she wasn't prepared for what she heard.

"They hung the dog in the barn."

Diana moaned and clamped her hand over her mouth, half rising from her seat; then she made herself sit back down.

"They disappeared afterward and didn't come back until after Cole left. If they had, I think he'd have killed them."

"Wasn't there somewhere else he could live?"

"He could have lived here, but his pa wanted him right there, doing a man's work. He said a thousand times that if Cole moved away from home, Cole's mama would pay for it. And Cole's mama—poor, weak soul that she was—wouldn't leave that bastard. By the time Cole left for college, she was so sick she didn't know where she was half the time, and she wasn't worth abusing for Tom."

Diana was still a little sick from the thought of the collie. "And what about Cole's father. How long ago did he die?"

"Last week."

Diana slowly made the connection between the conversation at breakfast and this piece of information.

"I told Cole he has to go back to the old place in case there's something of his mama's there for him. Truth is, I wanted him to see it as a man. In one of my books, it said that when adults confront the 'evils of their childhood,' they often feel better. I think, whether he's there or not, it would be a good idea if he knew you'd seen the place and it didn't matter. Personally, I think he'll go there."

"Will you draw me a map?" she said, pressing a kiss on his cheek and startling him. "I'll run up to the house and get the keys to the truck."

Cal started to offer her Letty's car since Cole had his, but Letty had left to do the grocery shopping.

Chapter 50

COLE STOOD NEAR THE FRONT YARD OF THE PLACE OF HIS BIRTH, A four-room shack with rotting boards for a floor—an ugly scab on a piece of barren earth.

His birthplace. His heritage.

He wasn't certain why he had come. His mother hadn't survived this place, so there was no reason to think anything of hers would be here for him. Perhaps he'd come to confront its ghosts and then to burn it down. . . .

There were no happy memories to preserve here; the only bearable ones were of his mother. She had died just after her forty-second birthday, while he was in his first year of college. He'd been with her for the birthday before that, though. He'd hitched a ride to town to buy her a birthday present, and he was late getting back. The house had been quiet, and for a minute, he'd harbored the false hope that his father was drunk in the barn or preferably further away than that. He'd almost reached his mother's room when his father's voice had uncoiled like a bullwhip from a darkened corner of the front room. "Where the hell you been, boy?"

346

He had reached for a light switch to dispel the gloom while mentally gauging his father's mood as ugly but not physically brutal. He'd been an expert at gauging his father's moods, because any mistakes in that regard would have dire results, not just for Cole, but for his mother.

"I had to go to town."

"You're a fucking liar. You've been over to Jeffersonville with your asshole uncle, lettin' him fill your head with all his fancy notions. I told you what I'd do to you if I caught you hangin' around with him again. You're just askin' for a lesson, boy!" Cole down-graded his mood to potentially brutal. As a child, he'd thrown up from sheer terror at moments like these. Later, his primary fear was that someday, he'd kill the man and spend his life in prison for it.

His father's attention was diverted by the flower-printed gift wrap on the box Cole was holding. "What the hell is that?"

"It's a present for Ma. It's her birthday."

Amused by the sentiment, his father reached for it. "What'd you get her?"

Cole held it back, out of his reach. "Nothing you'd want—a fancy brush and mirror."

"You bought her a fancy brush and mirror?" he taunted. "A fancy brush and mirror for that skinny old crow? That's even funnier than you thinkin' you're gonna become a fancy fucking college boy." His disposition improved by that, he picked up the bottle of whiskey from the table beside him, and Cole went into his mother's room.

She was dozing, propped up on pillows, her face turned away from him. On the scarred table beside her was a plate with a half-eaten sandwich. Cole turned on the lamp and sat down beside her hip. "Is this all you had for dinner?"

She twisted her head on the pillows and looked at him, blinking her eyes to adjust to the light. She smiled, but even her smile was somber. "I wasn't hungry. Was that your father yelling a few minutes ago, or did I dream it?"

"He was yelling."

"You shouldn't upset your father, Cole."

Her continual, lifelong submissiveness to his father's ugly disposition and vile temper was something that Cole had never understood. He hated the fact that she continually tried to placate the man, to make excuses for him. Sometimes he had to stop himself

347

from berating her for not standing up for herself and defying him. She wouldn't leave him, and Cole wouldn't leave her there.

"I brought you a birthday present."

She brightened, and for a moment he could almost imagine the dark beauty that his Uncle Cal said had once been hers. She lifted the present and shook it a little, prolonging the excitement; then she carefully removed the wrapping paper and opened the box. "It's so beautiful!" Her gaze flew to his face. "How did you pay for it?"

"Why should I pay for it when I can steal it?"

"Oh, Cole, no!"

"I was joking! C'mon, Ma, if I stole it, do you think I'd wait around to get it gift-wrapped?"

She relaxed back onto the pillows and held the mirror up to study her face. With girlish embarrassment, she confessed, "I used to be very proud of how pretty I was, did you know that?"

"You're still pretty. Listen, Ma. Things are going to get a whole lot better in a couple years after I get out of college. I've got big plans, and Cal thinks they'll happen if I want them bad enough to work hard. In a few years, I'll build you a special house out at Cal's place—one that's made of stone and cedar with lots of windows— and I'll put it over on the side of that hill with big porches all around it, so you can sit up there and look out all day."

She seemed to press back into the pillows as if she were trying to hide, her fingers clutching at his arm. "Don't go dreaming dreams! When they don't come true, that's when you end up like your pa. That's why he's like he is. He used to have dreams."

"I'm not him!" Cole said, appalled by her reaction. "I'm nothing like him." The only time his father ever talked about "dreams" was when he was looking for an excuse to go on a drunken tirade and he couldn't think of any other reason.

The orange truck died when she turned off the road, and Diana left it there and walked, picking her way through deep ruts that constituted a driveway. She saw Cole ten minutes later when she rounded a sharp bend—a tall, solitary man standing with his shoulders squared, completely motionless except for a breeze that ruffled his hair. A few steps more and she had a clear view of her husband's birthplace, the home of his youth. What she saw made Diana feel like retching. She'd expected something unappealing;

she hadn't been prepared for squalor. The house was a rotting wooden shanty that crouched at the base of a hill and was surrounded by broken fences and decades of accumulated litter. In blinding contrast to his surroundings, Cole was immaculately groomed, with brown loafers polished to a mirror shine, pressed khaki slacks, and a pristine white oxford shirt with the cuffs folded back on his tanned arms. He reached behind his neck to massage the muscles at his nape, and his shirt stretched taut across his broad shoulders. Shoulders that Diana wanted to put her arms around and lay her cheek against.

He didn't seem aware that she was there until she was right beside him, and then he said in a dead voice, "You shouldn't have come here." He looked at her then, and Diana swallowed in shock at the transformation. His face was completely expressionless; a face made of stone, with a jaw of iron and eyes of cold steel. And now she understood where that hard core had been forged. It had been here. It had given him the strength to break free of this place. "I had to come," she said simply, watching his face begin to relax as he broke free of the grip of this place. "You had to know I had been here and seen it."

"I see," he replied, his heart aching with tenderness. "And now that you've seen it," he added with an attempt to sound indifferent, "what do you think?" He turned to walk away, expecting her to come with him.

What did she think? In response, Diana did the only thing she could think of to vent her wrath and express her opinion. Looking around on the ground, she picked up a heavy rock and with all the force of her raging animosity, she hurled it. Cole turned to look at the exact moment the rock blasted through the front window. In open-mouthed shock, he stared at her beautiful, irate face and then at the broken window of the hellhole he had lived in. "That," she informed him, daintily dusting off her hands after having thrown a pitch that would have done credit to Sandy Koufax, "is what I think of it."

Cole's shout of laughter exploded louder than the window. In a sudden burst of exuberant freedom, he swooped her up into his arms and tossed her over his shoulder like a sack of flour. "Put me down," she laughed, wriggling.

"Not until you promise."

"Promise what?" she giggled, squirming.

"That you will never, ever, get mad enough to throw anything at me."

"I cannot make a promise I may not keep," she advised him solemnly.

He whacked her on the backside and continued down the road. He started to whistle. She started to laugh.

The merry sounds rolled backward to the hovel he had lived in. The only remaining piece of glass left in the window frame in the house crashed to the dirt floor inside it.

The lighthearted days and passionate nights became a routine during the rest of their stay at Cal's.

When the time to leave arrived, Cal drove them out to the airstrip and watched while the plane took off, his hand lifted in a wave. His heart felt heavy in his chest because they were leaving, but it did not feel weak. It felt very strong.

Diana's heart did not feel quite as strong when Cole left her at her apartment so that he could continue on to Washington. "I miss you already," she said. "This two-city living arrangement isn't going to work."

Cole tipped her chin up. "We'll work things out in a couple of days, as soon as I get things settled in Washington. The time in between will pass very quickly."

She furrowed her forehead. "How can you *say* that?"

"I'm trying to convince both of us."

"It isn't working."

Cole crushed her against his length. "I know."

"Don't forget to call me."

He smiled at that absurdity and held her tighter. "How could I possibly forget to call you, darling?"

Chapter 51

SAM BYERS WAS SITTING IN HIS CAR WITH THE ENGINE IDLING AND THE windshield wipers running when the Gulfstream streaked out of the sky and touched down on the rainswept runway at Dulles International Airport. He watched the plane taxi to a stop at a junction of the runways, waiting for instructions from the tower; then it finally executed a ninety-degree turn and rolled right past him. When the pilots got off, he pulled his raincoat up around his ears and ran forward through the puddles.

"It's a damn shame we have to meet this way," Byers announced breathlessly as the heavy-set sixty-year-old trudged up the last step and nearly collapsed onto the sofa, "but I wanted to give you this stuff in person, and it's a bad idea for us to be seen together." He reached inside his raincoat and removed a large brown envelope.

Cole took it and handed him a glass with vodka, ice, and a lemon twist—Senator Byers's drink of preference, he knew.

The senator noted the brand of vodka his host had just served as he glanced around at the luxurious, pale gray leather interior with its chrome-and-brass–trimmed lamps and tables. "You've got style and you've got taste, Cole," he said. "Unfortunately," he added as Cole sat down on the sofa across from him, "you've also got yourself a powerful enemy."

"Who is it?" Cole snapped.

He lifted the glass in a parody of a toast and said, "The junior senator from the Great State of Texas—Douglas J. Hayward. He's taken a very personal interest in putting you out of business and into the penitentiary." Without rancor, he added, "That boy has serious presidential aspirations. He'll probably make it, too. He has the look and the charisma of a young Jack Kennedy." Belatedly realizing that his audience seemed to be in a state of angry shock, he said, "Did you do something to aggravate him, or is he just out to get you on principle?"

The only possible explanation Cole could think of involved Jessica Hayward and a long-ago night when her husband, Charles, came home unexpectedly; yet it seemed insane that young Hayward would go to all this trouble after more than a decade to defend his mother's nonexistent honor. "The only reason I can think of is lame as hell," Cole replied curtly.

"That's not likely to concern him," Sam said dryly. "Every presidential hopeful needs a cause, a dragon he can slay for the public good. That's what gets them publicity, and publicity is what gets them elected. Reagan had the Ayatollah, Kennedy had Hoffa—you get my meaning?"

"I get the meaning, but I don't like the analogies," Cole said icily.

"Hear me out before you act on your impulse to beat the shit out of me," Sam said with a chuckle. "I was about to say that when high-reaching politicians can't find a legitimate public enemy to slay, they frequently create their own. For some reason, Senator Hayward has singled you out for that honor."

He paused to sip his drink; then he continued, "Cushman's board of directors is right behind Senator Hayward, urging him on in this quest for 'justice,' and they have some political allies of their own on the team. Between them, they've managed to convince the New York Stock Exchange, the SEC, and themselves that you started those nasty rumors that their microprocessor was faulty so that the value of their stock would drop and you could buy their company for half its worth. You already know most of that. Here's the part you don't know: The Cushman people are going to file a class-action lawsuit. In addition to a few hundred million dollars in damages, Cushman wants the court to grant them the rights to *all* profits Unified makes on the processor when it's marketed—*and*—they are also demanding that you hand over all future profits resulting from any other device, design, or formula of theirs that you may eventually use. My sources tell me that Cushman is particularly emphatic about the last part of that."

He took another sip of his drink and studied Cole's unreadable expression; then he shrugged. "I thought that was a little odd, but then I'm just a country boy. But even a country boy like me can figure out the obvious—If you are found guilty of any of the criminal charges in federal court, then Cushman's class-action suit is as good as won in circuit court."

"What's in the envelope?" Cole said, his mind on solutions and countermeasures.

"Nothing that will enable you to neutralize him, if that's what you're hoping, but it will give you an idea of where you stand. William C. Gonnelli, the administrative judge for the SEC who's going to hear your case, is already so sure you're guilty of something that he's helping the federal prosecutor decide whether the next step should be to haul you up before the grand jury and get an indictment, or take the short route and ask the judge for a warrant for your arrest. There's a copy of an SEC subpoena in there. Your lawyer will be served with it the day after tomorrow. Naturally, it will be leaked to the press. They'll be waving microphones in your face when you walk out your front door from that day on, I'm afraid."

Cole hadn't expected this much information or cooperation from Byers, and he was strangely touched that he'd gone to as much effort as he had—particularly because it appeared unlikely that Cole would be sponsoring any more fund-raisers for anyone.

As if he knew what Cole was thinking, the politician stood up and shook Cole's hand. "I liked you when I met you, Cole, and I liked you better later." With a grin, he said, "Nobody's ever laid a check for three hundred thousand dollars in my hand and told me to my face that they'd have handed it to a gorilla if he were the Republican candidate."

"I apologize for that, Senator," Cole said formally, and he meant it. "And I also appreciate your help."

"I thought your blunt honesty was refreshing. I'm not used to it."
He turned and squeezed between the sofas, then stopped again in
the open doorway of the plane and pulled the collar of his raincoat
up. "I also think you're innocent. Unfortunately," he finished, "I
won't be able to talk to you anymore after this. You understand,
don't you?"

"Perfectly," Cole said unemotionally.

He didn't feel unemotional, however. As he looked at the
subpoena with his name on it, he felt a rage that was beyond
anything he'd ever experienced. He wasn't afraid of subpoenas or
trials or groundless accusations or the damage to his good name.
The problem was that in two days, his name was going to be
synonymous with *fraud*.

And by association, so would Diana's.

A laugh welled up inside of Cole, then turned to anguish. Diana
had married him to save her pride and dignity. Now he was going to
destroy all that, along with her reputation, in a way that Penworth
never could have.

Last week, Diana loved him and believed in him.

Next week, she was going to despise him.

Cole leaned his head against the back of the sofa and closed his
eyes, trying to think of a way to keep her safe . . . of a way to keep
her at all. When he couldn't think of any, the unfamiliar constriction in his throat grew until it was painful.

Chapter 52

*D*IANA LOOKED AT HER WATCH AND THEN AT THE TELEPHONE, willing it to ring. By now, Cole would surely be finished with his meeting in Washington and either home or nearly there, but he hadn't called her, and she knew instinctively the news wasn't good. She'd turned the television set on to banish the silence, but she couldn't concentrate on it or anything else.

"And now for business news. The stock market closed up today, with mixed trading on a volume of . . ."

Although she believed completely in Cole's innocence, her over-wrought imagination continually presented her with pictures of Cole standing trial, being hounded by reporters and accused of vile crimes. He said that wasn't going to happen, but she had a horrible feeling that it was all beyond his control. He'd worked so hard to rid himself of the stigmas of his youth, and now he was facing the same fate his brothers had faced . . . only *his* would become a worldwide scandal.

"The biggest loser of the day was Unified Industries, whose stock closed at a fifty-two-week low. Analysts blame the plunge on rumors

that Unified's president and CEO, Cole Harrison, is about to be subpoenaed to appear before an administrative judge of the Securities and Exchange Commission. Reliable sources say that the SEC hearing will be a mere formality and that Harrison will be called before a grand jury . . ."

She had a sudden, insane impulse to call Doug and ask him for advice. No, what she really wanted to do was beg him to intercede somehow. He wouldn't help either her or Cole now. On the subject of Cole, he was completely irrational. She thought about his incensed tirade . . . *You have to unload him, now! . . . That bastard really has a way with females of all ages . . . even you!* The remark about Cole's way with "females of all ages" made her wonder if years ago Cole had stolen some girl that Doug had imagined he was in love with. Whatever the reason, Doug's loathing for Cole went so deep that he even hated Diana by association. He wouldn't be sympathetic to any sort of appeal from her now, not after he'd warned her. He'd predicted *exactly* what was going to happen.

Slowly, Diana straightened, a possibility taking shape that was almost too obscene to consider. Doug had warned her. . . . He had told her what was *going to* happen. He despised Cole with a virulence that was palpable.

She grabbed her purse and car keys and went to find the one person who was likely to know, and to tell her if he did know.

Corey opened the front door, and Diana realized from her dejected expression that she'd also heard the news. "Corey, I have to ask you something. It's terribly important. Has Spence ever told you that Doug hates Cole?"

"Yes. He told me that when you and Cole told us you'd gotten married the night before. You liked Cole and so did I, so I didn't think Doug's opinion mattered that much."

"I need to see Spence."

"He's out by the pool."

Spence was tightening the bolts on a ladder in the deep end of the pool. "Diana, what's wrong?"

"That's what I want to know from you. A few hours after the news conference to announce that Cole and I had married, Doug came to see me and he made it clear how he feels about Cole, but he wouldn't tell me *why* he feels the way he does. You two have been friends forever. You must know why he hates Cole."

"Honey, you have enough problems without worrying about Doug Hayward." He gave his wrench one last firm tug and stood up.

"I think Doug *is* the problem," Diana said.

"What are you talking about?"

She pulled him over to a chaise longue. "That day when Doug came to see me, he was furious because I'd married Cole. He ranted about how dishonest Cole's business practices are, but Doug wasn't just angry about principles, he took it personally!"

"What are you getting at?"

"I'm getting at something else he said. He told me that the stock exchange was investigating Cole. But, he also said the SEC would turn Cole over to the federal courts for prosecution."

For a split second, Diana thought Spence didn't realize what she was getting at, but then he said quietly, "He knew all that and it hadn't happened yet?"

"Exactly. He was completely certain of everything he said, and it's all coming true! Do you know why Doug feels the way he does about Cole?"

To her surprise and relief, Spence didn't try to tell her she was being ridiculous. "Charles Hayward is probably the only one outside of Doug who knows the real answer to that. Doug was drunk the one time he brought it up with me, but I got the feeling that somehow Barbara was involved in it."

"Barbara?"

"He wasn't making sense, so I'm not sure."

Diana got up. "Well, I intend to find out from Charles Hayward."

Spence stood up, too. "I'll go with you."

Diana bit her lip, considering whether Spence would be an asset or a liability. "I think I might get further with Charles if I am alone."

Chapter 53

CHARLES HAYWARD WAS IN HIS STUDY, SITTING IN A LEATHER WING chair with the VCR's remote control in his hand—rewinding and playing the CNN news story about Cole when Jessica took Diana in to see him. "Diana would like to talk to you, Charles."

Charles looked round from his chair and nodded; then he pressed the rewind button on the remote again. "Hello," he said, beckoning to the sofa across from him. "Sit down." He pressed the play button as Diana sat on the sofa, and to her disbelief, he watched the news clip again right in front of her, smiling a little as he did.

There was something almost ghoulish about what he was doing, and it was made worse by Jessica hovering in the doorway. Diana drew a careful breath, knowing this would be her only chance to find out what she needed to know and to try to neutralize it. "I wonder if I could talk to you privately, Charles."

"Of course," Jessica said and backed out of the doorway.

"Certainly, my dear," Charles said, stopping the tape then laying the remote control on the coffee table. He looked at her in

358

expectant silence, his face devoid of any of the cruel satisfaction she'd seen when he watched the television screen.

Diana felt her way forward very carefully. "Charles," she began quietly, "after my father died, it was you I always turned to for advice."

He nodded as if pleased by that.

"And when I decided to start the company, you were one of the people who loaned me money to do it."

"I *invested* in a promising venture," he said tactfully. It was what he'd always said whenever she tried to thank him.

"Now I need help again. Only this time it's much more important. It's about Cole."

His face turned as cold as his eyes. "In that case, I will give you the best advice I have ever given you. Get rid of him!"

"I won't do that."

He surged to his feet, towering over her until Diana stood up, too. "Right now, I'm trying to think of you as an innocent victim, Diana. But if you don't get rid of him and get out of the way, you're going to be covered with the same dirt he is. Congress has control over the SEC, and we have enough on Cole Harrison to hang him."

"'We'?" Diana burst out. "'We'? You're not involved with Congress, Doug is."

"*We are* going to hang him, and then we're going to bury him," Charles lashed back.

"Why are you doing this?" Diana cried. "What has Cole done to you to make you hate him so?" With an effort she forced herself to sound willing instead of combative. "Help me understand—then I can decide whether to do as you say."

The control Charles had been exerting over his temper suddenly snapped. "You want to know what he did to me?" he jeered in an awful voice. "I'll tell you what he did—He destroyed my family! That filthy son of a bitch was the real stud in my stable. God knows how many other of Barbara's little friends he molested—"

"'Molested,'" Diana said weakly.

He grabbed her shoulders. "You wanted to know and now you're going to know all of it. Do you remember my beautiful little daughter? Do you?" he demanded with a shake.

Diana jerked free and stepped back, but she couldn't make herself leave without hearing it all. "Of—of course I remember," she said shakily.

"That animal got my little girl pregnant. I almost walked in on them at the stable one night, and I ran him off, but I never dreamed he'd actually had sex with that child."

Diana shook her head. "Oh, no, Charles, you're wrong—"

"I'm not wrong!" he shouted. "I'm the one who has *been wronged.* When Barbara realized she was pregnant—almost five months pregnant—she told her mother and Jessica took her to have an abortion. I'd have never known anything about it except for three things. Do you know what they are?" he bit out.

Diana swallowed and shook her head.

"I found out because Barbara almost died, and because she had to have a hysterectomy to prevent it, and because my little girl has spent the rest of her life in the care of one shrink after another because of it! And do you know what reminds me of it every day?"

"No."

"Grandchildren! I don't have any. That fucking son of a bitch you married deprived me of a daughter and my daughter of children and me of grandchildren."

He pointed to the door and his voice shook with wrath. "Now, you get the hell out of my house and don't ever come back!"

Chapter 54

$\mathcal{D}$IANA DROVE HOME WITHOUT ANY CONSCIOUS EFFORT OR ANY awareness of doing so. At eleven, she was still sitting in the same chair, her legs tucked beneath her, a blanket wrapped around her shoulders and spread over her lap to ward off a chill that had turned her hands to ice and made her shiver convulsively.

Corey was calling every fifteen minutes. Diana let the answering machine pick up because she could not move.

Cole was not calling at all.

She was incapable of shedding a single tear or of throwing up another time. She was completely empty.

Cole was not calling at all.

At eleven-fifteen, Corey called again, and this time she wasn't worried, she was frantic and angry. "Diana, if you don't pick up the phone right now, I'm coming over."

Diana actually made an effort to answer it, but Corey had already hung up. She arrived with Spence in record time and used her key to get into Diana's apartment.

"Diana?" Corey said soothingly, approaching her with great

caution, Diana noticed—as if they both thought Diana had gone insane. Spence crouched down in front of her, handsome and caring. "Diana," he said gently.

"What did Charles Hayward say to you, honey?"

Corey crouched beside him, clutching his shoulder tightly, a brace against whatever hideous thing they were about to hear that had reduced Diana to such a mindless state.

Diana looked at both of them. "Oh," she said thoughtfully, "he said Cole molested Barbara and got her pregnant and Barbara had an abortion. Now she can't have any more children and that's why she's always been so unstable."

"*Whaat!*" Corey exploded, shooting to her feet.

Diana's gaze automatically followed her motion, and she tipped her head back. Her voice dropped to a whisper. "Isn't that *amazing?*"

"—'Amazing'?" Corey said, shooting a hesitant look at Spence as he slowly stood up beside her. "Is that what you think it is?"

It happened then, the thing that Diana had subconsciously feared for hours—she started to laugh and she couldn't stop. "Cole wouldn't have laid a hand on Barbara! He lived in daily fear of us coming on to him. Remember how hard we all worked to get him to notice us?"

"I remember," Corey admitted, but her brows remained pulled together in a watchful frown.

"It's so funny . . . so hideously funny."

"Is it? Funny?" Corey said cautiously, but she was beginning to believe Diana was thinking far more clearly than she'd first imagined when she saw her curled up in that chair.

"Yes, it is!" Diana said, nodding emphatically. "It's hilarious. I know, because I was the one who kept the bets."

"What bets?"

"The *bets!*" she laughed. "Everyone, including Barbara, put money into a box, and the first one to get Cole to kiss her was the winner." Diana laughed harder. "I was the treasurer. And *no one won!*" Suddenly she turned her face into the chair and the laughter turned to wrenching sobs. "No one won!" she sobbed. "They're destroying him . . . and no one *ever won!*"

Chapter 55

*D*IANA TRIED TO CALL COLE AT HOME THE NEXT MORNING, BUT THE man who answered his phone said that Mr. Harrison was at work. At his office Mr. Harrison's secretary said he wasn't in. Diana arrived at the obvious conclusion that she was a very dispensable commodity to men, and that Cole had just been amusing himself when they were together with Cal, playing with marriage. When other matters in his life became pressing, either he didn't want to be bothered with her or he forgot that she existed! Her brain accepted that, but her heart rejected it and went on aching.

Somehow she made it through the day at work. In keeping with her resolution to delegate more responsibility, she spent most of the afternoon working closely with two of her executives, to be certain they were all thinking alike. No matter where she went or whom she saw in the building, she maintained a cheerful and pleasant face. Cole's name and his current predicament actually came up several times in her presence, but it was simply a thoughtful effort by the people who worked for her to avoid acting as if he had either done something wrong or else died.

In retrospect, it was comical that she'd thought Dan's defection such a disaster. *This* was a disaster.

She left the office at five-thirty and, at her family's insistence, she drove to their house for dinner. Being there was even harder than being at the office. Unlike her employees, her family didn't hesitate to voice their opinions about Cole's situation or to insist that Diana talk about it, although Corey and Spence remained silent and supportive. Even Glenna had an opinion to express, but she, too, was part of the family. Besides, she was a flagrant eavesdropper. Everyone was sitting outside by the pool before dinner, when Glenna came out to tell Diana that she had an urgent call. The entire family brightened, thinking it was Cole.

"It's a reporter," Glenna said, holding a cordless phone in her hand with the *hold* light flashing.

"I don't want to talk to any reporters," Diana replied, and added to her family, "I don't know how they're getting this number, but we're probably going to have to change it."

"He wants to ask you about your divorce."

Everyone stopped talking and stared at the housekeeper. "My what?"

"He says he wants a comment from you on the 'grounds' you're going to use."

Diana took the phone, said hello, and then listened for a moment. "Where did you hear that?" she demanded. "Well, I don't think it's actually 'public knowledge,' Mr. Godfrey," Diana replied, slowly standing up, "because *I* don't know anything about it. Good-bye," she said, but a small feeling of hope was slowly dawning in Diana's heart. She turned and ran to the nearest television set with her family in close pursuit. The screen lit up just in time for a local Houston newscast team to confirm what the newspaper reporter had just told Diana.

"There's been a side development in the Cole Harrison–Unified Industries uproar," the woman on the screen told her male counterpart. "Diana Foster, his wife of less than two weeks, is filing for divorce on unspecified grounds."

"That didn't last very long," he said to the camera.

His coanchor nodded. "Sources close to Cole Harrison confirmed the rumor less than an hour ago. It seems that Diana Foster has chosen to disassociate herself and her company from the scandal brewing in Washington over Harrison's takeover of Cushman Electronics."

Henry Britton looked almost accusingly at Diana. "Is that what you're going to do, Diana?"

Diana slowly shook her head, her eyes glowing with relief and happiness. "That's what Cole *wants* me to do. Charles and Doug Hayward warned me to get rid of Cole so the scandal won't spill over onto me. Now Cole is trying to make sure it won't."

Corey looked at her husband and quietly pointed out, "So much for the theory that Cole married her to help his public image. He just blew it to pieces for her."

Diana didn't hear that; she was thinking and planning.

"What are you going to do?" Gram asked, but Mary Foster already knew the answer to that. Putting her arm around Diana's shoulders, she said with a soft laugh, "Diana is going to Dallas."

Diana was definitely going to Dallas, and for a woman who once couldn't function without a detailed schedule or leave on a short trip without lining every article of clothing with tissue paper, she accomplished that feat with amazing expediency. With Corey and her grandmother helplessly standing by, she stuffed whatever clothes she had at the house into two suitcases she owned; then she threw all her toiletries in on top of them. "That's that," she said, closing the last piece of luggage. After that she phoned her two top executives and told them they were in charge and to call her at Cole's numbers if they had questions or problems.

She took care of the items on her filled calendar by turning to Corey and saying, "Tell Sally to cancel all my appointments."

"What reason should she give everyone?"

"Tell everyone," Diana said as she dragged the two heavy cases off her bed, "that I'm in Dallas. With my husband."

By seven forty-five, Corey had dropped her off at the airport and Diana was in line to board her eight o'clock flight when she realized that the man who was sprinting past the rows of gates toward her was Spence. "Give this to Cole," he said, taking an envelope out of his pocket. "Tell him I said it's a belated wedding present and to use it if he absolutely has to as an equalizer."

"What is it?" Diana asked, moving forward as the boarding process continued.

"It is the end of Doug's political career," Spence said somberly.

Chapter 56

*T*HE MAN WHO ANSWERED THE INTERCOM AND LOOKED AT HER
through a tiny camera located at the gate of Cole's estate was
surprisingly easy to convince that Mrs. Harrison should be allowed
to surprise her husband by being admitted without advance notice.
In fact, the middle-aged man was positively beaming with delight as
he showed her through the silent house to the back door that
opened onto the patio surrounding the mammoth free-form swimming pool.

Cole was standing alone in the dark, his hands shoved deep into
his trouser pockets, his head tipped back as if he were looking up at
the stars. Diana opened the door and silently slipped outside,
watching him, trying to think where to begin when all she wanted to
do was fling herself into his arms. She'd rehearsed a dozen opening
speeches on the flight there, all of them designed to let her stay and
face his trouble together with him. She'd thought of pleading, of
reasoning, of demanding. She'd considered trying tears to weaken
his resistance. But when the moment was finally upon her, she
couldn't seem to begin. She took a step forward and saw him stiffen

with resistance the instant she spoke. "Cole?" He didn't even turn his head or look at her. "What are you doing out here?"

"Praying."

Tears stung her eyes when she remembered the way he had dismissed the idea as the last resort of fools—dreamers who won't face the fact that they cannot have something. "What are you praying for?"

"I've been praying for you," he said in a hoarse whisper.

Diana walked into his arms. They closed around her, yanking her against him, while he buried his lips in hers. When he finally ended the kiss, he kept her crushed against his length, his jaw resting against her head, as if he were afraid to let her go for fear she would vanish. Content to stay there, she rubbed her cheek against his hard chest. "I love you."

His hand slid up her back in a caress, and he brushed a kiss against her temple. "I know you do. The proof is in my arms."

"I know why you're having so much trouble with the SEC. Charles Hayward told me."

He went very still. "He told you what?"

"I went to see him last night. He told me you got Barbara pregnant and she had to have an abortion. She can't have children because of complications from it. She's been in and out of intensive therapy programs for years."

"He told you all that," Cole said, leaning back and studying her with puzzlement and disbelief, "and you came here, to me?"

She smiled at him in the moonlight and nodded; then she cuddled closer in his arms again. "I know it isn't true."

"Because you believe in me?" he speculated, confused.

"Yes. And because back then we all had bets about who would get you to kiss them."

A low chuckle rumbled in Cole's chest beneath her ear. "And no one won," he stated, understanding at once where she was going with that. With a smile in his voice, he whispered, "How much did *you* bet?"

His wife opened his shirt button and pressed a playful kiss on his chest. "Nothing. I only make idiotic bets in Las Vegas."

They were on their way to the bedroom when Diana remembered what she'd brought to give him. "What's this?" Cole asked, setting her suitcases at the foot of his bed. She handed him an envelope and

367

a hand-decorated sack. He opened the envelope first and then the sack. Spencer Addison had sent him a brief history of Doug Hayward's drunk-driving arrests, the last of which was while he was in law school and had resulted in serious injury to the face of the female passenger with him at the time.

Rose Britton had sent him a bag of homemade chocolate chip cookies.

Even after they had made love, Diana couldn't sleep. With her head resting in the crook of his arm, she stared out at the colorful waterfall beyond the bedroom's glass wall.

"I used to wear you out," Cole teased gently. "Now you lie awake pretending to sleep. That doesn't bode well for the next fifty years."

"What's going to happen at the SEC hearing?"

She sounded wide awake and very worried. "Would it do any good to tell you not to worry?" he asked.

"None at all."

He hesitated, hating to talk to her about the details of the snare that held him powerless right now, but she had a right to know and to understand. Based on his recollection of her camping trip stories and the way she ran her business, she had a greater fear of the unknown than of a visible threat.

"I know how stupid this sounds," she murmured in the darkness, "but you had a thriving company without the Cushman microprocessor. After everything that's happened, I wish you could just give it back to them along with their whole company."

"I didn't buy Cushman to get their chip. Intel is the leader at the high end. The low-end market is already being carved up into smaller and smaller pieces by a lot of foreign producers. In my opinion, the world doesn't need another computer-chip provider."

Diana rolled over onto her side and propped her head on her hand, facing him. "Then why in God's name did you go to all that trouble to buy them?"

"I wanted some patents they held and didn't know how to use. They owned a tiny piece of a puzzle that we needed in order to produce the most desired commodity in the world right now. We had everything else put together."

"Which is?"

"Which is an ultra-long-life battery that would power laptop

368

computers and cellular phones for days instead of hours. Everyone is working on one, and everyone is getting closer, including us, but whoever brings that battery to market first wins the game—and the stakes are almost beyond comprehension. The scientist who's heading the project for me used to work for Cushman and he knew about the patent. He works off-site, in secret, in a lab he runs with a few assistants who don't completely understand what he's doing. Neither do I, for that matter. His assistants think he's working on a super-thin computer monitor/television set, which he is—in his spare time."

"Could you possibly sell Cushman back their chip and keep the patents?" she asked helpfully.

"Not a chance," Cole said sardonically. "They don't want that chip. Based on what I learned from a friend the other night, Cushman wants the profits we'll make from that battery. The only chance they have of getting their hands on those profits is if they can convince the court that I cheated them by forcing the value of their stock down before I bought it.

"The patents were and are a matter of public record, so they can't accuse me of having insider information or anything like that."

Diana smoothed her fingers over the muscles of his stomach and chest. "What do you need to get out from under this right now?"

"I have a team of lawyers working on it. We'll find a way," Cole said with absolute conviction.

Satisfied that he would, Diana curled up against him and promptly fell asleep.

Cole was awake until dawn, because he already knew there wasn't going to be "a way." His lawyers had already told him to expect to be charged with fraud and to stand trial. Nothing short of a miracle would keep that from happening, he thought grimly. But then, Diana was lying in his arms, in his bed . . . and that was a miracle. She had come to be with him when everything she heard and saw should have made her run like hell. That was a bigger miracle.

Chapter 57

*A*T NOON THE NEXT DAY—TWO DAYS BEFORE COLE WAS TO LEAVE FOR his hearing in front of the SEC administrator—he made certain he wasn't being followed and took Diana with him to see Willard Bretling's laboratory.

Located in an old part of the city, it looked like a derelict warehouse surrounded by old Cyclone fencing and guarded by snarling dogs. The few cars that were parked outside looked older than the building.

Inside, it was antiseptically clean with every kind of state-of-the-art electronics equipment.

"This is right out of—of a James Bond movie," Diana exclaimed excitedly. Willard Bretling was thin and tall with slightly bent narrow shoulders, wire-rimmed glasses, and a perpetual, absent-minded frown. He was standing at a table in a corner of the lab, arguing with his two assistants about how to use their new toaster oven.

"Ah, Cole!" he exclaimed. "Do you know how these damned things work?" He apologized to Diana, who was trying not to show

370

her reaction to his dilemma. "Such knowledge is limited to those with lesser minds than ours," he said. He smiled at her, and it was the first time Cole had ever seen the eccentric old man grin.

"If that's the case," Diana said, downplaying her own excellent mind, "it should be right up my alley." The most important scientific brain in the world stood back and watched—his Pop-Tart in hand—in tense expectation as she fiddled with a knob and pressed a lever. Nothing happened.

"Useless gadget," Bretling stated.

"There we go," Diana declared. She pressed down all the way on the lever, and the smell of a new electric appliance being put into use emanated from it.

"What did you do?" Bretling demanded, looking a little affronted.

Diana leaned very close to him and put her hand on his sleeve; then she whispered in his ear as if she had sensed how sensitive he was about being made to look foolish.

He'd left Cushman Electronics because they'd made him look foolish by refusing to let him work on his patents and ultimately assigning him to work under a younger, less gifted scientist. Diana's simple action made the temperamental Bretling into a teddy bear, right before Cole's amused eyes.

While Bretling wandered around the lab, he chatted endlessly with her. Cole couldn't imagine what they had to talk about. He could barely spend an hour with the man without feeling as if his brain were overloaded with scientific mumbo jumbo.

On a table off to their left was another of Bretling's pet projects, an ultrathin television set with a perfect picture that Cole was determined to announce very soon and thus put to shame Mitsubishi's latest introduction. At the moment, Unified Industries' candidate for Television of the Century was a flickering, white screen.

Tables at the far end of the gigantic room were cluttered with rows of would-be ultra-long-life rechargeable batteries.

Willard Bretling watched Cole's restless movements from the corner of his eye; then he looked at Diana as he said, "Your husband is not a patient man. He is a man of vision, though."

Diana nodded, watching Bretling's arthritic fingers handle a wire as fine as a human hair. "He thinks very highly of you, too."

371

The fingers stilled, faded blue eyes stared sharply over the rim of his glasses. "Why do you say that?"

Diana told him all the things Cole had told her on the way there, and he seemed genuinely astonished. "He thinks you are going to 'save the universe' with that battery someday very soon," Diana said.

"The thin television first, then the battery," the old man announced stubbornly. "The Japanese already have one out, but the picture is not the same as a regular set. Ours will be."

Diana had the oddest impression that the scientist, and not Cole, was determining the order in which the two products were developed. "He needs the battery very badly."

Without replying, Bretling bent over a microscope, examining something Diana couldn't see or imagine. "Every entrepreneur has his favorite thing to want. Cushman wanted their stupid computer chip and took the people I needed to work on my projects to work on it. They put me in charge of testing. I am a creative genius, and they put me in a testing lab."

Diana had been around a few people with genius IQs before, and like Willard Bretling, they had seemed exceptionally sensitive to any kind of opposition. She answered with the answer she would have used to calm a frustrated child. "That must have been very embarrassing for you."

He changed slides without looking up. "I told them it was not reliable. So they fired me. The founder was a good man, but his sons, they are pigs. I had worked for them for forty years, and they fired me. They escorted me out of the building as if they thought I would steal something if I stayed longer."

Diana slid off the stool beside him and clutched his sleeve, unable to draw breath through her lungs. "You tested their chip and it's no good?"

"Yes."

It was all she could do not to scream or shout. "Did you tell my husband that?"

"I told him it was no good, yes."

"But did you tell him you had *tested* it?"

"Why would I boast at being reduced to a—a flunky? I told him it was no good."

"Mr. Bretling, don't you read the newspapers or watch television or listen to the radio?"

"No. I prefer classical music on disk. It is soothing to the creative spirit." He lifted his head and glanced at her; then he looked at her again, and his mouth fell open. "Why do you have tears on your face?"

Chapter 58

FOR THE NEXT TWO DAYS, COLE STAYED HOME, BUT DIANA HARDLY saw him when he wasn't on the telephone or meeting with people. The visitors arrived and departed from the house under the watchful eye of a new security guard posted at the gate to keep reporters and everyone else out.

Cole was a man with a mission now; he was mobilizing his own forces and he was awe-inspiring to see in action. She watched him sitting behind his desk in the library, his fingers steepled in front of him, as he listened to advice from his Dallas lawyers, discarded most of it, and issued orders of his own. He worked out strategies with attorneys from Washington, made plans with Murray, the chief of security, and simultaneously ran his company from his home. When she least expected it, he would suddenly materialize at her side, pull her into his arms for a long kiss, and then go back to the next meeting, the next phone call.

Diana loved to watch him, and she hadn't been entirely idle either. She had made some phone calls of her own, and she had finally located Barbara Hayward in Vermont and spoken to her.

Diana spent the rest of her time talking to her own office and reassuring Spence and Corey, her grandparents and mother, that all was well. And then reassuring them again. She even called Willard Bretling twice on a wild hunch that he was lonely and that with a little gentle urging and sincere compliments he could be hurried up with his projects.

Diana and Cole were to leave for Washington the following morning, and they expected to be there for two days at the most.

Chapter 59

WILLARD BRETLING, JOE MURRAY, TRAVIS, COLE, AND DIANA FLEW to Dulles in Cole's private plane; he made the attorneys fly commercial. It was a funny little quirk of his, Diana had discovered. Cole didn't like lawyers. Even his own. Also on board were four well-dressed men whose fashion accessories included concealed weapons, for which they had licenses.

Cole told her it was just a whim of Joe's, but Diana knew better. Joe was certain that Cushman had hired people to find Bretling, and within the next forty-eight hours, Cole was determined to give the Cushman brothers a reason to want him dead.

The Washington law firm that specialized in SEC matters met with Cole in his hotel suite at eight the next morning, before they went to his eleven o'clock hearing. They argued with each other, and with Cole, about Cole's nonnegotiable request for a hearing that would be open to members of Congress and the SEC.

Twenty miles away from the hotel, Barbara Hayward was walking into her brother's town house in Washington, D.C. Her father opened the door. "Barbara!" he exclaimed. "Honey, what are you doing here?"

She looked around him for Doug and saw him walking into the room, buttoning the cuffs of his shirt. He stopped cold, his pleasure in her visit shaking her resolve a little. "Is Mother here?" she asked, looking about the spacious town house.

"I'm here, darling," Jessica said as she floated downstairs in one of the silky, clingy peignoirs she always preferred. "The more important question is, why are you here?"

Barbara had the horrible feeling that of the three other people in the room, Jessica was already arriving at the correct conclusion. Barbara was sure of it when her mother began talking to her in a way that was calculated to make her sound feebleminded, even now, when she'd finally put her life together and built a good marriage with a husband who loved her.

"Why aren't you at your beautiful, peaceful place in Vermont?" Jessica said, rushing over to pour her a cup of tea. "You know how the big cities always upset you. Why are you in Washington?"

Barbara sat on the sofa and realized she'd finally arrived at the moment she had dreaded since she was fifteen years old. Her mother was going to despise her and make her sound like a maniac or a liar. Doug and her father were going to lose faith in her, no one was going to love her, she'd be abandoned— With an angry shake of her head, Barbara silenced that panicky inner voice that had chanted that same chant until she was nearly crazy with it.

"I'm here to have some tea," Barbara said with a calm smile as she took the cup and saucer and patted the seat on the sofa beside her. Doug sat down there. Her father and mother sat down in chairs facing them. "And I'm here to right a wrong that I helped Mother commit fifteen years ago."

Jessica shot to her feet. "You're having one of your spells again. I have some tranquilizers in my purse."

"Take one by all means if you need it," Barbara said, deliberately misunderstanding her. "Daddy," she said firmly. "Cole Harrison never, ever laid a finger on me. Mother was at the stable that night, and she ran up to my room and begged me to change clothes with her."

"Can you *believe* this!" Jessica shrieked. "You're completely insane!"

Her father wearily rubbed his forehead. "Barbara, don't do this to yourself. It happened, honey. That bastard got you pregnant."

Perhaps it was Barbara's calm that chipped away at her father's and brother's disbelief. Perhaps it was her sad smile. "The father of that baby was a boy I met at a rock concert, Daddy. I never even knew his name. I just wanted to see if I could seduce him. I just"— she transferred her gaze to her mother's white face—"wanted to be like you."

Chapter 60

"HOW DID IT GO?" DIANA ASKED WHEN HE RETURNED ALONE, LATE IN the afternoon.

Cole pulled her into his arms. "It was a trade-off," he said with a grin. "We gave a little and we won a little. And then we insisted the actual hearing be postponed until tomorrow morning at eleven."

"What did you win?"

"We persuaded the judge that since the SEC reports to Congress, I should have the right to request that members of Congress and members of the SEC be allowed at the proceedings if they wish to attend. I will also be allowed to make a brief opening statement."

She reached up and straightened the knot of the tie she'd given him.

"I just don't understand why an open hearing like that is so important to you."

"It's important because my name and my company's name have been dragged through the dirt over the Cushman deal." Steel threaded his voice as he added, "I don't like the reasons for it. I don't like the methods that were used. And I don't like the participants."

Making an effort to soften his voice, he said, "The Cushmans are an old and powerful American family, and they've used enormous political pressure and social influence to make certain I take a fall on this. The IRS has already been nudged to get into the act. I'm being tried by politicians and the media, and I don't like it. Most of all, I despise the hypocrisy behind it."

If there was one thing she had learned about her husband in the last few days, it was that, for a man who was supposedly ruthless and unscrupulous, Cole Harrison had some very strong personal convictions about which he was not willing to negotiate.

"And somehow," she speculated with a twinge of fear, "you think you can do something about all that tomorrow?"

"I may be able to demonstrate all that."

Diana didn't know how, and she was afraid to find out for fear it would worry her even more.

Instead she said, "You told me what you won this morning; what did you give up?"

"If I insist on making an opening statement, I have to give up my right to plead the Fifth Amendment."

"'Plead the Fifth Amendment,'" Diana said with a shudder. "It makes you sound like some mobster."

That made him grin. "I've been treated like a mobster. And that," he whispered, nipping her ear, "is what happens when nobodies from nowhere make it into the major leagues and start playing with the guys in the Brooks Brothers suits."

"You don't wear Brooks Brothers suits," she chided with a giggle as he continued to tease her ear.

"I know," he said with an unabashed grin. "And that's what pisses them off. They don't know how to deal with us. We're unpredictable. We're out of uniform."

In his place, Diana would have been frantic at the possibility of a trial and of being wrongfully convicted on some sort of circumstantial evidence and sent to prison. But Cole had such strength of purpose that it empowered him. He generated his own force and it swept people along with it.

Diana smoothed her fingers over his hard jaw. "Do you really *know* what's going to happen tomorrow?"

"No. I only know what can happen, and what I want to happen."

"What do you want to happen?"

He turned her face up for a kiss and said with a somber smile, "What I want to happen is this: I want to see your face on the pillow beside mine when I go to sleep and when I wake up. And more than anything else in the world right now, I want to give you everything you want."

"You?" she suggested and watched his gray eyes darken with tenderness.

"That, too," he whispered.

The phone rang and Diana reluctantly pulled out of his arms and reached out to answer it. Still in a lighthearted mood, she said, "You're the expert on human nature, tonight. Use your powers and tell me who this is."

Cole threw out the first name that came to mind. "Hayward," he guessed; then he had to hide his shock when he turned out to be right.

Diana covered the mouthpiece with her hand. "He wants to come up."

In answer, Cole shoved his hands in his pockets and nodded curtly.

Chapter 61

*D*IANA'S BRIEF FANTASY THAT DOUG WOULD APOLOGIZE AND OFFER to have the hearing called off was not only beyond his ability to fulfill, it was beyond his consideration. Instead, the two men looked at each other like sworn enemies. Cole kept his hands in his pockets and merely lifted his brows in aloof inquiry.

Doug was equally distant. "I won't stay long," he said. "I've come to apologize to both of you for everything I said and did that was the result of what I believed happened to Barbara."

"Does that mean you're planning to get off my back?" Cole mocked.

Doug not only refused to consider that, he was angered by the suggestion that he should. "Not a chance," he said with biting scorn. "You've built an empire by swallowing up solid, reputable, old companies like Cushman who can't fight you because they can't survive your tactics."

"Are you really that sanctimonious, or are you just plain gullible?" Cole inquired in a deliberately insulting drawl.

Diana saw Doug's hands clench into fists, and so did Cole and yet

Cole goaded him harder. "Isn't it interesting that you've forgotten to mention the people who profit when I take over—you know, the shareholders of those 'solid, reputable' companies with the lousy management and antiquated facilities that don't benefit anyone except the management at the top, who bleed off the profits before they can trickle down to the shareholders.

"You don't give a shit about my ethics or methods or motives. You need a high-profile conquest for your political image, and you made the mistake of selecting me. If I could prove to you that I'm guiltless on every charge you've gotten filed against me, you'd still press the issue tomorrow in hope the federal courts will rule against me."

"Does the term *libel suit* have any effect on you?" Doug retorted in a soft, deadly voice.

"Yes," Cole scoffed. "It evokes an urge to tell you to shove it up your ass."

"Stop it!" Diana cried, forgetting that Doug was no longer the same carefree youth who tried to teach her to drive a stick shift. "Cole is innocent of everything you believe he's done. I've seen the proof, dammit."

"He doesn't want proof," Cole said, sweeping Doug with a contemptuous glance. "He wants to make a reputation for himself."

For some reason, this time when Diana protested Cole's innocence, Doug faltered. "Are you saying that you can prove you did not start the rumors that drove Cushman's stock down to half its value?" he demanded.

Cole folded his arms over his chest and regarded him with more disgust than anger. "You're an attorney. You prove to me you did *not* tell any woman at any time in the last three months that she was pretty. Show me how you'd prove it."

Having made his point, Cole said, "The people who belong in front of a judge tomorrow are the Cushman brothers and all their cronies." Cole had meant to end the discussion there, but as he regarded Hayward, he realized there was something about the young senator's attitude that was—almost—genuine.

"Just out of curiosity," he added in a milder voice when Hayward turned and started to leave, "what would you do if I could prove to you that the Cushmans are as guilty as sin?"

Doug was completely convinced he was being manipulated by a master, but he was curious enough to stop and answer the question.

"I would get the judge out of bed tonight to have him sign a subpoena," Doug stated clearly and concisely. "And then I would make it my personal quest to see that they went to jail, among other things, for misusing the U.S. government."

Cole was so amused by that choirboy speech that he decided to call his bluff, if for no other reason than to get a little petty revenge for the misery Hayward had caused Diana in the last two weeks. "You're *completely* sure that's what you'd do?"

"That is only the beginning of what I'd do," Doug bit out.

"In that case, follow me."

Cole took him to a room down the hotel corridor, where two well-dressed men appeared to be waiting for a friend who was inside. They stepped aside when Cole nodded at them. "I'm going to introduce you to Mr. Bretling," Cole said. "And Mr. Bretling is going to tell you all about your allies, the Cushmans, and their alleged wonder chip. After you talk to Mr. Bretling, I'm going to give you a look at Mr. Bretling's companion who's traveling with us. She's on the table over there, inside that jumbo-size, deep-dish pizza box."

At seven-thirty that evening, while Diana was changing clothes for dinner, she heard her husband and her childhood friend return to the suite. Unable to stand the suspense, she opened the door and peeked into the living room.

Doug looked extremely angry. He yanked the telephone receiver off its cradle, jerked the knot in his tie loose, and started making phone calls. Diana sagged with relief. The thought of using the fact of Doug's car accident against him had broken her heart. Besides being a truly dedicated and ethical politician, his problem with alcohol had been a rare metabolic allergy and not alcoholism.

Cole walked into the bedroom and slipped his arms around her, linking his hands at the small of her back while a lazy grin worked its way across his rugged features. In answer to her unspoken question, he said, "The senator would like to join us for dinner."

"What did you say?" Diana asked warily.

"I felt bound by courtesy to consent," he piously replied.

"Of course," Diana said with sham solemnity.

"But not until he volunteered to pay for it."

Chapter 62

At TEN-THIRTY THE FOLLOWING MORNING, KENDALL AND PRENTICE Cushman and three other sponsors of the class-action suit being prepared against Cole Harrison and Unified Industries shoved their way through the curious crowd into the large room where the hearing was to take place.

Their friends and allies, Senators Longtree and Kazinski from the state of New York, had saved seats for them in the first row.

At ten-forty, an assistant to Senator Hayward walked up to the front row and politely handed the two senators and the five members of the Cushman entourage an envelope. In each envelope was a subpoena requiring their presence throughout the hearing today.

"What the hell is this for?" Senator Longtree said to Prentice Cushman.

Prentice Cushman didn't answer because he was watching a familiar elderly man with stooped shoulders walk up the aisle and sit down at Harrison's table.

Diana observed the unfolding drama from the back of the room, where she stood beside Senator Byers, who'd convinced the SEC security guard that she was a member of his staff and must be allowed to observe. Periodically he reached over and gave her arm a reassuring squeeze.

At first everything seemed to move with agonizing slowness. Cole's attorneys announced that if the judge would permit a degree of flexibility in the presentation of the case, the whole matter could be easily resolved. The judge kept looking at the crowd of two hundred in the room and seemed extremely willing to do anything that would bring the matter to its earliest conclusion. He was already convinced Cole was guilty, anyway, Diana knew.

After that, Cole made his statement. He said categorically that he had not started or caused to be started any rumors about the reliability of the Cushman microchip. He said that he had believed when he offered nineteen dollars a share for the company that the chip would perform and that he had been assured by responsible members of the Cushman board that the rumors about the chip were untrue—that their early test results had shown it to be a major improvement over other chips on the market.

The judge interrupted twice to challenge Cole's statements, which annoyed Diana and caused the senator to pat her arm reassuringly again.

At the conclusion of his statement, Cole said that the Cushman people had falsified their test records of the chip. The judge found that so ludicrous that Diana thought he would laugh. "Let me see if I understand you, Mr. Harrison," he said, tapping his pencil on the pad in front of him. "You are telling me that Cushman knew the chip was unreliable?"

Cole said that was exactly what he was saying, and the judge pounced on it. "Then would you care to explain to me why the former owners and shareholders of Cushman Electronics have filed formal complaints and are now endeavoring to get the rights to this chip back, and why you do not want to give it back, sir?"

Cole replied that neither he nor Cushman had any interest in the chip, and that sent a sudden hush over the room. It made the judge scowl impatiently. "Then what did you intend to gain when you bought Cushman Electronics?"

"Two patents," Cole replied.

After that, Cole's attorneys asked Willard Bretling to testify. He confirmed everything Cole had said. He accused the Cushmans of falsifying his test results, and with great ire, he related his ignominious ejection from Cushman's premises. He explained that he had told Mr. Harrison about his excellent credentials and warned him that the Cushman chip was no good, before Mr. Harrison bought it. Diana could feel the reaction to that in the room. Poor Willard looked to them like a disgruntled ex-employee who was now anxious to say anything to support his new employer.

Cole's lawyers interrupted the proceedings to remind the judge that the contents of patents are available to the general public and therefore do not constitute *insider information.*

The judge waved that off and asked Willard why Mr. Harrison had seen a use for these two patents that Cushman in their "shortsightedness" had not seen.

Diana wanted to applaud when the harassed genius said, as if he were patiently trying to explain to a child, "A creation is like a puzzle. Mr. Harrison had the whole box of pieces already. He just needed a couple more from my patents."

"To make what, if I may be allowed to ask?"

"I'll show you."

With infinite care and pride, Willard walked over to the exhibits table and, like a magician about to produce a rabbit from a hat, swept off the cloth covering a flattish square object. The whole audience seemed to lean slightly forward, but the judge saw it first. "Are you telling this court that you made a *pizza* out of one hundred and fifty million dollars' worth of patents?"

The roar of laughter that shook the walls made speech impossible, and so no one heard the voices coming from the box while Willard slowly opened it. He stood the object in it up and turned it toward the audience, and it was as if a giant hand clamped over the collective mouths in the room.

The picture on the eight-pound television set was in perfect color and had flawless clarity. The screen measured twenty-six inches diagonally. It was twenty-one inches high.

It was only five inches thick.

While Oprah interviewed two family psychologists, twenty

387

rows of men and women leaned forward in their chairs simultaneously and the whole silent audience seemed to flatten out and
tilt.

The judge looked chastened. "An ultraslim television. That's
quite an accomplishment."

"Mitsubishi's can't compare to it," Willard agreed. "And, of
course, theirs needs an electrical outlet."

"A battery-operated set?" the judge asked. "How long does it work
on that battery?"

"About five days."

A man in the row in front of Diana slowly stood up. The man
beside him followed him out. The next row filed out swiftly. It
reminded Diana of people in a hurry to make an orderly exit out of
church pews. Within minutes, three fourths of the room had
evacuated in a near stampede. The last quarter remained to get a
closer look at the *Oprah* show.

Beside her, Senator Byers leaned his shoulders against the wall,
crossed his arms over his chest, and laughed softly, his admiring
gaze riveted on Cole, who was talking quietly with his lawyers as
they all packed up to leave. "Diana," Sam Byers said, "your husband
is a very brilliant man. And he is also lethal."

Diana was more interested in the dark side of human nature that
made people assemble to witness a potentially scandalous spectacle
and leave when the promise of bloodletting disappeared. She
remarked on that to Sam Byers, "Once they realized there wasn't
going to be any bloodshed, they were in a hurry to get back to
work."

Sam Byers's chuckle became a laugh that rolled out from deep in
his belly. "They aren't going back to work, Diana. They're rushing
around finding phones to call their brokers to put buy orders in for
Unified's stock!"

"I see."

"I don't think you do see. Your husband has just created a vast
moral dilemma that will embroil at least one hundred politicians in
a round of accusations and counteraccusations with the SEC—who
technically reports to them."

"How?"

"This hearing wasn't actually open to the public; it was only open

to the Congress and members of the SEC. So at this moment, most
of the congressmen who rushed out of here are now busily buying
all the Unified stock they can afford, based on what could easily be
regarded as 'insider knowledge.'"

He shook his head. "It's the ultimate coup de grâce."

Epilogue

July Fourth

*T*HE SKY OVERHEAD WAS ALIVE WITH SHOWERS OF DANCING LIGHT AND whirling shapes that chased each other heavenward and tumbled back down in a shimmering waterfall.

Lying on a blanket with her head resting on her husband's shoulder, Diana watched the breathtaking display from beside the lake on the lawns at Unified's beautiful landscaped grounds. They had a ringside seat and the entire place to themselves.

"Do you think Cal can see this?"

"Yes."

"Do you think he's enjoying it?"

He chuckled. "I don't see how he could. He wanted to come along with us."

"We should have brought him."

"No," he said, kissing her temple, "we should not have brought him. Remember when he wanted heirs at any cost?"

"I remember."

"Now he has a brand-new one. He can watch the fireworks from

391

the house with Conner's nanny and help her keep an eye on his nephew."

"But—"

Cole muffled her protest with a kiss and rolled her onto her back on the blanket, pinning her beneath him. "Remember when you said I missed out on my youth?"

Diana lifted her hand, slowly brushing her fingertips across his hard jaw in a soft caress. "I remember," she whispered while fireworks exploded overhead in a crescendo of sound and light.

"Do you know the main thing I missed out on?"

"No, what?"

"I always wanted to make love to a woman who was watching fireworks over my shoulder."

She smiled at that, but she was remembering other things. She remembered when he held his son for the first time three months ago. He had carried him over to the windows of her hospital room, his expression filled with wonder, then turned him to the windows. "Conner," he said to the infant in his arms, "this is the city of Dallas. Daddy is going to give it to you."

Cole studied her smile. "What are you thinking about?"

"I'm remembering," she whispered.

"Would you like something else to remember?" he volunteered with a muffled laugh.

Diana withdrew her gaze from the fireworks. "Very much."